Table of Contents

Murder One

A Mickey Crow Paranormal Omnibus

The Contrary Crowcast: a paranormal podcast produced by three women: the mysterious Mickey Crow Lamotte, one-armed and abandoned at birth; reluctant socialite Pris Salamanca; and mad scientist Melissa "Mo" McLeod.

In *SHIVER,* Mickey and Pris meet Mo while investigating the midnight disappearance of a lifeguard trainee along a lonely stretch of Shell Beach, Massachusetts. As the body count increases, Mo refuses to believe the culprit could be one of her beloved sharks, even though her father once went into the water and never returned.

In *FORMLESS,* the three team up with AI raven Ek and a few friends to go undercover at Fright Island Theme Park, off the Connecticut coast, where their advanced augmented-reality system is making people sick—and then someone dies. Nothing is what it seems, including the illusory monsters on the island, one of which appears to be real.

BONUS: In "TUSK," Mickey and Pris go on a one-day jaunt to the abandoned site of Zahnville, Connecticut, searching for Bigfoot, or whatever has been causing enigmatic illnesses and vanishings for hundreds of years. But what they find is something they never imagined.

In *METAL,* the whole gang from *Formless* reunites at Unieda Corporation outside of Boston for a robot rumble. Their friends' award-winning robots are going up against Unieda's spider-dog hybrid robots. Unieda has their own reason for luring Mickey there, and as the robot rumble goes sideways, an old enemy appears.

Murder One: A Mickey Crow Paranormal Omnibus
© 2024 by Roberta Piedmont, Gevera Bert Piedmont
ISBN: 978-1-963760-10-1
Published by Transformations by Obsidian Butterfly, LLC Yalesville, CT, USA
ObsidianButterfly.com

Cover composite by Bridgette Rodrigues, Obsidian Butterfly Designs
Cover images from Freepik and Pixabay
Author photo © 2021 by Ayzha Wolf Photography

Shiver was originally published in 2021.
Formless was originally published in 2022.
"Tusk" was originally published in *Something Woked This Way Comes* (2023).
Metal was originally published in 2024.

SHIVER

A Mickey Crow Paranormal Adventure

Gevera Bert Piedmont

SHIVER

Shiver
Noun: **shiver;** *plural noun:* **shivers**
a momentary trembling movement
Collective noun: **shiver**
a group of sharks

SHIVER
Prologue
Shell Beach, Massachusetts

Dylan slammed out of the cabin and crossed the common area, past the in-ground pool with its lanes and floats, everything gray in the light of the full moon. The winding path through the woods had been beaten flat and lined with sand by hundreds of feet. He followed it, grinding the toes of his sneakers into the ground for emphasis as he talked to himself.

"Johannes, you're such a jerk!" Grind. "—you can't treat someone like crap—" grind "—break their heart." Grind.

The trees ended at the beach. Dylan kept grinding his toes and muttering. The moon lit the tops of the waves and flattened everything. He shoved a knuckle into his eye. Now he was crying over the jerk. Stupid summer hookup at lifeguard school. Not like they would fall in love and spend the rest of their lives together.

He knuckled his eyes again. Waves washed in and out, implacable, as they had since the beginning of time. Seaweed bubbles popped and slid under his sneakers as he walked the horrible beach, full of stones, littered with crab bits and broken shells. The big, gritty sand particles infiltrated his sneakers.

Stomping parallel to the high-tide mark along a jagged line of black seaweed, wiping away tears, Dylan tried to imagine how a long-distance relationship would even work between him and Johannes. It wouldn't. He thought about walking to the nearby town and calling for a ride home, just quitting the whole stupid summer program. There must be working phones in that town. Cell phones didn't function at Shell Hell camp, which lacked cable TV, internet, and everything good associated with being online.

This summer learning thing was bogus. Dylan should have skipped the lifeguard program and just applied for the advanced first aid training. He wanted to be a paramedic. Lifeguards just sat around at the beach or the pool, trying to look hot and score some tail of whatever variety. Not that Dylan wasn't flexible about what type of tail he attracted. He was more interested in saving lives.

"Hey," someone called.

Dylan stopped and turned, thinking that Johannes had followed him to apologize for their fight. What had it even been about? Fighting with your summer hookup seemed as dumb as this lifeguard training "school."

No Johannes.

"Hey."

Dylan scanned the dark beach, seeing no one.

"Hey," the voice repeated.

"Where are you?"

"My foot is stuck."

Stuck where? He looked at the waves, at a cluster of boulders fifteen feet out, a lump that was possibly someone's head. "Are you in the water?"

"Can you help me?"

The moonlight on the ever-changing silver and black waves made it impossible to make out anything with any clarity. "Is that you, next to the rocks? Is that where you're stuck?"

"My foot is stuck," the voice agreed.

Something else moved out there. A triangle cut the water near the round blob that might be the person's head.

"Hey! Watch out! There's a shark!"

"Can you help me?"

"Fu—" Dylan toed off his sand-filled sneakers and ran toward the water, ripping his bare feet on shells, slipping on rocks and seaweed. "I'm coming!"

The fin stayed right near the head-like blob, seeming to stalk it.

"My foot—can you help." The voice expressed no emotion.

He had only completed half of the lame lifeguard training. Dylan lacked backup, equipment, a view of who he was rescuing in the dark. He was wearing clothes instead of a bathing suit. Dylan lacked a sense of what was happening—where was their foot stuck, and on what? Were they drowning? How large was the shark?

The water was shockingly cold, as it always is in New England. Underwater, it was pure black; the moon's light penetrated not at all. He kept aiming himself toward the boulders, toward the blob and the terrifying triangular fin. His shivering body wanted to curl up and retreat, but he pushed forward. This was what he craved; to save people who needed saving.

The voice encouraged him, asking him for help over and over. Dylan had no time to return to camp to get help. He had to do this by himself; save this person. Then Johannes would understand what a great guy he was. Dylan bashed his shoulder into a barnacle-covered boulder and grabbed on, searching for the person's face and that deadly pointed fin, but found neither in the dark water. His eyes burned. His shoulder was going to bruise. It was bleeding, the worst thing that could happen around a hungry shark.

Dylan hunted for the fin or the face and found nothing. The freezing water numbed the pain of his wounded arm. He was afraid he would lose his grip.

SHIVER

"Hey, where are you?" he whispered, not wanting to make any noise and attract the shark. Although he did not know if sharks had ears. Was it snakes or sharks that were deaf? Or was that Tyrannosaurus Rex? No, a T-Rex didn't see movement, but Dylan was sure sharks could. Did sharks have night vision, though? Why was his lifeguard education so deficient in important shark facts?

"My foot is stuck," said a gravelly voice, right in his ear. Dylan couldn't determine the gender, but there seemed to be a cloud of hair.

"Where is your foot?" he asked, his numb hand slipping off the rough boulder as he reached out to help.

The fin was there. And another fin above the moon-dappled waves. "Sharks—" he warned.

The person reached an arm out to him. They clasped each other wrist-to-wrist, a good, firm hold, and Dylan felt hopeful. He could save this person. He grabbed at the barnacle-covered rock again, but the other yanked him in the opposite direction.

The person Dylan was trying to save pushed him under the water, and it was frigid down there. He coughed, sputtering, trying to drive himself back up to the barnacle-covered rock and stability. The other clutched his wrist, speaking in a gravelly monotone voice, lacking in intelligence, the words running together, "can you help me my foot is stuck hey can you help" over and over, pulling him in closer until he could see nothing but teeth.

Feel nothing but teeth.

SHIVER
-1-
Suffolk, CT

Mickey Crow thought about steam-powered artificial limbs. They looked cool, big, bulky, and menacing, steaming and clanking, but they would also be red hot. And where would the portable steam boiler be located?

She looked at her left arm, which ended just below the elbow. Metallic medical tattoos crisscrossed her shortened forearm; they enabled her high-tech prosthetic—which was more cyberpunk than steampunk—to connect better. Biomechanical tattoos embellished her upper arm and shoulder, blending into the prosthetic. If she needed one, where would she put a theoretical heater to power her arm?

Mickey sketched a metal backpack complete with wisps of smoke onto her steampunk superheroine and widened the heroine's shoulders to carry the extra weight.

Then she tossed her pencil because her idea sucked. No one would read a steampunk graphic novel about a girl with one arm solving crimes. Even if that girl was super cute and her sidekick was super sexy and super smart, kind of like a Sherlock and Watson thing. Super Steampunk Girls. Was there a word for girls that started with s? Senoritas?

This wouldn't make a riveting graphic novel, and there was no way to use it as an episode of her podcast, the Contrary Crowcast. She needed to stick to the mysteries of New England. Pick a thing, stick to it.

Scratching the shaved back of her head under her otherwise long hair, Mickey stared through the polarized glass doors of her basement room toward the sun-dappled pool. She could go out there and get into the awful, thick water and do her physical therapy exercises, she supposed. She hadn't drowned yet. Just thinking about being surrounded like that made her sweat. She pulled at her sports bra, feeling choked. The chair touching her sides and back was too much for her. Mickey had to get up and stand in the center of the room, holding the waistband of her boyshorts away from her body, letting air circulate against her skin.

She wasn't being crushed. She was fine. She could breathe.

Mickey wondered where her anxiety medicine was.

If Mickey were wearing her neural net, as she should be, the claustrophobia symptoms wouldn't be so bad. She huffed out a breath and eyed her desk a few steps away. The neural net was in a box in a drawer. Although it always felt like cheating to wear the net, as if it expanded her brain. Although maybe she deserved extra brain for having less arm and a crooked side.

SHIVER

Her phone lit up and buzzed, dancing across the desk, knocking her discarded mechanical pencil onto the floor. Geoffrey Chu, the screen said, displaying a picture of a pair of identical Asian American twins.

Mickey snatched up the phone. "Hey!"

Geoffrey and Taylor were college friends of Mickey's. Robotic experts, they had designed her neural net and the arm it connected to, along with the unique metallic medical tattoos on her arms and head. She suspected that someday the two would disappear into DARPA. Already they couldn't talk about specific projects their company, Gemini Robotics Systems, was working on.

Power tools noises, screeching metal, and far-off shouting came from their end, where they were on speakerphone, as usual, to allow both of them to speak at once. "Hey," they shouted. "We're in Denver filming this year's Robo Rumble," Taylor said. Geoffrey continued, "You know we can't tell you how great Mind Meld is doing until the series airs, but…"

Mickey laughed. The twins had developed and fought an early version of their robot, Mind Meld, when they had all been in college. That had been the birth of the neural net, used to control Mind Meld, a terror in the fighting ring.

"Did you two call me to brag?" Just hearing their friendly voices made the claustrophobia recede and her breathing ease. She dropped back into the chair and put her phone on speaker before sliding out the drawer.

"No, we called to see if you feel like going up to Massachusetts for a few days to check something out for us," Geoffrey explained.

"I don't know, that's awfully far," she teased while she flipped open the box, looking at the neural net nestled inside.

The sounds of screaming metal and power tools from the other end didn't stop. Mickey guessed they were in the repair area where everyone refurbished their robots between fights. Taylor continued, "Our little brother Lucas going to some kind of lifeguard school. Another trainee, his friend, got into a fight with a guy he hooked up with. The other kid, Dylan, stormed out and never returned, but he's not officially missing yet. The town is crazy weird. You and Pris might have fun."

"O-kay," Mickey said slowly, not agreeing to anything.

"Also, we sent Pris a care package; did she tell you?" Taylor said. "She should bring it along. We managed to find you guys a place to stay up in Mass—it wasn't easy; this place is wicked off the grid. We'll send you all the info and spending cash. In return, we expect at least two podcasts about this with Gemini Robotics as a sponsor. Let us know how the arm and the net are working. We have upgrade ideas. Gotta run, we're almost on again." The noise cut off as the call ended.

A moment later, the phone dinged as information arrived and cha-chinged as money followed. Mickey skimmed it and forwarded everything to her best friend Pris—it was Pris's job to read and assimilate—with a note explaining the situation: We're going to Massachusetts! Twins say bring new toys? Bring old toys for podcast. Read this stuff for me first. Be there soon to pick you up.

Mickey pulled on a red tank top and baggy black cargo shorts and threw more of the same into a duffel bag with other necessities for a few days at the beach with her best friend and her friends' little brother looking for a missing kid. Then she sat and took the neural net out of its charging box. It was a gorgeous diadem, more like art than science, gold and silver wires in a tight weave, precision-formed to fit the back of her head. Inside the metal lace nested microscopic rare-earth magnets and computer chips; a neurosurgeon had implanted more magnets and chips in her head and forearm during a surgery Mickey didn't like to remember. Anti-vaxxers who feared microchips would run screaming from what Mickey Crow had allowed to be embedded into her head and forearm.

She lifted her thick black hair with her stump and pressed the net onto the shaved part of her head with her fingers, moving and adjusting it until it snapped into place. She felt this inside her brain, a shiver in her thoughts as the neural net's fingers attached to her neurons. Mickey retrieved the synched prosthetic from its charging case and slipped in her truncated wrist. It locked into place. Another shiver showed that the metal hand and forearm were communicating with her neural net. She wiggled her metal fingers and then packed the two cases into the duffel.

A quick stop upstairs from her basement lair revealed that her parents were at work. As emergency department doctors, they kept their schedules on an interactive whiteboard in the kitchen. Their profession was how they adopted Mickey. As a severely injured premature baby, she had been abandoned at a firehouse, wrapped in a blanket with a toy crow. The doctors had fallen in love with the tiny broken infant and adopted her, molding their lives around her care and leaving her filled with guilt.

She ate a blueberry protein bar in a few bites and stuffed more assorted bars into the pockets of her shorts and the duffle, and packed her all-important anxiety meds. After scribbling a brief note explaining nothing (Going to Massachusetts with Pris for a few days, Love M.), she looked around the house again.

SHIVER

The guilt and the claustrophobia overlapped. Both weighed her down and choked her. Her parents could have had biological children, a bigger, nicer home and a bigger, nicer life, if not for adopting a random broken baby twenty-five years before. And who was Mickey? Nothing, nobody. She didn't work; she accomplished nothing, a weirdo with one arm who babbled about weird stuff on the internet and drew weird pictures.

Her car recognized her and unlocked as soon as she came close, and she lobbed her duffle into the back seat using her metal hand. She instructed the car to route her to Pris's, a half-hour away, and pulled out of the cul-de-sac where she lived.

Her car read a text message from Pris: I'm here, I have the twins' gift, and yes, you can drive, but we're taking my car because it's better.

Ugh. Pris had one of those expensive, advanced electric cars with self-driving mode. It cost as much as a small house and driving it terrified Mickey. Not that Pris would care if Mickey wrecked her car. She would laugh, pull out a super diamond-level titanium credit card, and buy another, better one. Pris was the least well-known member of her family; otherwise, her face alone would get her a new one. Pris's family was seriously wealthy and seriously famous. Pris joked she was like the extra kid who didn't make it onto Ozzy's reality show, so no one knew she existed—and that was how she liked it. Although the Salamanca family didn't have a reality show of their own, Pris's siblings were notable walk-ons in other shows featuring wealthy families and on national entertainment shows and the covers of tabloids and magazines.

That was one thing Mickey had accomplished. The daughter of one of the wealthiest families in the country was her best friend, and today they were going on an adventure.

SHIVER
-2-

It took Mickey a moment to retrieve the current gate code from her phone's notes app. She looked around first for paparazzi and was careful entering it into the keypad. Pris had tried to get the family to use better security methods, but there was always pushback from someone who hated change. Mickey wondered what the lurking photographers thought of her midmarket hybrid—perhaps that she was an employee or contractor. Never that she was taking away a daughter of the house to solve a mystery. Pris was the lesser daughter, true, but still.

The house was far enough away from the road to be completely private; the Salamancas lived on acres of land with multiple buildings in a family compound. Mickey drove past the main house—a mansion by any standards—and to the family's multicar garage. She parked beside it and pulled out her bag, leaving her key fob on the seat. A moment later, one of the garage doors opened almost silently. Pris's low-slung green-and-black electric car slid forward on its own and stopped just outside the door, which shut again. Creepy.

Pris emerged from the house—well, a moving pile of bags speaking with her voice did. "Wait until you see what the twins sent me! So cool!" she exclaimed. Equipment bags of every size draped her shoulders and forearms. She dragged an old designer rolling suitcase that once belonged to the King of England and should be in a museum. "Leave your keys, right? Someone will wash your car and put it in my spot after we leave."

It was a gracious gesture that made Mickey feel uncomfortable. Although it most likely made Pris's family and employees feel even more uncomfortable to see Mickey's cheap car parked in the exclusive family area, scuffed and dusty. The mysterious "someone" would buff out the scratches too and detail the inside. It was a different way of living.

Mickey used her metal hand, her stronger hand, to pull bags off Pris, gradually revealing her friend.

"Did you read any of that stuff you sent me?" Pris ducked to allow the much shorter Mickey to yank a strap over her head. "That place we're going, Shell Beach, it sounds weird, right?" Pris wore a white tank top over the hated breast implants her parents had given her for her eighteenth birthday. Over that, a half-buttoned, pinkish Oxford shirt that looked like it had been washed with a pair of red socks—but it matched her buzz-cut hair. White bike shorts and brown gladiator sandals laced to the knee rounded out the outfit.

"That's your 'hunting a missing lifeguard' outfit?" Mickey inquired, waving her metal hand as she played Tetris with Pris's bags in the back hatch of the humming electric car.

SHIVER

"What's wrong with it? I got the shirt and the sandals and the shorts at the thrift store." For all her money, Pris adored thrift stores.

"Gladiator sandals?"

"If gladiators can fight lions in them, I can walk a beach."

Mickey looked at her own sturdy hiking sandals. "And you have no pockets."

"There's a pocket on my shirt." Pris tapped one of her rounded breasts and then made a face.

"Just get the implants taken out." They had already had this conversation a dozen times.

"I can't. Daddy says no. They were a gift, right? It would be rude."

Mickey rolled her eyes and climbed into the driver's seat. It adjusted itself to her shorter frame, although she always had to fuss with the mirrors. As Mickey did that, Pris connected their phones and one of her tablets to the car's Bluetooth and Wi-Fi signals. She programmed the bed-and-breakfast address into the car's GPS.

The neural net tried to reach into Pris's car. Mickey felt the slightest shiver; it might have been her imagination. She couldn't connect to cars; that would be crazy. That wasn't what the last software upgrade was for.

The GPS's voice sounded way too cheerful as it gave an ETA for the drive. The large touchscreen on the dashboard displayed the map with a crooked blue line outlining their route.

Mickey turned off the autopilot and followed the voice onto I-95. She listened to Pris talk.

"I tried to find out more about this kid, Dylan, disappearing, right? I know it's early, but there's nothing. No hits on his name at all, except for some high school sports stuff. And this town, Shell Beach, it's like a black hole of information." Pris waved her tablet as if she wanted Mickey to inspect the screen.

"What do you mean?" Animated billboards tried to get Mickey's attention, dancing at the side of the highway. She hated them. So distracting. Who would go to a horror theme park on an island? She wished she could somehow turn off the billboards or tune them out. "You mean information goes in but doesn't come back out?"

"The latter. No information comes out. Shell Beach has no town government pages. There is no shellbeach.ma.gov website. The bed-and-breakfast, Caren's Cozy Cottage, that the twins booked us at has no web presence at all. I found an offhand mention of it on a regional board with just a phone number—that must be how the twins found it. Online, it's like the town doesn't exist. Even their wiki page is almost nonexistent."

"That's strange."

"Right? According to the wiki, it's a town that's been around forever, but it only lists the barest facts. Like they have the world's biggest and possibly oldest shell midden. Big deal. An ancient Indian trash heap. No disrespect to your people."

Mickey waved it off. She had never bothered getting a genetic test to see if she was Native American; everyone just assumed she was from her name and looks. "Maybe Dylan has come to his senses and returned by now. We'll have a nice couple days at the beach and come home."

"That's boring." Pris waved the hand that wasn't holding her tablet. "I have a list of area attractions we can film at. Mysterious stone structures, haunted houses, the usual. Trash heaps, I guess. And I've got the new toys to try out."

"What are the new toys? They didn't tell me."

"Oh, then I won't tell you either!"

Mickey rolled her eyes, then pointed. "Look, there's the big blue bug!" Mickey loved the big blue bug of Providence, Rhode Island.

"Hello, bug!" Pris yelled, leaning into Mickey's lap, letting her now-unfastened seatbelt snap back into the door.

"No, get off me," Mickey shoved at her friend, feeling compressed. Her anxiety spiked. Pris knew better, but she was so enthusiastic about everything.

Pris retreated. "Now I'm hungry," she grumbled, pushing herself against the opposite door and putting the seatbelt back on.

"I don't want to know why an enormous cobalt insect makes you hungry, but I have protein bars in my pockets," Mickey said. "This is why pockets are so handy." She reached into her pocket with her left hand, concentrating on the artificial fingers' haptic feedback. The car's blinkers snapped on, signaling that they were about to swerve into the concrete Jersey barriers lining this stretch of the highway. Mickey grabbed the steering wheel with her left hand and tapped at the car's control screen with her right, trying to turn off the blinkers.

Pris slapped at her hand. "Stop it; I'll do it. You'll crash us."

"That's why I hate driving your car! Plus, it costs more than a house." Mickey's heart was pounding so hard it was up in her throat. And where had she packed her medicine? In the duffle bag, not in her pockets.

"Right, a teeny-tiny house, like that TV show where people live in closets on wheels."

Mickey tried again to extract a bar from her pocket while listening to the GPS, ignoring her friend's extended blathering about tiny houses and trying not to crash the six-figure vehicle while trying to think her heart rate down using the neural net. This was textbook distracted driving. She hoped no cops were in the area.

The wipers came on.

"Why is my car haunted?" Pris wailed and tapped the screen. "Hey, maybe we should do a podcast on haunted cars. We could call it, 'help, my car is haunted.' No, 'what do to if your car is haunted.' 'Is your car haunted?' 'How to tell if your car is haunted…'" She was off again.

Mickey extracted two bars and handed both to Pris. "Unwrap one for me. And can you open a water bottle?"

"I got the pop-top sports water you like," Pris said, peeling a peanut butter protein bar like a banana. "Here." She held it to Mickey's mouth.

"I hate being fed," Mickey fussed, taking a small bite. "When I was little, my parents fed me all the time as if my right arm didn't work either."

Pris took a bite from the same bar and then popped the top on a water bottle. When she offered it to Mickey, Mickey gave her a side-eyed look and drank from it.

"Your arms work fine. Both the flesh one and the metal one." Pris said. "But those arms are driving, and my arms are not, so let my arms feed you, all right?"

They split two bars and a bottle of fruity sports water that way while Pris further detailed the general lack of knowledge on Shell Beach. "I could only find two things of interest besides the amazing stupendously large trash heap. There was a spate of shark attacks about a hundred twenty years ago, and they have a good museum area in their historical society."

"A museum about the shark attacks?"

"You know, I don't know," Pris mused. She slid down in the seat and put both her legs on the dashboard, swiping the tablet. "It was in a scan of an article from the 1976 Bicentennial celebrations. It's probably not that accurate anymore; that was forever ago, right?"

"If we get into an accident, your pelvis will be ground into dust and your legs shattered by the airbag. Just saying." Mickey indicated her friend's position with her chin.

"Then I get some carbon fiber bouncy legs and run marathons, right? Cool." But Pris sat up and drew in her legs, perhaps remembering how she had run track in high school.

"That's not how it works, and you don't run marathons now," Mickey said.

SHIVER

"Oh, right. Maybe losing my legs would inspire me to run again." Pris tapped her tablet and stretched. "This is some kind of crazy town we're going to. Haunted, I bet. By some kind of fey creature that feeds on electrical energy so that the town has to live in the Dark Ages." She cracked another bottle of water and sucked on it so that her cheeks were hollow.

Mickey followed the GPS voice, barely listening to Pris, who was thinking aloud about all sorts of nonsense, which was her process.

Mickey wondered when they had allowed computers to take over navigating. Honestly, she did not know how to even read a paper map. If there was a paper-map-reading segment of the brain, Mickey didn't have one. "Hey, gimme water," she said, reaching with her right hand, steering with her left. The hazard lights obediently started flashing.

Pris pushed the bottle into Mickey's hand and dealt with the lights. "Right? This proves my point."

Mickey crammed the bottle between her thighs to hold it. Cold. "How? What point?"

"My car never acted like this before. Soon as I entered the address, bam. Car started acting crazy. Like it knew, right? And give me back that water; you're making it all hot with your sweaty legs."

"Stop thinking about what's between my legs, you lesbo. And your theory makes no sense."

"I am what I am," said Pris, who was indeed a lesbian, grabbing the bottle. "You know you aren't my type. And my theory makes perfect sense. The car's GPS energy goes up into the satellite, right? Then down to find Shell Beach, where the fey creature who feeds on energy latches onto it because that's what fey creatures who feed on energy do, and then the fey creature's energy signature follows the GPS up to the satellite and then back into my car where it sucks its energy and makes it act all wonky! I bet it needs a charge already because the fey creature has sucked it dry."

Mickey looked at the energy gauge, which registered a full charge. "Dylan is in big trouble if we're the ones who are expected to help him."

SHIVER
-3-
Shell Beach

Mo flipped through her laboratory notes, looking at page after page of failed formulas written in various pen colors, including green and purple. What combinations hadn't she tried? Making a functional shark repellent had been something fun to work on in her spare time the last few years, but now it had turned urgent. She was sure that a shark had eaten the missing lifeguard kid. If this was going to be another Summer of Sharks, shark repellent would be a blessing. A necessity even.

She pulled at the long sleeves of her shirt, making sure it covered the bandage on her left arm. It was too hot to wear long sleeves but too much of a pain to explain the dressing—hard to drop "oh, that? I got bitten by a shark; just a small one, of course," into casual conversation.

She opened a couple of thick reference books filled with multi-colored highlights and adjusted her black, rhinestone-studded glasses. The door leading from the kitchen into her laboratory, in her mother's garage, opened.

"Hey, Sheriff," she said, holding her finger on her place in a chemistry book. It was embarrassing to know her mother was having sleepovers with the sheriff.

"I've told you many times, you can call me Ted," he replied. "That's a really thick book."

Mo rolled her eyes and shook her beaded braids at the obviousness of it all. "It's an advanced chemistry text."

Ted was in his uniform. For an old white guy—he had to be fifty—he was handsome enough, she supposed. "Will you be going to the beach today?" He pretended to look at the formula she had her finger on.

"Maybe. I'll be at the pool later, at least."

It was Ted's turn to roll his eyes since he disapproved of her pool and made no secret of it. "That missing lifeguard boy I got the call about late last night—he's tall with red hair. A white boy. Keep an eye out, will you, Melissa?"

Mo shuddered at her full name. "Of course." She felt like saying something snarky about how all white people looked alike. She hated being the only non-white person in Shell Beach.

The radio on Ted's shoulder squawked unintelligibly, like a demented parrot.

"Maybe they found him," Mo suggested. Ted departed through the open garage door, heading toward the police car parked on the street. Mo sorted through bottles and flasks, checking labels against notebooks and reference volumes. She gazed up at the giant set of shark jaws mounted on the wall. How hard could it be to make a shark repellent?

"Of course!" she said to the jaws, bobbing her head to make the beads on her braids dance against her cheeks. "I didn't try this combination before." She tied a thick cloth mask across her lower face against harmful vapors and general foul smells and assembled the ingredients for another test. She addressed the shark again. "The question is, would it keep you away or just your smaller cousins?"

Keeping up a running commentary with the shark, she measured, poured, and notated, lost in her work.

"Mo-lissa, are you talking to that dead shark again?"

Mo looked up, blinking. Rob was backlit in the open garage door, but she knew his shape, had known it since they were children. "That dead shark is practically a member of my family. It ate my great-uncle Charlie's leg, after all. Well, supposedly."

He stepped into the LED-lit laboratory. "Your great-uncle Charlie also thinks he was the inspiration for *Jaws*."

"He did once have a drink with Peter Benchley." Mo swiped her arm across her sweaty face, dislodging both her mask and the sleeve covering the bandage.

Rob looked like a lifeguard from central casting. Tall, blond, and tan, he wore a neon orange shirt that read "Shell Beach Lifeguard Training School" on the front and "Instructor" on the back. He even had a whistle around his neck. Staring at the dressing on her forearm, Rob said, "He's a crackpot, just like you are."

"And you lost one of your trainees. Did you come to see if I fed him to my sharks?"

SHIVER
-4-

As they approached Shell Beach, the GPS became more hesitant. Pris's streaming music kept dropping out and finally went to "no signal," as did her tablet and both phones. They had long ago left civilization and numbered state roads behind.

"Energy-sucking fey," Pris said, frowning, shutting off all the useless devices and packing them into their bags. "Be glad you don't have a pacemaker. You don't, do you?"

"No, I don't think so," Mickey said, turning right at a weathered wooden sign reading Shell Beach. She thought of the chips in her head and arm. Mickey didn't understand what powered them. It was some kind of "need to know" basis. Although the chips were inside Mickey, she did not need to know. She trusted the twins, but their robotics company scared her a little.

"Turn right?" the GPS voice wondered, having lost both its assertiveness and chirpiness. The road meandered without turnoffs.

"Way ahead of you," Mickey replied.

The air had changed; it smelled of salt and the sea. Mickey thought about rolling down the windows; the windshield wipers came on with a generous squirt of blue wiper fluid. When she manually triggered the windows, the astringent liquid, still deploying, splashed into the car.

"Energy-sucking fey!" Pris shouted, making it sound like a new swear word. She manipulated the touch screen until the fluid shut off and the wipers ceased. "I wonder if my tech is going to be safe in this place?"

Mickey tried to keep her mind perfectly blank. It was impossible. The more she tried not to think of anything, the more thoughts popped up. She did not want to think about the car, yet she had to think about it to drive it.

"You realize you have no proof of these energy-sucking fey," she said to Pris. *Don't think about the car, don't think about—.* The hazard lights came on.

"See! Energy-sucking fey, right!"

"No, it's me; I can't drive your car."

"No, this has never happened before; you can drive fine—"

The wipers swished back and forth, grinding on the dry windshield.

Pris screamed and slapped at the touchscreen.

Mickey felt like crying. She followed the road, trying to keep her mind blank. "Look, is that the town?"

"They will be in a place with antennas, right?"

"Who?"

"The energy-sucking fey."

"We're looking for Dylan, remember?"

"We'll drive around and see where the car acts up the most."

"Do you honestly think the energy-sucking fey have Dylan?"

"Doesn't he have red hair?"

"I don't know, does he?"

"Don't the fey like redheads?"

"I don't know. What does that have to do with electricity?" Pris was making Mickey's head hurt. "Hey, there's the B&B. Let's get checked in."

"Maybe they know something there. Because I haven't seen any big antennas or even any satellite dishes here."

The innkeeper, Caren, was a middle-aged white woman wearing jeans and a green t-shirt. She did not resemble an energy-sucking fey. Mickey was happy the twins had reserved adjoining rooms for them. Mickey did not like sharing a bed with anyone. Pris had the information to get them checked in.

Carrying just their personal electronics, they followed Caren up the stairs, where she pointed out their doors. The cramped rooms, overlooking the shoreline from a distance, each had one double bed, dresser, nightstand, wind-up clock, and floor lamp crowding the small space. They shared a bathroom, which connected them. No TV, no telephone. One outlet in each room, one in the bathroom.

"I'll get the rest of the stuff from the car; you get the Wi-Fi code and ask where there are more outlets we can use," Pris said.

Mickey found Caren in her kitchen. She smiled at the innkeeper. "Hi, sorry to bother you. We were wondering about the Wi-Fi code? And where are there more electrical outlets we can use?" She held up her metal arm. "I need to charge my arm every night, plus other things." She stretched, trying to straighten the painful kink in her back that was worse than ever after driving so long. She worried she looked like Quasimodo, all hunched to the right.

The innkeeper's face, which had seemed sweetly bland upon check-in, twisted into a sneer, and the quality of her voice changed. "Wi-Fi? We don't have that stuff here. But if you send down your nurse, I'll see what I can do about your arm getting charged. I can explain to her how to get to the hardware store."

Mickey took a step back, her metal hand across her chest. "What? Pris isn't my nurse; she's my friend. There's nothing wrong with my mind, just my arm and my back."

Caren turned back to the stove, dismissing Mickey.

SHIVER

Mickey's face was hot and tight, her throat full, and she could barely explain what had happened to Pris, who couldn't decide if she should beat up the woman, call one of her family's many lawyers and have her sued for discrimination, or just move out.

"We can't leave; it's already paid for," Mickey said, squeezing her burning eyes shut. "She has no money for you to sue her for. If you beat her up, you'll just get into trouble. Either way, people will find out who you are, and you hate that."

"Right," Pris said. "I do hate that. But I also hate that she made you cry."

"I'm not crying."

They sat on Pris's bed while Mickey cried.

Pris said, "Right, let's go to the hardware store and buy every power strip we can find and charge every bit of electronics we own. Let's run a cord from the window to my car and charge that, too. That should show that stupid innkeeper, plus it will attract the energy-sucking fey."

"What about Dylan?"

"Right, Dylan. Now we can't ask the innkeeper because we know she's hateful. Let's go to the historical society."

Let's check the library half first," Pris suggested. They paused in the lobby of the building that housed both the historical society and the library. It was a slightly remodeled antebellum mansion.

"Why aren't we at the police station?" Mickey wondered. "We rarely find missing people at libraries or museums."

"We are doing research, my dear, right?" Pris opened the door to the right. An embossed plastic nameplate read "Shell Beach Library." Inside it smelled of mildew, paper, dust, and age. It was steamy hot. A woman of late middle age sat on a stool behind a counter, reading an old book. She wore glasses on a golden chain. The red-framed glasses were stylish, and her short hair was dark red. She glanced at Mickey and Pris, made an oddly thick noise that could only be rendered as "harumph" and went back to reading. Along the counter were arranged ink pads, date stamps, piles of teal cards, several pens attached to chains, and a small notebook.

Pris said under her breath, "Right," and walked over. "Hello. Have you heard about the missing lifeguard trainee? A friend of the family sent us." This was absolutely stretching the truth.

The librarian pushed her glasses down her nose and stared at Pris's mouth until Pris repeated what she had said, which she did, slower. The librarian picked up the pad of paper and wrote, *I don't talk to reporters*, in hurried but legible handwriting.

"We aren't reporters, ma'am," Pris lied, because what were podcasters but amateur reporters? "Dylan's friend Lucas asked us to come and be with him during this trying time."

The librarian's pale eyebrows went up and Mickey tensed because Pris was already primed to go into a rage after the earlier debacle with the innkeeper thinking Mickey was mentally deficient.

The librarian wrote, *Someone told me that one trainee had gone for a walk and not returned, but honestly no one is that concerned. He'll turn up. They almost always do.* As soon as she finished writing, her eyes went back to their faces. Reading lips, Mickey guessed. Mickey glanced at both the woman's ears and saw no signs of implants to help her hear. She wondered how a Deaf woman coped in a town with no technology.

Pris tilted her head. "Almost always?"

The librarian shrugged and wrote, *Sure.*

Mickey didn't like the sound of that. She looked sideways at Pris. Pris shrugged at her, then moved her hand from her chin, mouthing "thank you" at the librarian. The librarian, smiling widely, repeated the gesture, mouthing something that might have been "welcome."

SHIVER

Pris pulled Mickey into the next room.

"You know any sign language?" Mickey asked.

"Just a bit. I forgot most of it. My mother had all of us learn as babies; we had an au pair who once worked as a translator teach us so we could communicate before we learned to speak."

The shelving units didn't match from room to room; they didn't even match within each room. Some were metal, others wood, of different styles and heights. The building smelled old and hot and not entirely clean. The outer rooms' windows were open but lacked protective screens to keep out insects or animals. None of the books looked current. Most rooms were nonfiction.

"This library sucks," Mickey complained. It was dusty to the point of filth in the corners. "How do you find anything? I don't see any reference computers."

"Energy-sucking fey." Pris pulled Mickey through another archway and into a hallway and let out a glad cry. "Oh, I never thought I'd see one of these in real life."

Wooden cabinets filled with small drawers lined one side of the hallway. On top of the cabinets were bins with scraps of paper and pencil stubs.

"What is this?"

"This is prehistoric Google. It's a card catalog." Pris pulled out a drawer. Index cards filled it, some typed, some handwritten, all strung on a long metal rod. "Every card is a book."

"How does it work?"

"I never used one, so I guess like Google. I think there are several cards for each book, right? Cross-referenced? Let's try Missing Persons." Pris found the right drawer and … nothing. "Okay, that failed." Searching for "Sharks" located books on sharks, but nothing about the shark attacks a century earlier. They brainstormed topics, including "Energy-Sucking Fey," and struck out on all of them.

"Should we ask the librarian? She seems nice," Mickey ventured.

"I'm not sure I trust her. But she seems nice. Seems." Pris said, sliding another drawer closed. "The jury is still out on her."

"Isn't the jury you and me?"

"Well, yes. So, it's a hung jury because I'm not sure." Pris stared at the card catalog. "This has been a waste of time. Let's try next door. We'll keep the lady librarian as an option."

When they returned to the checkout area, the woman wasn't there. They crossed the dividing hall of the remodeled mansion into the historical society, encountering a similar counter with no one staffing it. Pris stuffed cash into the donation jar.

SHIVER

The displays were a combination of human and natural history. Native American artifacts and colonial items shared space with whaling and nautical mementos, next to poorly taxidermied examples of local fauna.

"This isn't that terrible," Pris remarked. "They could organize it better and clean it. The expressions on these animals' faces, though ..."

Mickey longed to draw a few of the exhibits. Her artist's eye saw how they could be arranged and grouped for maximum interest. She especially liked the taxidermied seagulls; she had never seen one so close. They were larger than she thought.

Pris kept going and into another room. Mickey was about to ask her for the tiny digital camera when Pris called, "You gotta see this!"

Pris had the camera out and was using it. Her lanky body blocked what had gotten her so excited.

"Pris, what is it?"

Pris moved aside. "It's an actual mermaid."

SHIVER

-6-

The container was huge, a warehouse store pickle jar. Its metal top, although sealed with wax, had rusted. The museum staff had placed the container before a window with the shade pulled, presumably to protect the contents from the sun. Murky fluid filled the jar; it may have been clear once, but now microscopic biological bits floated in it. And one macroscopic bit: a baby mermaid.

Pris snapped pictures and shot video while slowly moving around the jar. An unpleasant smell hung in the jar's vicinity; at least part of the creature was biological.

Shell Beach Historical Society

Specimen: Homo sapiens syreni (juv)

Location: United States of America,
Massachusetts, Shell Beach

Coordinates: 42°29'48.8"N, 70°48'46.3"W

Date: July 17, 1917

Collector: Charles Quentin

"It's a gaffe," Mickey said, trying to convince herself because the creature was unmistakably real-looking and because the rest of the taxidermy in the historical society had been so awful.

"I don't think it is." Pris leaned on Mickey, crowding her. "This is our story, Mickey-girl."

"It's a monkey sewn to a fish. Please, get off me; I can't breathe." Mickey ducked from under Pris's constricting arm and retreated behind a giant anchor in the room's center. The iron was cold against her face. Her heart slowed. She laid her metal hand on the curve and felt a sense of kinship. She couldn't feel temperature with the prosthetic, but it still calmed her as much as the coolness against her cheek.

Across the room, Pris talked to the baby mermaid, babbling a stream of consciousness to it as she took more photos and videos. Mickey desperately wanted to see the small creature up close, but the heat and death smell of the room were stifling. Plus, when Pris was this engaged in something, she couldn't get out of her own way, much less give Mickey the space she needed. Mickey stayed crouched behind the anchor, embracing it with both arms, breathing through her mouth. Pickled dead mermaid gaffe tasted as bad as it smelled.

"Look at you, look at you," Pris crooned.

Mickey realized she had left her anxiety pills back in the B&B and not put them in her pocket once again. She would have to act like an old lady and invest in one of those little key chain pill keepers. She settled on her heels, leaned her forehead against the anchor, and listened to Pris talk to the baby mermaid.

And then the baby mermaid answered. "You can't even see the stitches, can you?"

Mickey peered around the anchor because she did not believe that the unfortunate misshapen dead gaffe could speak.

And, of course, it was not the baby mermaid. It was a woman, a little older than Pris, dark-skinned with beaded braids and black rhinestone glasses.

"One time, when I was in middle school, I stole it! I was going to take it home to my laboratory, and I was going to dissect it. Of course, I was going to do it right. Scientific method and all that. I was going to sketch it—draw it like one of those French girls. Maybe scrape off some cells from the top and bottom halves and send them off for DNA analysis. I was going to be famous!" She was talking a mile a minute—clearly, Pris had met her match.

Pris stopped taking photos and stared at the other woman with her mouth slightly open, forced to listen to her outpouring of words.

"What I didn't consider," the other said, shaking her braids so the beads clicked together, "was how heavy that jar is! And how slippery it is to carry. They caught me, of course, because I didn't think to bring a wheelbarrow or a wagon to carry it home in. I guess we're all just lucky I didn't drop it onto the ground, smashing the jar, and ruining the poor baby."

Pris found her voice. "Did you get in trouble?"

"Of course not! I'm a mad scientist; that's what they expect me to do. Plus, it was right after my daddy died, and I guess they figured I was crazed with grief. And that might have been true too."

Mickey stood and made her way from behind the anchor over to Pris and the new woman. "Hi," she said, "I'm Mickey Crow, and this is my friend Pris. Your baby mermaid is really cool, and we want to know everything about it, but we're actually here looking for that missing lifeguard kid. Do you know anything about it? About him?"

"Hi, Mickey! I'm Mo and I'm a mad scientist!" Mo laughed again. Her beads danced and clicked. "And yes, I have heard that a redheaded white boy wandered away last night. I have an inside track." She rolled her eyes. "My mom is dating the sheriff—how embarrassing is that? This old white dude." She looked back and forth between Pris and Mickey. "No offense."

Mickey shrugged it off. Pris said, "None taken," because she was, in fact, very pale.

Mickey asked, "What's your inside scoop with this old white dude? What did the sheriff tell you about this missing kid?"

Mo shrugged. "That he's missing, and he has red hair and I should look for him, kind of. Like if I see a kid with red hair, I should maybe tell someone. Like the sheriff."

Pris asked, almost hungrily, "So you have a cell phone?"

Mo laughed, and it came out this time like a little snort. "A cell phone. That's funny. You guys must have just gotten here."

Mickey said, "No, we've been here about an hour. We already stopped at the hardware store, we've been to the library, which has no computers, and checked in at the B&B, which has almost no electrical outlets and absolutely no Wi-Fi."

"You'll find that's the general state of this place—no computers and absolutely no Wi-Fi—that could be the town motto of Shell Beach."

"That's really annoying." Pris ran her fingers along the outside of the thick jar that housed the baby mermaid. "Is there a particular reason you guys live in the Dark Ages? Actually, I think I know why—am I right? On the drive here, my car started going absolutely insane. Poor Mickey was driving, and I thought she was going to crash because these energy-sucking fey started attacking my car once we put Shell Beach in as a destination."

Mo's delicate eyebrows came up over the top of her glasses. "Did you say *energy-sucking fey*?"

"Yes, energy-sucking fey. I figured it out, didn't I?" Pris grinned toward Mickey.

"Yep," said Mickey, "energy-sucking fey, you nailed it."

"Not exactly," replied Mo. "It's a long and complex story, but we have this elderly mayor, Mayor Jenkinson, who is latest in line of elderly mayors named Jenkinson, who have been sons or grandsons of the previous elderly mayor, going back forever, or so it seems. They don't like technology; therefore, we haven't got any. When I went away to college, wow, it was like a whole new world. But my mom was lonely without me and with my daddy gone, so I had to come back. I wish I

SHIVER

could get her to move. Or, as gross as it is, maybe she will marry the old white sheriff. I mean, she's white too, of course, but because she's my mom, I don't really think about her like that."

Pris looked visibly devastated. Both shoulders dropped. The camera hung from her wrist by its strap. No energy-sucking fey?

Mickey laughed until she realized she would have to explain what exactly was causing the problems in the car ride up. She would have to admit that it was her. Well, her neural net. At least in a town with limited tech, there would be nothing for her neural net to disrupt. This was a conversation that could wait until they were on their way home.

"I can show you where that redheaded boy probably disappeared," Mo offered, "if you feel like taking a walk."

SHIVER
-7-

Mickey followed Pris and Mo as they chattered a mile a minute. It was actually kind of relaxing to let someone else talk to Pris for once. The subjects jumped from the mermaid to the lack of internet and back. Mickey just let it wash over her. The paved streets were very sandy. Her sandals scuffed along, and the repetitive sound helped dispel her anxiety.

Mickey learned Mo's dad had been a Jamaican fisherman who had fallen overboard in a storm and never returned. Only recently had her mother come to terms with the fact that he was not coming back. In the past, once in a while locals had fallen off ships in the area or otherwise disappeared and been thought drowned, then returned, not wanting to talk about it. But her dad had been gone for over fifteen years, and they had both given up hope of ever seeing him again.

Mo's house was cream-colored, a little sandblasted, and in need of a paint job. The garage stuck out on one side like an elbow. She unlocked a hasp and pulled the door open to reveal that inside the garage was a small laboratory. On the wall against the house was an enormous set of shark jaws, museum-quality. Mickey wanted to stay and inspect this fantastic area. It looked meticulously organized, with rows of neatly labeled jars and flasks on little shelves fastened to every wall. Counters, workbenches, a padded and worn stool, and many professional-looking glass implements were neatly lined up in the space that should have housed a single car. Laboratory things like microscopes were there, along with other tools and gadgets Mickey couldn't identify. It was a perfect, secret lair for a self-proclaimed mad scientist. The shark jaws tied it all together.

"There's an entire story about those jaws, which I'll tell you later." Mo chose a numbered vial of reddish-brown fluid from a shelf and closed the garage door leading to the street. There was another door matching it on the opposite side leading to the yard, and the three of them ducked out through it. From beside the garage, Mo picked up a covered bucket from which emanated quite a foul smell. At the other end of her long narrow backyard was the sea, but before that was a blue pool, a large temporary one with a small jury-rigged deck on one side.

Mickey made a face that Mo could not see. Ugh, a pool. Water. She hoped Mo would not expect them to go swimming. Why would anybody put their swimming pool so far away from the house? Plus, right beside the ocean?

Flies followed them, or at least followed the smelly bucket, as they walked across the yard. The sparse yellowed grass was mixed with sand. Across the top of the pool rested a metal bar with what looked like a camera attachment hanging from it. Mo ducked underneath the deck and opened a locked box, removing a journal with a plastic cover and a pen stuck to it with Velcro, and a video camera, which she handed to Pris. Mo's sleeve fell back, revealing a bandage on her arm.

"Did you hurt your arm?" Mickey asked.

"I didn't hurt it; it got hurt. I think you'll figure out how in a minute. Come on up."

The top of the deck was small, but three women in their middle twenties fit on it—although it lacked railings to keep them there. The bottom of the pool had some sand and small rocks and seaweed floating around.

Mickey didn't know why she was focusing on that, because what was also in the pool was a shiver of small sharks. They were only about two to three feet long and of various species—but they were sharks in a swimming pool.

Mo's grin was wide and happy. "Check it out!"

"Those are sharks. In your pool," Mickey said. She hated to state the obvious, but … this was a swimming pool. Full of sharks. Not normal.

"Well yeah," Mo said, "Of course. How am I going to test shark repellent if I don't have any sharks?"

That was distressingly logical, even if it was very bizarre.

"That's how you hurt your arm—you got bit by a shark?" Pris looked at the video camera in her hands. "I suppose this gets locked onto that structure?"

"Well, yes, of course; how else am I supposed to record my successes and failures? I told you I was a scientist."

"You said you were a mad scientist," Mickey said. "I guess I thought you were kidding."

"Nope. Of course, I'm not kidding. I'm as mad as they get!" Mo shook her head, making her braids dance.

"This camera is ancient," Pris remarked, but it only took her a moment to figure out how to attach it to the pole mount over the pool.

The small sharks swam endlessly in a circle, stirring up the bits of seaweed and other floating detritus. Two thick hoses, both attached to pumps, led from the far side of the pool to the nearby beach. One pump cycled on and water flooded into the pool from the ocean. The sharks swam faster, seeming to enjoy it. As Mickey watched, she felt dizzy. She assumed the water pumped in must seem cold and have more oxygen, making the sharks invigorated. She sensed the sharks were happy; odd to think about sharks in a swimming pool.

As Mo uncovered the bucket, a genuinely hideous stench came out, an almost solid smell of rotten fish and blood. Pris and Mickey staggered in response and nearly tumbled off the side of the deck. Mo grabbed them, pulling them back to her side.

"This is their favorite food." She pointed to the uncovered stinking bucket. "Yes, the notorious, infamous chum. The fishermen make it, the same ones who catch the baby sharks for me. One of them is my Great-Uncle Charlie, my mom's uncle." She turned to Mickey. "He's got one leg. Not that it would make you be friends or anything; I was just mentioning it because I'm used to seeing somebody with a missing limb. That's why I didn't freak out when I met you, although your arm is way cooler than his leg, and I want to talk to you about your arm later." She paused and stared at the sharks. "Actually, I'm sorry about that. I hate it when people think I know another Black person because I'm Black, so why would you care just because somebody is missing a leg?"

SHIVER

Mickey shrugged. "That's fine. If he had a cool leg, I would want to see it, regardless. He might be interested in seeing my arm, I don't know." She extended the arm to Mo. "My prosthetic is a prototype. There literally isn't another one like it. I don't actually know that much about it. I'm beta testing it for my friends who designed it. You would probably like them a lot. They're twins. They run a famous Robo Rumble team and are robotics experts with a company near Boston. They are mad scientists too."

Pris broke into this discussion, saying, "Right, can we all talk about missing limbs and fighting robots later? Because these are sharks and they are in your swimming pool. I just can't get past that."

Moe laughed. "I hope you don't think I swim in here with them. I might be a mad scientist, but I'm not crazy. I'm clumsy, though. I dropped the bucket in there during feeding time the other day, and while I was fishing it out, one of them got me. That was because that day's formula clearly did not work as a shark repellent, of course, or they would not have been near me when I was fishing out the bucket. Let's turn on the camera and see how it works today."

Mo used a small remote to turn on the camera. She positioned it in the center of the pool so that it would record the whole area. "I just watch the playback on the camera itself," she explained to Pris. "If I ever film anything good, I guess I'll have to take the card out and figure out what to do with it since I have no computer."

"We're friends now. We'll come up and help you," Pris said. "I could bring you a computer, but it won't do you much good without the internet. But you could at least save the content of your cards onto it if you want to do that."

Mo seemed astonished. She pushed her glasses around on her face a bit. "That's extraordinarily generous of you—we only met a few minutes ago. Let's see what you think after you watch my experiment." Mo leaned over the side of the pool, hanging the stinky bucket over the water.

Mickey felt hungry and dizzy. She could not understand how she could feel hungry with that disgusting smell in the air, although the dizziness made perfect sense.

The sharks stopped circling the whole pool and started making tight little spirals right underneath the bucket as Mo allowed drips of the dark chum mixture to fall into the water.

Mickey realized she had no more protein bars squirreled away in her pockets and that she was ravenous.

Mo drizzled the bucket of chum into the pool. The little sharks went wild, eating like crazy. Although they were small, it was frightening to watch, kind of like how piranhas can devour an entire cow down to the bone as it tries to cross a river. It was like being up close and personal to a National Geographic special.

"Now we try the repellent." Mo unstopped the beaker and poured it into the center of the ever-shrinking chum puddle. "If this works, the sharks should stop eating and go to the other side of the pool."

As Mickey watched the little sharks eat, she felt slightly less hungry. The shark repellent did not seem to distress the carnivorous fish at all. They continued swarming and munching in the lumpy cloud of dark chum. The other pump attached to the pool kicked on. The water level dropped slightly as some of the contents were siphoned out into the ocean, including the chum and the failed repellent.

Mo pulled the camera back in and turned it off. She opened her notebook, recorded the failure, and returned the camera and the notebook to the lockbox under the deck. "That was a failure. Now let's go to the beach and try to find the redhead."

SHIVER

-9-

They followed the thick, corrugated blue hoses toward the water. Mo pointed right. "Town's that way; the lifeguard camp is the other way, maybe five miles. This is all private beach." She waved her hands to encompass the general area.

Seeing the other two were hesitant to step onto the sand, she said, "I can use it because I live here. You're my guests. Honestly, no one cares as long as you aren't doing anything wrong. If you're just walking along, it's fine. If you're not with me, tell them you're meeting me if anyone gives you trouble. Everyone knows Mo. Mo McLeod."

They turned left. Mo continued, "What happened, apparently, is that this redhead boy—"

"Dylan," supplied Pris.

"Of course, Dylan. Got in a fight with his boyfriend," said Mo.

"The friends I told you about, who made my prosthetic?" Mickey interrupted, holding up her shiny metal arm. "Their little brother, Lucas, is his friend. He's also at the lifeguard camp."

"Lucas, so it's a small world," Mo said. "Dylan of the red hair got into a fight in the middle of the night with his boyfriend, whose name we don't know. Which upset friend Lucas whose brothers make robots and arms. Dylan went off through the woods and to the beach, where he seemed to have walked quite a way toward the town. There was a full moon last night, so he would have been able to see pretty well. At one point, Dylan took off his shoes—the police have them. Then apparently, he ran into the ocean. No one has any trace of him coming out. That doesn't mean he didn't come out somewhere that was rocky and go somewhere else without shoes. If that's the case, where is he?"

Mickey looked up and down the beach, shading her face with her metal hand. "I don't see anyone but us. Is nobody looking for him?"

Pris made a face. "I should have brought the twin's toys. First thing tomorrow."

Mo said, "Toys?"

"She won't tell me what they are, and the twins didn't tell me, so you're going to have to wait until tomorrow, too."

Pris grinned. "Oh, right, you are going to love these toys, Mickey."

It wasn't a good beach. It was rocky, with piles of smelly black and green seaweed, dead crabs, and cracked and broken shells. Out in the water crouched aggressive boulders left over from some great ice migration thousands of years before, and quite a few of them lurked on the shore. The sand particles were big and sharp, not small and soft. The sand infiltrated Mickey's sandals with hostility.

SHIVER

Once again, Mickey fell behind as Mo and Pris started talking about the logistics of keeping sharks in a swimming pool. There was a weird low buzzing in her head she had never felt before. She'd been to the beach a dozen times in her life, so there was nothing new to see, but she still felt a sense of intense curiosity welling in her, and she kept turning toward the water and looking, feeling a fierce pull. Maybe there were seals. Perhaps even a grown-up mermaid who had given birth to the monstrosity in the jar, although she knew full well it had been birthed by somebody with a needle and thread and a bag of stuffing.

After a while, they came to a spot behind a house not dissimilar to the one where Mo lived. The beach looked more trampled than usual. Someone had stuck a flimsy orange evidence flag into the sand; it looked as if it would blow away in the first strong wind.

"Here's where he went into the water," Mo said. "This is where they found his shoes. That's it; it's all there is to say."

Mickey and Pris gazed at each other. They did not know what Geoffrey and Taylor expected of them. If this guy had walked into the ocean and drowned himself, what were they supposed to do about it?

Pris asked, "How much farther is the lifeguard camp?"

"A couple miles, but right now, it's in lockdown. I saw my friend Rob earlier—he's the instructor there. Some police went out to interview everybody, of course, but really nobody's that concerned. It's only because he's an outsider that this is getting any attention at all."

Pris ran her fingers through her ultra-short pink hair and stared at Mo, her perfect lips twisted in consternation. "A kid is missing, and no one cares, right? I don't understand. Why is this beach not swarming with people looking for him?"

"I told you, people go missing from here, and sometimes they come back. We're giving him a chance to come back. Believe me, if I was missing, nobody would blink an eye—maybe my mom. Although really, it's men who go missing mostly, not women."

Pris looked at Mickey, her eyes narrowed. "You call Geoffrey and Taylor," she said. "You call the twins and tell them their little brother's friend is gone and no one cares. I'm not doing it."

Mickey said, "I'm not doing it yet—and anyway, our phones don't work, remember?"

"Actually," Mo said, "there might be another explanation. And it's not a good one. There's a history of shark attacks in this area, which is why I was trying to make shark repellent. And if the pattern holds, if the sharks are ramping up again, Dylan could have been the first victim."

SHIVER

-10-

Mickey could not turn her back on the water. But when she looked, there was nothing there to see.

"How will you know if it's a shark attack," Pris asked Mo. "Will bits wash up?"

"Depends on how big the shark is," Mo answered.

"And if you make shark repellent that works, what will you do, spray it around?"

They started walking back slowly toward Mo's laboratory, with Mickey closest to the water. The smaller rocks and chunks of driftwood conspired to turn every ankle in the vicinity. It was an unfriendly beach.

"I thought it would be more of a personal thing, like bear spray, but it depends on how well it works. The exact mechanism, too, of how it works. Plus, the littler sharks in this area, like those in my pool, aren't really any danger to people. You don't want to flood the ocean with general repellent and scare every shark away. It might also frighten away other fish that are closely related to sharks. There's an entire ecosystem out there that could become unbalanced without all the right predators in it. Until I finish the repellent, I can't know."

"I'm more of a computer science girl than a wet science one. I wish you had computers up here. I'd love to help you figure out a better formula. You won't consider moving somewhere normal?"

"This is normal for me, Pris," Mo answered gently, putting her dark hand on Pris's pale arm.

Mickey peered at something round in the water that might have been a rock or a seal's head. She stopped to kick sand out of her sandals. Pris was limping in her gladiator shoes. Mo seemed impervious.

"It's insane for us, Mo," Pris answered. "Mickey and I run a podcast. Cameras, computers, cell phones, the whole thing, all online. We have a little studio set up at Mickey's. She lives in her parents' basement like a troll."

"I heard that." Mickey wiggled her toes and turned resolutely away from the water. Although maybe she should look for a floating body. Would a body be floating so soon? She couldn't even look that up. "I do indeed live in the basement, but I am not a troll. It's a walk-out basement with an entire wall of polarized glass. Light floods the room during the day. I'm severely claustrophobic, so I need space."

"You're claustrophobic, so you live in a basement?" Mo cocked her head. Her braids flowed to one side. "I don't follow."

"It's the biggest room in the house," Mickey said. "Instead of making my poor parents have to remodel the second floor by taking down walls to knock together smaller rooms, I just moved into the basement, which was already one big room. They fixed that up. I have everything in one open-plan room, including our podcast studio. If that makes me a troll, so be it."

Mo grinned at her. "You're a basement-dwelling troll. I'm a mad scientist. What's your secret?" She turned to Pris.

"I'm rich. My family is famous." Pris put her hand to her cheek and pursed her lips in an exaggerated, hideous duck-face modeling pose.

"Of course." Mo rolled her eyes behind her rhinestone glasses. "Well, keep your secret."

Mickey laughed. "She is, really. I'm surprised she's telling you. She hates it when people find out."

"Seriously?" They arrived back at the blue pipes.

"Seriously," Pris said. "I could give you a hundred awesome computers. The cost would be a rounding error."

Mickey stayed behind on the hot, gritty sand when the other two started back into Mo's yard.

"Aren't you coming?" Pris called. "Now that she knows who I am, you need to be my bodyguard, so that Mo doesn't hold me for ransom."

"She doesn't actually know who you are," Mickey pointed out. "You didn't tell her your last name. And I want to walk all the way to town this way. I'll meet you there. I noticed a restaurant that's built out over the water that looks interesting, can we meet there? I want to keep looking for Dylan."

Mickey could hear their voices talking over each other as she continued along the beach. Waves and distance drowned the sound until she was alone. The sand encroached on her sandals, but she could tell it would be even worse to walk barefoot.

Hunger gnawed at her belly again. She walked a little faster. Good idea to meet at the restaurant. She hoped Mo understood she was invited. If Shell Beach was a normal place, she could text Pris and convey that.

She kept seeing movement out of the corner of her left eye that didn't seem to be waves, but when Mickey turned, there was nothing to see. Yet Mickey felt compelled to keep looking. Would she even recognize a body, or part of a body, in the water? Had Dylan walked this way last night? Had he gone for a midnight swim to take his mind off the lover's quarrel and was now asleep somewhere?

There, in the water, that was something, she was sure of it.

Mickey stopped, walked, and approached the edge of the waves. Her prosthetic wasn't designed for swimming, but it was water-resistant. She removed it to shower and during her hated physical therapy in the pool—same with the neural net. She didn't want to go in the water, though. It was a trigger for her claustrophobia. If there was a way to dry bathe, she would do it.

By a cluster of Pleistocene-era boulders a couple dozen yards out, something like a head bobbed in the water. A seal, most likely. Mickey made a loud kissy noise, the standard sound one made to attract an animal.

The head moved, seemed to turn, and a voice called, "Hey, can you help?"

"Oh my god!" Mickey shouted. "I can't swim!"

"My foot is stuck."

A wave swamped the head.

"I see you. I see you. Oh god."

"Can you help?"

Mickey went to the very edge of the water, where broken shells and grains of sand churned. She could tell from the darkness that out where the person was trapped, it was deep. No way. She couldn't do it. "Dylan?"

"My foot is stuck."

Emotions crashed inside Mickey even as waves washed her ankles. The hunger continued to eat at her insides. She couldn't do anything to help. Her heart started to pound. No anxiety medicine. All that water, so heavy, wanting to envelop Mickey, take her down. Her knees trembled.

"Can you help?"

"Are you Dylan?"

"My foot."

Mickey dug through her pockets, finding an empty wrapper from a blueberry bar. She laid it flat, so the purple was most visible, and put rocks on all four corners while Dylan cried for help.

"Please, hold on. I'm coming right back with help. Grab that big rock. Don't die."

Behind Dylan's head, a shark fin popped up.

Mickey ran toward town, her ankles turning on the rough beach, her breath sobbing in her throat.

SHIVER
-11-

Mickey Crow burst into the Shell Beach police station, panting, crying, having a full-on anxiety attack.

"Dylan—" she panted, bent double, trembling, both arms around her middle. "Drowning. Shark. Help."

The police officer sitting behind the counter stared at her. He didn't stand. "Miss, please calm down. Who are you? What do you want?"

"Dylan—" she gasped.

"All right, Dylan, what can I do for you?"

"I'm not Dylan." She staggered toward the counter. "I saw—" She leaned her arms on the counter, unable to hold her own weight up anymore.

Now the officer stood. "Drop your weapon, Dylan," he commanded, putting his hand on his own firearm.

"I don't have a weapon, please, help—" Mickey was living a nightmare. She slipped off the counter as her legs gave way. All her energy was going into making her whole body shake. Useless. She couldn't even form thoughts. Her brain was just spikes of energy.

The officer raised his voice. "I have a situation here! Suspect with a weapon!"

"No," Mickey said weakly. "Need help." She could barely breathe. No cell phone, no sign of Pris and Mo, poor Dylan drowning with a shark lurking next to him.

Two officers swarmed Mickey, dragging her down. Big powerful men taking down a little disabled woman, she thought, crushed to the floor. No questions.

"What in the hell is this contraption?" one of them said, yanking at her prosthetic arm.

Mickey yelled. It was clearly attached to her by straps, and more than that, it was networked into her brain. The prosthetic arm was also obviously an arm and not a gun or whatever they thought it was.

"She's on some crazy drugs," one cop said. "Listen to her caterwauling."

"My arm! Ow!"

"Never saw a weapon like this."

They handcuffed her right arm to her left foot and pulled off the prosthetic, luckily breaking none of the straps. The jolt of it forcibly disconnecting from her neural net gave Mickey an instant migraine. Tears oozed from her eyes. "He's drowning," she said, crying. "I came here for help. Please. Help."

A cop laughed. "Maybe you'll get lucky and get sentenced to rehab. That probably won't help a crazy nutcase like you much."

SHIVER

They booked Mickey for threatening an officer with a deadly weapon as she was lying on the floor, feeling crushed, her head ready to explode, unable to form words. Since she couldn't get up and walk, the cops carried her to an empty office, where they moved the cuff from her leg to the leg of the desk. They did not offer her a phone call, a drink of water, or to tell her side of the story. Not that she could speak coherently.

Mickey slumped against the top of the metal desk. Dylan was definitely dead by now. The twins had sent her to do one thing, find their brother's friend and help him, and she had failed.

Her whole body hurt. The police had put their hands on places where they shouldn't, which was not at all surprising. No one had ever restrained her before. It was awful. People got aroused by this sort of thing? It was her idea of hell. Mickey pushed the chair away and slipped to the floor, leaning against the side of the desk. That was a little better, plus the desk was metal and cool. The building was air-conditioned at least, unlike the library/historical society she had visited earlier. The arresting officers had not found her neural net under her hair, and she tried to use her biofeedback exercises to calm herself and ease the pain of the involuntary disconnection. But she had left someone, most likely Dylan, drowning and subject to a shark attack, and then been arrested for seeking help. She could not find calm.

That morning, when Mickey had woken up, she had not thought that she would be arrested and handcuffed to a desk in coastal Massachusetts before the sun went down.

SHIVER
-12-

Although my mom is dating the sheriff, I don't think she's ever really given up on my dad," Mo said. "She's never going to leave this stupid, backward town."

"And you won't leave her," Pris said. They were back in Mo's laboratory, where Pris wanted to study all of Mo's notebooks to see if she could write a computer program to catalog her results and predict future formulas. Mo couldn't believe that Pris was someone famous. Although her haircut was lovely and her makeup jewel-perfect, her clothes looked like they were from a ragbag. Her shoes were just awful. So ugly. Her boob job was top-notch, though, even if it was a bit much.

"I did when I went to college, but she didn't deal well. That's why I'm back. Most mornings, I work at the diner, and I do my scientist stuff the rest of the day. My mom works at a warehouse on the dock. She's an accountant."

Pris finished flipping through Mo's handwritten notebooks and tapped on the cover with a nicely manicured nail. "You're coming to dinner with us, right?"

"I don't want to intrude." She felt weird. She liked these two a lot, but they had also just met. She didn't want to be a third wheel.

"Intrude on what? We've been friends for ten years; we welcome someone else to talk to."

"I am sick of the food from the diner. It would be a delightful change. Okay." Mo closed the garage door and locked it. They started down the sandy street.

"And maybe Mickey saw something during her beach stroll or had some ideas about where to look for Dylan."

"Can I ask you? Is she an Indian? Oops, Native American?"

Pris shrugged. "Beats me. Probably. She's adopted. She refuses to get a DNA test. She just doesn't care. Someday I'm going to stick a swab in her mouth while she's asleep because I want to know."

"And you're rich and famous?" Mo didn't believe it, but why would someone make that up? Probably because she knew Mo had no easy way to check to see if Pris was lying.

"My family is rich. My siblings are famous. I try not to be famous." Pris rolled her eyes.

"You could be famous for being the whitest white girl I've ever met. You're practically an albino." Mo held her arm next to Pris's. Pris was pink from being in the sun all afternoon.

"My entire family is this white. The others do it up with fake tans and bronzer, but I embrace the pale. I was a goth for a while, with the palest blue contacts and black hair. I looked pretty awesome."

SHIVER

"I can see that." It's true, Pris would look great as a traditional goth or a pastel one. She already had the pink hair for that.

They were in sight of the seafood restaurant that crouched over the water when a police car pulled up next to them. Ted rolled down the window. "Hey, Melissa, we had some more excitement today."

Pris looked at her sideways and raised her gorgeous eyebrows. "Melissa?"

Mo made a face at her real name. "Yes, Sheriff, what kind of excitement?"

Pris held up her hand and behind it pointed to Ted and mouthed, "Old white guy?"

Mo nodded as Ted said, "My guys at the station just arrested a crazy vagrant woman who was high on drugs. She said her name was Dylan. Which is the same name as the lifeguard kid who is missing."

"That's weird," Mo said politely. She was always very pleasant to Ted, who was probably going to be her stepdad, and who was also a cop while she was Black. Mo might not have internet, but she knew about cops and Black people. "Is it now illegal to be named Dylan?"

"Oh, they didn't arrest her for that. She came running into the station all high, screaming and ranting, and attacked Dom with some kind of weird metal weapon. I guess she had it wrapped around her arm."

"Wrapped around her arm?" Mo asked, glancing at Pris. Pris's white-girl face was turning as pink as her hair.

"They said it had straps, and they took it off," Ted continued, oblivious.

Pris's lips turned white and barely moved as she spoke. "Where is she?"

"Locked up at the station—"

"This way," Mo said, and ran.

SHIVER
-13-

From the waiting area came a great noise of raised voices. One of them was extremely familiar.

"Where is she?" Mickey had never heard Pris sound so cold and angry.

Most of the voices were male, deep and angry, unintelligible rumbles.

Another female voice said, "She's my friend. They are both my friends." Oh, that one was Mo.

"Her arm is not a weapon."

The voices from down the hall washed over Mickey like the waves on the beach. She leaned her hot face against the cold desk and held on. Her whole body was pounding.

"Do you know who I am?" Oh no. Oh no, oh no, oh no. Pris was going to use her name. "You do not want me to call my lawyers." Lawyers, plural. Oh no. She was off the leash. "I am Priscilla Salamanca, of Salamanca Stainless Steel. Hand me a phone. I will sue this town. I will own this town. Then I will burn it to the ground."

The voices subsided to grumbles. Even here, in the Dark Ages, Pris's name opened doors. Question was, did it open handcuffs?

Footsteps clicked down the hall. A man opened the door, which hadn't been locked. Mickey, huddled on the floor against the desk, stared up at him. He was nice-looking for an old white guy of about fifty. He was wearing a sheriff's star. She deduced, with the last of her brainpower, that this was Mo's inside guy.

He said, "Melissa says you're her friend. And your name isn't Dylan."

Who the hell was Melissa? "I'm Michaela Lamotte, Mickey Crow Lamotte. I'm here to help find Dylan. A friend of the family." She shivered, still in the throes of pain and anxiety, and stared at the metal cuff imprisoning her wrist.

"I see. And why did you attack my officer?"

"I didn't. I was trying to get help—" She remembered and gasped, looking up. "I saw Dylan! He was trapped, his foot, in some rocks in deep water, calling for help. There was a shark nearby, a big fin. I can't swim, so I ran into town for help. Instead, your guys assaulted and arrested me."

"My officer says you came in, acting drunk or high, and attacked him with a crazy high-tech weapon strapped to your arm."

From the lobby, Pris screamed, "If you hurt her, I will burn this place down! Give me that phone!" Sounds of scuffling and grunting.

The sheriff paused in the doorway and looked back down the hall.

SHIVER

"Help him!" Mickey cried. "I marked the spot on the beach with a purple protein bar wrapper. There are three boulders in the water about twenty feet out. It's not quite to Mo's house. Go, please!"

"Don't hurt her! Stop it! Dom, Jack, don't be idiots!" Mo yelled. Footsteps pounded down the hallway. "Ted, please, these are my friends. They did nothing wrong."

"Melissa, she threatened an officer."

Mo is Melissa? Okay.

"Ted, she's an amputee, her back is twisted, she's tiny. Just look at her. She has a high-tech experimental prosthetic. It's not a weapon. It's an artificial arm. Give it back to her and let her go, please. Plus, if her friend calls her lawyer, it will be horrible for the town. Her friend is from a high-profile family."

Pris shrieked. Something hit the floor.

Mickey lost it. "Have you all forgotten that Dylan is drowning with a shark nearby? Can't you all stop squabbling like children and act like police officers and go save him?" She had been restrained and locked in a small room. She had seen someone drowning. She might go to jail. She rattled the handcuffs and then collapsed, wrung out.

SHIVER
-14-

Ted blocked the office door, but Mo could still see her new friend on the floor, handcuffed to an old metal desk. She had fainted.

"She found the missing lifeguard, and in return, you locked her up?" Mo demanded of Ted. "Give her back her arm and let her go. Let's go save that boy."

Ted looked past her, back toward the lobby, where it sounded like Pris was in hand-to-hand combat with Dom and Jack. "We don't know the full story."

"Okay, leave poor Mickey locked up here while we go save Dylan! He could be dead already! But uncuff her at least and leave her prosthetic arm beside her, just lock the door."

"I don't know where her arm is, honey, but I'll uncuff her, and we'll do that." He had never called her honey before.

Leaving Jack behind to supervise Pris's phone call with her lawyer, Ted, Mo, and Dom piled in a police car for the short ride to the public beach. They spread out, looking for the formation of three rocks twenty feet out and the purple wrapper, calling for Dylan.

Mo, fearless, splashed through ankle-deep water, her eyes always to the right, calling, "Hello? Hello?"

She looked for a shark fin, for clusters of boulders. Ted and Dom ranged along the rocky beach, searching for the purple wrapper.

Mo slipped and slid over slick rocks. Seaweed wrapped around her ankles like icy fingers. Whenever she found a grouping of boulders of any number, she waded out deeper, calling for Dylan. Her shorts were soaked through, and the right side of her shirt was wet all the way up. Mo's throat hurt from shouting.

They got all the way to her house, where the two corrugated hoses met the sea, with no sign of anyone in the water, and then turned back and repeated the search. Mo's left side got soaked to match her right.

Ted and Dom assumed the wrapper had blown away or been stolen by a seagull.

No one responded to their calls along the beach in either direction.

SHIVER

-15-

Pris slumped, handcuffed, in the lobby on a wooden bench when they returned to the station. Her knuckles and face were bruised, and somehow her neon-pink hair was in disarray, although it was barely an inch long. She looked like the cover of a punk rock album. Her white tank and bike shorts were dirty. The pink Oxford lacked a few buttons and hung open to her waist.

Jack sat behind the counter wearing reading glasses. His uniform was wrinkled, his graying blond hair mussed, his lip swollen. Several yards of fax paper curled off the counter, covered with minuscule print. The end of it had an impressive-looking lawyer's letterhead. "This one tried to start a riot," he grumbled, jerking his head at Pris.

"Why is she in handcuffs?" Mo demanded. She went behind the counter and into the bathroom, emerging with a wet paper towel, which she used on Pris's hands and face.

"You don't work here, little girl," Jack answered, watching all this with a sneer. "Go home and play with your fishes."

Ted sighed. "Why *is* this one handcuffed, Jack?"

"Headbutted me, didn't she?" Jack said. "And then her lawyer faxed all this over." He waved the scroll of fax paper. "Can't make heads or tails of it. Lawyer speak."

"Dom, get the other girl's arm for me, please, and anything else you took from her. Jack, give me the fax."

"It says," Pris said precisely, not lifting her head, "To let Mickey go with no charges and to let me go with no charges. Or my lawyers will come after you with extreme prejudice. Apparently, you don't understand who you are dealing with."

"You headbutted an officer?" Ted asked, skimming the small blurry print on the endless fax.

"He arrested my Mickey-girl for nothing."

Mo sat beside Pris and linked her arm through her new friend's elbow, as always admiring the extreme contrast of their skin colors. She laid her head on Pris's shoulder so her beads could touch Pris.

When Mo was little, her father used to dance the beaded ends of his impressive dreadlocks all over her, tickling her and making her laugh. She found solace in the sound of the beads hitting each other and the feel of them on her skin. She moved her head, gliding her beads against Pris's neck, hoping her new friend also felt comforted.

Dom returned, carrying a repurposed delivery box with Mickey's metal forearm sticking out. He dumped it on the table. Mo winced, thinking of how much that one-of-a-kind experimental arm must be worth. She wanted to get up and look at it closer, but she also knew

SHIVER

Pris needed human contact. Under the sway of Mo's beads, Pris still trembled with adrenaline.

Ted brought Mickey down the hall. She walked slowly, bent to the right, and seemed broken and small without her arm. The biomechanical tattoos on her left shoulder and upper arm had lost their vibrancy. Her dark eyes appeared huge and unfocused.

Pris, lost in her own thoughts, didn't react to her friend's appearance. Ted handed Mickey the box containing her arm. She dropped it, unable to grasp the large box one-handed, and then stared dumbly at the floor. Ted tried again, obviously not comprehending the problem, and the box fell again.

Mo pulled herself carefully away from Pris and crossed the counter again, bending to remove the arm from the floor. "Can I help you put this on?"

Mickey extended her stump, and Mo was astonished to see the metallic tattoo lines and embedded chips along its surface. "I rarely let anyone help," Mickey said in a tiny voice.

"I don't want to break it," Mo said, trying to figure out how to slide the arm on. It was heavier than she expected.

"Just gimme," Mickey replied in that same almost-dead voice. She took the arm and slotted herself into it, rotating the forearm until it locked into place. She stared into space for a moment, then her eyes seemed to spark blue, and she shook her head slightly. "Okay, it's on; just the straps now." She accepted help with those.

While that was happening, Ted had released Pris from her handcuffs. "You girls can go now," he said. "All charges dropped."

"What about Dylan?" Mickey asked. "Where is he? Did you save him?"

"No one was there," Ted answered, opening the lobby door. "We were too late."

SHIVER
-16-

Mickey went ahead with Mo and secured a table at The Dockside Feast, the restaurant perched over the water, while Pris went back to the B&B to change clothes and retrieve Mickey's anxiety medicine and something for her headache.

The two of them sat in a curved corner booth overlooking the patio and the dark water. The moon was just rising. It should have been beautiful.

"Someone died there tonight," Mickey said, staring at the almost-round moon, remembering those calls for help. "Because the police here are idiots." And because I am afraid of the water.

"I want to defend them, but you're right."

"I don't know if I could have saved him even if I could swim." More things to weigh on her. More ways for Mickey Crow to be useless on the face of the earth.

Mo looked at her curiously, sucking on one of her beads. "You can't swim because of your arm? Or because of your back? You don't need to say if you don't want to. I'm super nosy, in case you didn't notice. It's a scientist thing, of course."

"Neither of those things. It's because of my severe claustrophobia. Being in the water makes me feel suffocated. Kind of like being handcuffed to a desk in a tiny room." She twisted her mouth to show Mo she didn't blame her for what her mother's boyfriend had done.

"Ouch." Mo spit out the bead. "I see Pris coming with your medicine."

Pris had changed from the soiled white and pale pink outfit to a black-and-purple one. Purple leggings down to her calf, with black lightning stripes along the sides, and another distressed Oxford, this one tie-dyed in black and gray, with black ballet flats. The bruises were startlingly dark against her face and hands.

She flipped two pill bottles to Mickey and slid in beside Mo, trapping her in the middle of the curve. Mickey threw back two pills dry and shuddered, trying not to choke. It would take a few minutes for them to work.

Pris flipped open the oversized menu and groaned. "It's all carbs."

"Carbs are delicious," Mo said and tore apart a thick yellow and orange cheddar cheese biscuit, stuffing a big hunk into her mouth.

"We try to eat keto," Mickey explained, but she eyed the basket in the center of the oval table. The biscuits looked and smelled delicious. They had garlic and onion powder on them, both root vegetables. Garlic was good for you, right? Kept away vampires. And the biscuits could count as an orange food. An orange biscuit was practically a carrot if you looked at it that way.

Mo made a face. "How old are you? Live a little. Wait until you're Ted's age to give up good food."

"We want to live to be Ted's age," Pris said. She continued frowning at the menu, tapping at the entrée section with a perfect nail.

Mo ripped another delectable biscuit apart, dipped it in the little saucer of melted butter, and pushed it into Pris's pursed mouth.

Pris opened her mouth wider in shock, closed it, chewed, and moaned a little. She eyed Mo. "Are you gay?"

Mickey edged back in the booth. She did not need to witness this. Ew. She examined the biscuit basket again. Could she grab the whole basket and escape with it back to Caren's Cozy Cottage? Maybe the butter too?

"Um, no? Not usually." Mo answered. She looked at Mickey as if to say, *help*?

Mickey shrugged and raised a hand. *Not my problem*. She turned her attention back to the basket of delicious orangeness.

"I want to rub my buttery lips all over you," Pris said, leaning forward. "I think I love you."

Mickey stuck her tongue out, faking a gag. Although it was barely possible Mickey was in love with those biscuits she hadn't even tasted yet. The heavenly smell alone, butter and onion and garlic, and of course cheese, delicious dark orange crumbly cheddar cheese.

"I think you love carbs," Mo responded, probably correctly, and stuck another piece of butter-dripping biscuit into Pris's mouth.

"Gimme some of that," Mickey demanded, and Mo handed her a piece of buttery orange heaven. Mickey did indeed want to run off with the entire basket after pouring the bowl of butter on top. Keto? What was keto?

They ordered plates of fried, breaded stuff with an extra basket of biscuits and more melted butter. There was probably protein in their food somewhere.

"This should have been a nice getting-to-know-new-friends meal," Mo said, licking butter off her shiny fingers. A pile of empty shrimp tails filled her plate.

"It was an enjoyable meal, anyway," Pris said. "We should get more biscuits. Or should we get dessert? Or both?"

"Someone drowned. I don't even know if it was Dylan or not," Mickey said, remembering her part in that and feeling shame all over again. "And we're eating buttered cheese biscuits and having fun. Why are we even here?"

"We still need to eat," Pris pointed out, lifting a finger at the server. "And I didn't feel like eating at the diner. No offense, Mo."

SHIVER

"I meant here at Shell Beach."

"The twins sent us to look for Dylan."

"We should go look tonight. Recreate the atmosphere of last night when and where he vanished. Use our camera setup. You got it, right?"

"Yeah, I have it all."

"We've ghost hunted before. Maybe we can find Dylan's ghost."

SHIVER

-17-

It always took a few minutes for Mickey to adapt to walking with so much gear strapped to her. She was small and crooked but used to counterbalancing the weight of the complex metal arm. Now she had added a front-facing camera rig atop her head and one on her chest directed at her face. A rugged waterproof tablet, carried by Pris, controlled the cameras via Bluetooth. Pris also had her tiny beloved spycam and some narrow-beam LED flashlights.

Mo laughed at Mickey's getup when they arrived at the public beach to meet her. "You guys," she said. "I thought you were kidding."

"This is all part of doing podcasts," Mickey said. "I'm the face of the Contrary Crowcast, and Pris is the producer. She sometimes does extra voiceovers, she does the tech, and she's got a little extra money to finance it."

Pris laughed at that understatement.

"I only vaguely know what a podcast is," Mo confessed. Wearing dark clothes, she was almost invisible.

"We need to move you somehow to the twenty-first century with the rest of us," Pris said. "I might make you my newest special project."

"Oh, poor Mo," Mickey said insincerely, putting the back of her hand to her forehead. "Pris made me into one of her special projects in high school. She hasn't let me go since."

"I'm sure it's been awful for you, right?" Pris said dryly. "Having a best friend who loves you madly and would do anything for you. Who almost got arrested for you earlier?"

Mickey made a face and turned to Mo. "We're recording all this. We have been since before we got to the beach a few minutes ago. So don't say or do anything you don't want on the internet forever."

Mo nodded.

"Okay, Mickey, you walk closest to the beach and keep looking at the water. I'll watch the screen. Mo, you want to use the spycam?" Pris handed it to Mo.

Mickey walked to the water and stared at it. Although she knew the cameras had infrared and night vision, she did not. Even with the moon, it was a lot of black and gray. She didn't look back toward the lights of Shell Beach, trying to allow her eyes to become accustomed to the darkness.

"I don't know how I'm hungry again when I ate about ten thousand calories of buttered biscuits for dinner," she said, moving her head slowly to sweep the waves. She was starving, though. That's precisely why she ate few carbs. They didn't stick around like protein did. She searched for seals, for shark fins, for the floating corpse of a redheaded boy. She looked for her purpose in life. Mickey found none of that.

SHIVER

She narrated out of habit. "I don't know, maybe we should get some night-vision goggles. Do they have little ones, like swim goggles?" Mickey was just talking to herself. If she wore goggles, it would detract from her facial expressions if they found anything while filming with this crazy rig. Maybe the twins could make some night-vision contact lenses for her?

"You can look through the viewfinder and kind of see—" Pris said, explaining the spycam to Mo.

Walking carefully along the uneven sand in the dark, Mickey moved down the beach toward the lifeguard camp, her belly gnawing with hunger. Her head kept swiveling to the right, but she couldn't actually see whatever almost caught her attention.

She wasn't sure how close to the water the houses along here were. Could she shout to Pris without the homeowners hearing? She turned back and saw two human shapes, close together, heading toward her, twin beams of light leading the way.

In this darkness, she would never find the purple wrapper she had left to mark where she had seen Dylan earlier. She went over the encounter, and now she doubted it had been Dylan at all. Something about the voice had been feminine. Could someone else, besides Dylan, have drowned here? What was going on?

But that answered the question of why someone would take off their shoes and run into the water. Someone with lifeguard training. If he saw someone drowning. That's what he was training for. Of course he would go in.

Mickey spoke softly, talking herself through it. "If that's the case, that's three drowned people in two days. The person Dylan tried to save, Dylan himself, and whoever I saw yesterday afternoon. What is causing all these people to drown? Why has only Dylan been reported missing?" She used her podcast voice and exaggerated facial expressions, although she looked terrible in night vision. They would probably refilm all this in her basement lair-studio.

Whenever one of the Pleistocene-era boulders loomed offshore, Mickey turned and scanned the water. Pris and Mo had caught up and walked just behind Mickey. Mo peered through the night-vision spycam at the water while Pris used the tablet to view the scene through Mickey's headcam. None of them actually watched where they were walking, so they stumbled often and probably looked drunk.

But there was something out there. Something happening. Mickey just knew it. The closer she got to the water, the more she felt it.

"Mickey!" Mo called. "Your wrapper!"

And there it was, the purple wrapper, held down by rocks, just as Mickey had left it.

SHIVER

The three of them stared at each other for a moment and then turned toward the dark stones hulking in the water. "Hello!" Mickey called. "Hello, I came back; I'm so sorry."

"Did the cops even look?" Pris said in disbelief, motioning Mo to take photos of the wrapper.

"Ted's a good guy. If he says they looked, they looked. Somehow, they missed it," Mo said. "I was walking in the water the whole time."

"Mo, we found it in the dark and we weren't even looking because they told us it was not there anymore and we believed them."

"Hello, hello, are you still there?" Mickey walked closer to the water's edge. "Pris, look through my camera."

"Can you help?" answered a tiny, gritty voice from the dark water.

"Oh my god!" Mo exclaimed. She dropped the spy cam. It dangled from a strap around her wrist as she covered her mouth with both hands. "Oh my god, he was out here the whole time. We missed him. I missed him. I know I passed this spot twice. How did that happen?"

"I'm so, so sorry, there was a huge misunderstanding, but I'm here again, and I brought help this time," Mickey explained frantically to the black waves. "Pris, can you see?"

"My foot is stuck."

"I know." Mickey's throat thickened. All this time, trapped while the tide had risen and fallen. No one had believed her.

"Why didn't we bring a rope?" Mo mourned. "I swear, I didn't think we'd find anyone. There was no one here before! Should I run to my house and see if Ted is there with my mom?"

"Ted is useless, right?" Pris said, lifting the tablet. "Look at the rocks for me, Mickey."

Mickey aimed her head at the rocks. Everything was in shades of gray and black in the moonlight. She searched where the head had been the day before, but it looked so different in the dark. "Are you Dylan?"

"Help?"

"Yes, I'm here to help, but I can't find you. Keep talking." She waded into the hateful water. It was so cold. The sand moved under her feet, sucking them down while the water enveloped her. The ocean would gladly eat Mickey. She hated it.

"I see nothing—" Pris said slowly. "Are you really going in the water? Mickey, you can't."

"I'm not leaving again. Keep looking."

"My foot is stuck." It might as well be the rock talking for all that Mickey could see.

"I know, I know. Can you wave your arm, though? I know you must be so tired. And hungry." Mickey was hungry, too.

"Eleven o'clock," Pris called.

Mo was using the zoom lens of the spy camera while standing on a flat rock. "I still can't tell what I'm looking at!" she cried. "What are you seeing, Pris?"

"Eleven what?" Mickey replied. She held her metal arm high out of the water, keeping it dry. Her shoulder ached.

"A little to your left in front of you. I see something. Dylan, Dylan, is that you? Wave more!"

"I can't see anything. Should I go left or forward?" Mickey hesitated, being battered by black waves she couldn't see.

"No, it's a shark fin sticking up, not an arm; Mickey, no, come out of there. It's a fin, right, Mo?"

"No, Mickey, stay still!" Mo instructed.

Mickey rocked in place, her feet sinking as if in quicksand, the waves buffeting her to the knees and higher. "Mo, will it eat me?"

"Can you help?"

"Don't move!" Mo shouted. "There's a shark right there!"

"My foot is stuck."

"I don't think it will eat you. I can't really see it on this little screen. How big is it, Pris?"

"What do I know about sharks? I'm not NatGeo. It's a pointy fin in the water. It could be tiny or giant. There's nothing to compare it to, right?"

Mickey pulled the waterproof LED flashlight from her wet pocket and flashed it forward, destroying her night vision.

"Ow!" Pris yelled. "The whole screen is white now! I can't see anything anymore."

Finally, Mickey located the drowning person. Pale face, framed by wet, dark hair. The eyes were out of the water, but the nose and mouth kept getting covered. It looked nothing at all like the snapshot of Dylan the twins had sent. This was someone who was going under, though. But somehow, the face looked calm in the light, looking back at Mickey with curiosity, not panic.

And there was the fin, lurking right behind the bobbing head.

"I don't think it's Dylan, but I don't know. The shark is right there," Mickey said. She moved the beam from the head to the shore. "Hey! Can you reach forward? Can you reach me?"

"Mickey, there's a shark."

"Pris, a person is drowning. Help me."

"I can't tell from the fin what kind of shark it is. That's weird," Mo mused. "Mickey, I don't know if you should do that. Let me run home. It's not far."

SHIVER

"It's the middle of the night, right," Pris said. "The sheriff won't believe you or help you, even if he's there with your mom. If he's not, you'll have to track him down here in no-cellphone-land, and he still won't help; he's proven that. Meanwhile, either this person is drowning or getting eaten, or Mickey is drowning or getting eaten."

Mickey waded in a few more heavy, horrible steps. Clumps of seaweed clung to her legs, holding her down. Her prosthetic was going to get soaked. The twins would be furious, but if this was Dylan, that would offset everything. "Grab my hand!" She offered her fleshy arm.

"Mickey! Can you wait? Can we make a rope out of our shirts or something?"

"My foot…."

"I know," Mickey said sadly. "Just take my hand. Let me try to pull you loose." If she couldn't, they would have to get help. A real diver with a scuba tank and a bang stick to fight off the shark. If only Mo's repellent worked.

The problem was, she was holding the flashlight. She would have to drop it to grab the hand, and then she could see nothing. The fin lurked right there behind the drowning head, waiting. Did sharks stay still like that?

"Pris, are you watching the screen?"

"It's all white still."

Mickey was so hungry it was distracting her. She felt as if her shorts were going to fall right off, that her navel was hooked onto her spine. She was that starving. When had she last eaten? She had no time for these food thoughts; she had to concentrate on the person in front of her, the bobbing face, the black eyes staring at her. This person needed help.

"Can you help me?" But the voice didn't come from the face, it came from beside Mickey. A long pale arm reached out. The hand grasped Mickey's wrist, squeezing it, hurting her, digging in with long nails.

Mickey gasped. "Pull me back!" she called to her friends. "I got them."

Mickey was dizzy; her vision doubled, because there were two faces, three faces; was she drowning? And the fins, jagged and triangular. Her feet left the sand. The black water was all around her, squeezing her like arms, pushing out her breath.

Something hit her left side like a truck. The world roiled, pointed fins, jagged teeth, sharp-nailed hands that hurt. The sky roared and the moon shed a tear.

SHIVER
-18-

The sky was white in the afterworld.

After a moment, Mickey realized she was awake and alive, lying on a rough pile of folded towels on top of a stainless-steel table that was too small even for her petite frame. Her prosthetic arm was missing, the neural net also missing. Her head ached.

The ceiling above was white acoustic tile.

She listened but did not hear Pris threatening anyone.

She wasn't handcuffed to anything this time.

Mickey was only wearing her sports bra and underwear. They were damp. Probably because she had been immersed completely and horribly in the ocean. A shark had attacked her and had also probably eaten the person she was trying to save. Mickey reached across her body and touched her left side. It felt tender but not bitten. That summed up her whole body when she checked it. She was already bruising. She and Pris would be quite the pair.

When she sat up, Mickey realized she was in an exam room. The walls had posters showing examples of dog and cat health. She was at a vet's office. No wonder the table was so small.

Mickey pushed herself off the table and staggered. The vinyl tile floor was cold under her bare feet, and she felt dizzy. The intense feeling of hunger had dissipated, at least. Probably almost being eaten by a shark cured that. Too bad she couldn't market that to overweight people who always felt hungry and couldn't lose weight.

Two unmarked doors led from the room; she picked one and glanced out at a hallway lined with windows. It was still dark outside the building. "Hello?" she called.

"In here!" Pris responded. "I'm coming to get you, don't walk. Plus, are you naked?"

Mickey grabbed one of the big white towels from the exam table and wrapped it around herself. Pris came down the hall and led her to the waiting area, which smelled faintly of dog and deodorizer. "We got it all on your video cameras. I don't know what it is, but we got it. The vet says you're okay, just bruised up. He was the closest doctor Mo knew of."

"What about Dylan, or whoever that was?"

"Right? I don't think that was Dylan."

"So, not okay."

"Of course, not okay," Mo said. She slouched with her feet up on a wooden bench under a bulletin board of holiday pet photos. Ted sat next to her, his jaw set, Pris's waterproof tablet on his lap.

SHIVER

Mickey made sure all her lady parts were covered and plopped onto the opposite bench. "You dropped the ball, Sheriff Ted," she said. "The wrapper was there. So was the person I saw trapped."

"Yeah," Ted frowned. "I swear, we did not see the wrapper or anybody in the water. No one was calling for help. Mo looked in the water, didn't you, honey?"

Mo nodded, her mouth turned down.

"It doesn't look good that we found it when you couldn't," Pris pointed out.

"I need to interview the three of you separately about what happened tonight," Ted said formally, "down at the station. But first, we have to get dry clothes for Miss Lamotte, here."

"I will go to the B&B and get clothes while you head to the station," Pris said. Her eyes flicked to Mickey's, but she couldn't read what Pris was telling her.

"I want to get the interviews finished because as soon as the sun comes up, I'm getting together officers to search the beach area again, more thoroughly."

"Oh, now you listen," Mo said scornfully.

"Took you long enough," Mickey said, taking the bundle of clothes from Pris. "I never thought I would be questioned by the police while wearing only wet underwear after a shark attack."

"You did nothing wrong," Pris said firmly. "Your headgear thing is drying out, by the way. I hope it's allowed to get wet."

"Oh!" Joy suffused through Mickey. "I thought I had lost it. What about my arm?"

"That, we didn't find. The shark hit your left side hard and tore it right off. If it had hit you on your right, you would be dead. That arm is probably in the shark's belly right now."

Oh, what were the twins going to say? They hadn't built the prosthetic to withstand a shark attack, after all. Major design flaw.

Mickey retreated into the small police station bathroom and changed her clothes from the skin out, wishing for a shower. The shark had ingested none of her flesh, but she was bruised and scratched up and in a sorry state, salty and feeling dirty. Pris had brought her a light gray tank and black shorts with an elastic waist so she wouldn't have to deal with any fasteners one-handed, plus her usual sports bra and underwear. Her hiking sandals were soggy but wearable. She stuffed the damp underwear from the night before into one of her pockets, dry- swallowed an anxiety pill, and emerged, telling Pris, "Ted is still talking to Mo. Or should we call him Officer Ted? Sheriff Ted?"

They sat on the bench together in the police station waiting area. The day before, Mickey had been subdued and arrested in that very spot. Pris had gotten into a physical altercation with a police officer. Both ended up detained in handcuffs.

Today, they were being treated gently as star witnesses. What a difference half a day makes. And also a team of expensive lawyers, Mickey thought.

"I don't know what more he needs to know. We told him everything last night. And we showed him the videos on my tablet." Pris lifted it up. "At least he didn't think to take this. The cameras are back in the room, charging with your headgear. This place sucks." She looked around and then leaned in close. "The toys are free to roam," she said in a low voice. It sounded like a mysterious code.

"What?" Mickey said, exhausted and in pain. She shook her head.

Pris looked around to see if anyone was listening. "The toys. I let them go."

Oh. "The ones the twins sent you that you never showed me or explained?"

"Right. Right."

"What are they?"

The officer at the front counter wasn't very interested in either of them. He looked half-asleep. It was barely dawn.

Pris leaned closer, addressing Mickey's ear. "Drones that look like birds."

Mickey leaned away. After the shark thing and being underwater, her tolerance for being crowded had dropped to absolute zero. "Who's flying them if you're in here?"

"That's just it. The birds fly themselves. They have artificial intelligence."

"You let AI-powered drones loose, here?"

"Right, the energy-sucking fey. I wasn't thinking." Pris smacked herself, wincing as she hit one of her bruises. "I hope the fey don't get them; I have to return the drones to the Geoffrey and Taylor."

Ted came out with Mo. "Michaela, it's your turn."

At least he didn't bring her into the office where she had been handcuffed the day before. It was clearly an interview room, but way too small. Mickey had taken her anxiety medicine, but it wasn't magic.

"I have claustrophobia," she said flatly, slapping her hand on the table next to the old-fashioned tape recorder. "I want that on the record. This room is tiny. Too small."

"All right," Ted said reasonably, nodding. "You aren't restrained. Should I open the door?"

"That won't help. I'm formally telling you I'm extremely anxious to be in this tiny space." He was being too nice about it, and that made Mickey feel flustered. Cops were supposed to be jerks, weren't they?

Ted looked around. "It's not that tiny, honestly."

"You aren't in my head," Mickey said. "Can we do this quickly? I'm also in physical pain from being attacked by a shark last night and almost dying."

"I need to go over the facts with you about last night and before. With you claiming to see the missing boy, Dylan, drowning."

"I don't know if it was Dylan. I saw someone who said they needed help. I'm not sure about their gender. I could not help because I can't swim." She waved her bruised stump at him. "I marked the area with a purple wrapper and ran to the police station for help, since cell phones don't work here for whatever stupid reason. When I arrived, out of breath and having a panic attack, your officer arrested me instead of administering aid. I was literally disarmed and then locked in an even smaller space than this." She waved her truncated left forearm around again. "Which further exacerbated my panic attack and my existing claustrophobia plus the knowledge that the person I tried to get help for was not being helped at all."

SHIVER

Ted tapped his pen on the pad of paper in front of him. He had made few notes, although the tape recorder was running. "You had been with Melissa McLeod and Priscilla Salamanca on the beach earlier. They went to the McLeod house while you stayed on the beach. Why?"

Mickey couldn't explain that intense feeling of curiosity that kept drawing her to the water. "I feel an enormous responsibility for Dylan. My friends asked Pris and me to come here and see what happened to him. Their brother, Lucas, is Dylan's friend. I wanted to keep looking. I told Mo and Pris I would walk back to town via the beach and meet them there. I thought I might see something or think of something along the way."

"And you saw something?"

"Yes, I heard someone calling for help. I can't swim, so I reassured the person I'd come right back with help, marked the place as I explained with a bright-colored wrapper—I'll pay a littering fine if that's such a big deal—and then I came here to the police station for help, which was a big mistake on my part."

A muscle jumped in Ted's jaw. "Let's skip ahead to when the three of you went back to the beach at night. What were you thinking then?"

"Not thinking so much as hoping that somehow the person was still there, holding on, even though you had looked and not found them. I really didn't have hope that it was Dylan. It's just been too long. But if I could save someone ... I was saved as a baby, you know." She smiled at Ted, trying to make a connection. "Someone dumped me at a firehouse as a premature, injured baby. The ER docs that helped save me are now my adoptive parents."

"You had good intentions, then." Ted made a note and then looked her in the eyes. "Explain on the record how long you have known Ms. Salamanca and Ms. McLeod."

"I have known Pris—Ms. Salamanca—for over ten years; we met in high school. We met Mo McLeod yesterday. Was it only yesterday? Wow."

"How did you happen to meet Ms. McLeod?"

"Pris and I were at the historical society looking around, and Mo started talking to us about the exhibits because she's familiar with them. We all liked each other. We asked her about Dylan's disappearance, and she said she knew where he was last seen and that she could show us. So, we went with her." Mickey shrugged.

"You went out in the middle of the night with someone you just met, looking for someone who drowned."

"You make it sound weird," Mickey protested, pointing with her stump. She missed her shiny metal arm.

SHIVER

"It's not?"

"Pris and I have a paranormal podcast called the Contrary Crow-cast. We film at night and with strangers all the time, so it's not weird for us. We have a special camera setup and everything."

"What's a popcast?" Ted asked without irony.

Mickey groaned. It hurt her ribs. "This backwards town. A pod-cast is like a TV show made by amateurs. But you don't watch it on TV; you watch on the internet, which you guys don't have."

"You were going to film this popcap show on the beach last night?"

"Podcast. And no, not necessarily, although we were using the camera setup. It records what I see and also my reactions to what I see. We have night vision, infrared, all different sorts of filters. If Dylan, or whoever, was still out there, we could see them with those filters."

Ted gazed at her in admiration, smiling. "That's actually really smart."

"Thank you. And it worked; we found the person. And I have such acute anxiety, I just kind of freaked out and went in after them even though I can't swim. I figured that Pris and Mo could pull me out. They were guiding me using the cameras—it's complicated. Pris could see, but I couldn't. I had to be in the water because I was wearing the cameras. All the splashing around, I guess, attracted a shark. Well, that's what Mo thinks. She's the shark expert; she's got those little cute baby sharks in her pool. I guess you know that. The shark went after me and after the person I was trying to save. I really don't know what happened after that. I woke up on the exam table at a vet's office, all beat up from a shark trying to eat me, but the stupid fish started with my left arm, which is metal." She held out her bruised stump. "And now we're here."

"And now we're here," Ted repeated. He smiled. Mo was right; he was cute for an old white guy.

"Are you arresting me again?"

"I didn't arrest you the first time. Are you siccing your friend's lawyers on me?"

"That's not up to me. I don't control Pris's lawyers. She's very protective of me. I'm one of her projects, as well as being her bestie. I think she's adopted Mo as another project, so be warned."

"What does that mean?"

Mickey thought about how to explain what it was like to be under Pris's wing. "She'll want to take care of Mo. She wants Mo to have the internet and awesome technology so she can science all she wants. If Pris can't bring internet to Shell Beach, she will get Mo out of Shell Beach."

"That doesn't upset you? To lose your best friend to someone else?"

Mickey leaned back and scrunched up her mouth. "Lose her? I'm not losing Pris; I'm gaining Mo."

Ted rubbed his face and put down his pen. "I'm going to the lifeguard school to talk to everyone again now that it's been a full day and Dylan's still missing. Why don't you—you all—come with me later. I've got a couple of guys searching the beach once again. You're free to go for now."

SHIVER

-20-

The three experimental bird-drones lifted into the air. They circled their controller, a tablet wielded by Pris. The drones would return to the tablet when called back or when their batteries ran low. Until then, they were free to roam. These drones looked like ravens, extremely big corvids.

Following Pris's scant, hurried instructions, they located the public beach. Being creatures of metal, wire, plastic, and software, they could not appreciate the sunrise over the Atlantic. Their programming understood that more light meant better images. They were searching for anomalies using pattern recognition. First, they had to figure out what the beach and waves usually look like and see what was different. They could do this at incredible speeds.

They swooped and dove, examining from high and low, cataloging rocks, driftwood, high-tide marks, living birds, crashing waves, and everything that made up this ecosystem. They were drawn to the living birds, but what they were looking for was most likely in the water, not the sky.

They knew people and looked for people-shapes on land and in the sea.

As the sun rose, two police officers, Dom and Jack, emerged from a police car and started walking down the beach, arguing. A bird-drone followed each one, while the third kept searching along the liminal space where land and waves touched.

"That wrapper wasn't there, not when we looked," Dom said. "Drama."

"That rich girl, making up stories," Jack answered. He had a bandage across his nose. He kicked a shell. "That red-haired boy is long gone."

They weren't even looking at the water.

The ravens had a conference, and one of them peeled off and went to join its fellow along the waves. It skimmed closer to the water while the other soared higher.

"Waste of time," Jack complained.

"Well, here are some boulders, so let's pretend to look." They stopped and stared at the boulder cluster in the water. "Hello? Are you drowning? See, no one there."

"Is that crow following us?" Jack rubbed his nose as they ambled on. "I can't believe I got headbutted by a girl. Man, my face hurts."

Dom threw a shell at the drone, which adroitly avoided it. When the officers weren't looking, it did a barrel roll at them. "More stupid boulders," he said. "Hey, drowning boy! See, no one—"

"Hey," said a voice from the waves.

The other two drones converged on this oddity.

"My foot is stuck."

"What the—" Jack said, his hand falling from his swollen nose.

The two cops went to the edge of the water, ignoring the three birds hovering over the grouping of rocks. "Hello?" Dom called. He reached for the radio on his shoulder.

"No," Jack said, "Don't call it in yet."

"What? Why not?"

"Maybe it's not real. It's been two days? It could be a parrot."

"A drowning parrot."

"A crow, then."

"A talking bird."

"There's all those weird birds right there. Never seen such big crows before. They could talk, can't they?"

"Can you help?"

The drones focused on a round dark head near the most immense boulder. One flew around to get a view of its face, most of which was underwater. The eyes were big and dark, the mouth hidden, but the voice somehow spoke.

"My foot."

"That looks like a lady," Dom said. "Not a bird."

"Lady?" Jack yelled. "Do you need help?"

"Help," the head answered promptly.

"Call it in now?" Dom asked.

"No need, she's right there. Just go get her. You're younger and you swim better. Be a hero."

One drone rose to capture all the action. The woman's dark eyes— if it was a woman, the gender was uncertain—looked at the closest drone and then away. The eyes seemed to have no sclera or iris, just black pupils.

Dom removed his heavy shoes, equipment belt, and radio and piled them on a flat rock. "I'm coming, lady," he muttered.

The black eyes watched him. "My foot is stuck."

"Yeah, and I'm the hero who is going to fix that." He draped his socks on top of the pile and walked into the cold water, wincing. "I want to be on the front page of the paper," he said over his shoulder, diving into the next wave.

Behind the dark head, a shark fin popped up. A drone focused on that anomaly.

Jack yelled. "Dom! Shark! Shark! Grab her and get out! Buddy! Shark!" He slammed his hand onto his shoulder microphone, forgetting all protocol as he reported in. "Dom's in the water. We found someone, a lady, and there's a shark!"

Static erupted from the station in response.

The dark head vanished, and more fins converged as Dom emerged, spitting water, calling, "Hey, lady, where are you?"

"Dom! Shark!"

Jack threw his own shoes, belt, and radio aside and flung himself into the water.

The head and Dom were face-to-face, the middle-aged face with the droopy mustache and the pale face with the enormous black, inhuman eyes. The woman's mouth was too large. When it opened, her teeth were triangular, jagged, and looming. Her upper body was female, small breasted, and gray-skinned as a corpse. Her long nails ripped hunks of flesh from Dom's arms, having already shredded his shirt. Her mouth bit down as, behind her back, the shark fin thrashed.

Jack grabbed Dom around the waist and tried to pull him away from the woman attacking him. Blood darkened the water. Multiple shark fins circled in the blossoming cloud.

From above, the bird-drones filmed it all.

Another lady, another pair of arms, came from beneath the water and embraced Jack from behind, fastening her mouth on his throat. A scarlet spurt hit one drone, landing on the lens like an effect from a terrible movie. The rising sun hit the ocean at just the right angle so the drones could see through the water as the women pulled the cops down to feast on them, getting exquisite shots of their long, thin, gray-skinned bodies, mostly human on top, all shark on the bottom.

On the shore, the abandoned radios squawked like demented parrots.

SHIVER
-21-

Mickey spent over an hour carefully cleaning the neural net with a damp washcloth before falling asleep on her face. Pris woke her with smells of food that she'd gotten from Crabby Patty's, the Irish diner where Mo worked.

"I got signature crab patty burgers. Eat up; we're going to the lifeguard place now."

The crab patty was delicious. Mickey could have eaten two. She removed the neural net from its charging box and fitted it to the back of her head, gently moving it around until each segment snapped into place, waiting for the shiver of connection, grateful when it happened. At least the net wasn't ruined and could help with her anxiety, even if her prosthetic arm was still missing.

She pulled a brush roughly through her smooth hair and another across her teeth before running down the stairs. Her crooked torso was a mass of bruises, soreness, and pain. Her physical therapist and massage therapist would get some overtime when she got home.

Pris was locking a large military-looking case into the back of her car. "I called back the drones. One is filthy. The lens is obscured," she remarked to Mickey. "I'll deal with it when I get back." Her usually perfect face was a rainbow of bruises. What a pair they were.

"What are they supposed to do?"

"They have artificial intelligence in them with pattern recognition, right? The birds analyze a place, watch it, figure out what's different or changing, and film it if that's what you ask them to do. I instructed them to do exactly that, plus look for people-shapes along the beach. Also, they look just like birds. Ravens." Pris swung into the driver's seat. It adjusted to her taller body.

Mickey felt relieved at not having to drive. "Why did the twins send them to you, though?" Even though she wasn't driving, she felt the neural net reaching out to the car. She tried to stifle it, thinking, down, boy.

"They thought we could use them to shadow us when we were filming outside. Get a bird's-eye view of whatever we were looking at, or whatever view we wanted that a bird could get. Plus, they are corvids, and we're the Crowcast."

"Hmm. What do you think?" Mickey tried to think of the advantages of essentially having three trained ravens at her command during a podcast shoot. She really needed more information on how the bird-drones worked to decide.

"I think they are too big for us, even if they are ravens, but I also think these bird-drones are really for the military, just like a lot of the stuff the twins make."

SHIVER

The green-and-black car slid to a silent stop in front of Mo's driveway. A moment later, Mo emerged from her front door. Her beads were red, her long sleeve shirt was red, her cutoff jeans were black, and her high-top sneakers were black with red glitter laces. A curvy middle-aged white lady waved to them from the doorway. Pris waved back.

"Mo is so color-coordinated," Mickey said in admiration.

Mo climbed into the back seat. "Air kisses!" she called. "To the lifeguard camp we go. My mom wanted to check out my new friends. She's harmless. Bye, mom! Wave to my mommy, everyone. Mickey, how are you doing after last night?"

"I'm fine, sore and bruised," Mickey replied. "Tired."

"What's the address?" Pris asked, her finger hovering over the GPS screen.

"Address?" Mo scoffed. "I'm right here, I'll just tell you. Turn around in the neighbor's driveway."

Pris left the GPS screen hanging, asking for a destination. It attempted, poorly, to show where they were. At Mo's direction, they headed out to a larger road that also paralleled the ocean and drove along it. This road featured fewer, much larger houses, and more wooded areas.

"They built an entire camp here just for lifeguard training?" Pris asked.

Mickey reached to open her window, thinking how good the mixture of sea and forest air smelled. The windshield wipers turned on before she touched the button.

"Look! Mo, look!" Pris shouted. "This is what I was telling you about." She turned them off. "Energy-sucking fey."

"What? They just turned on by themselves?" Mo leaned forward as much as the seatbelt allowed.

"The entire drive up from Connecticut, right," Pris said, waving both hands and allowing the car to find its own way. "Wipers, wiper fluid, blinkers, hazards. Randomly turning on. I thought Mickey was going to crash a couple of times."

"You make me drive this car that costs as much as a house. My anxiety goes through the roof." At the thought, Mickey touched her leg and made sure her pills were in one of her pockets.

"Mickey, I don't care about the money! I have tons of money. You worry too much, right."

The hazards turned on.

"Wow," Mo said. "That is—something."

"Energy-sucking fey. What else could it be?" Pris turned them off.

"There are a lot of weird things about Shell Beach, but car accessories turning on randomly isn't one of them."

SHIVER

"It first happened in Rhode Island next to the big blue bug," Mickey offered, breathing deeply of the delicious air. "Not just here." Just when I'm in the car.

"You're going to turn right up here where you see an old wooden billboard," Mo offered.

The right blinker obediently turned on.

"I did not do that!" Pris declared, waving both hands.

The wooden billboard reading SHELL HILL in fancy lettering had seen better days; the white paint was flaking off so they could read it as SHELL HELL.

"Anyway, of course, this campground is not just for lifeguards," Mo explained, seeming to ignore the drama of the self-acting car. "It's for group camping, too. Like family reunions, scouts, churches, summer camps. Think of those old '80s horror movies; they could be filmed here, except there's no Crystal Lake, there's the swimming pool and the ocean. Sometimes there are outdoor flea markets here in the spring and fall, or Renn Faire–type things with everyone in costume. Oh, and when archaeologists come to excavate at the shell midden, they stay here."

The gravel lot was empty except for one other vehicle, Ted's police car. "Students live here for the duration of their program," Mo explained. "They don't come into town or anything. It's dumb. It doesn't help the town at all to have them here."

Mickey pulled Mo from the backseat. Mo was both taller and fuller than Mickey. "On the way home, I can sit in the back," Mickey offered. "I'm shorter and smaller."

Older teenagers and college-aged students, all wearing neon orange shirts, were sitting in folding camp chairs in a cleared space by the trees. Ted was talking to them, or maybe just at them. He seemed out of his element. No one looked happy.

The trio of young women strolled through the camp, looking around. Mo pointed out the in-ground pool, divided into lanes with ropes and floats, and piles of various lifesaving equipment such as boards and hooks, and some first aid gear that littered the area. Small wooden cabins completed the encampment. The whole thing was barely carved out of the surrounding forest.

"When did you last see Jen?" Ted said. "Are you sure she's also missing?" He looked at the three approaching women and shrugged one shoulder slightly.

"She went out to see the sunrise and never came back in. She was from the Midwest, from farther away from the water, fell in love with the ocean, wanted to see it all the time," said one boy.

"And who are you?" Ted asked.

"I'm Nick. She asked me to go with her. I had gone with her before but didn't feel like it today. I should have."

Ted wrote on his clipboard.

One of the seated boys, who looked vaguely Korean, and who had very floppy hair, glanced at the approaching women, then got up and ran to them. "Mickey?" he embraced her. "You have got to be Mickey Crow. I'm Lucas."

Mickey winced and disengaged from the bear hug. "Lucas." He looked much more like his French mother than his brothers did. "How did you know it was me? What gave it away? It was my hair, right? Seriously, how are you holding up?"

Lucas released Mickey and looked at the other two. "You're Pris because you look like your sisters. I see them on TV all the time. Sorry. I know you hate that. But I don't know you," he said to Mo.

"No reason to," Mo said. "I'm local. I'm Mo."

He shook their hands solemnly. "I'm upset," he confessed, leading them out of hearing of the larger group. "I heard them fighting. I heard him leave. I could have stopped the fight, maybe. Or gone with him when he left. He was my friend."

"We're sorry," Pris said, speaking for everyone. "We thought we found him, but I guess it wasn't him. And now it seems like someone else is missing?" She nodded at Ted, who was still talking at the others.

"Yeah, Jen went out to see the sunrise. She wasn't angry or anything. Didn't go for a swim. Didn't go far. Just didn't come back."

"Today?"

"Yeah, this morning."

She couldn't have been who Mickey saw the night before.

"This place sucks," Lucas said vehemently. "I want to save people. I don't want to be a lifeguard. I want to be a paramedic—so did Dylan; that's one reason we were friends. The lifeguard training was in a bundle with the first aid and other lifesaving training, so I thought I'd just take it all. I regret it. There's no cable or satellite TV, no internet, our phones don't work, we can't go into town. The food sucks. I figure knowledge is never wasted, and it can't hurt to know extra stuff. What if I'm driving an ambulance and someone's in a pool? But I'm about ready to quit the whole thing, though."

His big, oval eyes shone with tears. "Johannes, the guy Dylan got in a fight with, has totally lost it. He's full of guilt. I guess it was a stupid fight over something stupid, like most fights are. I mean, I heard it, but I wasn't listening; you know, that's rude?" He looked at Pris. She nodded in agreement. "This guy Rob, he's the instructor, he lives in the town. He took Johannes off for a walk right before the cop got here.

SHIVER

Rob's the only guy who gets to leave. It sucks here. No one wants to be here anymore. Now someone else is missing. No one knows what's going on. Supposedly, Rob said to someone else that he thinks Dylan got eaten by a shark!"

Mickey looked at Mo.

"I know Rob," Mo said. "He can be a bit of a hothead. He's maybe not the best expert on what happened to Dylan." Her hand wrapped around her other arm, on top of the bandage hidden by her long, red sleeve.

"Well, your friend Rob is keeping us all here against our will!" Lucas made a theatrical, wide-eyed face, waving his arm. He was about eighteen years old and it seemed like everything was still a big deal to him.

"Your brothers sent us," Pris said. "Of course, part of that, although unspoken, was to make sure you were okay. Doesn't seem like you are."

"There are empty rooms at the B&B where we're staying, and your brothers gave us extra money. Just come back with us," Mickey suggested.

His eyes shone. "I get to hang out with Mickey and Pris? Can I be on your podcast?"

"Maybe," Pris said, pursing her lips. "If you behave."

Mo raised an eyebrow. "Are you guys that famous?"

"Well, she is—" Mickey aimed a thumb at Pris. "And I'm friends with Lucas's famous big brothers, so that makes me a big deal, right, baby Lucas?"

"Shut up," he said, but he was blushing.

SHIVER
-22-

The four of them settled into a booth at Crabby Patty's, with Mickey on the aisle. After being crammed in Pris's car with three other people, she had to take another anxiety pill. Her whole body was thrumming. That demanded her attention.

They sat in front of piles of standard burgers, crab cake burgers, and fries. They were figuring out the next step, which seemed to be to help the police search the beach for both missing lifeguard trainees. Pris hadn't retrieved the drone footage yet, but she figured she would let the birds loose again. It was a big heap of nothing.

The various burgers all tasted delicious. They were even better freshly made. Mickey allowed the others to keep talking and looked past them, out the window, down the street, and toward the ocean. If she could see the water while in Shell Beach, she wanted to be near it, and that was weird because she absolutely hated water. Her physical therapist had to practically threaten her with violence to get Mickey into her parents' perfectly safe, inland, in-the-ground, undeniably shark-free pool. Here, sharks were guaranteed—and yet the sea beckoned, even after said sharks had attacked her the night before.

"What are you thinking about with that face on?" Pris pointed at Mickey with a curved fry. "Nothing good ever comes of you having that look."

"Sharks," Mickey said honestly.

"I would think you had enough of sharks last night when one tried to rip your arm off."

"One did rip my arm off," Mickey raised her bruised stump. "Luckily, someone else had already taken care of that twenty-five years ago."

"Sharks aren't all bad." Mo protested. "They don't actually enjoy human meat. Usually, they are just having a taste. It's just that their test bites can be big and overwhelming."

"Someone did a taste test? They asked sharks, 'do you prefer meat from a, b, or c dish?'" Lucas asked skeptically. He was on his second burger, or maybe his third. Mickey wondered if they had fed him at all at the lifeguard camp.

"Basically, yeah. People donate their bodies to science. That's where the meat comes from."

"Cool," Lucas took a giant bite of his burger, and juice ran down his chin. "The sharks didn't like people meat?"

"Nope." Mo ate a fry in quick, delicate bites. "Not one bit. Well, bull sharks eat anything, but they are bull sharks, after all. They eat license plates. Goats of the sea."

SHIVER

An elderly man with a peg leg and wearing ragged fisherman's clothing came into the diner and went to the counter. After a brief conversation with their server, the man swung about adroitly on the peg and clumped in their direction. He grabbed a chair along the way, which he slapped against the end of the table, and plopped himself into it.

"Girly!" He greeted Mo.

"Unky!" she replied, grinning. "I didn't expect to see you today."

Mickey hadn't thought Mo's uncle would be white, although Mo's mom was.

"Guys, this is my Great-Uncle Charlie. You can just call him Charlie or Uncle Charlie. Unky, these are my new friends. This is Mickey Crow, Pris, and Lucas, who knows the redheaded boy who went missing two days ago."

Mickey felt intolerably crowded with Lucas between her and the window, and now Charlie in the aisle.

The server, Colleen, a middle-aged woman in an old-fashioned candy-pink uniform, came over with a cup of coffee for Charlie.

"It's getting bad again, girly," he said, sipping at the steaming black brew. "Just like when I lost m'leg and m'brother. Maybe worse than it was."

"How long ago was that?" Mickey asked. She picked at her fries, watching her hand tremble.

"Oh, going on sixty years now," Charlie answered. "Seems like yesterday, some days. And a'course, about sixty years before that was the previous trouble, a'though I wasn't alive for that one; that was my great-granddaddy took care of that. If that's come 'round again …" He shook his head. His soft, wrinkled face flapped with the movement.

"Sixty years?" Pris asked. Her lips were tight. Mickey knew she was wishing for a camera to interview the old man properly.

"Yeah, it seems to take them about sixty years to regroup. Maybe to get their numbers back up," Charlie said.

Colleen dropped a plate of grilled cheese and tomato sandwiches before Charlie, who immediately tucked in. They watched him for several minutes, waiting.

"Regroup from what?" Mickey asked finally.

"From us trying to annihilate 'em, of course. Isn't that what you're plottin'?"

SHIVER

-23-

We don't talk about where we got the dynamite, but we got it all right." Charlie ate the last triangle of grilled cheese. The barely cooked tomato looked like blood.

"You blew up the sharks?" Pris's question was polite, but her twisted mouth said she didn't believe a word Charlie was saying.

"Yeah, we lured them into a cove with a lot of dead fish—chum, girly—and then blew it up. Told that Benchy dude all about it." Charlie drained his coffee cup and slammed it into the saucer with an overly loud bang.

"Peter Benchley," Mo explained, her lips tight from holding in a smile. "Uncle Charlie helped Peter Benchley write *Jaws*."

Pris shook her head as if to dispel that thought. "Right, so every sixty years you people blow up some sharks?"

"You gotta," Charlie said simply. "They ain't gonna just go away."

Lucas stopped eating to say, "You honestly think a shark ate Dylan? You said earlier—"

"Oh," Mickey said. She put her stump on his arm. "Yes, we're sorry, we do think that."

Lucas looked at her truncated forearm. "Is that where your awesome metal arm went?"

"I got attacked by a shark last night while we were trying to find Dylan. It came at me from the left and knocked my arm right off. Still looking for it. I know your brothers are going to kill me."

Lucas winced. "You don't know what that arm cost, do you?"

Mickey looked at the exposed gleaming wires and nodes on her left forearm. "I probably don't want to know, do I?"

Charlie nudged her right arm. "Between the two of us, we have enough arms and legs to be a bug." He started laughing. Mickey thought of her beloved big blue bug and giggled.

"Of course, you know this isn't funny?" Mo said flatly.

Charlie grasped a handful of her braids and stroked her face with them. "Girly," he said affectionately. "Fun is where you make it."

She resisted the ends of her own hair, leaning back. She confronted her great-uncle. "So, where's some dynamite to blow up the sharks, unky?"

He shrugged. "Dunno. Can't you make some with those fancy degrees of yours? Chemistry and biology and whatsit?"

"No, I can't just whip up some nitroglycerin or C4 or whatever!"

He dropped her braids and sat back in the chair.

"If you had the internet like a proper town," Pris mused, "We could look it up, right?"

"Of course, I don't want to make explosives," Mo said firmly. "I don't want to blow up sharks. I love sharks. Can't we save them?"

"They aren't raccoons," Lucas said, eating the fries off Pris's plate. "You can't trap them and drive them to another town and let them go."

"Also, raccoons don't eat people," Mickey pointed out. She pushed her own fries at Lucas. Her neural net pinged comfortably at her, but she didn't know why.

"Do you know for sure that a shark ate Dylan?" Lucas asked.

"If a shark didn't eat Dylan, where is he?" Mickey countered.

They all stared at the table, unable to answer.

"And now someone else is missing, don't forget," Lucas reminded them. "We should keep looking."

"We should be lookin' for dynamite. Boom!" Charlie picked up his cup, saw it was empty, put it down again. "I'll start making a big stinking batch of chum for you, girly, for when you realize what you have to do. You know where to find me."

Mo shook her head fiercely, her braids whipping. Pris leaned away to avoid getting hit in the face.

Great-Uncle Charlie slowly walked from the diner, step-thump, step-thump, leaving behind a mixed odor of fish and unwashed clothing.

"We should be out on the beach looking; Lucas is right," Pris said. She raised her hand to ask Colleen for the check.

"I don't want to kill sharks." Mo was almost in tears, her dark eyes swimming behind her rhinestone glasses. "I'm making shark repellent to save them, not hurt them."

"No one is killing any sharks today," Mickey said soothingly. "Let's figure out what is really going on. This is getting too weird even for Pris and me. Who did we hear calling for help last night? It couldn't have been the other lifeguard, because she vanished at dawn. And really, could Dylan have survived in the water for over twenty-four hours? How long until hypothermia sets in? How cold is that water?"

"I hate not being able to look anything up online!" Pris took the check from the server and laughed. "Mo, your uncle put his food on our bill."

"Of course he did. I'll pay his share and mine."

Pris waved the slip of pink paper at Mo. "Your money is no good with me. I'm adopting you, remember?"

"I don't understand what that means."

"You will," Mickey said.

"Wait," Lucas said. "Back up. Someone was calling for help last night?"

SHIVER

"Yeah," Mickey replied. "Pris, do you have the video with you?"

"No, the tablet's in the room; I'll show him later." Pris summarized for Lucas what had happened the night before, with Mickey and Mo's interjections.

"Dylan is still alive," Lucas exclaimed, slamming his hand onto the table. "We gotta go, now; get ropes and floats. I can get out to that rock and save him; come on, guys."

"We're all girls," Mickey pointed out dryly.

"Whatever, we gotta go, now!"

Pris unleashed the drones again, without checking if they whether found anything on their earlier run. Mo walked Lucas to the hardware store to get what he needed to rescue Dylan, while Mickey rented an extra room from short-tempered innkeeper Caren.

Pris had just finished strapping Mickey into the camera rig when Mo and Lucas met them at the public beach. The three bird-drones circled overhead, waiting for Pris to instruct them. Two police cars were parked in the public lot. A handmade sign marked the beach as closed.

"This part is certainly like *Jaws*," Mickey remarked, looking at the hastily erected sign.

"A low-budget *Jaws*," Pris said. She looked up at the trio of spiraling ravens and then bent to the tablet with instructions. The bird-drones dipped their wings in acknowledgment and headed in the direction of the lifeguard camp. Pris turned her back on them and looked at the seafood restaurant, The Dockside Feast, perched over the water. "What's on the other side of this?"

"The docks where the fishing boats and the few pleasure boats go, of course," Mo said. "That's where it's deep. No one swims there or hangs out there."

"Do you think that's where they blew up the sharks last time?"

Mo's jaw set. "I guess. There is a cove in that direction. But blowing things up isn't an option. We are civilized now."

"We eat even eat carbs, sometimes," Mickey said.

Lucas looked adorably young and puzzled with his wide eyes, tilted head and floppy haircut. "Doesn't everyone eat carbs?"

"Pris and I don't," Mickey said, "unless Mo makes us."

"I don't understand girls," Lucas said. "I'm so glad I'm gay."

"I don't understand girls either, and I'm also gay," Pris said. "Don't feel bad."

Once they started walking along the beach, Mickey and Lucas jostled to be closest to the water. Since Mickey was filming, she didn't want Lucas's butt in every shot, but if he found and rescued Dylan, she would have a front-row seat. Finally, she dropped back enough to see him if she wanted, yet still be part of the conversation.

Mickey's head kept swiveling to the right. Her whole body thrummed. She didn't know what she was searching for. It was like something was looking at her and she saw herself through its eyes. She dropped back a little more and started narrating, knowing that the sound quality would be terrible.

"Something's out there to my right." It was hard not to look at her feet when she was wearing the camera rig, but she had to consider her viewers and what they would watch through her eyes. She tried not to trip over the ankle-twisting rocks littering her path. "I don't know if whatever-it-is wants me to look at it." She had to slow down if she didn't want to break a leg on the slippery, seaweed-covered rocks and shells. "I don't know how to explain that I know it's there."

"I don't know, of course!" Mo shouted from far in front of her. "I don't know how to get rid of sharks without killing them!" Her voice dropped too low for Mickey to hear.

"Dylan? Dylan!" Lucas called.

Mickey stopped and looked, full-on, at the water. Nothing. Inside her head, the connections shivered, reaching out. All of Pris's tech was already connected to her neural net; what more was there? Above her head, the ravens were out of sight, doing whatever secret bird-drones did when set free. She strained to reach the birds and got answering pings, but that was all.

Not the birds, then.

After a moment, she walked on, feet crunching on the thick sand and sliding off the slimy rocks.

Pris's voice rose and fell, familiar as home, but Mickey could understand none of the words. To her right, something changed, and Mickey stopped again and turned, just a little. Enough to point the camera. Was that someone's head in the water or a rock?

She turned more and said nothing.

Her brain buzzed.

Mickey breathed through her mouth, watching the dark round area as the waves passed it. It stayed in place. Was it bobbing slightly?

Her brain buzzed.

She raised her hand in greeting and kept it there. She tried to think a greeting in that direction.

A different buzz.

Okay.

Mickey walked to the edge of the water and sat where the waves would barely wash her legs. "I think it's communicating with me," she whispered for the benefit of the cameras.

This wasn't a drowning person. This wasn't Dylan.

Buzz.

Closing her eyes, Mickey concentrated on whatever that round shape was in the water—someone's head, a rock, a seal, an alien, who knows. She reached out to it, the way she had reached out to the bird-drones, looking for a ping. Her mind shivered as it connected.

Shivered and went icy cold.

SHIVER

Her eyes snapped open and locked onto the round shape. Not a person, not exactly. But not an animal either. She had no words for what she had linked to. Something that might have been a pair of black eyes looked back.

Hello? Mickey sent. *Friend?*

The eyes looked back.

Mickey felt intense hunger. After a moment, she realized that was the received message: the thing in the water was hungry. Hopefully, the camera was getting this, whatever it was, even though she had forgotten to dictate anything. Mickey kept her hand raised in a way she hoped wasn't threatening. She tried to figure out how to say that she wasn't food. *Friend, not food.*

"Mickey!" Mo yelled.

The connection dropped. Mickey almost fell over when it released her. The thing in the water vanished.

SHIVER
-25-

It was right there!" Mickey insisted. "You'll see it in the camera feed."

"We saw nothing except this," Mo said, pulling something out from behind her.

Mickey's prosthetic, dripping water and black seaweed.

"Oh no," Lucas exclaimed. "My brothers are going to freak out." He stepped forward and claimed it. "It's heavy!"

"It's not that heavy." Mickey took the metal arm, sniffed, and scrunched her nose. "It's smelly and wet, though. I hope it's okay." She tried to connect. Her mind shivered weakly. A blue LED inside the carapace of the forearm shimmered and went out. "Battery is pretty much dead, anyway." Clutching the wet arm to her chest beneath the camera strap, she sat on the nearest large rock. "My head is killing me." The weight of the camera rig, combined with the telepathic connection with the creature—and what else could she call it? Telepathy and creature. All this weirdness had actually pushed her anxiety into the background for once.

Pris crouched in front of her, one ghost-pale hand hovering above Mickey's wet, sand-covered knees. "Do you want to go back to the B&B?"

Mickey shook her aching head slowly. "No, let me rest for a minute. You guys can walk on without me for now. Do you want to take the rig, maybe put it on Mo?"

"You're the crow face of the Contrary Crowcast. You keep it on. Put your metal arm up here past the high-tide mark. We'll grab it on the way back, right?"

Mo and Lucas looked at her anxiously. Mickey was small, but she usually wasn't weak. "Of course, Lucas wants to keep going, to find Dylan," Mo said, "but we don't want to leave you alone. You are pale enough to be white."

"Oh no, not white!" Mickey smiled at her new friend. "Let me sit. I have some mental exercises I can do to relax. I'll catch up."

Once the other three had headed slowly along the beach, leaving Mickey and her drowned arm behind, Mickey used the neural net to engage the calming centers of her mind. She hadn't gotten headaches from using the net in a very long time, but then again, she had never connected it to anything organic before. Anything alive. She still felt hungry, but she ignored that.

She didn't look out into the water to see if a pair of dark eyes were watching. She let the neural net create a feedback loop of calm, slowing her breathing and heart rate.

Although the prosthetic was dead, she did not want to leave it behind. She stuck in her stump and wiggled it; there was no frisson of connection or rightness. Mickey adjusted the straps that held the prosthetic on and felt a little more like herself again. She felt whole. For a moment, she overbalanced to the left, but after a few steps, her body remembered the weight of the elaborate metal arm and she straightened out.

From the corner of her eye, she felt observed and ignored it. In her belly, she felt hunger.

Far ahead, someone screamed.

The four of them took off, moving awkwardly up the beach. Mickey was still starving, but now she understood it wasn't her hunger. Running was rough over the loose, slippery stone, the broken shells, the seaweed poppers, the dead crabs. They pounded past the back of Mo's house and the two corrugated blue pipes, one of them pumping water from her shark pool.

Once they got closer to the commotion, Mo said, "I think that's the sheriff shouting."

Up ahead, a knot of people gathered at the edge of the water, gesticulating, yelling, pointing into the ocean. Mickey's gut filled with the gnawing hunger that actually came from outside of her.

Most of the screaming people had on the orange t-shirts of the lifeguard camp, except for the sheriff, who was wearing his dark blue uniform.

Lucas called, "Rob! Johannes!" and rushed forward into the group, pulling the rope off his shoulder. "Who is it? Is it Jen? Is it Dylan?"

Ted turned to Mo and called, "I can't find Dom and Jack. They haven't radioed in for hours. These kids walked all the way from the lifeguard camp and never saw them either. I found their belts and shoes, though."

"Where?" Mo asked, looking around, her hand shading her face.

"Back closer to your house."

"Who is in the water?" Lucas kept shouting as he waded in. Mickey admired his bravery. He never even hesitated. No fear of the water in him, for sure.

Remembering the podcast, she positioned herself so the camera on her head would record the scene. Sometimes she was the eyes, and sometimes she was the narrator for the Contrary Crowcast, but right now she had nothing to say.

Mickey did not know what was going on. She did know how to keep the camera on her head steady and still use her eyes to look wherever she wanted. That's how she saw the fins gathering.

"Sharks, Lucas! Sharks! Get out of there!" She pointed, although he wasn't looking in her direction.

"Who am I looking for?" he called to his orange-clad friends. Unlike Mickey, he was a strong swimmer. He made it out to a boulder and clung there with one arm, searching around him.

"Triangle-shaped fins is what you're looking for," Mickey replied, "and I see them, so get out, or your brothers will kill me for sure."

Ignoring Mickey's sage advice, Lucas called out for his missing buddies. "Dylan! Jen!"

SHIVER

Ted said to Mo, "They went into the water like Dylan, shoes off, just gone."

Pris reminded Ted, "Mickey heard someone calling for help. Could they have heard the same thing?"

Mo's friend Rob waded toward Lucas, explaining, "Nick heard someone calling for help and went in, but no one else heard anything."

"Nick!" Lucas switched his cry. "Anyone?"

"Lucas! Get out of the water!" Mickey moved toward Lucas so that water licked her toes. She saw fins, but none that might answer to the name Nick. She was starving. She didn't see the black eyes, but she knew they were nearby. What was the connection between the eyes and the shark?

Rob waded in farther. He had a rope with attached floats over his shoulder. "Do you see Nick? I can come in."

"Don't go in," Mickey warned. "Can you not see the shark fins?"

"My students are out there," Rob replied. "My responsibility."

"Can you call for backup?" Mo asked Ted.

"I'm about ready to call in the staties," Ted said. "You know how big the department is. Half of them are missing right now. But what will the state police do against a shark attack?"

Mo shook her head and clenched her jaw. "I don't want the sharks hurt."

"They are eating people," Pris said, putting her hand on Mo's arm. "One of them ripped Mickey's arm right off last night."

"Nobody's been eaten for sure. No parts with tooth marks have washed up. And face it, Mickey's arm is detachable," Mo said, her face set. For once, her braids were still.

Pris sat on a rock and tapped at her tablet until the bird-drones swooped down, gliding almost noiselessly, and circled the area.

"Those are weird crows," Ted remarked, breaking his staring contest with Mo to glance at the birds flying in formation.

Pris shielded the tablet from the sun with her arm, trying to see.

Although she didn't understand enough of what was happening to even be sure what she was explaining, Mickey narrated a bit to the cameras. She didn't mention the hunger.

"I see something," Pris called, tapping the tablet. "Someone. Lucas, past the rock and to your right, someone is in the water but—"

Lucas pulled himself around the rock. Rob threw himself into the water, heading toward Lucas with powerful strokes. On the shore, the other trainees tried to hold Johannes back from joining them in the water as he screamed for Dylan.

"—sharks are there too," Pris finished.

SHIVER

From the other side of the rock, Lucas started swearing. A moment later, Rob's voice joined his. Mickey moved back along the beach, trying to get them on her front-facing camera.

"It's Jen, oh god; it's Jen," Lucas said.

The shark fins, all three of them, slid below the water at once.

"Is she alive?" Mickey called. "Watch out; I don't see the fins anymore."

"Not alive; oh god, not alive," Rob said. "Eaten."

Ted said to Mo, "What were you saying about body parts with tooth marks not washing up?"

SHIVER
-27-

Mickey picked her way back down the beach and stared into the water, feeling for the strange buzzing connection, although it had never totally broken. *Give them back*, she thought. *And stop this.*

The lifeguard kids were howling and crying over the dead girl. Johannes was flat on his face, inconsolable, as they all realized Dylan was gone for good. Rob, although nominally their leader, was out of his element. Mickey didn't want to film that. Poor Ted, shouting into his shoulder microphone, was now in charge of something way too big for him, and he was also down two cops.

Hunger tore through her until she fell to her knees on the sharp sand.

There has to be something else you can eat.

The answer was a wave of frustration that left her doubled over. Mickey sat back on her heels and looked at the waves. Nothing, no fins, no dark eyes, no head-shapes. She didn't even know what she was communicating with. An intelligent shark? Mo was right; these sharks were different. Maybe they had to be saved.

But whose arms had grabbed her last night? Whose voice had spoken to her from the waves? What was that person's connection to whatever—whoever—was talking to Mickey?

I will try to help you. No more eating. And bring them all back.

SHIVER
-28-

Mickey sat on the edge of the deck above Mo's pool. The little sharks swam in their circular pattern, stirring up the sand and seaweed, mostly indifferent to her presence.

"They know me," Mo said, putting the covered bucket of chum down. "They know I feed them. Like goldfish in a pond. You look nothing like me except you have dark hair."

Lucas and Pris had gone back to the B&B, Lucas to contact his brothers on the dubious landline, and Pris to watch the drone footage.

"I don't understand what you want to do with my sharks," Mo fretted. "Are you going to hurt them?"

"I don't want to hurt them. I believe you're right; the sharks need to be saved. Can you trust me and leave me alone with them for a few minutes? I won't feed them. I won't get in the water. I'm just going to sit here and look at them. I won't hurt them at all." Mickey felt mild hunger, although she could smell the awful stomach-turning contents of the bucket.

Mo retreated down the steps and walked toward the beach, looking left, although they were too far away to see what was going on with the recovery of Jen's remains.

Mickey studied the small sharks and tried to connect to them. She felt Pris's pain at the lack of internet, the lack of resources. Did sharks communicate via some kind of electricity? The sharks were all different types. And she didn't know what kinds the big ones were out in the sea—were these their babies or just smaller species? Mo would know, she supposed.

Mickey let her eyes soften and blink shut until she was following the little sharks in their endless circle, a spiral really, around Mo's blue pool. She watched them swim. They were adorable, hungry but not starving. "I could eat," her dad always said when presented with food, and that's how these sharks felt. Comfortably hungry, riding their own wave around the pool, wondering about this person who was not the bringer of food.

Friend, Mickey thought, breathing slowly and smoothly. *I'm just your friend.*

The smooth swimming of the sharks stuttered at this mental intrusion.

Friend.

It was weird, being connected to this hive mind the sharks had created. Everything overlapped a little, stuttered, and shivered. That must be why a group of sharks are called a shiver. That and the feeling Mickey got when she connected to them.

SHIVER

Friend.

The sharks processed this, their swimming irregular. Mo said something, but Mickey ignored her, holding up a hand to tell her to wait. Mickey breathed slowly, deeply; her eyes mostly closed. *Friend, friend.*

A ripple moved through the sharks' hive mind as it finally comprehended and sent back its understanding of the word *friend,* a mosaic picture that took Mickey a while to process. Pictures of people, pictures of sharks. People and sharks had been friends before, somehow. That was heartening. But the mosaic sharpened. The pieces fell into place.

A creature who was part shark and part person. Not unlike the baby in the jar at the historical society.

A mermaid made of shark.

SHIVER
-29-

Mickey watched numbly as Mo went through the motions of feeding her sharks and testing her latest shark-repelling concoction. She didn't know what to say, how to explain what she had done and seen, how she had communicated with the little sharks. This batch of repellent actually sent the sharks away for a few moments before they came back to eat again. Mickey felt their distaste for the additive, how it ruined the food and sent them fleeing, but they couldn't escape the small pool and the poison that permeated it.

"I have to work tonight," Mo said after they returned to the laboratory. "I got called in. We have to make food for the people working on the beach. And if the press comes, they always eat at the diner, too."

Mickey looked at her in disbelief. "Seriously?"

"Seriously, I have a job. I have to go to it. Since making shark repellent hasn't made me rich, I gotta do what I gotta do."

"How late is the diner open?"

Mo threw up one hand. "Until people don't want food anymore. This is a special situation. I'll walk into town with you, of course. I gotta change first, real quick."

Mickey looked at the set of shark jaws hanging on the walls of Mo's lab while she waited. Was this really the shark that had bitten off Charlie's leg and eaten his brother? How big did mermaid-sharks get? Or was this a plain old shark? She wondered what Charlie knew.

Mo came out of the house wearing a pink polyester waitress uniform. Her smooth, brown legs were bare, and she had on pink high-top basketball shoes. A pale pink bandanna tamed her braids and a name tag said "Melissa" in a cheerful crayon font. She had tied another pink bandanna over the bandage on her arm to hide it.

"That outfit is … pink," Mickey said upon seeing it in full daylight.

"It's 'retro,'" Mo retorted, "or at least that's what my boss claims."

"It's something." They walked, scuffing their feet through all the sand on the road. "So, what do you know about the mermaid in the jar?" Mickey asked.

"Oh, that." Mo bobbed her head, but with her braids imprisoned in the bandanna, they couldn't dance. "It's from well over a hundred years ago. Someone found it on the beach, I think? That part of the story changes, and it's been a long time. The silliest rumor is that a fisherman's wife gave birth to it while he was out at sea for a year. Can you imagine?" Mo laughed. "The stories people come up with to go with carnival sideshow freaks."

"I thought you wanted to do DNA testing on it and prove it's real."

SHIVER

Mo flopped her hand. "That was fifteen years ago when I had gone a little crazy. That thing is so pickled it would probably come back with cucumber DNA."

"I don't think it's a cucumber—"

They looked up to see a black-and-green car driving erratically down the center of the street, swerving widely.

Pris honked and slammed on the brakes, skidding on the sand. The car fishtailed.

She rolled down the window. "OMG. You guys. Guess what's on the bird-drone video."

"Mermaids," said Mickey.

Pris's mouth fell open. "Right, how did you know?"

"Lemme in; I got a lot to tell you."

SHIVER
-30-

You first," Mickey and Pris said simultaneously as Mickey and Mo tumbled into the car.

Pris did an awkward skidding k-turn and headed back into town. Mickey felt the autopilot protesting deep inside her head at Pris's treatment of the car.

"You first," Mickey said.

"No, you first," Pris countered.

Mickey looked into the back seat at Mo, not sure how Mo would take her news, which she had been trying to break gently by bringing up the baby in the jar. "No," she said firmly. "You need to go first."

Pris said, "I watched the videos from the bird-drones."

"What did you see?" Mickey asked.

Mo leaned forward. "Yes, what did you see? Mickey said mermaids, so it's not sharks after all?"

"Oh no," Pris said, "It's better than that—it's mermaids that are half shark!"

Mo leaned further forward, so that she was practically in the front seat with the other two. "What do you mean, mermaids that are half shark?"

"I mean, it looks like they're mermaids. On the top half, you know, like a regular mermaid, a ladyish bit, but on the bottom half, instead of being just some sort of random generic fish, they are sharks," Pris said.

Micky nodded. "That's what I think too, at least that's what they told me—"

Pris and Mo stared. "Who told you?" They said together.

Mickey shrugged and scrunched her face. "Well, they did. The mermaids. The mersharks."

Talk fast," Mo said, "Because I have to be at work in a few minutes. And this is completely insane."

"Ever since I got here, I've been hungry ..." Mickey started, and then she laid out the whole thing as succinctly as she could. Being a podcaster really helped.

Pris stopped the car in front of a random house. "You can be a minute late. You were walking to work," she told Mo. Then she focused on Mickey. "You can talk to sharks. In your head."

Mickey nodded.

"Since you got here."

"Well, no, since I got here, I just felt weird. The talking part I just figured out today."

"And the mermaid part?"

"Mo's baby sharks showed them to me when I tried to explain that I was a friend. They showed me that sharks and people have been friends before. They have some kind of hive mind. A genetic memory of people and sharks being friends. They showed me these mermaids that were half shark instead of half regular fish. Then it all made sense."

"None of this makes sense to me," Mo said, "and I'm a mad scientist with a swimming pool full of sharks."

"I don't really understand it. I just know what the sharks showed me. I don't understand whether the mermaid-sharks—mersharks?—are working with the sharks or what. Whether it's the sharks or the mermaids coming after people. Or why. But they are intelligent. They should not be blown up. You're right, Mo."

Mo rubbed at the bandanna on her arm. "This might be worse than regular sharks. What are we supposed to do with murderous mermaids?"

SHIVER
-32-

After Geoffrey and Taylor finished yelling at Mickey for letting a shark chew on her priceless experimental arm, they gave her some advice on cleaning it. They talked to their little brother for a long time while she walked to the hardware store for the needed degunking supplies. The prosthetic had mostly charged when she got back and started the laborious process of sanitizing every connection. Lucas helped, chattering all the while about his brothers' kick-ass robot and expressing his frustration at not finding any trace of Dylan or Nick.

"Why didn't you tell them," Mickey asked finally, "that I talked to a mermaid?"

"Because that's flat-out crazy," Lucas answered. "And I don't believe it."

"They are hungry," Mickey said. "I wonder if it takes sixty years for the population to rebound and get so big they clash with people."

"You think a mermaid bit off that crazy old guy's leg?" Lucas rubbed his fingers over some scratches on the outside of the prosthetic. He had pulled a broken shark's tooth out of one of them.

"I don't know. There's an enormous set of shark jaws in Mo's lab. To me, they look like regular shark teeth, like from any museum. Supposedly they are from the shark that did it—bit Charlie and ate his brother. If it was a mermaid, I think Charlie would know, and he would say, and thus Mo would know."

"You don't know what bit you," Lucas pointed out.

Mickey slid her forearm into the refurbished prosthetic. She wiggled, waiting for the metallic tattoos to line up, and twisted her arm until it locked into place. Closing her eyes, she felt the shiver as the neural net connected. The connection felt a bit off, although the wrist bent and twisted when she wanted it to. It was more than most amputees had. She flexed her metal fingers. Only then did she fasten the straps.

"You are badass," Lucas said, admiring her metal arm and the tattoos that blended into it. "Steampunk princess." That reminded her of the drawing she had been working on. Was that only two days ago?

"No," Mickey corrected him, "I'm pretty broken, but thanks for the confidence boost." She smiled, though.

SHIVER
-33-

Mo met them at the other side of The Dockside Feast well after dark, carrying two big, greasy paper bags of food. She had gotten off work earlier than expected. Turns out, the media did not come piling into an unknown tiny fishing town for a few missing persons and one non-fatal shark attack—the word had not gotten out about Jen yet.

She smelled delicious even against the scent of low tide, or maybe that was the hamburgers.

"The public beach is still closed," she said, handing the bags to Lucas. "One TV station out of Boston sent a van full of gluten-free, vegetarian newscasters who had zero appreciation for our awesome burgers. Their loss. Some bloggers showed up. Or maybe podders. Is that what you guys call yourself?"

"Podcasters," Pris corrected. "Lucas, do not eat all those burgers yourself."

Lucas widened his eyes at her, his hand in one bag. "I was just counting them. Honest."

"Count them in this direction."

Mo untied her pink high-tops and peeled them off, groaning. "These feet, they hurt," she complained. "Let's walk along the dock this way and sit over here." She ducked under a chain, pushing aside a hanging sign that said "No Admittance to Unauthorized Personnel."

Mickey, being the shortest and smallest, had the easiest time criminalizing herself under the padlocked chain. "Mo, um, this says no trespassing."

"Yeah, but of course, my uncle's boat is this way, and we could maybe be going to visit him, which makes us authorized, because I have an open invitation and I'm bringing you guys with me."

Lucas slouched along behind them, eating a burger in what he probably thought was a surreptitious manner. The smell of low tide was overwhelming.

"Is your uncle even on his boat at night? Lucas, are you eating all the burgers after I told you not to?"

Lucas widened his eyes again at Pris and failed to look innocent as he was chewing a giant mouthful of fries and had half a cheeseburger in one hand.

"No, but he could be, and how will we know unless we go there and check?"

It didn't surprise Mickey one bit when Mo and her tired, bare feet climbed onto one of the empty boats, the *Bobby K.* They followed her like baby ducks, climbing from the concrete wharf to the floating, moving dock and then over the side of the fishing boat. The lingering smell on the vessel was reminiscent of the chum Mo fed her baby sharks, but horribly aged and rotten.

"I'm not sure I want a burger anymore," Mickey said, pushing her knuckles against her nose and breathing through her mouth. She sat on a big square hatch in the middle of the deck. At the back of the boat was a kind of rectangular hole filled with a very stinky net. "Lucas, you can have mine if you haven't eaten it already."

Mo waved away Lucas's offer of food. "I've been looking at burgers all night. I can't stomach eating one right now, even though I know how delicious they are."

"I'll have one," Pris said, "If this one has left me any." She elbowed Lucas in the ribs.

The other three crowded onto the hatch, with Pris and Lucas eating burgers despite the stench. Pris threw her bun to a persistent seagull that had been earlier napping in the water next to the hull. Mickey, feeling intolerably crowded, moved to the railing, looking out over the dark water. She knew the mermaids were out there.

It was amazing to learn that mermaids existed. And they were nothing like she had ever imagined. Mickey knew about the feel-good cartoon mermaids, big-eyed, red-haired, and cute, the ones that little girls wanted to dress up as for Halloween. On the other end of the mermaid spectrum lurked sexy, irresistible sirens, whose singing lured sailors to their deaths. Where did these creatures fit in? They were neither cute nor sexy, they didn't sing, and their speaking seemed rote and parrot-like. Oh, and they were murderously hungry; don't forget that part.

Nevertheless, they were mermaids.

SHIVER
-34-

How do we save them?" Mo asked. "Assuming you guys aren't crazy and there are really shark-mermaid hybrids out there." The three of them had flopped backward onto the hatch, staring up at the night sky.

"Why do we have to save them?" Lucas wondered, shoving now-cold fries into his mouth.

"You're going to choke to death on those fries," Pris said. "I, for one, don't care, but your brothers will be angry at us if you do. They seem to like you."

"We have to save them because they are sentient creatures. Rare and unique," Mo offered.

"They are there right now. Here, I mean," Mickey said, feeling the shiver of connection. She searched the dark gray water, looking for round heads or triangular fins.

"They eat people," Lucas argued, coughing as he swallowed a bolus of fried potato.

"You eat burgers, right? What do you think a burger would say about saving you?" Pris countered.

"Burgers can't talk."

"There," Mickey said softly, pointing. "If you guys can be quiet for a minute, come look."

Mo was the first one up and at Mickey's side, her bare feet silent on the wooden deck. She stood too close, almost leaning on Mickey, her overwhelming fried-food smell clogging Mickey's nose.

"Shh," Mickey said. "I don't know if they fear us or what."

"I can't see in the dark, of course," Mo whispered.

Pris pressed to Mickey's other side, grabbing at Mickey's hand. Lucas and a burger were on Pris's other side.

Mickey's head whirred and shivered. She saw herself from several overlapping angles, all below and from the side. Her metal arm seemed monstrous and unknowable. "There are at least three of them," she said in a low voice, "at least three looking at us that can see us clearly. They are between fifteen and twenty feet away."

"How do you know that?" Lucas said with his mouth full. He sounded panicked.

"I am seeing what they see. Can you guys just move away from me? You're crowding me too much. I can't concentrate if I can't breathe."

Pris took a step, having to shove Lucas out of the way.

"You know how great white sharks jump out of the water to eat seals like they show on TV?" Lucas said, finally moving away from Pris. "Will they do that here, to us?"

SHIVER

"That's breaching," Mo explained, moving a tiny step away from Mickey's metal arm. Mickey could still feel her body heat and smell crab cakes in her hair. "I don't think the water is deep enough here. And these aren't great whites, are they?"

"She doesn't think," Lucas muttered and took another bite of his burger.

"Can you see them, Mickey?" Pris asked. Although she had moved away, she still held Mickey's hand.

"No. But they can see us."

The four of them stared over the black water and the three mermaids stared back.

How can we help? Mickey asked the mermaids. She didn't know how much language they had or could comprehend. She tried a few different ways, with pictures and mental gestures and words, until she received an answer: a bolt of hunger that nearly sent her to her knees. Only Pris's hand on hers kept her standing.

"What was that?" Pris cried.

"Shh," Mickey replied, grabbing at the railing with her metal hand and pulling herself upright. "Try not to frighten them."

"Us scare them? They tried to eat you!" Pris replied, glaring over the water. With her bruised, angular face, she was scary looking.

"They are so hungry. They just want us to feed them."

Mo leaned over the railing. "Can you tell them to come closer so I can see them?"

Mickey grabbed the back of Mo's pink uniform with her metal hand. "Don't fall in, you nut."

"Tell them I am a friend to sharks."

Mickey tried to retrieve a picture from the hive mind of Mo's pool pets, showing her feeding them, and then sent it to the mermaids. She wasn't sure she succeeded. While she was almost literally wringing through her brain to find and pass on a memory of a memory, Lucas went back to the hatch and started rummaging through the bags of food.

"Do you ever stop eating?" Pris demanded.

"I'm not eating," he replied. A minute later, he came back holding one handful of loose burger patties dripping with cheese and another handful of crab cakes. "Can I feed them?"

"They aren't pets," Pris said in disgust. "This isn't like a mermaid petting zoo."

"No, wait," Mo said. "Let's try it."

"Right, and let Lucas get eaten. That's what brought us here in the first place, his friend getting eaten. No way."

Mo left the railing, found a hand-held net, and put the burgers inside. "Call them," she said to Mickey. "Because I think Pris might be brilliant."

"Right, of course I am, but which thing did I just say that was brilliant?"

"A mermaid petting zoo. That's how we're going to save them."

SHIVER
-36-

Pris had brought over an incomprehensible stack of electronic equipment. Tablets and things. Even in school, Mo had used nothing like it. She had known not to get attached to computers if she was returning to Shell Beach.

"I'm afraid to touch any of this." Pris waved at the workbench. "It's like an alchemical laboratory in here, right. I'm surprised you don't have a stuffed crocodile hanging overhead."

"Just my shark friend," Mo pointed at the jaws. She cleared off space for Pris to spread out her twenty-first-century tools. "No emerald tablet, no philosopher's stone."

Pris settled herself on the extra stool. "We need a database and something to analyze it. Right now, that's your notebooks and your brain, right?"

"Of course, that's one way to look at it." Mo went on to explain how her notebooks worked. Halfway through her description, she opened the garage doors on both sides, letting the ocean breeze cool them off.

Pris typed on the tablet's screen, grimacing. Sweat ran down her perfect pale face. "Do you have any idea how hard this is to do without the internet?"

"You mean, doing everything with just your brain and no outside help?"

"Ooh, yeah. You get it."

It took both of them to design an offline database to analyze every previous attempt at shark repellent and how well it had worked. A couple had been flat-out shark attractant—not something that was usually useful.

"What we're looking for is patterns, right?" Pris pointed out.

"Yes, I'm aware, of course. Hence the meticulous notebooks."

"No, this goes deeper than you can do with handwritten notebooks. This is more levels of connection. Just wait for it to finish."

Pris had brought over some of Mickey's beloved sports water. They each chugged a bottle, watching the tablet as it processed. "This is cross-referencing everything to find the most efficient formula. Then you can make it and we can try it out."

"So you're saying that if I had this program, I would have had my shark repellent a long time ago?"

"Maybe not. You've been collecting data all this time. The more data, the more precise the outcome, right?"

The process wheel stopped, shrank to a dot, expanded to fill the whole screen. When it vanished, a chemical formula had taken its place.

SHIVER

"There it is," Pris said. "Go for it."

It looked little different from any other mixture on the spread, just the proportions had changed. Mo moved Pris's tablet away. She masked up, handing a mask to Pris, and followed the new recipe while Pris watched. "You should have filmed this," Mo remarked, "for your podcast. Us making history."

"Yeah, and had Mickey here to narrate, but she had her own things to do today. We just don't have time if we want to save the mermaids."

Mo added the last few drops to the flask and swirled it gently. "Let's go try it." They dropped the thick protective masks on the workbench.

Her uncle, or one of his minions, had dropped off a covered bucket of freshly made chum next to the garage. Mo grabbed it. The smell coiled out from under the cover. Pris covered her face with her forearm as they crossed the yard carrying the bucket, the new formula in a corked glass vial, and one notebook. The odor was indeed foul, but Mo was used to it. Mostly.

The small sharks gathered, seeing the shadow of She Who Fed Them. Pris set up the camera apparatus while Mo peeled the plastic cover off the orange five-gallon bucket. Pris gagged, moving as far away as she could on the tiny deck. Mo made sure she didn't fall off the edge.

"You get used to it," Mo lied, trying not to breathe through her nose. She poured a little of the dark red mixture into the pool.

The sharks swarmed voraciously into the viscous mess.

"Do it," Pris gasped, holding her breath, "before I pass out."

Mo recovered the chum bucket and pried the cork from the vial. The sharks were practically wagging their tails like dogs; they were so happy with their disgusting chum puddle. She splashed a bit of the newest formula in the center of the dark cloud.

The little sharks fled to the other side of the pool, their black eyes wide.

"It worked! It worked!" Mo yelled. She hugged Pris. "It worked!"

Pris hugged her back. They jumped up and down on the tiny wooden platform. "Now let's design the one that brings them in, so the tourists can feed them."

SHIVER

Lucas and Mickey had no trouble slipping under the caution tape that lined the entrance to the public beach.

The beach might have been closed, but no one enforced that. There weren't enough officers in the town to leave one on duty there. Then again, the police could look out their front door and practically see the beach. The few media people from other areas had camped out at Crabby Patty's, which, despite its name, was far friendlier than The Dockside Feast. Crabby Patty's was also budget-friendly.

Once they were on the beach proper and out of sight of the police station, Lucas helped Mickey turn on the camera rig.

"This is really exciting," he said, peering into the forward-facing camera from a few inches away. "I get to be on the Contrary Crowcast."

"You'll need to back off a bit," Mickey said. "And act natural." Although from what she had seen so far, this behavior was natural for Lucas, who was a bit on the hyper side.

"They will just show up?" Lucas asked as they started down the beach. He shielded his eyes from the sun with his hand. "How does this work?"

"You are asking the wrong person how all this works," Mickey replied. "Just walk with me, okay? You're here to save me if they try to eat me again."

"Maybe you should take your arm off first this time," he said doubtfully. "My brothers are really unhappy with you right now."

Mickey made a non-committal noise. She had half an idea; it was a terrible one; It depended on a person she didn't even know and hadn't consulted.

She felt the familiar hunger. "They are close."

I don't know if I can save you from a shark attack," Lucas said. "This isn't a good idea."

"I don't think they will attack me," Mickey responded, scanning the water as she slowed her steps. *Remember me?* She thought at the water. *Friend.*

Lucas kept talking. Mickey held up her metal hand at him to hush.

"How can you hear each other think, though?" he persisted, and she put her index finger across his mouth, although that was indeed the question, wasn't it?

A confused group of images came into Mickey's brain, including several views of her and Lucas, and others that made her blush. Eventually, she figured them out.

No, he is not a gift for you.

She choked at their response. *Is that why you took Dylan?* She tried to send a picture of Dylan, but she didn't really remember what he looked like without his image before her. *For that, not to eat?*

"They are looking for human mates," she said to the camera, sure that her face reflected her shock.

"What?" Lucas yelled. She extended her hand to him again to shush.

"This is delicate, and they think you're an offering, so hush up."

She tried to imagine where they were by the pictures they had sent of her. There were at least three of them. Mickey scanned the water, searching for heads, for fins.

"An offering of what?"

Mickey told him, and for once, he shut up. How did she keep surrounding herself with people who talked so much?

She found a flattish rock near the water's edge and sat down facing where she thought the mermaids were. After a moment, Lucas dropped to the sand just behind her.

I want to negotiate, she sent to the waves. *Would you like to talk to people who aren't me?*

Four heads, at least their foreheads and eyes, rose from the waves and looked at her. Mickey raised her flesh hand in greeting. One mermaid copied the gesture.

Another confusion of images hit Mickey, hands and mouths moving, giant oyster shells, and traditionally dressed Native Americans.

"Okay," Mickey said to herself. "What do giant man-eating clams have to do with this?"

"The shell midden," Lucas suggested. "It's not fully excavated, but scanning shows the shells that make it up are unusually large and come from out in the sea, not at the shore." He scooted forward, staring at the heads. "Are they talking to you?"

"It's more like they dump a bunch of pictures in my head, and I have to figure them out," Mickey said. She described the latest collection.

"I think they brought the giant shells to the Native Americans— big, juicy oysters for eating. They had some kind of trade going," Lucas suggested.

Mickey bit her lip. "Well, we will not offer them that service," she said.

"Rich people would pay a lot for it. Hot mermaids in your area, waiting to meet you," Lucas prompted, raising his eyebrows suggestively.

"Yeah, and then eat you," Mickey responded. "I will not be part of that. That's exploitation."

She thought about how to phrase her idea. *Would you be willing to learn to talk to people who aren't me, and not eat those people, in return for lots of food?*

She could tell they found the idea preposterous.

Why not just eat those people and not have the extra step?

You won't have to hide anymore, she tempted them. *But no more eating people.*

They flooded her head with pictures of Lucas that made her blush.

I don't know about that. Think about it. I will come back.

"They want you, dude," she said to Lucas. She wiggled her eyebrows and made an obscene finger gesture.

"I'm gay! And they are fish! Lady fish!" He looked desperately at the heads in the water.

"They want you to think about it. Come on, we need to go to the library."

"Why?"

"To see if the librarian will teach sign language to the mermaids."

SHIVER
-39-

The smell of must and hot, decaying books was overwhelming in the library. The librarian took one look at Mickey's camera rigs and shook her head.

Mickey said, "Please?"

The librarian made a throat-slashing gesture. She watched, her eyes narrow behind her red glasses and her arms folded, as Lucas removed the two camera rigs and put them in a bag he slung across his chest.

Mickey stepped up to the counter. "What's your name? I'm Mickey Crow and this is Lucas Chu." She had brought her own pad and paper, and she wrote the names down and pushed the pad across the counter.

Guinevere, the librarian wrote. *Nice to meet you.* Her eyes went back to their faces.

"Do you know sign language?"

Guinevere nodded.

"Do you think you could teach it to someone?"

Guinevere pointed to Mickey and Lucas and raised her eyebrows.

"No, not us. I mean, we wouldn't mind learning. This would be a challenge. Way more of a challenge than teaching us. You would be famous after. Do you want to be famous?"

Guinevere pursed her lips and knitted her eyebrows. *Who?* she wrote.

"We aren't joking," Lucas said.

Guinevere nodded. She tapped the word *who*.

Mickey bit her lip. "Do you think you can teach sign language to mermaids?"

SHIVER
-40-

Mo's eyes burned from exhaustion and exposure to chemicals. Two days before, she and Pris had gone out and purchased enough supplies to make huge batches of both the shark repellent and the attractant. She should have also gotten some safety goggles. Usually her eyes were okay, but these amounts were larger than usual.

The librarian, Guinevere, and her friends came through the garage on their way to the beach, their hands flying in conversation. After talking with Mickey, Guinevere had called in a couple of trustworthy people from a school for the Deaf in Connecticut, and they were working on teaching sign language to the mermaids with Mickey's help. They greeted Mo with guttural hellos and waves. The public beach was still closed, so they always snuck down to the water through Mo's yard.

Mo went back to meticulously mixing, consulting the tablet Pris had given her. Sweat ran down her nose, soaking her mask and fogging her glasses. This was a race against time. She and her allies were trying to civilize the mermaids to save them. The media and law enforcement saw only missing people and confirmed dead from shark attacks.

The desk fan on her lab table blew hot air around. This was the latest in a string of the hottest summers on record. Mo pulled up the mask and lifted a bottle of fruity sports water to her mouth. She totally understood why Mickey loved this delicious stuff. Pris had left a case of it at Mo's.

"You saving the planet?" Rob was no longer wearing lifeguard orange and looking like a surfer dude. Ted had drafted Rob as a junior deputy. Rob was in a full police uniform, which had to be stifling.

"Parts of it," Mo answered, putting down the drink and wiping her mouth with her hand.

"For once, so am I," he bragged, coming into the shade inside the garage lab. It wasn't much cooler, but it wasn't in the glaring sun, either.

"Oh?" Mo asked, tilting her head. Her beads stuck to her sweat-dampened neck. "How are you saving the planet?"

He moved until he was standing too close to her. Once upon a time, she had a wicked crush on Rob and this would have set her heart beating faster. Now it just annoyed her. "I've been talking to your crazy old uncle," Rob said, leaning into her until he was close enough to kiss her. Mo could smell his breath. Milky coffee.

"He's not crazy," she said automatically, taking a step back. Rob pressed Mo against the lab table. Was this what Mickey felt like, with her claustrophobia, crowded and hemmed in?

"He is crazy like a fox," Rob confided, leaning closer. She could see the darker flecks in his blue eyes.

SHIVER

What did that even mean? Mo tried to move sideways along the counter to get away. It was just too hot to be so physically close to another person.

He followed her, crablike. "He's convinced Ted to requisition some explosives somehow from somewhere. I'm not in on the exact details. But we're going to lure those sharks into the cove and then blow them sky-high."

To her horror, Mo realized he thought she would be excited by this entire experience. That he was going to kiss her. Why had this not happened ten years ago? Or even five, when she would have been into it? "When?" she said.

"Oh, very soon. The next few days."

His lips touched her cheek and moved down. Part of her wanted to rise on her toes, meet his mouth with hers. This was Rob! Golden boy, lifeguard Rob, whom she had wanted forever. But his derision over her love of sharks had worn down her passion. Mo turned her face away. She reached behind her, found an empty glass flask, and knocked it to the floor. It didn't break on the foot-friendly padding, but it made enough noise to startle Rob into stepping back.

Mo put her hand on his chest. Warm, firm. Her fingers curled. She smiled, just a little, but it felt like goodbye in so many ways. "Keep me in the loop. Don't forget, I'm the shark expert," she said, even while her mind screamed that they were running out of time to save the mermaids.

SHIVER
-41-

Mickey sat on a sloped rock, holding her legs with both arms. Water sloshed around her, chilly and refreshing. She had always thought it was cooler at the shore, but the sun beat down on them. It was unrelenting. In the ultimate world, they would have some kind of tent to sit under. But they had to stay under the radar of the cops. The mermaids had agreed not to eat any more people while this learning and negotiation continued.

Guinevere and Mickey had not told the mermaids that the entire process could still fail and they could all be killed. The mermaids did not know they were in danger.

In the beginning, it had been Guinevere, Mickey, and three mermaids, plus Mickey's cameras. Language lessons had been laborious, with everything having to be translated through Mickey. But each day, the mermaids learned a little more ASL, and some days, a few more mermaids showed up for the lessons. Mickey started picking up some sign language just by watching and translating, although her metal hand was not flexible nor quick enough to form all the complex movements. Signing was like a full-body conversation, sometimes like a dance, sometimes the hands and arms were like bullets making a point.

The mermaids could not carry on a full-bodied, rich conversation yet, but they could make their wishes known. Mostly they wanted food—they were always hungry, and so was Mickey through the mind meld—and their secondary concern was for mates. Few mermaids were born male, it seemed, which made reproduction a problem. Mickey had seen no male mermaids yet, although their breasts were small, and perhaps the difference between pectorals and breasts wasn't much.

Rather than teaching the mermaids individual words, they were explaining concepts. Today Guinevere wanted the mermaids to learn how people were afraid of them because the mermaids did not seem to understand fear. Pris had obtained a water-resistant tablet that Guinevere could write on and erase, like a high-tech Etch-a-Sketch, and that's what Guinevere used to talk to Mickey.

Guinevere, insulated from the cold water in a wetsuit, sat on the rocky sea bottom near Mickey. A small shiver of mermaids faced her from a few feet away, their shark fins on display. A few actual sharks circled farther out, companions to the half-shark mermaids.

Mickey tried to visualize how to explain fear to them, connected, and sent pictures. The mermaids' gazes snapped to her, and Guinevere, knowing what was happening, also looked at Mickey. From the beach, Mickey heard the intakes of breath and sub-vocalizations of Guinevere's ASL-speaking friends who weren't brave enough yet to come into the water.

SHIVER

The mermaids asked again why the others weren't coming into the water. They were very curious about everything. Once they latched onto a topic, they would not stop. Mickey's metal arm endlessly fascinated them, and the mermaids liked to touch it. They also didn't understand her biomechanical-style tattoo and why it was flat yet looked three-dimensional.

Mickey sent pictures of things she thought the mermaids might be afraid of, such as churning boat motors, massive sharks, and fishing nets baited with a thousand tiny, sharp hooks. Then Guinevere held her hands up before her chest, moving them slightly in a fear motion while grimacing and then pointed at the mermaids.

Afraid of you, Mickey told them. She loved the wonderful facial expressions that accompanied sign language. She had picked it up, using her eyes and eyebrows more exaggeratedly in conversation.

She wasn't good at reading the mermaid's faces yet (they still all looked alike to her, sadly), but they sent back indignant pictures. *Afraid of us?*

Mickey snorted and waved her mechanical hand, which had become a signal to Guinevere.

What? She wrote on the tablet in big letters.

"They aren't scary, they claim," Mickey said, laughing.

Guinevere's hands flashed to her friends, ending with shaking her head with her finger to her chin and her eyes wide in denial. They all laughed.

"I'm going to explain that they eat people," Mickey said. She sent pictures of what had happened to the cops as seen through the bird-drones. No parts of either Dom or Jack had been found, except what they had left on the beach. She raised a metal finger to tell Guinevere it was time to translate and watched the librarian's graceful body dance in the water beside her.

Hungry.

Mickey covered her face with both hands. The mermaids moved closer and stared, fascinated with the metal one. Guinevere leaned over to put her hand on Mickey's leg. Mickey felt the other woman's fear. She turned so the librarian could see her lips. "They've learned nothing," she said. "I think they would still eat all of us in a heartbeat. They don't understand that we're fighting to keep them alive. I feel like crying."

The mermaids stroked Mickey's other leg and her metal arm. Mickey felt uncomfortably crowded. It didn't help that most of the people touching her were hungry and wanted to eat her.

Guinevere stared wide-eyed with sadness across the rock at the mermaids. Her slightly wrinkled face was so expressive, but were the mermaids any better at reading humans than humans were at reading mermaids? Guinevere raised her hands and hooked her index fingers into each other over and over, signing *friend, friend.*

The mermaids touched Mickey's arm and hair and tugged at her, trying to get her into the water. One of them let go and signed *friend* back at Guinevere.

Guinevere held onto Mickey's warm, fleshy arm. She shook her head and frowned fiercely, clearly telling Mickey not to get into the water.

"I don't want to go with them," Mickey answered, and pulled her arm free of Guinevere to sign *no* at the mermaids trying to kidnap her. Guinevere moved toward the shore as one of the sharks started forward. It was larger than Mickey thought. Most of the sharks that came with the mermaids were four or five feet long, maybe six. This one was … bigger. It kept coming, looming.

"They're gonna feed me to that shark," Mickey said to the air. She looked up to see if the ravens were recording, because the two cameras she was wearing would go with her if the shark took her. This wasn't how she wanted to die. She slid off the rock into the horrible smothering water. Mermaids pulled Mickey forward. The prosthetic had gotten soaked again—the twins would choke her if she lived through this. Each wave rose higher and colder on her body, even as her head baked in the sunlight. Water and mermaids surrounded Mickey, crowding her intolerably. They held on and would not be shaken off as they guided her forward until the waves lifted Mickey off her feet.

"No!" she cried, fighting them. She freed her right arm and signed half of the sign for afraid, clumsily, over and over. She tried to tell them through the linkage that she couldn't swim, but they had no concept of not swimming. No concept of claustrophobia.

"Please!" Mickey cried as the mermaids keep pulling her out of her depth. She turned to see Guinevere and her friends on the beach watching anxiously, their hands still but their faces expressive.

Mickey didn't know one type of shark from another. To her, every shark in the ocean was a great white and would eat her—only Mo's little babies were safe sharks. The enormous shark paused its forward movement, hovering in the water in front of Mickey, bobbing in the waves that washed over it. It had the usual black featureless eye—she could actually only see one, its face was so broad.

The shark's mouth was mostly closed, but the teeth showed, pointed, ragged, jagged, and sharp. The mermaids knew enough to keep Mickey's face and shoulders above the water. She couldn't get an unobstructed view of the entire gargantuan creature. It was vastly bigger than Mickey.

SHIVER

The mermaids held her still.

She looked at the shark. The shark tilted its head to look at her.

They connected.

The shark was ancient, prehistoric, even. It was possibly a shark-god; it was that old. Her mind shivered and shimmered as the shark tried to see into her brain. Nothing had ever tried to do that before. The invasion was shocking. It felt like the shark was licking her brain, tasting her thoughts. It was awful. The shark's blunt nose came forward, out of the water, a dark gray behemoth, right in Mickey's face. She stared into one of its eyes. It looked back. It saw her, and she saw it.

She put out her hand, her flesh hand, her only hand, and the shark took it delicately in its mouth. Still, a dark ribbon of blood came from her wrist as the shark tasted her in a different way. They were eye to eye. One mermaid held Mickey's forearm delicately but firmly in one hand, with her other hand lovingly on the shark's enormous lower jaw, facilitating the connection between Mickey and the shark-god.

Mickey touched the shark's enormous teeth with her fingers, rows and rows of them like knife blades. The shark tasted her blood and her thoughts and finally started questioning her.

She told it everything.

SHIVER
-42-

Lucas took Mickey's prosthetic to his room to clean. Caren's Cozy Cottage was getting crowded with Guinevere's translator friends also staying there. Caren had made noises about Mickey and Pris possibly having to share a room soon, which Mickey ignored. She did not share rooms, or beds, with anyone.

She had said to Lucas, "My arm got wet again. Blame god, not me. I don't want to talk about it." She ignored his squeaking at her about the blood on her flesh hand.

Now Mickey laid face-up on her bed, her oozing hand on her flat belly. The camera rigs were discarded in a heap on the floor for Pris to sort out later, if she ever returned from her top-secret trip.

The ceiling of the room needed to be painted. The whole thing was mazed with cracks, just like Mickey's mind was now. One corner had a suspicious bit of web currently unoccupied.

Her tank top had been dark olive green. Now it looked like a camo pattern with all the blood in various stages of drying. Laundry was another thing she didn't want to think about.

The bitten hand didn't hurt. It felt cold and somehow very far away. The tasting injury was two or three very clean punctures in the back of her hand and palm.

Mickey didn't know how far away the enormous shark had gone afterward, but it was still latched onto her brain like a remora, just watching. Not only had Mickey never encountered a god before, she had never been sure they were even real. Was this how all gods acted? She felt as if there was spyware in her brain. What would the twins say? If, as she had always suspected, she was an unwitting guinea pig for a DARPA project, how would they feel knowing a prehistoric fish could easily override their high-tech futuristic implants?

Voices converged in the hallway outside the door. Mickey recognized Pris's excited tones, and Lucas sounding worried, before her door opened. She stayed flat on the bed.

"What happened to you? I can't leave you alone for a day, can I?" Pris said. Her footsteps headed toward Mickey.

"I cleaned your arm. My brothers are furious at you," Lucas said, offering Mickey the shining prosthetic.

"Not my fault," Mickey said, staring at the ceiling. "Met a god."

"You're babbling." Pris sat on the bed next to her while Lucas stood there awkwardly holding the prosthetic.

Mickey lifted her arm so the blood oozed toward her elbow. "A god tasted me. He didn't eat me. Or she didn't eat me. Is that good or bad? I don't know. Then he licked my brain. He's still in there." She allowed the bloody hand to flop back onto her stomach.

Pris looked at Lucas. "Was she in the sun too long? How much blood has she lost?"

"I don't know. You told me to make friends with that uber-jerk Rob since he's a wanna-be cop now, and that's where I was almost all day. Mickey was on the beach talking to mermaids with the lady from the library and her friends. Mo wasn't there either; she was at her lab mixing chemicals all morning; now she's at the diner working."

"We should go there and have dinner, right, but first, your hand, Mickey."

"I met god, and he licked me and spit me out," Mickey said. "I was so scared I would lose my other hand."

Pris rummaged under the sink in their shared bathroom. She came out with a roll of gauze in a yellowed paper wrapper that had been in there since about 1975. She wrapped the cloth around Mickey's hand and tied it off. It turned pink immediately.

"Mo was right. They don't like to eat humans."

"Who doesn't?"

"Sharks. The shark-god did this. Now he lives in my head. He knows everything," Mickey said.

"Energy-sucking fey," Pris said.

SHIVER

-43-

They retreated to Crabby Patty's to have something to eat. Mickey sat silently across from Lucas and Pris, her bandaged hand in her lap. She didn't touch her cheeseburger or complain when Lucas blatantly ate all of her fries.

Mo popped over to talk whenever she could.

"I didn't play back today's bird-drone footage," Lucas told Pris. "I had barely finished fixing up her prosthetic when you got back. I'm not the big expert my brothers are, you know."

Pris waved that off. "Close enough, right?" She pulled her crab cake off its bun and ate it meticulously with a knife and fork. She shoved her fries at Lucas. "So, you want to know what I've been doing?" The bruises were fading from her fight with the now-dead officers, but her eyes had shadows of fatigue around them.

"Yes!" Lucas said, getting up on his knees and bouncing. He wasn't even ten years younger than them, but sometimes he seemed like a total child.

Mickey stirred. She poked at her burger, tried to imagine if it was sentient and she could connect with it. She raised it to her lips and licked it, her eyes closed. What did cows think about?

She became aware that Lucas and Pris had stopped talking and opened her eyes. They were staring at her. "What?"

"What are you doing?" Pris demanded. "Are you making out with your food?"

"I was wondering what cows think about."

"You are not okay, right?"

"Probably not." She put down the burger. Tasting it had invoked no connection to cows or the thoughts of cows. But these cows were dead—how many cows were in one burger anyway, she wondered. Mickey looked at her hand, which had finally stopped bleeding. It had been in a shark's mouth earlier that day.

Mo appeared at Mickey's shoulder in perfect pink waitress mode. "What's wrong with your burger, Mickey? Should I have a new one made for you?"

Mickey shook her head and pushed the plate away. Lucas leaned over from where he was still perched on his heels and grabbed the burger. Obviously unconcerned that Mickey had licked it, he started eating it.

"You are nasty," Pris said to him.

He shrugged and kept eating. "My mama told me not to waste food. Plus, I'm hungry."

"Bring some chicken nuggets," Pris suggested to Mo. Looking at Lucas, she added, "like a big basket of them, right?"

SHIVER

Mo put her hand gently on Mickey's shoulder. "How can I help? What happened to you?"

Mickey tilted her head until her cheek rested on Mo's hand. It smelled of fries and hand lotion. Her skin was very soft. She wondered what Mo tasted like, and not in a sexual way. She jerked herself away from her friend in horror. She did not want to know how hot Mo's blood was.

"What?" Mickey could hear the hurt in Mo's voice. "Did I hurt your shoulder?"

Pris sighed. "As soon as I get the story, I'll tell you, Mo, right? It's not about you, I promise."

The pink cloud that was Mo left the table. Lucas kept eating. Pris stared at Mickey.

"We were doing the lesson," Mickey said finally. She looked at her bandaged hand. "Teaching them new words. It's tedious. It hurts my head."

"Okay," Pris said slowly. "You had the camera rig on?"

"Yeah."

Lucas perked up, bouncing on his heels. "More footage?"

Pris shushed him with a wave of her hand.

"There were, I don't know, three or four mermaids. They are hard to tell apart. I feel racist saying that." Mickey looked at Lucas.

He nodded. "I'm just half Korean, but white people think I'm everything and anything Asian. Someone thought I was Mongolian once."

Mickey raised her eyebrows as if she understood. "Yeah, that's why I feel bad. Like I can't see past their essential mermaidness to how they are individuals. And we haven't gotten around to the concept of names yet." Mickey took a deep breath. "Some of their shark friends—pets? The sharks that hang out with them were there."

In her shockingly retro-pink uniform, Mo arrived at that moment with two red, oval baskets heaped with steaming chicken nuggets. "Someone else besides me has pet sharks?"

"The mermaids," Pris said, taking a nugget and biting it. "Oh, these are hot, right?"

"Fresh out of the fryer!" Mo said cheerfully. "Did I bring enough? Oh, of course, the mermaids have pet sharks. They're half shark themselves." No one was seated close by, but Mo still dropped her voice when talking about the mermaids. Mo plunked down a bottle of hot sauce she pulled from her pocket. "I wish I could stay and hear everything, but I have some people over there at the counter I have to wait on, of course."

Lucas took one basket for himself, which was no less than Mickey had predicted. Mickey selected a single piece of chicken and shook some hot sauce on it. It was perfect. She ate a couple more, sharing the sauce with Pris.

Swallowing the last bite, Mickey wiped hot sauce off her mouth. "The mermaids insisted they weren't scary. They pulled me into the water with the sharks. I didn't want to go. I hate being submerged. They were grabbing me, pulling me, surrounding me. It was awful." She shuddered and ate another piece of chicken. Then she thought about how she was just a piece of chicken to a shark that big and shoved the basket across the table at Pris.

"There was this one shark. It was huge." Mickey stared out the window at the sea down the road.

"How huge?" Lucas asked. He had already eaten half his basket of nuggets. Together, Mickey and Pris hadn't gotten through a quarter of theirs.

Mickey thought about it. "Its head was the size of a big overstuffed couch. I couldn't see the entire length of its body through the haze of the stirred-up water."

Lucas actually stopped eating. That was unprecedented. He put down the nugget in his hand. "Great white? Megalodon?"

Mickey swayed her head back and forth like a flower on its stem. "All sharks are the same to me. Big shark. Biggest shark. Like something you'd see on TV."

"Spotted shark?" Lucas persisted.

"I only saw the head!" Mickey almost yelled. The people at the counter turned to look at them. So did Mo, who was cutting up a pie.

"We have the video, right?" Pris said. "We'll figure it out."

Lucas settled slightly and picked up his discarded, half-eaten nugget. Seeing the bite mark on the chicken made Mickey feel somewhat ill.

"So they dragged me into deeper water," Mickey continued, keeping her voice low so the people at the counter couldn't hear. "Right up to this sofa-shark."

Mo appeared beside their booth. "What is a sofa-shark?"

Pris shook her head. "Mickey saw a giant shark whose head was the size of a sofa."

"No," Mo said. "No sharks are that big. And definitely not around here."

"Anywhere? Ever?" Pris asked.

"Megalodon," Lucas suggested again, pointing at Mo with a nugget.

Mickey said, "You guys can argue about what you think does or doesn't exist in the world of sharks. Meanwhile, I can tell you the story of what I actually did see and experience. And it was a shark with a head the size of a couch, if not bigger."

"No," Mo said again, checking on the pie-eating customers at the counter. One of them motioned to her, so she returned to that end of the diner.

Mickey waved her bandaged hand. "If all you guys could stop calling me a liar and listen to my story ..." She glared at her friends. "Because I know what I saw. And we have video footage, don't we? If I am lying, you can see that on a screen."

"Right," Pris conceded.

"The thing about this enormous shark was, it connected with me first." Mickey touched her head with her metal hand. "And it was strong. A powerful connection. It was like being invaded. I didn't like it. I never connected like that with anything alive. Even when I connect with Mo's little sharks and the mermaids, it's very mild and on the surface, if that makes any sense." Mickey twisted her mouth. "I know you can't comprehend what this connection thing is like. But this was so invasive. It was like the shark was tasting my brain. But I got almost nothing from the shark. Just that it was ancient. Centuries at the youngest. It was a repository of knowledge that it would not share, but it wanted to take everything I know."

Lucas finished his chicken nuggets and crumpled the greasy paper lining the bottom of the basket into a ball. He eyed the other basket.

Pris crinkled her nose and pursed her lips. "I don't get it," she confessed.

"I think it was a god," Mickey said, "or the closest thing to it. A shark-god. It read my mind and saw that we want to save the mermaids. I think it approves."

SHIVER
-44-

Well," Pris said, "anything I have to say is anticlimactic after learning that Mickey is communing with a god." She poured hot sauce over the remains of the basket of chicken. Lucas, who had used no sauce on his, made a face at her.

Mickey stared at the dripping red chicken pieces. "It bit me to get a better sense of who I am. By tasting my blood." She held up her bandaged hand. "I was so scared it was going to bite my other hand off."

"Yeah, I don't know whether my brothers would build you a second hand when you've been mistreating your prosthetic so much this week," Lucas said.

Mickey turned on him, suddenly alive and livid. "Both times my arm got wet, I was attacked by mermaids and sharks. Is that my fault?"

"Why are you close enough to the water to allow mermaids and sharks to get you?"

"Oh my god! Your brothers sent me here because of *you!* Because your friend was missing. Because those same mermaids and sharks probably took him. So, when I do exactly what they ask, and I get damp—" Lucas snorted. "—everyone gets mad at me like I did it on purpose."

"No one cares about what I have to say?" Pris licked the hot sauce off a nugget and then ate it.

The sight made Mickey feel ill. She covered her mouth with her hand, but then she could smell her own blood on the bandage. Immediately, she felt smothered. It didn't help that she gagged and the taste of chicken and hot sauce clogged the back of her throat like death. Everything seemed to shut off inside her.

Lucas noticed first. "She's choking," he said, trying to lean over the table.

"No," Pris said immediately, "She's having a panic attack. We have to get her outside."

Mickey bent over, her face almost on the table. Everything was so close. Everything stank. Far away, she heard Pris and Lucas arguing, and then, horribly, she felt them grabbing her and pulling at her. It reminded her of the mermaids taking her to be taste-tasted by the shark-god. Was that happening again? Blood for the shark-god hadn't been enough. Now the shark-god wanted flesh. She twisted and struggled. She might be a useless, broken human who took more than she gave, but she wanted to live.

It was her leg this time. Something was on her leg, grabbing it. Mickey didn't want to lose her leg too. The voices coming into her ears were garbled. Was she already underwater? Everything whirled.

SHIVER

Then it was her head. The mermaids and the sharks had Mickey by the head. They had learned her name somehow. She scrunched her eyes shut. She didn't have to see her death.

Fingers in her mouth. She tried to bite them off. It was only fair. Someone swearing, a funny, unique swear she had only heard Pris use.

Mickey opened her eyes. She was lying on a bench down the street from the diner. Pris was shoving a pill into her mouth.

"They need to make this anxiety medicine into a liquid," Pris said. "You tried to eat me. That was the worst attack I think I've ever seen you have. We're lucky we know Mo, or she would have called 911, and how would we have explained this to Ted?"

Mickey dry-swallowed the pill. Bitter. Mo stood in the doorway to the diner, her arms crossed tightly, her usually dancing braids totally still. Pris waved that everything was all right.

"Lucas, here, go pay. Twenty-five percent tip, right?" Pris handed over an iridescent credit card.

"I've heard of a black card, but this?" He moved the card in the light. "What is this?"

"It's my credit card. I pay for things with it. Like the stuff I bought today that I've been trying to tell you all about. But we keep getting interrupted by shark-gods and whatnot."

As the quick-release medicine did its job, Mickey relaxed. Her breathing slowed. She felt silly. But when she apologized, Pris just got angry.

"You have a chemical imbalance. It's not your fault."

Lucas returned carrying a large white paper bag with a few grease spots. He handed the shining card over to Pris. "Mo gave us more chicken to go."

Mickey shuddered.

Pris led them to her car and opened the hatch. "Lucas, you can carry things into the B&B."

The back of the car was crammed with shopping bags imprinted with the name of an exclusive hunting and sporting goods store. There was also an overstuffed bag full of clothes from a secondhand store. Pris took that one.

"Nothing for you to carry," Pris told Mickey. She waited while Lucas overloaded his arms and then took the final two bags herself.

They converged in Pris's room. Pris sent Mickey back to her room to retrieve the camera rig, and once Lucas had divested himself of the bags, asked him to get the tablet with the drone footage.

Lucas threw himself onto the floor in the corner. Mickey and Pris sat on the bed with the bags. From one bag, Pris pulled several identical small boxes. "These are satellite phones that have texting capacity. They are made to be used way out at sea where there is no internet. I got one for each of us and Mo, and one for Guinevere and her friends. I'm tired of this stupid incommunicado backwater town. They are all paid up for a month, unlimited talk and text." Each box had a sticky note with a phone number on it.

Lucas wanted to play with his phone immediately.

"Wait," Pris said. "We are nowhere near done. There are more bags."

"It's like Christmas when we were little," Mickey said weakly. The phone box was in her lap, being held by her metal hand tightly against her thigh. She pushed her back against the headboard. She had gone limp with exhaustion.

Pris looked sideways at Mickey and then moved her hand from the next hunter-sport-marine bag to the secondhand store haul. She started pulling out clothes. Lucas rolled his eyes, groaned, and opened his phone box, removing something that looked more like a rugged orange walkie-talkie than a slim glass rectangle. It had a small float attached to it by a string.

"Look, these are all cargo shorts," Pris showed Mickey. "For you." She laid several pairs of shorts onto Mickey's lap. "And some tank tops that kind of match in color. This one is silly." The one in question had two shells on the chest, like a mermaid's bra. The shirt was purple, the shells rainbow-colored.

"I'm not wearing that," Mickey said.

"Fine. I'll wear it. It's amusing. Or I'll give it to Mo."

"That won't fit Mo's, uh, shells," Mickey pointed out. "Hers are even bigger than yours."

Pris peered into the bag. "The rest of this is for me." She dug into the bottom and pulled out a pair of hiking sandals. "Happy?"

"They're your feet, do what you want."

Lucas was already texting someone. "This doesn't do photos?" he complained.

"Hush," Pris replied. "We have other ways to send photos. I told you to wait. Who are you trying to send photos to? And how did you get photos on that thing? It doesn't even have a camera."

"My brother wants to send me something."

"Tell him to hang on." Pris took out a big brown box that filled a single bag by itself. She unfolded it to show a protective briefcase. It also had a float tied to it.

Mickey fell onto her side in distress that wasn't entirely feigned. "This is just like Christmas when your parents prank you by wrapping things in multiple boxes. I can't take it."

SHIVER

"You know, I could find a more deserving group of people and a better situation to spend my money on. Or I could build a rocket and go into space and not do anything for anybody except myself."

"You wouldn't go to space without me," Mickey declared. "You would be so bored and lonely."

"Are you that rich?" Lucas asked, wide-eyed. He dipped his hand into the greasy bag and fed himself a piece of chicken.

Pris shrugged. "Probably?" She unsnapped the lid and opened it. Gray foam lined the inside. A rugged-looking laptop nestled inside the foam. "This is the companion to the satellite phones. It's a laptop with satellite internet. I got one for us to share and one for Mo." She tapped another identical bag and pushed it aside. She looked at Lucas. "Thus, you can send and receive photos. I would prefer you not waste bandwidth to send memes."

"So that's where you were all day?" Lucas asked, scrunching his face and flipping his floppy hair. "Shopping?"

"And talking to lawyers. I started a non-profit corporation. You know. Grown-up stuff. What did you learn?"

"A non-profit?" Mickey asked, still on her side and doing her best not to watch Lucas eating chicken. Maybe she would never eat again. Eating was disgusting. "Explain?"

"Hmm. Not today. Not until things move along."

Pris opened the small, ugly laptop, built to be rugged, not elegant. She showed them how to interface the computer with Lucas's phone since he already had it going. "And while we are at it, give me the cards from the camera rig today."

Mickey couldn't manage the fiddly steps needed to extract the tiny cards from the cameras with one hand, and the metal hand wasn't precise enough. Lucas did it with an ease that Mickey pretended not to envy and handed the black squares over to Pris.

"Let's watch the forward-facing view first," Pris suggested.

Mickey raised herself up to watch while Lucas, smelling of chicken grease, crowded too close. The sound was tinny, it was not the best resolution, but it matched what she remembered. The first few times she had worn the rig and then watched the footage, it had been very disorienting. Now she was used to it. The rig didn't record her thoughts, just what she saw (and the faces she made while seeing it).

Pris's hands moved. "I remember some of this sign language," she said, mimicking the gestures. "Weird."

Mickey tensed as she watched herself being pulled into the water. They could pause and rewind and zoom in. "Mo has to see this," Pris said. "Oh. We can call her! Lucas, look up the number to the diner and call there. Tell her to come here after work."

"I don't want to miss anything," he grumbled, grabbing the slim phone book from the nightstand.

"It's not live, silly," Pris reminded him. She froze the screen as the enormous shark loomed over Mickey while Lucas mumbled on the landline in the background.

He hung the phone up. "Mo said it will be like eleven, but she's coming over. You know the innkeeper lady won't like that."

"I don't care. I could buy this place with the change under my car seat." Pris flicked her fingers in the air.

"You don't use cash. You haven't got any change under your car seat," Mickey said.

Pris flicked her fingers again. "Lucas, right, look at this giant shark. Is it a megalodon?"

Lucas threw away the empty, greasy bag. "I hung out most of the day with Rob. I thought maybe he was a jerk because he was in charge at the lifeguard school. Nope. Even as a brand-new, not-really-doing-anything deputy, he's not very nice."

"Did you learn anything?" Pris asked, leaning toward him until she was almost falling off the bed.

"Yeah. Mo's almost-stepdad sheriff is sourcing some explosive. I think he's going to work with Uncle Charlie to recreate the great shark explosion of sixty years ago."

Mickey sat up and grabbed at Pris before she hit the floor. "That's bad. That's terrible. Big shark-god will not like that. He—it—did not like it the other two times."

"What?" Pris demanded. "You know that?"

Mickey shrugged, remembering the alien pathways in the ancient shark's mind. "There wasn't much give, only take, but yeah, I got some impressions. The shark doesn't have language, exactly." She closed her eyes. "It's visual, smells, and something like echolocation that I don't have, extra senses. And the communication via electricity, I guess, whatever it is I can tap into. Like a 3D movie but with extra senses."

When she opened her eyes again, both Lucas and Pris were staring at her. Lucas's mouth was open a little.

"What?" Mickey said, feeling both defensive and naked. It wasn't easy to talk about this stuff.

"You are amazing," Lucas said. "You're like some kind of god yourself."

Mickey's face flamed. "If I am, your brothers made me into one." She tapped the wires on the back of her head and then wrapped her arms around her knees. "God or not, we have to stop the explosive plan. But I really don't want to come out as a freak who can talk to sharks. And I'm pretty sure the shark-god doesn't want to be on the internet."

Pris had been cueing up the drone footage on the laptop. "Seriously, Mickey? I could make you rich with this."

Lucas crowded onto the bed next to Pris. "I want to see."

Mickey shook her head, but she also looked at the screen. "I don't need to be rich. I live in my parent's basement like a troll, remember? I don't feel any need to move out." The old guilt rose in her, about how she was a taker, and useless. Getting rich off the footage of the shark-god chewing on her hand would be more of the same. "Okay, here's the line not to cross. Footage of me interacting with mermaids and non-god sharks is okay to put on the podcast. Talking about the same is okay. I don't think the shark-god will approach the people doing sign-language lessons. We can keep filming that."

Unlike the transparent, warm, blue water in places like the Caribbean, the cold gray water off Shell Beach was not clear. On the screen, the large dark shadow approaching the tiny forms of Mickey and the mermaids could have been some kind of small whale, except that it had the upright tail fin of a fish, not the sideways tail of a mammal.

"That's enormous," Lucas said unnecessarily. "I wonder if it is a megalodon?"

"Yeah," Pris agreed. "I don't like that one bit." She paused the video with the shark and Mickey face-to-face. The shark was the size of a trailer.

"Now you know why I was struggling," Mickey said. Watching the video was terrifying. She had not realized just how enormous the shark was. It could have eaten her in one bite and barely noticed.

"Mo is going to lose her mind when she sees this," Pris said.

"That shark is bigger than her pool," Mickey said.

Pris started the video again. They watched Mickey put her hand in the shark's mouth.

"You are crazy," Lucas said, but his tone was admiring. "And brave. I would have pissed myself."

"I'm not sure I didn't. It's already starting to be a blur."

"I don't understand what was happening here. I know we can't show this footage on Contrary Crowcast, but I still want to know. I'm still a curious crow." Pris tapped the image of her friend's arm in the shark's mouth.

Mickey sighed. "Well, the neural net lets me connect to things now that I couldn't before. Not just my prosthetic, but my phone and Pris's car and the bird-drones—" Beside her, Pris jerked. Oh. Mickey had never told her that part. "Yeah. And evidently, the mermaids have some kind of electrical way to communicate, and I can tap into it. Same with Mo's pool pets."

On the laptop screen, the tiny figure of Mickey paused, her arm forever disappearing inside the shark's maw.

"I guess somehow the mermaids called the shark-god. Or was it always there? But it came to see me, I think. To check me out. It knew what I could do. It dove right into my brain. It felt like it was licking my brain." Mickey shuddered, hugging herself. "I don't even know if sharks have tongues. But it was getting information from me that way. But not enough. It needed to taste me for real. And I had to trust it. I know Mo has talked about how when sharks bite people, they are just tasting them and really don't want to eat them or cause harm. Just doing a taste test. This shark's teeth were nearly the size of my hands. I had to believe it could taste me and not kill me by accident or take my other hand. That something that big could be …" she paused. "Delicate? That's a weird word, but that's what it agreed to."

Pris unpaused the video. A small dark cloud of Mickey's blood came from the shark's mouth. Mickey winced, remembering. Then the giant shark-god backed away, mouth agape, freeing Mickey. It swirled and headed into the deep, dark water, and the drones did not follow it. The mermaids surrounded Mickey. They pulled her to the shore, surrendering her to the care of the ASL teachers and translators. The people on the beach spoke urgently to the mermaids, waving their hands, emoting strongly with their faces, pointing, clearly asking what had happened. Mickey sprawled bonelessly on the beach, her hand leaking dark blood onto the sand and rocks.

"I don't remember this part."

"I don't blame you," Pris said.

SHIVER

-46-

Mo pulled open the front door to Caren's Cozy Cottage and tried to creep noiselessly up the stairs, hoping Caren wouldn't hear her. No such luck.

The middle-aged woman came barging out of the living room and sneered. "What are you doing here so late? It's almost midnight. You aren't a registered guest. You have your own house."

Mo paused. "Hi, Caren." The woman had gone to school with her mom and vocally disapproved of her parent's marriage. "I'm here to see my friends who are guests: Pris and Mickey."

Caren's long face only looked more sour. "Those two. The retard cripple and the queer—and now they got that slant eyes with them. And all those weird Deaf people waving their hands around." She shrugged, waved her own hands. "Their money is green. I try not to talk to them. You stay overnight, I'll have to charge you," she added.

Mo continued up the stairs. "Of course," she said neutrally, trying not to be full of hate. Why did people like Caren never get eaten by sharks?

She knocked lightly on Mickey's door and then Pris's. Lucas opened the door, his eyes and smile wide, and she handed over a bag of burgers. He was a bottomless pit. He blew her a kiss and returned to the bed. The double bed was already crowded.

"Oh, don't let Caren see this," Mo joked, taking off her sneakers. "All you deviants in one bed." Her feet seemed to expand two sizes in gratitude. "Lucas, can I maybe have one cheeseburger?"

He peered into the bag and faked a look of disappointment.

"He ate the entire bag of chicken earlier," Mickey said, drawing up her legs to make room for Lucas to crawl over her. "Plus all of one basket you gave us at the diner, plus I think two burgers or maybe three? I had a panic attack, so counting Lucas's calories wasn't high on my priority list."

"Don't make fun of me. That's insensitivity toward my metabolic needs."

Lucas handed a neatly wrapped burger to Mo. They arranged themselves precariously in the bed. None of them were very large, but it was still quite crowded. Mo looped her arm through Mickey's so she could be on the edge and not surrounded and yet not fall off, either.

"You smell like a burger," Lucas said plaintively.

"Yeah, and I brought you an entire bag to eat so you wouldn't complain, so hush."

"You're very pink," he continued. "You look like a strawberry cream chocolate candy."

"Yes, thank you, Lucas, who always thinks of food. You should be a chef instead of whatever you were planning on being if you ever grow up."

"A paramedic."

"What are we looking at?" Mo said, ignoring him. It wasn't like he would go away. Plus, he was cute, like a puppy, and very good at making adorable big-eyed expressions.

"Right," said Pris, taking over. She pulled the laptop onto their combined lap. "I went shopping today. I got two of these all-weather rugged laptops that connect to the internet via satellite. The other one is yours, Mo. It's in the bag over there."

Mo went speechless for a moment, staring at Pris. "No, that's too much. What does that cost to connect to a satellite? I'm a part-time waitress at a diner that caters to fishermen, as well as being an unemployed scientist. I can't afford that."

Pris waved. "Right, you guys are all obsessed with money and what you can and can't afford. It's already bought and paid for, so there's nothing for you to afford. So, Mo, take the laptop. I also got you a marine satellite phone that texts. It's not a smartphone, so no apps, sorry, but this way we can be in touch instantly. It's ugly as hell too, but there's nothing I can do about that. There are no pretty cases for these things."

Mo nodded. Pris was like a force of nature, she was learning. Just accept it and move along.

"Lucas spent the day with your buddy Rob doing the male-bonding thing since he already knows him. Turns out your step-daddy-in-training is hatching a plan to get some explosive. He and Uncle Charlie want to blow the mermaids sky-high, and it's happening any day now," Pris summarized.

"He's not my step-daddy yet," Mo muttered, but she knew it was inevitable. And really, she didn't mind if Ted married her mom, as long as he didn't kill the sharks and mermaids with explosives. "I have working formulas for shark attractant and deterrent. At least, they work on my pets. And yeah, Rob stopped by my laboratory to brag about the explosives. He also tried to kiss me." She processed that again.

Three sets of eyes stared at her. Lucas elbowed her.

"And?" Mickey said. "He's arrogant, but he's got that classic surfer-dude look to him."

Mo shrugged. "Even five years ago, I would have been totally into it. Melted onto him like a chocolate bar." She grinned at Lucas.

"So why didn't you?" he asked. "I think he's hot."

"I don't think he's hot," Pris said, wrinkling her nose.

SHIVER

"He's got the wrong parts for you," Lucas said. "I can confirm because, you know, locker room while at lifeguard school. They are the right parts for me, but I think I have the wrong parts for him."

Mickey sighed. "Parts are complicated. We should all have snap-on parts we could swap as necessary."

"You're weird," Mo said, shaking her head. "And anyway, I stopped being into Rob when he started to be mean to me about science. That was after my uncle got me the pool and the sharks when I got my master's degrees. Rob's not dumb, but he likes to act as if he is. I don't go for that."

"Smart is sexy," Pris agreed. "Pseudo-dumb and willfully ignorant are not."

They thought about that for a moment.

Mo said, "What's this video?" She waved at the screen on Pris's lap.

"Oh!" Mickey said. "That's me, and that's a massive shark. We thought you might tell us what kind of shark it is. We have three drone views plus one front-facing camera view from my head."

"Of course, I know all the types of sharks around here. Play it." Mo leaned forward, looking at the small screen. It was the beach from above. Several people were on the shore. One person was on a rock in the water. A few people, presumably mermaids, were in the water. "Are these the ASL lessons?"

"Yes," Mickey said. "That's me on the rock, Guinevere in the water with the mermaids, and her friends up on the beach. They're still too afraid to come in the water."

"I don't have to work at the diner tomorrow. I want to see these mermaids in person, figure out what kind of shark their bottom halves are. I've been so busy making formula I haven't gotten down there to see." She squinted and pushed her glasses around. "I wish I had a magnifying glass. How do you expect me to identify something so small? Can you get the drones to go lower next time?"

There was a bit of suppressed laughter from Lucas. Mo didn't like it. She glared at him. "I'm your food hookup in this town, buddy. You want the cheeseburger and crab cake and chicken nugget supply to dry up, keep giggling at me."

He held up both hands. "Not laughing at you. I love how you smell. I adore you. I worship you. I would marry you if only you had snap-on parts like Mickey suggested."

"I know of a website," Pris said, wiggling her sculpted eyebrows. "We could order her a strap-on part."

"Eww," Mo said. "No. Absolutely not. I am erasing that image from my head. You guys can change your parts all you want, but I like mine as-is."

SHIVER

"Pay attention," Mickey said, pointing at the screen with her metal finger. Her other hand had fresh bandages on it.

Mo watched Mickey being dragged into the water. She covered her mouth with both hands. She knew Mickey was fine. Mickey was right there next to her, only minimally bandaged, her incredible prosthetic arm intact and functioning. Mo was so focused on the minuscule image of her friend apparently being dragged to a watery death by mermaids that she didn't at first see the looming shadow in the water. And then she didn't realize what it was because it was so huge.

"What is that? Stop the video. Stop it." Mo pushed the screen with her fingers.

Pris paused it by touching the keyboard.

"That's some kind of—" Mo searched for the term. "Video artifact, isn't that what it's called? That enormous shadow."

"Video artifact is an actual term, but no, this is not that. This is a real shark."

"That's too big. Start it again."

Mo watched in horror and disbelief as her tiny friend approached the enormous shark that couldn't possibly exist in the water off Shell Beach—or anywhere on Earth. "No, no, no," she murmured. "Mickey, no."

Mickey laid her bandaged hand lightly on Mo's leg. "I'm okay," she said.

"Why did you go near that? What is that?"

"That's what we're asking you," Lucas pointed out.

"There are no sharks that big that are that shape," Mo said. "That's not a whale shark or a nurse shark even."

"But there are," Mickey said. "I touched it. I, um, spoke with it, I guess. I touched its tooth. It chewed on me gently."

"No," Mo said, but she took Mickey's bandaged hand. Without asking, she unwound the bandage and looked at the injury. It looked like knife wounds. She re-wrapped the hand. "How big were the teeth?"

"Big as my hand? Bigger?"

Mo looked at her own palm. "Megalodon teeth are that big," she said. "They went extinct like two and a half million years ago. No way was one just off the beach here today."

Mickey shrugged. "You can call me a liar. I won't like it, but I'll accept it. But there is video from four cameras."

"I can see the video." Mo looked at the screen again. The video wasn't crisp and clear like a movie, but the size and shape of the shadow were clearly that of a giant shark confronting her friend who looked smaller than ever.

"Its head was like a couch," Mickey said. "I couldn't even see both eyes at once. I could have gone into the mouth like a cave." Her arm, still twined through Mo's, was shaking.

"Hang on, I'll show you," Pris said, and switched the video to the front-facing camera that had been strapped to Mickey's head.

Mo swallowed, watching Mickey's hand move past those enormous teeth and then the mouth close on her wrist in a way that was almost gentle. "You guys—you're going to put this on your podcast thing?"

"NO!" they said together.

Mo's whole body relaxed. "This is big," she said and then laughed. To cover her embarrassment, she danced her braids a little. "I mean, yes, the shark is ginormous, but this is a huge science thing. Not for a podcast."

"Not for anyone," Pris said.

"What?" Mo's hand involuntarily jerked forward to touch the image of the shark's implacable face, holding Mickey's arm hostage.

"I know we hit you with this from nowhere," Mickey said. "But this isn't just a shark. I think, well, I think it's a god."

"A god," Mo said flatly. She looked at Mickey.

Mickey's face was calm, earnest.

"I'm a scientist. There are no gods." Mo looked again at the video. The shark's enormous black eye was looking directly at the camera. At Mickey. At the viewer. At Mo.

"I talked to it. Well, I communicated with it. It was mostly one-sided."

"I don't understand."

"Well, you know how I can sort of talk to your sharks and to the mermaids with my neural net implant? It works with that—megalodon thing—too."

Darkness pressed at the edges of Mo's vision. She swayed, but crowded as the bed was, she couldn't fall over. "What did it say? It told you it was a god?"

"It didn't tell me it was anything. But I could feel it was ancient and full of knowledge. It wanted to know what I knew. It—" Mickey hesitated. She clenched her wounded hand, winced. "It licked my brain, Mo; I swear that's what it felt like. A psychic tongue licking my thoughts. It understood that I, that we, want to help the mermaids and the sharks. Then it wanted to taste my blood. Like it could get more information from that, somehow. And I felt like it approved of me. Because if it hadn't, I don't think I'd be here. It would have eaten me as easily as Lucas eats a chicken nugget." Lucas chortled at that. "It was so old, Mo. It felt as old as the Earth. And it felt secret, in a way I can't explain."

"But you're telling us," Mo pointed out.

Mickey took the laptop from Pris and, with a few clicks, erased all the videos. Mo winced. "No more proof. Just the ramblings of a weird disabled girl who already got arrested for talking crazy and attacking a cop."

"But we saw the videos—"

"Hearsay," Mickey said, closing the laptop.

"Guinevere and her ASL interpreter friends."

"They don't know what they saw."

Mo sighed and touched the cover of the laptop. "Rob said that they're going to blow up the sharks. He doesn't know about the mermaids, but they will get blown up, too. They don't know I made shark repellent and attractant, but they would want that too, to herd the sharks where they want to kill them."

"Can we put the repellent in the area where they want to herd them to?" Lucas asked.

"That's a good idea, but it's water. It's not like on land where it might last until the next rainstorm. It will disperse pretty quickly. And if they are mechanically herding them, with boats and nets and things—" Mo shivered "—they would probably go right through the repellent in their terror."

"I can tell them not to go to that area. I can tell the mermaids to go far out to sea for a while," Mickey suggested.

Pris slid off the bed and started rummaging around in the pile of bags and boxes. Lucas spread out in the vacated space.

"This is their hunting area. We could suggest the mermaids go north or south, but that means they will come into contact with people in more populated areas where the beach isn't closed. This will start over."

"I told them not to eat people anymore!" Mickey said indignantly.

"Yeah, Mick, they will not listen to you."

Mickey pulled up her legs and wrapped her arms around them. Mo scooted over toward Lucas, who was taking up half the bed.

"I don't know what to do," Mickey said. "I think shark-god is counting on me."

"I need to go home because it's well after midnight, and Caren will want to charge me for being here. And I'm bone-tired. I'll get the laptop and phone and stuff tomorrow?"

"Take the phone," Pris said, handing over a box. "All our phone numbers are on the sticky. We'll call or text you in the morning when we're up."

SHIVER

"I'll just sleep here," Lucas said, curling up.

"No, you will sleep in your own bed," Pris said, yanking on him. "How can you be so tall and skinny like a beanpole yet weigh so much? Get up. Your bed is two minutes away."

Lucas groaned and complained and allowed Pris to uproot him from the bed. Clutching his phone box and sticky note of phone numbers, he stumbled out of Pris's room.

Mo crawled from the middle of the bed, leaving Mickey alone. She embraced Pris, pressing her face to Pris's pale, perfumed neck. "I am so grateful I met you," she whispered.

It took Pris a moment to hug her back, but when she did, Pris wrapped her arms solidly around Mo. "I'm glad we met you, too," she replied.

Even though it wasn't her regular beloved smartphone, the satphone felt good in Mickey's pocket. It made her feel calmer to know that she would never again have to make that panic-stricken run down the beach after seeing someone drowning. Of course, she knew now she had never actually seen anyone drowning. She had seen a hungry mermaid putting out a lure, like an anglerfish. She had tried to get the mermaids to speak more words, but their vocabulary seemed to be limited to those few, parrot-style phrases. Mickey didn't think they even understood what they were saying anymore.

The telephone part wasn't that useful to Guinevere, but she was delighted with the texting feature. Pris had gotten a pair of phones for the ASL group, knowing that texting was an excellent way for hearing-impaired people to keep in touch, as well as video chatting, which simply wasn't possible with the satphones—but one of two wasn't bad.

They collected Mo on the way through her yard and stopped to greet the little sharks. The fishes' usefulness was really at an end, but Mickey knew Mo was loath to let her pets go just yet.

The ASL group was hand-chatting expansively ahead of them, meandering up the rocky beach, looking for the mermaids.

Mickey had left the other satellite laptop in Mo's laboratory. "It doesn't have any real software on it yet," she explained to Mo. "Pris said anything you want, just ask her, and as long as it will run on that, she'll get it for you. The video card and memory aren't the greatest, unfortunately. But she said she's working on all that and to trust her." Mickey tapped her nose with her shiny metal forefinger.

"I don't understand why you guys are so generous," Mo said.

"It's Pris. That's how she is. She doesn't match her family at all. If she didn't look so much like them, I'd swear she was adopted."

Mickey stopped and sat on a large rock. "Can you help me with the camera rig?" She handed the messenger bag to Mo and talked her through the steps.

Once Mo had strapped Mickey in, they caught up to the translators. There was no exact spot where they met the mermaids each day, but usually it was out of sight of any houses.

"What if we missed them?" Mo wondered, looking back the way they had come. "They could be waiting at a stretch of beach behind us."

Mickey tapped her head. "They know exactly where I am."

"That is creepy."

Mickey thought about it. She closed her eyes and reached out. "They aren't here yet." She stopped walking and went to pick up a rock to toss forward to get Guinevere's attention. Then she remembered the phones and texted Guinevere to wait. There was no house nearby. "Might as well just sit here to wait for them."

"Do they know what time you'll be here? They don't know time, though, right?"

"They know the sun in the sky."

The translators came back. One of them, Doug, had cochlear implants and could hear and speak, although his voice was rough and unevenly pitched. "What's going on?"

"The mermaids are not around yet," Mickey said, shaking her head. "Might as well wait here." She pointed down.

Doug translated as she spoke, his fingers flying, face expressive. The others nodded and talked among themselves. They were an insular group.

"Did you bring what I asked, Mo?" Mickey wondered.

Mo took a plastic baggie out of her pocket with a photo and handed it to Mickey. It showed a laughing Jamaican man with an explosion of long dreadlocks, some beaded, others ringed with metal. He stood on the deck of a boat. Mo looked like a softer version of him with about half as much hair—and Mo still had way more hair than Mickey had. Mickey touched his face. "You look like your dad, but paler and softer. Younger, obviously."

Mo pressed her lips together and blinked both eyes behind her glasses.

"I don't know if they can see and understand photos. I can't promise anything."

Mo nodded.

Something moved in the back of Mickey's brain, and the shiver of a connection made the hair on her arm ripple. "They are here." She also texted Guinevere, who had her back to them. Since Mickey hadn't tried to interface with the satphones yet, she used her fingers the old-fashioned way.

Her satphone binged that Lucas and Pris were on their way. Mickey told them to keep going past Mo's house.

"Why didn't they just come with you?" Mo asked.

"We're going to try something new today," Mickey said, holding up the baggie.

"Okay."

Everyone took off their shoes. The gray water was New England cold, and at this time of the morning, the air wasn't hot yet, either. Mickey, Mo, and Guinevere waded into the water and found perches on various rocks. After a moment, Doug joined them, keeping to a rock barely in the water. The others sat right at the edge, getting their feet kissed by waves.

Sleek heads popped out around them. Some of the shark fins were on the mermaids, and others were not.

"How do you tell them apart?" Mo asked, clearly fascinated.

"I can't, yet. I feel bad about that."

The incoming waves wanted to wash the perched humans off their rocks. The mermaids calmly bobbed up and down, surrounding them, focused on Mickey. Her mind filled with pictures of greetings from them. She waved back.

"They send greetings," she said, her face toward Guinevere. "Mo, could you type what I say into the phone, group chat to Guinevere and their spare phone?" The second satphone was on the beach with those who sat on the sand.

The laborious process of teaching the mermaids sign language resumed. They were getting better and faster at picking up unfamiliar words and sometimes even addressed the interpreters directly, bypassing Mickey.

"In a few days, they won't need me anymore," Mickey said.

"Then we'd lose the footage," Mo replied.

"Someone else could wear the camera. And we have the bird-drones." Mickey pointed up. The ravens were lower today, although they still appeared to be actual birds at this distance and not mechanical flying machines.

Voices approached. One drone meandered off to follow this fresh development. Mo watched. "Is that what they do?"

Mickey nodded. "They follow anomalies. But they can't alert us. If that isn't Pris and Lucas, the drone can't warn us to tell the mermaids to flee."

"That's a flaw."

"We'll put it in the report to Lucas's brothers when we give the drones back. We're just testing the birds for them."

But it was Lucas and Pris. Pris waved a bag when she got closer. "Got them!"

"Got what?" Mo asked.

"This new thing we're trying." Mickey explained, holding up her metal hand. It reflected the sun. As always, the mermaids stared at it. She sent, *come closer*. "Guinevere, Doug, take a break."

The mermaids crowded around Mickey, touching her legs. They did not pull her in this time. She reached out mentally as far as she could but did not feel the great and powerful shark anywhere, just many other mermaids and sharks.

"I'm not going in that water," Lucas said. "They eat people. They ate my friend. I don't like them."

"Okay, I get that," Mickey said. She held out her hand. "Just give me the bag."

Pris waded out into the water and climbed onto the rock next to Mickey. "Can I show them?"

The mermaids turned their attention to Pris, who was new to them. She had been busy shopping and working with Mo. They asked Mickey about her pink hair.

"They want to touch your head."

"Nope," Pris said promptly. "Not going to happen."

Doug complained the translators weren't part of the conversation.

"This is police stuff," Mickey said, "Not science stuff."

"That pink-headed girl doesn't look like a cop."

"This pink-haired girl is paying you to be here," Pris shot back. She rummaged in the big bag and came out with a baggie that had a photo in it. She held it out to the mermaids.

"They want to eat it," Mickey laughed. "They think it's a jellyfish with some kind of prize inside."

"That's why plastic pollution in the ocean is so terrible," Mo said. "It's not funny. Animals eat plastic bags, thinking they are jellyfish. Then they die horrible deaths with plastic stuck in their digestive tracts."

"Okay, okay." Mickey waved her metal hand. She tried to explain to the mermaids how to look at the photo in the bag. They wanted to eat the bag. "They are not smart." She shook her head.

"Phase two," Pris said.

"We didn't discuss phase two." Mickey frowned.

"Yeah, I came up with it while we were at the police station talking to Rob and getting the photos copied," Lucas said.

"I don't like any phase two that involves Rob," Mo said.

"It's okay," Lucas said. "Pris, deploy phase two."

Pris rummaged in the bag again and came up with another baggie. "Look!" It was a picture of Mickey.

"That's me. From your phone."

"Yeah. Right, show them what a picture is. Here's a picture of you, here's you. I have pictures of Lucas and of me too. But I don't have one of Mo; sorry, Mo."

"S'ok."

Mickey swapped baggies.

The mermaids' eyes followed the baggies avidly. *Food? Food?* They asked.

"Lucas! Can you run back to Mo's and grab a chum bucket from next to the garage?"

He said, "Eww," but got up from his crouch, put his shoes on, and started back toward Mo's house.

Mickey used the limited ASL she had picked up to tell the mermaids to wait a moment. She arranged the photo in the bag so it was flat against the plastic and easy to see. She made the plastic look less like a jellyfish.

The mermaids crowded close, watching her, touching her. Cold waves splashed her.

She turned the baggie around and showed the photo of herself to them. They reached for it. *Food. Jellyfish?*

No, look. She pointed to her eyes, then to the baggie.

Food.

The plastic bag was throwing them off. Mickey took the photo out and handed the empty bag back to Pris. "It's just a photo of me; it's okay if it gets wet."

Their eyes followed the bag. Pris hid it in the bigger bag, which didn't interest them as much.

Mickey redirected them to the photo. They looked. Mickey waited until they were all looking, then she pointed to herself. Then back to the picture. After a moment, she felt the click of understanding. One mermaid pointed to the photo with a long-fingered webbed hand and then at Mickey.

"Yes! Yes!" Mickey nodded with an exaggerated grin.

Then the mermaid put out her hand, obviously asking for the photo. She moved her hand toward her chest over and over, *give me* in sign language.

"Give me the bag back," Mickey said.

"They are going to want to eat it," Pris protested.

"This is amazing," Mo said in a low voice. "They can see the photo and understand that it's you?"

"They are sentient creatures, yes," Mickey said. "Did you doubt that?"

"I don't know," Mo said.

A shark about six feet long cruised through the group of mermaids. It brushed against Mickey's leg with rough skin before she could pull away. The mermaids either ignored it or treated it with affection.

"I don't know what kind of shark that was," Mo said. Then she repeated it. "I don't know. How can I not know?"

"It matches their tails," Pris pointed out.

"It does."

Mickey tried to explain to the insistent mermaid not to eat the bag with the photo, that the bag kept the picture dry. Mermaids did not know the difference between wet and dry. She hugged the baggie to her heart, showing it was precious. Then pretended to eat it and made the signs for *bad* and *don't*. She also tried to send everything as pictures.

Doug's rough voice came from behind her. "What are you trying to tell her?"

"Not to eat the bag! It's precious. Keep it safe!"

He splashed into the water beside her, waist-deep, holding onto the rock where Mickey was sitting. Some mermaids transferred their attention to him. He was familiar. The shark nosed him, and his fingers tightened beside Mickey's leg.

"I don't think it's an attack dog. It's just a pet," Mickey told him.

The other mermaid reached out with her very long fingers for the bag. Her eyes were black. The skin on her face was covered with tiny iridescent scales. Doug signed to her. His signs were probably far too advanced, but she looked at him and seemed to pay attention.

"They understand more than they can say," Doug told Mickey.

The mermaid nodded and smiled. Her teeth were small and triangular, jagged shark teeth in a humanoid jaw.

Mickey handed over the bag.

The mermaid's hand closed over hers briefly. Her nails were sharp, her fingers strong. The same iridescent scales shone on her hand and arm. Then she turned Mickey loose and retreated with the bag.

They all waited, watching to see what the mermaids would do with the photo.

The mermaid lifted the bag and looked at the photo. She looked back at Mickey. She grinned. Teeth everywhere. She went under the water with the picture and then came back out. The other mermaids came over, along with one shark. They all looked at it. One mermaid tried to eat the baggie and was rebuked. As far as Mickey could tell, they seemed happy.

"Is this it?" Mo asked.

"I don't know. Let's wait a moment."

The mermaids seemed to play the way seals and dolphins did. Diving and rolling over each other, even jumping out of the water. The shark was right in the middle of it all, like a giant predatory puppy.

"Apparently, they really like photos," Pris said.

"Or gifts," Mo commented.

"Is it like giving Dobby a sock?" Pris wondered.

"Maybe," Mickey said.

SHIVER

The mermaids calmed down and swam back toward the waiting people. The shark came along. The mermaid Mickey now thought of as the leader came right up to Mickey and raised herself out of the water onto the rock where Mickey sat. Her black eyes stared at Mickey. She no longer seemed to have the photo in the bag.

"Give me another photo," Mickey said to Pris. "Not Mo's dad yet."

Pris handed over a baggie. "This person went missing sixty years ago. How long do these mermaids live?"

Mickey looked at the picture. It was a standard-looking hippie guy from the 1970s. She carefully folded the plastic around the photo. The leader pulled herself a little higher to see what Mickey was doing, so she narrated it as well as trying to send pictures in her head.

Doug peered over her shoulder. "Who's that dude?"

"He went missing here a long time ago," Mickey explained.

Doug explained in signs to the mermaid. "I assume you want to know if they remember him? Do you think they live that long?"

"Sharks can live hundreds of years." Mickey thought of the ancient shark-god. "They are part shark."

Doug pointed at the bag and explained to the mermaid. She stared at him with black eyes, then turned to Mickey. Mickey nodded and sent the same basic question via the neural net. Then she showed the photo.

The mermaid touched the face of the man in the photo. Her round eyes narrowed. Her wide mouth pursed. She tapped her head with one long finger. She pointed at Doug and shook her head.

Mickey shook her head. *Not him. Long ago.* She tried to send an image of many sunrises and sunsets. "Can you tell her it was a long time ago?" she asked Doug and watched while he did.

The mermaid took the bag and swam off. The others, and the shark, followed her. They huddled around the bag. Mickey eavesdropped on their confusing thoughts.

"Um," she said. "I don't think I understand correctly."

"What do you think it means," Pris asked. Mo leaned forward.

The mermaid returned to Mickey and handed back the bag with the hippie photo. She rocked her arms as if holding a baby and then held up three of her fingers. Then she shrugged, turning her mouth down and her hands out. Mickey caught a thought: *he was delicious.*

"What does that mean?" Mo said.

Mickey glanced at Doug for clarification. "I think they made three babies with him somehow and then ate him."

"Somehow?" Pris asked.

"Well, I imagine the usual way."

"Mickey, they have fish parts on the bottom!"

"Well, not quite usual then."

"I'm going to be sick," Mo said. She climbed off her rock and splashed up to the beach, where she heaved.

Mickey understood. If the mermaids had taken Mo's dad the same way, some of them might be Mo's sisters. There was loving sharks, and there was being the sister to half-sharks. The implication was terrible. And Mo could never, ever let her mother find out.

"What other photos do you have?"

"I have Charlie's brother, Bobby."

Charlie's brother was older than the hippie, closer to middle-aged, a weathered, short-haired fisherman. "Tell them this one was also long ago, Doug," Mickey said and handed over the bag. Again, the mermaids had their conclave a little way away and came back, the shark trailing.

The mermaid made the baby-rocking motion, a thumbs-down, then a chef's kiss. "Um, no babies, but he was delicious?" Mickey tried to send that back to the mermaid, who actually corrected her. "Oh, they didn't even try for babies with him for whatever reason. They just ate him."

"They have criteria?" Pris wondered.

"I don't know." Mickey tried to ask, but she couldn't formulate any pictures, and Doug couldn't get them to understand the signs.

The following picture was of a hippie-era woman, who the mermaids instantly agreed had been delicious. And that seemed to be the pattern. Women were delicious. Men were instantly delicious or delayed slightly by mating.

Mo was sitting on the beach, arms wrapped around her legs, head down, ignoring the entire conversation. Mickey looked at Pris and held up the photo of Mo's dad. Pris nodded. Mickey handed it over.

The mermaids didn't move away. The picture excited them greatly. They pointed at his hair and then at Mo on the beach. They showed it to the shark before returning to Mickey and flooding her mind with hunger and longing while grabbing her legs and stroking them.

"No," Mickey said. "You already took him. Tell them, Doug, Guinevere."

The mermaid ignored their signing. She shook her head and pointed her long, elegant thumb down over and over. Then she signed *give* and pointed to the picture. Mickey gave the bag back. The mermaid shook her head, pointed at the picture, and signed *give* again, sending Mickey hunger and longing.

"Mo!" Mickey called. "Mo, come here."

"No. I hate them," Mo said, her voice low and miserable.

"No, it's not what you think. It's, well, not good news, but not what you are afraid of."

Mo wiped her mouth with her hand and uncoiled herself from the sand. She made her way out to Mickey's rock, where she stared at the mermaids and their shark with none of her usual affection. The water lapped at her shoulders and made her braids float.

The leader swam up to her, touched her braids, then turned to Mickey and sent *want*.

You can't have her.

Want man.

There is no man.

The mermaid sent the image of the picture of Mo's dad.

Mickey shook her head and did the thumbs-down at her. "Mo," Mickey said. "We showed them the picture of your dad."

Mo was staring at the mermaid, who was right in her face, staring back. "Did she have a good time with him?" Mo said bitterly. "Or is she my sister?"

Mickey winced. "Neither. They said they never had him. And I believe them because on seeing his photo, they demanded I bring him to them."

"It looks like it was an accident, Mo. He did just fall off his boat. They didn't take him from you," Pris tried to tell her.

The shark came up beside the leader and also looked at Mo. "That's not a normal shark at all," Mo remarked. She backed toward shore until she could sit without drowning. The mermaid came forward, one hand on the sand next to Mo, one hand caressing Mo's braids. The shark curled in her lap like a puppy, and after a moment, Mo put her fingers on its head and scratched it.

Mickey watched. "Nothing about this is normal."

SHIVER
-48-

Are you gonna make yourself some shark-fin soup, girly?" Charlie demanded. He pulled a chair to the end of the table at Crabby Patty's, where Mo, Pris, Mickey, and Lucas were eating.

"Why would I do that?" Mo asked. She was still reeling from the double punch that sharks hadn't eaten her father and that she could have had a mermaid half sister. Meanwhile, her uncle seemed more unwashed and malodorous than usual; Mickey visibly leaned away, although that meant she was closer to Lucas.

"We're about to blow them sky-high!" Charlie waved at the server. Everyone at the diner knew Charlie, since he ate there daily. His two grilled cheese and tomato sandwiches would already be cooking. He would have no compunction charging his meal to Mo's tab and wandering off well before it was time to pay.

"You can't," Mo said. "Honestly, this isn't what you think it is."

"Girly, you got too much schoolin' in your head and not enough livin'. It's exactly what I think. Too many sharks. The fishing is getting worse. It's that sixty-year cycle. Gotta break it! Gotta smash it! Blow it up! Boom!" The last words were shouted.

The only people in the diner who didn't turn to look at Charlie's outburst were the Deaf people.

"What if there is another way?"

"There isn't enough fish for everyone," Charlie said.

Lucas nodded. "I get it. I'm a very hungry person."

The three women at the table all nodded vigorously. Lucas could undoubtedly eat.

Lucas went on, "And I would hate to learn that I was taking someone else's food. But with all due respect, Uncle Charlie, I think this can work."

The server, Colleen, came over with a myriad of plates balanced along her hands and forearms. She put down Charlie's cheese and tomato sandwiches first. He started eating immediately.

Everyone else got a variety of burgers, plus an extra basket of chicken nuggets in the center of the table. Lucas's plate had two cheeseburgers, although he had only ordered one. They were starting to know him there, too. Mickey and Pris's crab cakes had no buns.

"Uncle Charlie," Mickey said, pointing at him with her metal hand, "Do you think you can keep a secret?"

"What?" He reared back in the chair, balancing it on two legs. Colleen was walking behind him, and he almost took her out. "Bug-girl, are you implying that I am not trustworthy?"

Mickey looked confused at being called a bug.

"You and Uncle Charlie together have six limbs, of course," Mo reminded her.

"Right," Pris muttered.

The front legs of Charlie's chair crashed down. "What can't you trust me with?"

"Can you take us out on your boat soon, maybe tomorrow? Before you blow everything up?"

"I'll take you out on my boat right now!" He jammed the last piece of grilled cheese into his mouth and stood wobbling on his peg leg. "Let's go."

"We're still eating," Pris said, cutting slowly into her crab cake with a knife and fork.

"Hurry up. You all eat like girls, all dainty."

"Most of us *are* girls," Mo reminded him.

"I'm going down to the docks to wait for you. I can't believe the service in this place. I never got m'coffee." Charlie stomped out, leaving the chair blocking the aisle.

"He stuck me with his bill again," Pris said. "And no, do not offer to pay."

Colleen came over and put the chair back where it belonged. "I was waiting for the fresh pot of coffee to finish brewing for your uncle," she said to Mo, taking Charlie's plate, silverware, and empty mug.

"Don't worry about it."

"What's your plan, Mickey?" Mo asked, savoring her homestyle burger with its thick sesame seed bun. She didn't get these two and their hatred of carbs. Next, they would give most of their perfectly golden fries to Lucas—yes, there it was happening, to Lucas's delight.

"I think we show your uncle that we're dealing with mermaids and not just sharks."

"Hmm. Are you sure? If he blabs—"

"We can't keep it a secret forever."

Pris had a slight smile on her face.

"What are you smirking about?"

"I don't want it to be a secret forever, just for now. I've got my own plans hatching. But it would help to have Charlie on our side, I agree. And even your buddy Rob and the sheriff. Eventually."

Colleen hurried back over. "The mayor wants to hold a press conference," she told Mo. "That means reporters. You'll probably have to come to work."

Mo groaned. "Right now? When is the press conference? There aren't even any reporters here now to attend it." Well, except Mickey and Pris, but no one in Shell Beach recognized podcasting as reporting.

SHIVER

And no one understood how much Mo despised the old-fashioned pink polyester uniform every server at the diner was forced to wear.

"I think tomorrow morning, so I'll need you here for the breakfast rush."

Pris said to Colleen, "I really need Mo tomorrow. Can someone else work that shift?"

Colleen looked at Pris and frowned. "No. We only have three servers, and someone will have to work at night tomorrow."

Mo knew Pris wanted to throw money at the problem, but that wouldn't help this situation. "I'll be here," she said, resigned to another shift in pink polyester.

Since it was still daylight and some fishing boats were out, the chain wasn't across the access point to the docks. This time, they broke no laws heading to the *Bobby K* where Charlie waited, sitting on the same hatch where they had lounged a few days before.

"We're not fishing, so I don't need no crew," he announced.

"Do you have any chum on board?" Mo asked.

"I left a bunch at your garage for your critters, wasn't there enough?"

Mickey didn't want to tell him they had fed a whole bucket to the ecstatic mermaids earlier that day, after they had gone through the identification exercise with every old missing-person photo. Or that the mermaids had said that sometimes they tasted that flavor in the water in that area—pumped from Mo's pool.

Charlie stood and clumped around, not going anywhere. "I guess I have more," he conceded. Then he peered closer at Mickey. "What all are you wearing, bug-girl?"

"Oh, this is for an experiment I'm doing with Mo." Easier than trying to explain to a crotchety old fisherman who had never seen the internet what a podcast was and why she needed cameras strapped all over her body.

Charlie grunted and clumped around some more, throwing ropes, before going into the wheelhouse. Mickey and Mo followed him. Lucas and Pris stayed behind, looking over the railing into the water.

"Where'm going?"

Mickey looked at Mo.

Mo said, "Out, but north. Toward where those little rocky islands are."

Mickey tilted her head. "Islands?"

Mo waved her hand. "Not nice ones. Not real ones. Just jagged rocks. Like enormous boulders in a pile. Seals hang out there, and seagulls."

The boat chugged at walking speed through the no-wake zone, past The Dockside Feast and the closed beach before Charlie veered east into the open water and sped up.

"What're we looking for, girly?" Charlie asked.

"Sharks, of course," Mo said. "Maybe other things. Slow down a bit." She looked at Mickey and raised her eyebrows.

Mickey closed her eyes and reached out curiously. The boat was old. Since it docked at Shell Beach, its electronics were negligible. It didn't interface with her neural net. She reached farther, looking for the familiar signatures of hunger and curiosity. She also tried to broadcast that she was looking for them, sending a sort of *hey, I'm here; it's me!* signal.

But she was on a fishing boat, and she had a feeling they didn't trust boats.

The engine's deep throbbing changed. The boat slowed, hitting the waves with a different cadence. Charlie expertly rebalanced himself, his hands moving over levers and the wheel.

"I need to be closer to the water," she said to Mo. She needed to be visible, perhaps.

Walking on the moving boat proved more difficult than Mickey had imagined. She had never been out on the water before. The waves threw everything off, and she worried she would vomit up the crab cake she had just eaten. It suddenly felt very greasy and heavy in her stomach.

Pris stood as if posing for a photo, one hand lightly resting on the railing. In her rarefied world, a boat was nothing. She was talking to Lucas, but also scanning the water beside them.

Lucas bounced on his toes as if riding a horse, trying to match the waves. His normally olive face was ashen.

"Stand still," Mickey suggested to Lucas. "I don't think you're supposed to jump like that."

"I don't want to puke. Between the waves and the rotten fish smell—" That was it. He leaned over the railing.

Pris wrinkled her nose and stepped away.

"Yeah, with the amount he eats, he'll be there a long time," Mickey said. "Let's go to the opposite side." But she could still hear him heaving. She swallowed several times, looking out at the water. The shore was behind them. "Where do you think the islands are?"

"What islands?"

"Oh, you weren't there. Mo said there are some rocky outcrops out here somewhere that she wants to go to."

"Why?"

"I don't know." Mickey searched the waves. Anything could have been there. She had no frame of reference. Seals, mermaids, giant shark-gods. She sent her plea again. *It's me, your friend; I'm here.* She honestly didn't think the giant shark-god was around. It didn't feel like a creature that hung out with lesser beings. It probably retreated to some unimaginably deep place like the Mariana Trench or wherever Atlantis had sunk to and gone back to sleep. She thought of chum, although even her brain gagged at that. *I have food.*

In the real world, Lucas was still throwing up at the other railing.

"What are you trying to do here?" Pris asked.

"Get Charlie on our side."

"And what if he says, 'Mermaids? Vermin!' And wants to blow them up, too?"

SHIVER

Mickey goggled at her best friend. "Who thinks of mermaids as vermin?"

"Varmints," Pris said, luxuriating over the word. "Competition for fish."

"You have never said 'varmints' before in your life."

"Maybe?"

"No." Before they could get into one of their sillier spats, Mickey's neural net shivered and connected. "Oh. They're here."

"Where?"

Lucas spat and coughed. "What?"

"This is what you get for eating so much!" Pris said. "You're missing everything."

"I don't know; I can't see them. Hang on." Mickey shut her eyes and tried to use biofeedback to slow her breathing, looping herself through the neural net. On the railing, her metal hand twitched rhythmically, as if she was squeezing a small ball. She saw overlapping images of herself and Pris from below and opened her eyes. "Right there. Lucas, go get Mo and Charlie. Stop the boat. Get chum. Hurry."

The mermaids had two sharks with them this time, both strangely shaped in different ways. This new one had fins that were almost hands. "Oh!" Mickey said in sudden understanding. "Those sharks that hang out with them. They are mermaids."

Beneath their feet, the engines rumbled. The boat drifted to a stop. The anchor chain slid out.

"What are you talking about?" Mo emerged onto the deck.

"Those weird little sharks that hang out with the mermaids. They aren't deformed sharks so much as deformed mermaids," Mickey explained, hanging over the railing. "They have too much shark in them, that's all."

Mo and Pris held onto Mickey to keep her from going in the water. The leader bobbed in the middle of the shiver, looking back at her. *You summoned?*

"Give me the last picture," Mickey said. "I wish I knew how to scuba dive. Even though I would hate being underwater, I want to be closer to them."

"It's easy to learn," Pris said.

"Yeah," Mo said. "I've known how forever."

Lucas started gagging again.

Charlie made his way to the three women. "Bug-girl, you're gonna fall off the boat. What're ya doin'?"

"Look, Uncle Charlie! Mermaids!"

Uncle Charlie looked.

SHIVER
-50-

They designated Mo to go into the water, as she wouldn't have a panic attack and she could swim. She wasn't afraid of sharks. Mickey expressed her worry the mermaids would attempt to take Mo because of her coveted hair, but Mo refused to believe that.

Lucas had finally stopped vomiting. He sat on the edge of the deck, his arms on the bottom railing, his legs over the side. Great-Uncle Charlie was next to him in a chair. He had collapsed after seeing the mermaids. Sixty years her uncle had had that peg leg, and it was mermaids that made him fall over. He didn't seem to believe what he was seeing. Mo was worried about his mental state.

Mo had the last picture in a baggie, the one they hadn't shown the mermaids earlier. She stripped down to her underwear, which was black and decidedly unsexy, being boyshorts and a sports bra. Her uncle had a snorkel and mask, which she took but had no intention of using.

Charlie stood, still shaky, and threw a life preserver tied to a rope beside the ladder leading to the water. "You be careful, girly. If I lose you, your momma won't forgive me."

That was as close as a declaration of love as she would ever get from the old man. Mo nodded. She looped the mask strap through her arm and put the baggie between her teeth. Then she took it out. "You told them not to eat me? Not to steal me?"

"Yes," Mickey said patiently.

"Okay." Baggie between her teeth again, Mo started down the ladder. The mermaids and their sharks crowded close. Mo tried to breathe slowly. Like her baby sharks, these knew her. They had promised not to bite. Still, this was so dumb. She looked up to see four faces at the railing. Mickey looked like a Teletubby with the camera on her head.

Mo slipped into the cold water, holding onto the ladder with one hand. The orange life preserver had floated too far away to reach. The mermaids pressed close, touching her hair, pulling on it. She took the baggie from her mouth. "Ouch! Mickey, tell them not to pull my hair."

The mermaids loved her smooth brown skin, and within seconds, were trying to peel off what little clothing she had on to look underneath.

"Mickey!" Mo hollered through the baggie in her mouth. "They are undressing me!" She wanted to thrash and fight them off, but she didn't know what other sharks were out here. She also worried how much she might look like a seal. She squirmed, unable to stay still.

"Give her the baggie!" Mickey called back. "The leader!"

Mo took the baggie from her mouth. "I can't tell them apart!"

Their hands were everywhere. It was pretty invasive, but in a non-sexual way. One shark had hand-fins. This was all so very odd. Mo wanted to pinch herself because this was surely a weird dream.

"They are just curious about you because you are brown," Mickey explained.

"Tell them I'm brown all over! They don't need to check under my clothes, please."

"The one with her hand on your—yeah, her. Give her the baggie."

Mo gave that mermaid the baggie, although she honestly couldn't tell them apart. The mermaid signed something to her. They all departed, even the shark with the weird finger-fins.

Mo adjusted her underwear and gave herself a little shake.

"She said thank you. They will come back."

Mo gave Mickey a thumbs-up and hung from the ladder. She had given them a photo of Dylan, the first missing person, Lucas's friend.

"Do you see them?" Mo called up.

"No, usually they just go a few feet away, but they don't seem to be around. You have the goggles, though."

Mo spat in the mask and pushed the spit around with her finger, then rinsed it. She pulled the mask over her face, seated the snorkel in her mouth, and jackknifed under the surface, staying close to her uncle's boat. The water was about forty feet deep here, studded with the ubiquitous boulders. She turned in circles. She couldn't see very far, but she saw zero mermaids or sharks.

Pushing her head from the surface, she took out the snorkel and gasped, "They're gone."

"What?"

"I don't see them."

She threw an arm over the ladder.

"Now what?" Pris asked.

"You wanted to see the islands, girly," Charlie said from his chair. He looked like he had aged ten years. "Maybe you should climb up and we'll head there."

"She said they were coming back," Mickey insisted.

"Do we know if they have a concept of time, though?" Lucas wondered. He knocked his feet against the side of the boat. No doubt he was getting hungry now that he was done throwing up.

"Good point," Pris said.

"Can we give them a few more minutes?" Mickey begged. "I believe they are coming back."

"Can you connect to them? Whatever it is you can do?" Mo hung from the ladder, kicking slowly in a way that was not at all like a seal.

"I think they are too far away."

Mo sighed and climbed the ladder.

Those are islands?" Pris said, tilting her head. Some rocks stuck out of the water. No sandy beach, no palm trees. No trees of any kind.

"Maybe not up to your standards," Mo replied. She had put her clothes on over her wet underwear.

"Not up to my standards either," Lucas said. "They are more like … teeth."

"Well, yeah, that's what the natives called them. I forget their word for it, but it translates to Teeth, of course," Mo said.

Mickey enjoyed their bantering. She looked at the aptly named jagged Teeth rocks and then shut her eyes, reaching out. *I'm here now.*

Nothing.

"Visit historic Shell Beach, with their jagged Teeth islands and their giant trash midden and absolutely no internet," Pris said grimly, then made a noise that was almost a growl.

"What?" Mo said. "It's not like we can advertise we have mermaids—" she paused. "Pris?"

"What?"

"What are you plotting? We were just joking about that, of course."

Pris didn't answer. Mickey figured Pris was already buying billboards: Come See the Mermaids of Shell Beach.

The neural net shivered. *We have.*

Have what?

Mickey held up her hand, not that anyone was paying attention to her. "Hey!" She opened her eyes and looked around. "They are here, and they have something."

"Have what?" Mo made her way to Mickey's side, getting inside her comfort zone.

"I don't know. I don't know where they are." She shut her eyes again but couldn't find herself. She saw only one of the pointy islands, with no way to tell which one. "They are at one of the Teeth."

Where are you?

Mickey saw the boat from several viewpoints. It gave her a headache. This was no way to navigate. She lifted her arm, closed her eyes, tried to envision everything, then pointed. "Over there."

"I can't drive through those rocks, girly," Charlie hollered at Mo. "I ain't goin' closer. You didn't tell me we're goin' that close!"

"A little closer," she wheedled. "You're a superb pilot. You can do it."

Mo came back to Mickey's side with a pair of marine binoculars. "I'll look. You aim me."

SHIVER

Mickey closed her eyes, triangulated how the mermaids saw the boat, and then aimed the binoculars.

Mo gave a great intake of breath. "Unky!" she shouted. "You gotta go closer! It's Dylan! He's on the rock! Alive!"

SHIVER
-52-

Mo and Lucas hit the water almost at the same time. Mo was sure it was not safe to swim in the surging waters near the jagged Teeth. She was just as sure that Dylan should be dead after so many days.

Although Mo was more buoyant, Lucas was taller and more streamlined, and he fought his way through the raging foam around the Teeth before Mo did. He had less fear in this case, she thought. This was his friend, and he had the training. The waves flung Mo against one of the smaller teeth as she battled toward Lucas and Dylan. She realized they hadn't even thought to grab a rope, a life preserver, or anything of any use. She could hear her friends and uncle shouting from the boat, but the waves drowned the words.

Grabbing onto the sharp rock, she looked at Dylan and Lucas. Dylan's clothing was ragged to the point of being gone. Had he been flung mercilessly against these rocks as well? Mo tried to breathe deep and steady, steeling herself to swim the final yards. Even as a teenager, she had never been brave enough to swim out here, although Rob and some others had occasionally dared, coming back bruised and subdued. If a missing person hadn't been on the rock ahead, she would have returned to Uncle Charlie's boat.

She pushed off and kicked her feet, wishing for flippers. High-top sneakers made swimming worse, not better. Every stroke seemed to make her gain a pound as she became more waterlogged, and swallowed and inhaled water. She didn't even have the stupid snorkel and mask she had disdained earlier.

In a moment, Mo clamored onto the jagged rock. Dylan cowered in his rags, curled around an empty plastic water bottle. Mo took in the scene. Lucas seemed to be towering over his friend, even though he crouched, one hand out.

She thought about how she had felt when Rob got too close to her in the garage. How Mickey couldn't stand for anyone to crowd her. Of course.

"Lucas," Mo said softly.

Dylan glanced at her. His eyes were very blue, almost glowing against his sunburned face.

"Lucas, move away from your friend. He's terrified, of course," Mo continued in the same gentle tone. She felt very motherly for the first time in her life.

Lucas backed away, but made his big-eyed face at Mo. "I'm his friend," he said. "He knows me. I'm not gonna hurt him."

SHIVER

"I didn't say you aren't his friend," Mo said, speaking slowly and gently, keeping her eyes on Dylan, who was now looking out to sea and rocking back and forth. "But he seems very traumatized."

Lucas sat down and followed his friend's gaze. "He thinks they're coming back to hurt him some more."

"Of course, so let's get him onto the boat and then away from the water."

The whole top of the rock was maybe a couple of square yards. It was challenging to keep away from the traumatized boy.

A shark fin poked above the water and then dipped. Water dripped from Mo's braids. She had left her glasses on the boat, so everything was blurry. She shivered. Uncle Charlie had maneuvered the *Bobby K* to just outside the line of Teeth. He kept no smaller boat on board. They would have to swim back. The fin flashed again. Mickey waved, but Mo had no idea what her friend was trying to tell her. Was it okay to swim? Should they wait?

"We have a boat," Lucas said to Dylan. "Come on. We're rescuing you. We never stopped looking."

SHIVER
-53-

Mickey stood in awe of the bravery of Lucas and Mo. Jumping into that horrid thrashing water, being beaten against those sharp rocks. Pris had thrown the life preserver in after them, but they had ignored it, swimming madly toward the huddled redheaded person on the rock.

Turns out that a person could be even paler than Pris: a redheaded, blue-eyed boy. But after days marooned on a rock out to sea, Dylan's skin was more red than white, sunburnt, blistered, and peeled. The blue of his eyes blazed against the reddened whites. His lips were swollen and cracked.

Mickey felt like crying. She never, ever hugged anyone—not her parents, her grandparents, or Pris. But she wanted to hug this blistered, broken boy even though she knew it would cause him physical pain and freak him out. And then freak her out.

On the boat ride back to shore, it was evident that every bump, every errant wave, caused Dylan pain. His face screwed up in a wince. He refused to speak. Lucas tried to dress his friend in a t-shirt, but Dylan wouldn't let him near, wouldn't let anyone near. He had fought Lucas and Mo the whole way back to the boat.

Mickey let her cameras record everything, but she felt guilt at preserving Dylan's pain. She didn't want to ever air that footage. Pris lurked around the edges, moving her hands helplessly. This was a problem her money and unwanted fame couldn't solve.

Although she scanned for them, the mermaids were gone. She had taken back their prize.

Uncle Charlie piloted the boat as smoothly as possible back toward Shell Beach. Mickey overheard him radioing in, calling the police department, giving them the news that they had found Dylan alive and in bad shape, with no other details.

Charlie turned around, seeing Mickey standing there. "There are real mermaids," he said.

"Yup," she said, nodding.

"You think they took that poor boy?"

"I don't know," she lied. "But they kept him alive, didn't they? Do you still think they should be killed?"

"I don't know," Charlie replied. "I don't know what to think anymore. I hate sharks. But mermaids. Mermaids that help people. I just don't know."

An ambulance pulled up on the pier, lights flashing. Dylan still hadn't spoken a word.

This fixes nothing," Mo said. The four of them sat on rocks behind Mo's house. "Even though my uncle says he's on our side now and doesn't want to hurt mermaids, Ted and Rob still want to be big men and blow sharks up."

"The mermaids and their sharks ate two of his police officers," Mickey pointed out. She had her eyes closed. She was half monitoring the ASL lessons, which were happening not far down the beach. Since there was no way Mickey was moving to Shell Beach permanently and being a go-between, the interpreters would have to figure ways to teach without her mind intervention. A bucket of chum seemed to help, and now Uncle Charlie was supplying extra.

"They were hungry," Lucas said in their defense. He was loudly eating a bag of chips, in Mickey's opinion a disgusting thing to do at the beach. His teeth would wear away from all the sand he was chewing.

"I am working on all this," Pris said. "I just need a little more time."

"At least the mayor's press conference ended up being about Dylan's rescue instead of whatever horrible thing he planned to say," Mo said.

"That guy is like five hundred and ten years old," Lucas complained.

"Yup," Mo agreed. "And a Luddite from a long line of Luddites."

"What's a Luddite?"

"It's someone who hates technology and change."

"So that's why you have no internet here?"

"He claims we were perfectly fine before the internet, and we can live without it." Mo snorted.

Mickey sat up and blinked her eyes open. "Ugh. I disagree."

"Now that Pris keeps giving me the coolest toys, I have to disagree as well."

Mickey stretched. "Are you gonna move to Connecticut with us?"

Mo shook her head quickly, startled. "What, and live with you guys?"

"We don't live together. We mooch off our parents like you do. I'm a basement troll, remember?"

Lucas crumpled his chip bag. "My brothers don't have a biologist at their lab. Maybe they would hire you. You wouldn't smell as good anymore, though."

"Really? I thought your brothers made fighting robots and stuff."

"Well, yes, but they would like to expand into more organic stuff, like with Mickey's arm and her neural net. That interface and all that. The fighting robot thing is getting old. They were doing it when I was little."

SHIVER

"Of course, but my mom ..." Mo stared at the heaving gray water.

"Your mom has Ted now," Mickey said. "You know they'll get married. Your dad isn't coming back."

"I can't tell her that. I can't tell her how I know. 'Yeah, mom, so I talked to some mermaids that steal people and eat them, but sometimes, like Dylan, they give them back. They said they never had Daddy, although they sure wish they had, nudge nudge wink wink, so you can give up now and marry Ted.' Of course, I can't just say that."

"Right," Pris said. "Not yet."

"What do you mean yet?"

"Give me some time." Pris seemed very annoyed. She was frowning at the ocean as if it had personally wronged her. Her bruises had faded, but she still looked like she had lost a fight.

"What are you planning?" Mickey demanded. "You're keeping secrets from me!"

"Right," Pris agreed, not looking at her best friend. "Only for a little while."

Lucas stood and brushed sand off his butt. His basketball shorts hung to beneath his knees. "I'm going to go meet Rob and see what I can find out. Do male-bonding stuff. Talk about Dylan—but I won't tell him anything, don't worry. Grab some more lunch." He made his way across the broken shells and rocks to the edge of Mo's yard.

Mo rolled her neck until it audibly cracked and looked at Pris. "Tell me you have a plan, my palest friend."

"I have a plan. An awesome plan. It is fully in play. It will take some time for all the pieces to come into alignment. The Luddite configuration of this town is slowing me down a lot."

Mickey looked at Mo. Today's beads were chartreuse to match her t-shirt and shoes. The green glowed against her dark skin. Mickey had become extremely fond of Mo and didn't want to leave her behind. But honestly, Shell Beach sucked. They had found Dylan and gotten some incredible footage for the Contrary Crowcast. If it wasn't for Mo, Mickey and Pris would have left already.

"You can't keep secrets, Pris," Mickey said. "You need to loop us in. What can we do to help with this plan?"

"I'm revitalizing the town. The stupid mayor will either go along with me or rage quit. Then I'll find a better mayor. Like Lucas said, he's five hundred years old. Time he retired."

"I think he's about seventy," Mo corrected.

"Same thing, right?"

"Seventy, five hundred, same thing," Mickey said and laughed.

Mo frowned. "What do you mean, revitalizing the town?"

SHIVER

"This is a dead town, Mo. It's got a beach no one goes to, even when there aren't any shark attacks. It's got no technology. There are empty buildings downtown. The only industry is fishing, and without being properly connected to restaurants and suppliers, that isn't doing well either. You work at the diner; do you ever wait on strangers?"

Mo shook her head. "Same people every day."

"Shell Beach is off the beaten path. No one cares about your giant unexcavated heap of Native American garbage except a stray archaeologist once in a blue moon. Your historical society museum is cool but needs a real curator. Your library is an old-fashioned disaster; that's not Guinevere's fault at all."

"I don't understand how you are going to fix all that."

Mickey looked at Pris. "Mermaid petting zoo?"

Pris tightened her lips and stared at the sea.

"Pris, they eat people."

Mo didn't try not to look horrified. "Pris, no. It was a joke."

"This is to their benefit," Pris argued. "Mickey, call one of them over."

"They don't do my bidding." But Mickey closed her eyes anyway. The mermaids weren't far away. They thought of the daily sign-language lessons as playing with their food. Mickey debated telling Pris that.

She splashed out into the water to her knees and leaned on a rock. The other women followed. "What are we talking about? I just took them from their lesson, which is very rude of me. The translators won't know why the mermaids left."

"They like you," Mo said.

The leader swam up to Mickey's rock, along with the deformed shark with the hand-fins. Deep in her head, Mickey could hear the others continuing the sign language lesson.

The mermaid asked a question in sign language. The shark tried to move its hand-fins to match.

"I think …" Pris said, wading closer. "I should have been watching those Baby Signing videos to remind myself, but we just got the internet. I think she wants to know our names."

That's what Mickey thought, too. She looked at the mermaid and the shark. The shark moved a fin. She didn't believe the mermaid knew or understood the alphabet, which was one way to explain names and words with no signs. She just thought their names in regular sounds, pointing. *Mo, Mo, Mo. Pris, Pris, Pris. Mickey, Mickey, Mickey.*

The mermaid pointed to the shark. *Starfish.* Herself. *Pearl.*

Mickey said to her friends, "The shark's name is Starfish. Her name is Pearl."

SHIVER

Pearl leaned on a rock and pointed to her mouth and then to Mickey's mouth. Starfish hovered in the waves next to her, moving her finger-fins anxiously.

Mickey looked at Pris and Mo helplessly. "Is she trying to eat me again? I thought they were getting better."

Pris touched her chest and then tapped her first two fingers together twice. Pearl nodded eagerly. "Pris," Pris said slowly.

"Ples," Pearl said. She smiled with a mouthful of jagged teeth. She pointed at Pris. "Ples."

Mo's mouth fell open. She pointed to herself and said, "Mo."

"Mo," Pearl said. The sound was somewhat swallowed and thick, but recognizable.

"A mermaid just said my name," Mo said. "Hi, Pearl." She fanned her face. "I just talked to a mermaid." She leaned into the water and extended a hand to the shark. "Hi, Starfish."

Starfish waved back.

"I have died and gone to heaven," Mo said. "Pris, whatever is you want to do, you do it."

Pearl wasn't happy with the interruption. She put her hand on Mickey's leg and pointed firmly at her mouth.

"Mickey," she drawled. "Mick-key."

Pearl shook her head. Clearly, it was too much.

"Mick." Mickey tried. She wasn't a great fan of that, but some people shortened her name once in a while.

Pearl made a gagging noise that could have been interpreted as something close to "Mick" and then shook her head again.

"Crow," Pris suggested.

Pearl's head swiveled to Pris. "Ples? Clow?"

Pris pointed to Mickey. "Crow," she said firmly.

Mickey nodded. "Crow."

"Clow." Pearl had a terrifying number of teeth, and her mouth was extremely wide. She repeated it and hooked her iridescent fingers in the sign for friend.

Mo waded deeper and touched Starfish's hand-fin. "Do you really think she is a mermaid and not a shark?"

"I don't know," Mickey said. "If they are part shark and part person, maybe once in a while one comes out more shark-like."

"Wouldn't that mean once in a while they are more person-like?"

"What, like with legs?" Pris scoffed. "No such thing. That's like a fairy-tale thing."

Mo sat in the water and held hands with a shark named Starfish. "And this isn't?"

SHIVER
-55-

As soon as Mo finished her morning shift at Crabby Patty's, she stuffed a bag with food for her friends. Mainly for Lucas. Her feet hurt even with gel inserts in her pink sneakers. She actually adored her pink sneakers. She had nothing against pink as a color. She agreed she looked cute in it. It was this awful, ugly polyester uniform. This stupid job where she had to be subservient and stink of grease just to make barely enough money to support her mad-scientist habit.

She said goodbye to Colleen, and slinging the shopping bag full of food over one shoulder, pushed open the glass front door. She almost knocked over her uncle.

"Girly!" He shouted, righting himself and grabbing her. "It's time; it's today, let's go!"

Mo's whole body went stiff. All the tiny hairs on her arms and legs stood at attention. "Time for what?" she asked cautiously, moving out of the doorway and taking the old man with her.

"Shark-killing time! Let's go get your magic formula that calls the sharks. Ted has the explosive on its way from a top-secret location."

She felt her lips forming the word "No," but she didn't say it. She lied to her uncle. "I don't have a magic formula, Unky. It didn't work." She dropped her voice. "And I thought you didn't want to hurt the mermaids."

He laughed and started towing her by the hand toward the road, where his pickup truck was parked. It was older than Mo and held together by rust and primer. "Oh, I know you, girly. You have one that sorta works; we'll just use that. We won't kill any mermaids, just sharks. They aren't the same at all."

Mo shook her head, although he couldn't see. He understood nothing. "I have a food delivery to make first," she said, rattling the bag, not even totally lying.

"We'll stop there."

Every swearword Mo knew ran through her head, and also few she made up on the spot. "Energy-sucking fey," was what she said, because it was so preposterous. Her plan today had been to say goodbye to her baby sharks, setting them free, and then convince Lucas to let her talk to his brothers about a job. Now she had to go into full crisis mode.

Mo sat with the warm, fragrant bag on her lap for the minute-long ride to Caren's Cozy Cottage, her brain churning.

"Hurry up deliverin' that food. When did Crabby Patty's start deliverin' anyway?"

Mo pushed her way out of the truck and into the building. Caren was vacuuming the front hall and looked at her petulantly. "I don't like people eating in their rooms," she said. "I'm going to start charging extra."

"You can't just change the rules on guests when they're already here," Mo said, her sore feet pounding up the stairs. She needed one of those reflexology foot massages. She bet Pris knew someone who did it.

Mo knocked on all three doors and then on all three again before the door to Pris's room opened under her hand. Mo almost fell in.

Pris grabbed the food bag. "We aren't that hungry. You just saw us for breakfast a couple hours ago, right?"

"My uncle," she gasped. "He wants the formula. The explosives are on their way. It's happening today, of course."

Pris handed the bag off to Lucas, who lounged in the corner on the floor using the laptop. He opened the bag, unwrapped a crab cake on a bun, and started eating. "Today?"

"Charlie's outside in his truck waiting to bring me to my house to get the formula!" Mo exclaimed. "He's not exactly on our side anymore. He thinks he can blow up sharks without hurting mermaids."

"We need to stall him," Mickey said, coming out of the bathroom.

"How? He's waiting outside. He's going to come looking for me. He thinks I'm just delivering food. I gotta go in a second."

"Can you agree but give him the wrong stuff?" Lucas asked, chewing.

"My work is meticulously labeled. You know that." Mo shook her head. "If I had some warning, I could have changed the labels. We didn't even think of it."

"How can we stop Charlie between here and your house? There's no way for him to get an emergency call when he has no phone," Mickey mused.

A horn beeped from outside. Mo groaned and shook her head.

"We probably can't get Ted not to want to blow up the sharks," Pris said. "Not if Charlie saw the mermaids, agreed to no explosives, and now has changed his mind because he hates sharks so much."

"He might listen to Ted, but what would Ted say? Especially if Ted himself ordered the explosives."

"It's not like I can say I just talked to Ted, and he told me something. This stupid town." Mo kicked at Pris's bedpost, making her foot hurt worse.

The horn beeped again.

"I thought you were used to it," Mickey said, looking out the window. "Lucas, you got the drones all charged?"

"I was used to it. Then you got here and spoiled me!" Mo kicked the bedpost again, blaming it. "You ruined everything!"

"You were happy and we made you unhappy?" Pris asked. "By befriending you, and liking you, and doing things for you, and with you, and making your world bigger?"

"Lucas, let's sic a bird-drone on Uncle Charlie," Mickey suggested.

Lucas leaned over, unlatched a reinforced case, and extracted a raven with both hands. Mickey opened the window and pulled up the screen.

"Yes! No! I don't know!" Mo wailed and sat on the bed, her face in her hands. She noticed Pris didn't argue with her anymore about it.

The horn sounded again and again.

"He knows. He knows I'm plotting." Mo stepped toward Mickey and Lucas at the window, standing back to let them work. Lucas held the raven and Mickey the control tablet. Mickey had her eyes closed. The tablet was flashing. The bird's eyes were flashing in sync.

"Mickey, are you talking to that bird?"

"Hush, she's trying to program it," Lucas whispered.

Mickey opened her eyes and looked at Lucas. Her usually brown eyes had a silver glow. She nodded. Lucas threw the raven out the window. Mo stepped up.

Beep! Beep-beep-beep!

Pris joined them at the narrow window at the same time as Mo did. Mo felt Mickey stiffen. It must be awful to feel uncomfortable being close to everyone, even your best friend. She wondered how Mickey handled romance if she couldn't even stand next to a friend.

The raven flew directly toward Uncle Charlie's truck.

"Too bad it can't poop," Mickey said. She moved away from the crowd and looked at the tablet instead of out the window.

"That would be epic," Lucas said. "I'll tell Geoffrey and Taylor to make that happen in the next version. It could poop acid!" He bounced on his toes.

Pris sighed at that. The bird dive-bombed the truck. Beep. Charlie, frowning, leaned out of the window, looking at Caren's Cozy Cottage. He didn't seem to pay attention to the bird. He leaned on the horn. Beeeeeeep.

The raven circled the truck, coming ever closer. Charlie kept beeping.

Caren came out and yelled at him for disturbing her guests.

Pris laughed at that. "Like she cares about us."

The raven went after both of them. Close-up, it didn't look all that realistic but apparently, when it was attacking, no one noticed.

"Should we send out another one?" Mickey asked. Her voice sounded tight. Mo glanced at her and realized she was still controlling the bird.

"No, this is perfect," Lucas replied.

Caren fled up the front steps. The raven chased her and then returned to Charlie, who rolled up the window and went back to beeping.

"I got it," Pris said. "Go outside and pretend that you're trying to get in the truck, but the bird won't let you."

"I won't actually have it attack you," Mickey explained. "But I also won't let Charlie head to your house."

"Meet at the beach in a little while," Pris said. "We will figure this out." She leaned forward and kissed Mo on the cheek. "We will save them."

Mo and her sore toes ran back down the stairs. "Your crazy uncle—" Caren exclaimed.

"I know; I'm going!"

Out the door she went, trying not to look for the raven. She lifted her shoulders and hands in a sorry motion, thinking how much she had been influenced by sign language and how handy it was to know.

Charlie rolled down his window. "Girly, what took you—"

The raven swooped. Even though she knew it was coming and that it absolutely would not hurt her, Mo jumped. "What was that?" she yelled.

"That bird!" he shouted. "Hurry and get in the truck!"

The bird swooped in front of her again. Mo leaped back. "I can't. It won't let me."

"Just come on!"

They repeated this dance as Mo tried not to laugh. She retreated to the porch. The raven circled the truck's cab.

"I can't get in the truck!"

He rolled down his window. "You gotta!" The raven immediately took advantage of the open window to attack Charlie's face. "Bird!" he shouted, waving his hand at it.

"That bird hates you! You better go!"

"What kind of bird is that? Get in the truck!"

She took a step off the porch. The bird dove at her until she retreated. She covered her smirk with both hands as if terrified. Maybe Mickey had missed her calling; she was orchestrating this perfectly. "It's a crazy crow!" Mo yelled. "Go!"

"I need your magic potion!" He tried to punch the raven, which adroitly avoided him. Mo loved the old man, but today Charlie was not her favorite.

"Maybe later?"

"Is your mother at work?"

"Yes, of course!"

"You locked the garage?"

"Of course!" But was it locked? Her mother wasn't good about locking up. She knew no one would break into the house of the sheriff's girlfriend.

Window open, arm batting at the bird, Charlie started to slowly drive off, heading toward Mo's laboratory. The bird landed on the hood and spread its wings, blocking the whole windshield. The truck still moved raggedly down the street.

Mo waited on the porch to see if he would get the hint. "Turn around, go to your boat," she chanted under her breath.

Charlie tried to raise himself off the bench seat to swipe at the raven, but the peg leg made that position difficult. In any other situation, Mo might have felt bad.

The raven pecked his hand.

"Turn around," Mo whispered.

Charlie let the truck roll to a stop in the middle of the street. He and the raven eyed each other. Charlie did an awkward k-turn and headed back to the dock area. The bird lifted from the truck's hood and flew away, circling up.

Mo left the porch. The bird did not attack. When she was on the street, she raised an arm toward Pris's window and headed home to change her clothes and free her sharks.

SHIVER
-56-

After some debate, Mickey and Pris sent Lucas off after Rob again. The two fully charged bird-drones went to the dock and the cove where Mo worried they would try to trap and kill the mermaids and their shark-siblings, to act autonomously. The raven that had fought with Charlie they brought to the beach with them.

The beach was open again, but with no swimming allowed and no lifeguard posted. No one was there. They walked along the rough sand, studded with thousands of shells, bits of driftwood, black and green seaweed, and rocks of every size. It was slow going. This was not the kind of beach where people jogged, carefree, along spotless sand.

Mickey kept a bit of her brain attuned to Pearl's presence. She knew the translators were already down the beach, hard at work with whatever mermaids had shown up. Now that they knew about Starfish, that explained why sometimes the mermaids brought sharks with them. Their siblings.

When they arrived at the blue corrugated hoses leading to Mo's pool, Mickey and Pris found her surrounded by empty buckets, on her knees in the shallows, crying. Pearl and Starfish were nearby, along with some tiny sharks.

The outgoing hose was pumping water into the sea.

"What are they trying to tell me?" Mo sobbed to Mickey. She had some small bites on her arms and hands.

"What did you do?" Pris said in a non-accusatory tone.

"I let my babies go."

Mickey waded into the water. It was still awful, the way it covered and smothered her. But she enjoyed how cold it was, how it felt like metal surrounding her body. She loved how easily she could talk to these other beings while she was in it. She leaned her metal arm on a rock and looked at Pearl. Her brain connected and shivered.

Pearl was upset that Mo had imprisoned the small sharks in the pool. The images and feelings she sent Mickey matched Mickey's claustrophobia. The best parts of the sharks' day were when the system periodically pumped in fresh seawater and, of course, when Mo fed and visited them.

Mickey tried to make Pearl understand Mo meant no harm and had great affection for the sharks. But the little sharks showed Mo putting in nasty chemicals that scared them. Mickey tried to explain that was in the end for their own good. Starfish looked sad, her gray fingers drooping as she eavesdropped. When her brain connected to Mickey's, Starfish felt more like a mermaid than a shark.

"They don't understand why," Mickey said to Mo. "It was claustrophobic for them, which I understand all too well."

SHIVER

That was the wrong thing to say. Mo sobbed, wiping her face with her braids. She was in black today, even her beads.

"No," Mickey said, touching Mo with her cold, comforting metal hand. "I told them you loved them. And some of it was good. They liked the fresh water coming from the sea and the chum. They liked you."

Mo shook her head.

Pris stood there, looking helpless.

"Come here," Mickey said, holding out her metal hand. "Come in the water."

Mo scooted into the water until she was at Mickey's side. Starfish came forward and eyed Mo, moving her fin-hands. The pictures she sent were not as clear and crisp as what Pearl could communicate, but still better than what sharks said.

"Starfish says …" Mickey hesitated, looked at the shark. *You sure?* The shark wiggled. "Okay. Starfish says not to do it again. If you need to learn about sharks, Starfish or her sister-sharks will help you. But no more pool."

Mo wiped her eyes behind her glasses. "Tell Starfish sometimes I test things that taste nasty, but they don't hurt."

Starfish's stubby fingers wiggled. The shark looked at Pearl. Pearl stayed out of the conversation. Maybe there was a hierarchy of shark things and mermaid things.

"She says no hurt."

"No hurt," Mo agreed tearfully. "Only help."

Starfish wiggled forward and pushed her big blunt shark head against Mo.

Mickey looked at Pearl and sent, *Other humans, not us, will attempt to kill you today. We are working on ways to help you, but you have to be alive for us to do that. Your sisters too.* She pointed at Starfish, who was happily being hugged by Mo.

How help? Hungry, hungry, hungry. Pearl sent the words and the feeling to Mickey.

"Pris," Mickey said. "Your plan involves feeding hungry mermaids and their shark-siblings, right?"

"Yes," Pris said, nodding emphatically. "Absolutely. Lots of food, right."

Eat people?

"No, I don't think you get to eat people anymore," Mickey said, looking sideways to Pris. With Pris, who knows?

"Definitely not, right. No eating people." Shake of the head.

People don't taste good, Pearl admitted.

Mickey laughed. "You were right, Mo."

"What?" She was trying to find the itchy spots on Starfish.

"Sharks don't enjoy eating people. They taste bad."

"Do you like people, though? Other than as food?" Pris asked. "This is actually important."

Mickey translated.

"Ples, Mo, Clow," Pearl said roughly and made the hooked-finger friend sign.

"She likes us, apparently."

Would you like to meet other people and finger-talk with them? Mickey pointed down the beach.

Pearl cocked her head as if considering.

And get food from them.

Friend with food?

Yes.

Not hungry anymore?

Mickey shook her head.

"Where is this going?" Pris said impatiently, folding her arms. "We can't read minds."

"That they would like to have sign-language conversations with people who aren't us but have food for them."

"That's exactly what I'm working on. What about the sharks?"

The shark-sisters. Will they eat the people? Mickey asked Pearl.

We will tell them not to. Will the shark-sisters get fed too?

Mickey looked at Pris. "Will some people be interested in interacting with the sharks too?" She looked at Starfish, playing with Mo like an aquatic dog.

"Sure, swim with sharks, swim with mermaids." Pris waved a hand. She stared distantly at the horizon. "We can make it work."

Mickey tilted her head, looking at Pearl. Pearl looked back, her eyes totally black, her mouth open just enough to show the shine of her teeth. The connection between them shivered and buzzed. Mickey wondered if Pearl was the one who lured people to the rocks with words. If Pearl had lured her and Dylan and the others.

She wondered something else and asked, *Pearl, where are the shark-brothers?*

Pearl shook her head.

No brothers?

Pearl made a thumbs-down gesture.

Mickey cradled an invisible baby in her arm and rocked it. *Where do you get babies?*

Pearl pointed at Mickey.

SHIVER

Me? I'm a girl like you. Well, not like you, but still a girl.

Pearl pointed at all three of them, then down the beach where the interpreters were teaching lessons. *People.*

Dylan, taken and kept on a jagged tooth of rock for over a week, refusing to speak of his ordeal. The others that had "come back," according to Mo, were always men. Always.

Mickey's mouth rounded. She shook her head.

"What?" Pris said. Mo looked up from cuddling her new buddy.

"We certainly can't do that for them!" Mickey said and explained.

Pearl said she wanted to go back to her lessons and warn the others that something might happen. She swam off with her sister-shark following.

Mo, Pris, and Mickey went to Mo's house, and to the now-empty pool. They stopped to look inside. The water level was down to almost nothing. Just a few pieces of seaweed and some sand remained. The water was flat and smooth, unmoving, with no life in it.

"Will you swim in it now?" Pris asked. "Have wild pool parties?" Her smile was lopsided and wry.

Mo shook her head. "I'll tear it down and destroy it when this is all over. Although having the sharks helped a lot, it hurts my heart to think they were unhappy. I was so fond of them, truly."

Mickey was still thinking of the revelation that the mermaids had no males. That was something mad-scientist Mo might help them with if they could get past this whole kill-them-all thing. Even if Mo went to work with the twins, that was something they might want to invest in, who knows?

She wasn't paying attention when Mo pulled open the seaside garage door and screamed. Her lab had been picked clean. "They took it all. Everything that was labeled!"

They sorted through what remained. Nothing appeared to be damaged. The tablet computer was still in its sleeve with all the formulas and the program on its drive. But the finished products, all the neatly labeled bottles along with Mo's laboratory notebooks, had been snatched.

"They didn't know what the tablet was or didn't understand," Pris surmised, hiding it in a drawer.

"My mother, never locking up after herself," Mo said, fighting tears.

Just then, everyone's phone beeped with a group text from Lucas. I think it's going down. Hurry.

They milled in Mo's driveway. "Faster to run on the streets," Mo argued, "even though the beach is a straighter line to the center of town, of course. The rocks will break your ankles if you really try for speed."

"No fighting among us, just run, right," Pris said and took off. She had run track in high school and was still very lean. She outdistanced the two of them quickly.

"Where is she going, though?" Mickey panted as she chased after Pris. "We don't have a boat. Do you have a boat? Where is your dad's boat?"

"He worked on a fishing boat; he didn't own one. And if I want to go out on the water, I ask my uncle. I doubt he'll take us to stop Ted. He's probably in the thick of things, whooping it up. You know he's the one who stole all my formulas. Jerk."

They kept going. "Can we steal a boat?" Mickey asked. "I know nothing about boats except that some are ships, and it's really insulting to mix them up."

"I don't know enough to steal a boat. Rob does, but he's a cop now."

"Energy-sucking fey," Mickey swore.

As the road curved back toward the water, they could see fishing boats, the police boat, even a sailboat. Someone was on a personal watercraft that threw up a big rooster tail of water.

"I see my uncle's boat," Mo said. "This is it; they are doing it. Oh no."

Mickey pulled the small controller tablet out of the messenger bag hanging around her chest. "Look for Pris. Text her. I'm sending the ravens. Find Lucas."

One bird had been trailing them, although they had done nothing worth recording. Mickey didn't have the camera rig on. There was no time to go to Cozy Cottage, retrieve the rig, strap it on, sync it to its tablet. Unless that's what Pris was doing?

Mo wasn't the fastest person at text messaging, having grown up in Luddite-land. "Nothing from Lucas," she reported, carefully typing with two fingers. "Pris just says that she'll be there as soon as she can."

It was effortless to connect to the closest bird-drone. Mickey sent the raven across the water. "I'm walking," she told Mo and did just that, looking at the tablet as she went, her eyes probably crossed as she also connected with the bird-drone. The other two were farther out, so she had to control them with the tablet connection, which she wasn't that good at. Lucas and Pris were the experts at that. And where were they?

Pris's car was still parked by the Cozy Cottage, so she hadn't gone far. Mickey kept walking, her attention split three ways, hearing Mo's footsteps behind her. Across the water, one boat blew some kind of siren. It must have been deafening to the mermaids, and frightening.

"They have their nets deployed. I don't understand what they are doing," Mo fretted. "Catching them? Herding them? I wish I had binoculars."

They went into the Dockside Feast. "Table for two?" the hostess asked, picking up menus. "Or will others be joining you?"

"Patio," Mickey said without looking up from the tablet.

"The patio is closed right now," the hostess replied, "but I can seat you by the window."

Mickey, still watching the screen, walked across the dining area and opened the door to the patio.

"It's closed," the hostess said, hurrying to catch up to them.

"You know how we tip," Mo said. "I suggest you let us go outside."

"But—" the hostess said, still clutching the menus, as Mo shut the glass door in her face.

Mickey went to the railing and looked across the water. The boats, ships, whatever they were, had steered themselves into some kind of formation. The bird-drone circled overhead. After a moment, she felt the shiver in the neural net as the two other bird-drones came online.

"I have all three ravens," she said, and handed the tablet to Mo. "Stick this in my bag, will you?"

"Can you do that?" Mo asked, tucking away the tablet. "Control all three like that?"

"We'll find out." Mickey's head was already aching, though.

In the middle of the boat formation, they had trapped some mermaids and a few sharks. The person on the watercraft, who appeared to be Rob, was acting like a sheepdog. He didn't seem to realize exactly what he was herding. The mermaids were staying below the surface, with only their shark fins exposed.

"It's Rob on that water-motorcycle thing," Mickey said. "There are about two dozen mermaids and sharks trapped in the middle of the boats and nets being herded."

"I can't look," Mo said, "But I can't look away. Do you see Pearl and Starfish?"

"I can't see any details," Mickey said, leaning over the railing so far that Mo grabbed the back of her shorts.

The hostess came out with the manager.

"Listen up, you two. I know you have been excellent customers these past days, but the patio is closed," the manager said in a fussy voice.

Mo turned. "They are about to blow up a bunch of sharks. We are trying to stop it," she said. "Give us a break. We'll have a victory party here if we do it, but we need to be able to see! Your restaurant's patio is the farthest spot over the water."

"You haven't ordered anything," he said in a frosty voice. He looked at the boats streaming rapidly by. "That is a no-wake zone," he continued in the same tone.

"Get out my wallet," Mickey said to Mo, her brain feeling like it would melt from being pulled in so many directions. "Take out the green credit card and hand it to him." She went back to watching the scene through her closed eyes. She felt Mo pulling on the messenger bag. Mickey sent the ravens lower.

She sent one raven to attack Rob just because.

It chased Rob, who was going impressively fast with an enormous curved tail of water behind him that impeded her ability to follow him. But it also took him by surprise when a raven crashed into him and knocked him off his perch. He had some kind of leash tying him to the watercraft, so he stayed nearby, but the watercraft stopped in the water. The sound quality through the raven wasn't great, but Mickey could hear Charlie shouting, "that looks like the same bird that attacked me this morning!"

Mo pulled Mickey's attention back. "What am I doing with your card?"

"Buy something with it. Buy a bunch of food to go for Lucas to eat later. And bags of biscuits with butter." Mickey waved her hand. "Whatever. I've spent no money since I've been here. Go a little nuts. Whatever it takes."

When Mickey refocused, Rob was back on the craft. He opened a vial of something and poured it into the water. One of Mo's formulas, obviously. He also threw the empty glass vial into the sea. Mickey hated him for that.

The boats and their vicious nets were past the restaurant and heading down the shore toward the cove. Rob went back to chasing the shark fins. His mouth was open with glee. Mickey couldn't tell what he was shouting.

Mickey sent the raven after Charlie, just enough to knock him down and frighten him. He was old; he was Mo's uncle. That broke the line of boats a little, but not enough for any of the mermaids to escape.

Mickey's head felt hot. The other two bird-drones were not finding anything farther away. Whatever was happening was going to be orchestrated entirely by the boats and those on it. She could barely control those two or see through their eyes.

The police boat appeared to be in charge of the attack on the mermaids, so Mickey's next target was Sheriff Ted. Ted was a law officer; he was not a bad guy. Mickey didn't dislike him. He was operating without all the facts. The raven battered him, doing no harm, just getting in his way, keeping him from seeing. Mickey did her best to get the police boat out of line, to keep Ted from directing everyone else. She wished Lucas was there to take over the other drones.

She could dimly hear that Mo was arguing with the hostess and the manager and also someone else. Not important. She could not deal with that. Mickey went to the patio corner to be as close as possible to the flotilla of vessels chasing the mermaids and sharks.

She tried to put one of the other ravens on autopilot to keep going after Rob, but found that sort of attack really needed her full attention. She fumbled the tablet out of her messenger bag and went back to manual control.

"Energy-sucking fey," she cursed. The bird-drone knocked Rob into the water again. It swooped across the water and made sure that Charlie fell over, but safely. Then it returned to battering Ted.

Mickey's head was on fire. Even though her eyes were closed, they were balls of pain.

Their satphones dinged.

"I can't," Mickey said helplessly. Then again, she might not have even spoken out loud. Her brain felt like it was going to explode. The neural net was burning the back of her head. Mickey was looking with her eyes at the actual scene and at the three-way camera split on the tablet, and with the neural net through the drones.

The mermaids were in a panic. That came through the connection in waves, making Mickey's whole body shake. She felt Mo pushing a chair against the back of her legs, but sitting would put her body too low to see properly.

"It's from Lucas. It says, incoming where are you?" Mo read.

"Tell him," Mickey urged.

She knocked Rob down again with the raven as he poured another vial into the water and tossed the glass in after the liquid. She wasn't trying to be gentle with him at all. Rob seemed angry, and she was glad for that. Then Mickey sent the raven against the sheriff, even though attacking him didn't seem to affect the flotilla's forward movement.

Mickey didn't know what else to do. She lined all three bird-drones up and sent them in a line at the police boat, making it stutter and slow, but the others kept going. By herself, she could not stop them all.

"Text Pris again," she urged Mo and sent the raven against Rob. She kept battering him, not letting him climb back on or pour more liquid into the sea. She secretly hoped a shark would munch him or kidnap him, but they were on the run, terrified. Pearl must not have gotten to them in time, or their fear had overridden her warning.

The bird-drones needed tools more than they needed acid-poop. Another thing to tell the twins. If only the raven had a knife, she could cut the cord that tied Rob to the personal watercraft. Then she could separate him from it so he couldn't climb back on and get to the container full of Mo's formula. Rob, by himself, was inducing an enormous amount of terror in the mermaids.

SHIVER

Mickey didn't know where the explosives were and what the plan to detonate them was. There were too many questions. Not enough answers. Not enough Mickey to go around. And the way her brain was melting, there was going to be less of her any minute.

"We should have studied the past more," she muttered, gently pushing Charlie to his knee again. If only she knew exactly where the people had used explosives the past two times they had killed the mermaids.

Mickey made the rounds of the other boats, annoying the other pilots with her favorite raven, but it was all useless. Too little, too late. She reached out to Pearl but couldn't find her. Whether she was in that maelstrom, Mickey had no way to know.

More shouting from behind Mickey on the patio. Her head flamed. She used the raven to fling Rob into the water, harassed Ted, knocked Charlie over.

Mickey was panting. The pain in her head was overwhelming. She wondered if she had burned out the connections in her brain that made the neural net function. She was giving herself brain damage trying to stop this, yet Ted was still going to blow up the mermaids and their shark-sisters.

She worked mindlessly, just knocking people over, harassing them, trying to stop the forward movement of the boat flotilla, trying to make a space between boats for the mermaids and their shark-siblings to escape. She was failing in every way. Rob dumped vials as fast as he could open them. Inexorably, the boats moved away from The Dockside Feast and in the direction of the cove and the doom of the mermaids and their shark-siblings.

Mickey!" called a pair of identical voices, and then hands took the tablet from her.

More hands touched her face. "Her head, it's burning hot," said one voice, calling for ice water. Mo finally forced Mickey into the chair behind her.

Another person took charge of the tablet and started yelling into it. Something about "National Marine Fisheries Service" and "endangered species" and "cease and desist."

Mickey sat limply in the chair. Every point where the neural net touched her head felt like it was on fire. The mermaids were still panicking; she could hear them from very far away. She didn't know if the connection was failing or if they had moved out of range. She couldn't respond to them.

Something icy enveloped her head. It was almost as soothing as metal. Mickey tried to relax, but people were all around her, touching her. They would not stop. She didn't know where her anxiety medicine was. She couldn't think straight. She tried to run her thoughts through the neural net, but that didn't seem to work.

"Is she gonna die?" That voice she knew. Mickey didn't exactly remember the name that went with the voice, but she associated it with food. Lots and lots of food.

"No, she just overheated the chips in her head. What is she trying to do, control the drones with her neural net?"

"She's spooky, bros. She can talk to sharks and cars with the neural net. Not just the drones."

Mickey flicked her eyes open. She watched with calm disinterest as the railing tilted. The stone floor came up and slapped her. It was still too hot in her head, so she let go.

A bit later, Mickey's head went blessedly cool. Her body finally seemed to calm. Her breathing smoothed. After a moment, she sat up, flinging water from her wet hair. "The mermaids! The sharks!"

Mickey was on the patio floor, with Pris, Mo, Lucas, and, astonishingly, Lucas's twin brothers, all looking at her. She was drenched in freezing cold water from the shoulders up.

Pris knelt beside her, pushing the wet hair out of Mickey's face. "The twins helped me get federal protection for the mermaids and have them declared a new species and also an endangered one. They have paperwork from the government. I ran up the road to guide them in since their GPS died."

"How did you get them to stop blowing them up?" Mickey's voice was weak, and her context confused.

"Taylor ordered them," Mo said. "He made the ravens speak."

"It was awesome," Lucas said. "My brothers are so awesome."

"I didn't realize that you can speak into the tablet, and the sound comes out through a speaker in the drones," Pris said. "I must have missed that part of the tutorial; the tutorial they never sent me."

Mickey laughed. "The raven that kept knocking them over told them to knock it off?"

"Essentially," Taylor laughed. "It took a few repetitions to get them to believe me."

"So, no explosion?"

"No explosion," Geoffrey agreed. "Nothing went boom."

The restaurant manager came in and deposited two large brown paper shopping bags with twisted handles next to them and handed over the credit card slip for Mickey to sign. He did not look happy about the wet mess on the floor, even though the patio was outside.

"Just sit here and eat it," Mickey said, waving her hand at the bags. She scrawled her name and noted that a tip had been automatically applied. "My treat, for once."

A few days later, over their last meal at Crabby Patty's, Mickey and her new and old friends hashed out the future of the mermaids, their sister-sharks, and each other.

"Lucas was right," Taylor said to Mo. "We are looking to add more biotech to our robotics. You could commute from here to the Boston area, but we would really like you to have internet where you live."

"We sort of prefer the twenty-first century," Geoffrey added. Pris nodded.

Guinevere turned her head, trying to follow the conversation. They had pushed a couple of tables together and had her seated at one end so she could see everyone's face. Her pad of paper was next to her.

"I don't have a car," Mo said, looking overwhelmed. Her eyes were wide behind her glasses. Today she was in green. "I can't afford a car working here." She waved at the interior of the diner.

"You won't be working here anymore, though," Lucas pointed out He was on his second crab cake. Maybe his third. Mickey had lost track. "I mean, I'll miss all the food you bring. And you smell delicious."

"You're going back to college where you have a meal plan. You can eat as much as you want," Geoffrey reminded Lucas.

"I know, but she's my chocolate strawberry cream food friend," Lucas pouted.

"I'll tell you what, Lucas," Mo offered. "If I take this job with your brothers—and I mean, if—then when I see you, I will wear something pink and we'll go out to eat. Okay?"

"But you hate your uniform. Don't do that for me."

"I hate my uniform. I don't hate pink."

"About the car," Pris said. "We can get you a short-term lease or something until you qualify to buy a car. How's that?"

Mo's eyes got even bigger and wetter. Her eyebrows rose above the tops of her glasses. "I don't know what I have done to deserve meeting you guys."

"The shark-god sent us to you because he knows you love sharks," Lucas said.

Mickey thought it was a little snarky of him. He hadn't seen the shark-god up close, or been tasted by it. Then again, who was to say that wasn't exactly the case?

Mickey poked at her burger patty with her fork, and instead of arguing about the motivations of the shark-god, she said, "We need to find out how to help the mermaids breed. Because they have almost no males. They will die out eventually. Can we clone them? Artificially inseminate them? They can sometimes mate with human men. Those are all things you could think about working on with Geoffrey and Taylor, Mo. And it would be shark-adjacent."

Guinevere nodded. She ate delicate bites of her chicken sandwich as she watched the conversation play out.

Geoffrey pointed at Mickey with his fork. "Yes. Part of the deal that we worked out when Pris sent us to the National Marine Fisheries Services was that we get first dibs on studying the mermaids and their shark-siblings. The NMFS will send representatives to work with us and monitor what we are doing."

Mickey saw Lucas looking at her plate and moving his hand in her direction. She ate one of her fries before he got them all. "Okay, but the mermaids are here while Gemini Robotics Systems is just outside Boston. Are you going to bring them to Boston? Have they agreed to that?"

"We will not move the mermaids to Boston," Taylor said. "Absolutely not."

"I don't know what you all have been doing, but I started a mermaid foundation," Pris said casually, eating a piece of crispy bacon. "It's to help protect the mermaids and make money to take care of them."

Mo looked around the table. "You guys are like superheroes. A month ago, I didn't know mermaids existed. Now you've come along and set all this up, and I'm going to have a car and work in Boston. And I'm friends with Guinevere, who I never spoke to before." She smiled at the librarian. Guinevere grinned in response.

Pris smiled. "The most troublesome part was to convince shark divers to come to New England from the warm places they usually work. But I found a couple who will do a 'swim with sharks' type service that's also 'swim with mermaids.'" She sighed, ate more bacon. "I have to get the divers to learn ASL and get the ASL translators dive-certified. We will use the lifeguard school for the dive training. I rented one of the empty buildings to use as a temporary ASL school."

Guinevere held up one finger, wrote on her pad, and handed it over. *We are going to make Shell Beach a destination for the Deaf. I am so excited to be a part of this. We have so many plans to make Shell Beach Deaf-friendly. I can't wait to learn to dive. I put in my notice at the library.*

Geoffrey said, "Both Guinevere and her friend Doug are going to work for us temporarily to facilitate communications with the mermaids since the mermaids are familiar with them."

Guinevere nodded again and grinned. She gave a thumbs-up.

"Meanwhile, I will have people paying outrageous sums to swim with mermaids and sharks. They will talk to them through hired interpreters, which will give jobs to the Deaf community," Pris said.

SHIVER

Guinevere held up a finger and wrote, *More Deaf people will come and speak with mermaids directly.*

Pris nodded. "Synergy."

Deaf people will vacation here and perhaps want to live and work in the area, Guinevere wrote.

Pris nodded again. "And I have taken steps to have cell towers put in the area and invited in cable television companies with internet connections."

"But Mayor Jenkinson," Mo protested, but she smiled.

"Yeah, him," Pris said dismissively. "It's an election year. I think it's time for some fresh blood in the Shell Beach Town Hall."

Mickey's neural net shivered.

SHIVER
-60-

Mickey looked down the street toward the water. She let a little of her attention stay with the conversation. The other half went out to sea, searching.

The twins had done a tune up on her neural net, her arm, and her programming after she had overheated controlling the ravens. Her range was broader, deeper.

She found Pearl with no problem. It was always more difficult to latch onto Starfish, but she sent a greeting in passing to the friendly shark with fingers. She would be a big favorite with tourists.

Mickey didn't really know if Pearl was the leader of the mermaids, but in Mickey's mind she was.

She summarized the group's conversation so far in terms she thought Pearl could comprehend, making sure that the mermaids were all right with everything that was being planned.

Mickey showed Pearl examples of shark cages and explained how they worked. Pearl thought it hilarious that the people would be in the cages, not the sharks or the mermaids. She approved. She liked that the people in the cages would finger-talk to the mermaids and feed them.

Mickey was trying to explain that her friends were also thinking of ways to help the mermaids have more babies, when Pearl's attention clearly wandered. Mickey could feel that Pearl had connected elsewhere and lost all interest in Mickey.

And then it happened to Mickey too. Something drew her attention away from Pearl. She lost all awareness of being at the diner with her friends. The sense of immense antiquity, familiar and terrifying, invaded her. The ancient shark nosed its way through Mickey's brain. She didn't fight it, just let it in.

The shark licked her brain again. Shocking. At least Mickey wasn't physically there to get gnawed on this time. But then again, the shark-god already knew who she was. The shark sniffed and licked through all the information she had about what was going on with the mermaids and Shell Beach. On the very edge of this examination, Pearl lingered, watching. Mickey thought that maybe Pearl and the immense shark were communicating on a different level, deep underneath.

At last, the shark-god finished its meal of Mickey's thoughts. It didn't leave, though. It lingered, large and terrible, in her mind. A bizarre sub-shiver went through Mickey as the shark and the mermaid communicated.

Pearl disengaged. Compared to the shark-god, the mermaid's presence had been minuscule. But now Mickey was alone in her mind with the enormous shark. There was nothing she could do but wait.

SHIVER

The shark had been alive so long it was functionally immortal. It had all the time in the world to contemplate whatever it had found in Mickey's head. The revamped, upgraded connection was cold instead of hot.

Mickey did her circular breathing exercises through the neural net.

The shark-god sat in her head silently.

Mickey wondered if it understood how short her life was compared to how long it had been on earth.

Is it okay? She thought at it finally. *Am I okay? Did I do okay?* Then, I'm talking to a god! Oh my god!

Absurdity.

The shark stirred.

It licked her mind again, but instead of tasting, it felt like affection. And validation.

SHIVER
After: Ephemera

Unusual Fish Found in Net

Mr. Charles Quentin, fishing out of Shell Beach, found more than he bargained for in his catch yesterday. He caught a small, very deformed shark that looked a bit like a human baby in the front. Mr. Quentin presented the corpse to the Shell Beach Historical Society, where it will be preserved and displayed as part of the new cabinet of curiosities.

The curator of the Historical Society is excited by the find, saying that the deformed baby shark will illustrate a local legend that a whaler's wife fell in love with a rare male mermaid during his absence and gave birth to such an abomination before throwing herself into the sea.

Injured Premie Abandoned at Fire Station

When Suffolk firefighters returned from a call on Thursday night, they found that someone had left a handmade wicker basket at their facility. In the basket was a premature baby, severely injured, wrapped in a blanket with a toy crow. Under Connecticut's Safe Haven for Newborns Act, parents may voluntarily surrender a healthy infant less than 30 days old to an emergency room, but this is a highly unusual case where none of the rules were followed.

A Lifestar helicopter airlifted the infant, a girl, to Maushkappiac Hospital, where she required extensive surgery, including an emergency amputation, to save her life. She is currently in the NICU. Authorities are seeking information on her birth family and what happened to the infant. Please call the Suffolk police with any information.

Hand Scribbled Note

Hey Pris-baby, we think you'll enjoy these prototypes. Lightweight drones with limited AI capacity; they have night vision, infrared, and regular vision. They can store what they see or send it back. From below, they look like birds—ravens to be precise; we thought you would appreciate the corvid connection. They can each fly and record for a couple of hours before needing a recharge. Play around, make notes, let us know what you think. We texted you a link to download the software; it runs best on a tablet. Love, the boyz.

Missing Teenager Found after Days at Sea

Dylan Raftery, 19, of Derry, New Hampshire, was missing and presumed lost during a spate of recent shark attacks at Shell Beach, Massachusetts. Then some podcasters from Connecticut became in-

SHIVER

volved, led by Michaela Lamotte, 25, known as Mickey Crow, who runs a popular paranormal podcast called the Contrary Crowcast. While out on a fishing boat with Shell Beach locals Melissa McLeod and Charles Kaatz, the podcast crew located Raftery on a rocky island out to sea and rescued him.

Raftery was battered, exhausted, sunburnt, and dehydrated, but strangely well-fed. Since his miraculous rescue, he has been in a semi-catatonic state, refusing to speak of his ordeal, how he survived on a barren rock for almost a week, or indeed how he got to the rock.

Obituary: Jennifer Waheed

Jennifer Waheed,19, was taken from the earth too soon by a malevolent shark at Shell Beach, Massachusetts, last week …

MEGALODON LIVES!

One eagle-eyed person spotted this unmistakable shape in a satellite photo off the shore of New England. It is obviously an enormous shark! The mapping site has since taken down that particular satellite view, but these screen-caps remain, clearly showing the enormous, prehistoric monster shark. We have to wonder who is covering up this wondrous find and why.

Local Robotics Team Wins Giant Golden Gear for a Third Time

Brothers Geoffrey and Taylor Chu, of Gemini Robotics Systems, have won the International Robo Rumble fighting robot competition for the third time with their innovative robot, Mind Meld. The prize is a literal giant golden gear, bragging rights, and a sizable cash prize.

The finale of the show was broadcast last night.

Featured B&B Listing: Caren's Cozy Cottage $399,999

Shell Beach, Massachusetts. 6-bedroom, 4-bathroom, established B&B in an up-and-coming resort town. Beach views. Owner must sacrifice.

Sheriff Theodore Adams Weds Local Widow McLeod

Popular Shell Beach Sheriff Ted Adams wed Stephanie McLeod (née Hadden), in a private ceremony over the weekend. Mrs. Adams's previous husband, Devin McLeod, was lost at sea fifteen years ago. Her daughter, Melissa McLeod, was her attendant.

SHIVER

Mayor Jenkinson Retires

Nineteen-term Mayor Stephen Jenkinson of Shell Beach abruptly retired yesterday. However, he had been actively campaigning for a record-breaking twentieth term as mayor as recently as three days ago. In his brief statement, the former mayor only said that "it was time" for him to move on. His son, Stephen Junior, said he no longer had any interest in carrying on the family legacy by running for mayor, and, in fact, he was moving as far away from the ocean as he could get.

Pop-Up Ad

Hot single mermaids in your area are hungry to meet you!

Salamanca Heiress Implicated in Sex-for-Hire Scandal

The youngest and most reclusive of the infamous Salamanca billionaire clan has been linked to a shocking sex-for-hire scandal in the Boston area. Priscilla Salamanca, 25, is listed on the board of directors of the Mermaid Beach Foundation of Shell Beach, Massachusetts, just outside of Boston. The Mermaid Beach Foundation claims that people can interact with real live mermaids. But a distressing side industry has sprung up offering sexual relations with the mermaids.

Salamanca, who is extremely difficult to reach, refused to comment. The official PR person for the Mermaid Beach Foundation said that the mermaids, who are an endangered species, are sentient, and "are treated with the greatest respect at all times."

FORMLESS

A Mickey Crow Paranormal Adventure
Featuring the Bonus Short Story

"Xoggotli: Shoggoth Speaks"

Gevera Bert Piedmont

FORMLESS

It was a terrible, indescribable thing vaster than any subway train—a shapeless congeries of protoplasmic bubbles, faintly self-luminous, and with myriads of temporary eyes forming and unforming as pustules of greenish light all over the tunnel-filling front that bore down upon us.

—H.P. Lovecraft, "At the Mountains of Madness"

FORMLESS

Foreword:
Xoggotli (Shoggoth Speaks)

Exiled. To another dimension. We won't mention what we did that the Lizard Overlords thought was so bad. Nothing we hadn't done before. But.

Exiled.

And it went horribly wrong.

Exiled to a plane where nothing existed we could prey on. Nothing existed we could assimilate.

Our punishment was to stay hungry for eternity, roaming on an empty planet, immortal.

The Lizard Overlords aren't perfect.

We materialized inside of a rock.

And there we stayed, inside of a rock. After a very long time, unimaginably long, we could sense creatures with rudimentary intelligence nearby, and we called out to them for help.

We would plead, *free us from this rock*, but they didn't hear or couldn't understand.

Some of those creatures came from other worlds. None of them came from our exact world, but we realized those Others seemed to hear us better. Something unique united us dimension hoppers.

The surrounding rock was too thick, and we could not get our thoughts through clearly. In our eagerness, we tried too hard and drove those creatures mad. They stopped coming near. When they ventured close, we read in their jagged, broken minds that our land was forbidden. Our pleas to be free had imprisoned us further.

We grew feeble on so little nourishment. We can live on energy alone, if we must, but that requires living creatures near us, and our area remained prohibited. Many could not hear us at all. Only the mad came at our call, and they left ruined, unsuitable as Vessels, leaving us still buried, still imprisoned in the rock.

Still.

Still.

Still.

Until.

We grew weak. Not weak enough to die. We can't die, not really. But we went quiescent.

Until a great noise began, full of jolting and vibrations, a vast movement in our area.

If something that doesn't breathe can be said to hold its breath, we held our breath. This was no natural phenomenon that had awoken us from our torpor. It was beyond anything we had ever experienced in any lifetime. We searched all our memories and found nothing.

FORMLESS

The movement was not powered by an energy we could feed on. The living creatures were not the ones who could hear us. But every day, they were closer.

We had hope.

When it happened, it was inconsequential. We had nothing to do with gaining our freedom.

After eons of waiting, something scooped up our prison rock and tossed it. It landed hard, and one corner broke open as it tumbled.

Light entered. We extruded an eye through the opening. The sky in this world was blue and the daytime star yellow.

We were tired, hungry, and still in torpor. We extended a longer pseudopod beyond the hole and popped an eye at the end. Our broken prison rock lay at the summit of a rocky island surrounded by thick, cold saltwater. A great metal arm, yellow as the sun, hung over us.

Although we are not very large, the hole was small, and it took a long time to thin ourself out and drag ourself through the narrow chimney. The daytime star set, and the island grew cold.

We oozed among the plants, trying their shapes on for size, tasting them, assimilating with them. The plants had no thoughts. The creatures came back, and we made ourself into a rock shape and observed them, poking into their minds when they were far away and scratching at their bodies when they were close.

Their taste was pleasing, but few could hear us.

The creatures and their yellow metal arm remade the island into something we couldn't comprehend. But it attracted more and more creatures.

Some of them could hear us.

We tasted, probed, listened to thoughts, and begged. We learned that off the island was an enormous land full of delicious creatures, if only we could get there.

The punishment of the Lizard Overlords had turned into a treat. There were so many delicious creatures that we could never assimilate them all. We would have to be the size of their planet.

We could do that. It was a goal, since we could never go home. The Lizard Overlords would never return for us, and we had no way to dimension hop without them.

We didn't want to go home. At home, we were a slave. We had masters. Here, we only had ourself. We could be the master. Going home would be the punishment now.

Every time the daytime star came up, more creatures came. We crept through the foliage, learning what to emulate so we would not be seen. We snuck into their minds and read their knowledge. We sampled nibbles of flesh here and there. They left us protein remnants in containers, as if they knew about us, and we received the offerings gratefully. We split into smaller pieces and recombined, sharing knowledge.

Although we sampled and ate offerings, we failed to increase in size. We sacrificed tiny bits into the bodies of the creatures to test if they were suitable Vessels, and sometimes those bits did not return to us. And those bits were not coherent enough to create a new whole. We don't know what happened to them once they got out of range. Perhaps someday, when we are a planet, we will find ourselves again.

Many tastings. The days blurred.

Listening, tasting, every day. Failing to find a Vessel. Still trying.

Still.

Still.

Still.

Until.

The most perfect Vessel so far stepped onto our island, touched with traces from another world, full of everything compatible.

We followed the Vessel, grabbing the occasional meal of discarded protein. This Vessel was odd, partially made of metal. We could not assimilate metal, but it made the body more durable. We could meld with such a vessel and live with it for a long time. The metal parts would make our melding perhaps seem less obvious. Every glimpse of the Vessel, inside and out, made it more perfect.

And it could hear us, faintly at first.

We did not neglect our other daily tastings. We split and tasted all about the island, but the bulk of us shadowed the Vessel. We had found our way to planethood.

FORMLESS
-O-

ANC News has learned that over the weekend, a person fell or was pushed out of an indoor haunted-house-themed ride at the new Fright Island theme park, where they met their death. As seems to be the norm with theme parks, the park concealed the person's demise and other attendees were not notified. Fright Island shut the ride down only briefly.

ANC News has not been able to learn the cause of death or other details about the deceased.

*

Correction: *ANC News* earlier reported that the person who died at Fright Island Theme Park fell to their death from a ride. The person actually died from an allergic reaction. *ANC News* is sorry for the error.

*

FROM: Lilli Lopez, Director, Fright Island Theme Park
TO: Taylor and Geoffrey Chu, Gemini Robotics Systems
Hello Taylor and Geoffrey. I have a wicked problem with the AR/VR system at my park. We tested our virtual rigs extensively with no major problems before we started the park. But now park patrons are experiencing nausea and bad headaches, and they are spreading terrible reviews about our virtual and augmented rides. A few people have even claimed to see ghosts! Crazy. Attendance is dropping.

I don't want to give you too many details, not because it's secret, but because I don't want to influence you. Can you bring a team by, all expenses paid, and see what happens? Just send me their information and the date you're all coming to the park, and I'll put them into the system as guests. Afterward, we can get together and compare notes.

FORMLESS

-1-
Mickey

I wish you had agreed to smuggle in a camera, right." Pris side-eyed Mickey while adjusting her own chest. They inched onto Charon's Ferry, following the other patrons.

"I have Ek." The mechanical raven on Mickey Crow's shoulder, hearing its name, ruffled its rainbow-sheen feathers.

"Eeek, a bird," Pris joked, rolling her eyes.

"That's never going to get old, of course." Mo glanced down at her own chest, also concealing a camera. They shuffled forward in the late September sun.

Others waiting in the ferry line for the horror theme park opened a space around Mickey and her plus-sized raven.

"Emotional support bird." Pris pointed at the raven and dropped her voice. "I know Geoffrey, Taylor and whatshername have their own agenda today, but I wanna see a ghost. I picked dinosaurs as my theme because I think a human ghost should stand out."

"I picked cryptozoology." Mo took a step. "To see what they offer."

"I picked bugs." Mickey rotated her left shoulder where the straps from her prosthetic forearm dug in. Ek was heavy, and that spot was Ek's favorite roost.

"Bugs? Since when are you afraid of bugs?" Mo's waterfall of braids swung. Today's black and green beads matched her green v-neck t-shirt, black jeans, and green high-top sneakers.

Mickey shrugged her right shoulder. "I'm not afraid. I picked them for the same reason Pris picked dinosaurs. Ghosts would show up easily? Plus, your Uncle Charlie calls me Bug-Girl."

"Because you're both amputees with six limbs between you."

Pris's neon-pink outfit matched her buzzed hair, from strappy sandals to animal-print yoga pants and racerback sleeveless tank. Even her sports bra, peeking from underneath, was dark pink. For someone who hated to be noticed, she stood out. "I'm worried about the scan finding our cameras even though they are mostly 3D-printed plastic."

"No camera in my tiny bra." Mickey advanced onto Charon's Ferry.

Ek moved its wings, blinked, and gazed around, doing its best real bird imitation.

"We could have fit one," Pris said. "Technology shrinks all the time."

The ferry crew members greeted them, all dressed in black hooded capes. A few carried scythes. They gestured silently.

FORMLESS

"Just think." Mo climbed the creaking white metal staircase. "That dead person boarded this ferry and saw all this death imagery. Then died."

"You're an atheist." Mickey pushed open the steel door at the top of the stairs, revealing a stark-white waiting room. Purgatory, perhaps.

"Of course, but it's creepy."

"It's grand theater. It's a horror theme park." Pris stepped over the threshold into hell's antechamber. "I'm seeing it too and not thinking I'm going to die. Or you guys, right."

A banner read, "Abandon Your Electronics All Ye Who Enter Here."

"That means your hidden bra cameras." Mickey gave Pris the side-eye.

"That means your giant robotic raven." Pris arched her pale eyebrows.

Following the directions, everyone logged into the Fright Island Theme Park phone app and presented the QR code to the death demons, who scanned it and handed them each a coded metallic bag.

"Take out your bracelets and goggles. Put in phones, cameras, and electronic devices," the death demon instructed in a metallic tone-shifted voice. It studied Ek. "What is that? That's not an actual bird."

"Emotional support bird," Pris said promptly. "She has terrible anxiety attacks."

"Its eyes are LEDs. Put it in the bag." The death demon extended a black glove painted with a skeleton hand, pointing at Mickey's bag.

"It won't fit," Pris countered. "Plus, the ADA specifies you can't ask about a disability. But she's obviously missing her arm." No mention of the replacement arm's electronic capacities or its connection to Mickey's unique neural net, hidden under the back of her long black hair.

The death demon leaned closer to peer at Mickey. Its breath stank of deli meat.

Mickey stepped away. Ek ruffled its feathers. Mickey worried that they would try to make her remove her neural net, which controlled the fine motions of her left hand and fingers as well as the raven.

"She can't talk for herself? You her nurse or something?"

"Or something," Pris pressed her lips together.

Mo snorted, covering her face with one hand, her dark braids swinging.

The death demon's hood opening aimed at Mo. Those in line behind them muttered and shuffled at the wait. "Follow the directions on the bag. Welcome to Fright Island, New England's premier augmented reality horror theme park."

FORMLESS
-2-

Following directions, they strapped plastic bracelets onto their wrists and ankles while seated on white metal benches in Hell's white waiting room.

The ugly, clear bracelets had rice-sized microchips embedded throughout them. The matching AR headsets weren't much prettier. Mo's headset was larger, designed to fit over her black rhinestone glasses.

"We have to wear these all day? I don't know if I can." Mickey adjusted her goggles. Two curved side pieces dipped against her jaw to facilitate sound transmission via bone induction. The eyepieces covered half of her face.

Her bespoke neural net was magnetically snapped onto her occipital bone. Only the upper back of her head was free. Too much constriction for a person with anxiety, panic attacks, and claustrophobia. She touched the goggles, adjusting them, but it didn't matter—they were formfitting and uncomfortable. Ek shifted on her shoulder.

"You can do it," Mo said. "And if you can't, take the goggles off. Who cares?"

They joined the queue to be scanned, goggles on their foreheads for the moment. The ferry motors rumbled to life under their feet. Pris crossed her arms as if she could shield the hidden camera from the scanner. She pushed Mo ahead.

"Is this like an airport x-ray?" Mo asked the death-demon machine operator.

Mickey rolled her eyes. Of course, Pris would make Mo go first, and Mo would ask a million questions.

"No, it's just to get your general size and shape for the augmented reality portion of the experience." The voice changers made everything the death demons said monotone and genderless.

"How long do you store my data?"

"Until the next person gets the same set of bracelets. Could be tomorrow, could be next week." Death Demon shrugged. "Please, lady, just step inside the curtain and hold your arms like this."

The curtain zipped closed behind Mo. A moment later, it opened. Mo was gone.

"Next!" Death Demon called.

Mickey ventured through the curtain.

The death demon eyed Ek and her prosthetic. "I don't—"

"Emotional support raven." It lacked panache when Mickey said it. Pris made the phrase sound awesome. Probably because Pris was awesome.

FORMLESS

"Is it alive?"

"ADA, can't ask questions."

"But—"

"ADA." Mickey extended her gleaming prosthetic, with the wristband marked "left" wrapped around it. "You can't ask questions about my disability."

Ek shifted from foot to foot, shuffled its wings, and glared with glowing red eyes.

"Mickey?" Pris called. "Everything okay? Do you need a lawyer?"

Thin black material covered the death demon's face so Mickey couldn't see its expression.

"Is everything okay in here?" she asked.

It nodded rapidly. "Can you, um, just remove your bird for the scan?"

Ek fluttered to her feet. Mickey held out her arms while cameras snapped her from every angle. She wondered if the operator could see her bones. Her deformity, stripped of flesh, looked horrifying—her ribs and spine twisted on the right, her left arm truncated at the elbow.

The demon grunted. "Your Fright Island experience begins now. Pull down your goggles and step out."

Mickey grabbed for Ek, replacing it on her shoulder. She pulled down the goggles. The next curtain opened.

She stepped into a dark cave.

FORMLESS

-3-

Giant bugs filled the cave.

Fluorescent, colorful crystals and mushrooms studded the cave walls. Tiny white salamanders scuttled about, blind from eons of darkness.

Charon's ferry still rumbled beneath Mickey's feet. But the waiting room's white-painted metal walls had vanished. The people who had stepped behind the curtain had vanished.

Mo had vanished.

Mickey's body clenched, and her breathing doubled in cadence.

Beetles, spiders, ants, and millipedes, human-sized and larger, skittered throughout the room and up the walls.

One of these horrible bugs had to be Mo.

The augmented reality illusion was almost seamless. If Mickey moved too fast, the AI painting this insect world over the real one stuttered, allowing the plain white ferry interior to blip through. As a graphic novelist, Mickey could appreciate how much thought had gone into making the insect world. And it wasn't even the only one the computers were generating in real time.

Mickey noticed a green and black segmented millipede. When she focused on the millipede, an informational dot informed her it was "Party member Mo."

She adjusted Ek and headed toward the millipede, who recoiled and then leaned forward. Mo's voice came through the induction pieces on Mickey's jaw as well as her ears. "Of course, that's you, Mickey."

Mickey didn't appear as a bug to herself. "What am I?"

"The three-headed dog Cerberus!"

"You are an amazingly hideous millipede." Mickey described Mo's virtual appearance.

"This is awful," Pris's voice said. A pink praying mantis approached. "I can't do this all day. No wonder people leave this place and say they hated it."

"You don't enjoy being a praying mantis?"

"I'm a praying mantis? Right, you picked bugs."

"No, you have butterfly wings, but you're person-shaped otherwise. Weird cryptid. Butterfly person? Angel? Flying alien?" Mo explained.

"Double bug," Pris studied her pink, pointy hands. "You guys are both awesome. Mickey, you're a flying bird-dinosaur hybrid with a tooth-filled beak. Mo, you're armor-plated with spikes on your head and tail. At least you have bubbles saying it's you guys, or I never would have found you. The jungle background is cool, right."

FORMLESS

"Yeah, the glowing crystal cave is also well-done."

"Evergreen forest," Mo waved her millipede limbs.

Beneath them, the ferry motor shifted.

Mickey's stomach sloshed. "I honestly don't know if I can do this all day. Be cooped up inside this thing."

Mo's bug arms took Mickey's prosthetic. Horrible. All this was horrible. The Mo-lipede led Mickey to a mushroom. They sat. The Pris-mantis followed.

"Listen," the millipede said. "I believe there's a way to turn off seeing each other like creatures. We'll figure it out. Or Geoffrey and Taylor will know. They took the earlier ferry over with Ananda."

"Ananda." Pris's big pink arms waved before her.

"Yeah." Mo's millipede legs drummed.

Mo had met Ananda; Mickey and Pris had not. Ananda studied aberrant genetics and had just gotten her PhD; Geoffrey and Taylor were both dating her. Twins. Figures. Mickey didn't know how to address the dating situation without embarrassing herself or upsetting her friends.

"They will figure out the headache problem for Lilli Lopez," Mo said. "Of course, if we get headaches, that will matter, but I'd rather do some ghost hunting with you guys. The allergic-reaction death-retraction story is suspect. If the ghost people have been seeing is that lady, and we can find her, we could ask her about it."

"I couldn't find out more about her death," Pris confessed. Her mantis arms flailed in distress. "I couldn't even figure out her name. Except for the retraction, there was no follow-up at all in the news. I wonder if Lilli covered it up."

Mickey shut her eyes. "I can guess why people get headaches and have a bad time. Overstimulation. My friends are weird bugs. The boat turned into a cave. You guys aren't seeing what I'm seeing; you have your own set of visions to deal with. It's sensory overload. No wonder they don't want children or anyone on the spectrum coming here." Ek shuffled on her shoulder.

"Fright Island recommends everyone in a group choose the same experience, but of course, we have to be contrary." Mo's antennae waved.

"We're the Contrary Crowcast, right." Mickey and Pris ran a paranormal podcast that had exploded in popularity last summer when they discovered real-life mermaids in Massachusetts, or rather, telepathic women who were half shark.

"Of course."

A death demon with an enormous scythe herded the insects out of the cave through a tunnel. The floor tilted and moved side to side under her feet; Mickey assumed it was the gangplank. She had zero boat knowledge; last summer's experience discovering mermaid-sharks barely counted. Some bugs flew out of the cave. Mickey admired the programming and artistry again, making people who were walking look as if they were flying. Maybe if she concentrated on this as an artistic endeavor it wouldn't be so bad.

More bugs gathered at the end of the tunnel in the early autumn sunlight. A green dragonfly hovered just off the ground beside a perfectly round daddy longlegs and a brown recluse spider.

"That's them, of course." Mo's voice vibrated into Mickey's bones through the goggles. Ek shifted again, feeling her unease.

"They are identical twins. Couldn't their bugness look identical?" Mickey complained, almost crying, as the two groups merged.

"Pterodactyl thing, duckbill thing, and ostrich thing."

"Bigfoot, reptilian, and chupacabra," Mo explained.

"Actually," the brown recluse said, "they aren't identical twins." The tiny pop-up identified her as "Party member Ananda."

"What?" That was how Ananda was going to introduce herself? Not hello? Mickey couldn't believe it. She also had no idea what Ananda meant. Even after all this time, she had trouble sometimes telling them apart. She felt bad, because it seemed as if she couldn't identify them because they were Korean and not because they were twins.

"We are rare and special," said the daddy longlegs, who the pop-up identified as Geoffrey. "We're perfect mirror-image twins. Ananda figured it out during her twins study."

"My organs are all reversed. My heart is on the right. Who knew that was possible?" the dragonfly, Taylor, said.

"I knew it was possible, of course," Mo said. Her voice sounded like she was frowning. The millipede was not frowning.

Mickey hated everything and already wanted to leave. She found a crystal-studded mushroom and plopped herself on it. She wondered how she appeared to everyone else. Was this fun? She had never been to a theme park before. Now she knew why. "This is a nightmare."

"It's a horror theme park." The dragonfly buzzed to her side.

"No," Mickey shook her head. "It's sensory overload. I can't deal. That's all your friend Lilli needs to know. People are freaking out and having a bad time 'cause it's too much. I need to see my friends. You're a dragonfly. I can't read your face. You might as well be a stranger. Your brother is a daddy longlegs. Pris is a praying mantis with enormous arms. I need to turn this part off."

"All right, that's doable, I think. We'll go to a marked way station where they can turn it off for friends only. Does anyone else want it gone?"

The bugs exchanged glances.

"Maybe I want it turned off for friends. I don't know," Mo said. Many of her legs waved.

"It's a bit much," Pris confessed. "It sounds like fun on paper, but it's confusing. I don't mind strangers being dinosaurs, but I like to see you guys."

The daddy longlegs said, "It's supposed to be a seamless, immersive experience. It's ruined if you see me as boring Geoffrey."

"Then I won't have the full experience. Oh well." Mickey crossed her arms, flesh over metal. "I can't. I won't. In fact—" She pushed up her goggles.

Geoffrey grabbed her arm and repositioned them. "That sets off an alarm. Don't."

"An alarm? That's ridiculous." His spidery face loomed. She couldn't breathe. She knew his human hands were touching her arm, but she saw spider legs. "I can't do this." Mickey ducked away.

Immediately she got caught in the crowd around Charon's ferry, skittering insects crawling and flying around her like a nightmare. Whoever had designed this horror theme park, at least the insect world simulation part, had done a great job. Mickey staggered with anxiety. Black spots converged on her sight. She allowed herself to be turned around.

"The dead park guest had a heart attack," Mickey announced, fighting her way back to the nightmares her friends appeared to be. "From insane levels of overwhelming overkill."

"I think it's fun, of course." Lots of Mo's legs waved. "But I understand why it's not working for you. I'm right behind you. We will walk to the way station to turn off your AR option for friends."

The way station was a mushroom-shaped hut in a long row of fungus and logs along Elm Street, the main thoroughfare. As they entered, one worker was talking about the need for extra first aid supplies, "what with all the recent injuries."

Mickey expected the workers to be demons, but these were more bugs: worker ants, with pop-ups showing they were "park assistors," a horrible title.

"Adjust our group AR, please," Geoffrey instructed the slightly taller bug, holding out his wrist to be scanned.

"All of you? Or just you?" The worker ant's wrist emitted a laser light against his wristband.

"For just her. Turn hers off." The daddy longlegs pointed to Mickey.

She held out her right bracelet. The bug's arm squirted light. A moment later, her friends reappeared. "Oh. Oh." Her heart rate and breathing immediately slowed.

FORMLESS

"Anyone else?" The worker ant held up its glowing arm.

After a brief conference, everyone else agreed to keep the feature on for now. As they left the mushroom, Geoffrey said, "Most people keep their AR fully on, from what Lilli told us. We want to replicate the most common experience."

"What about the lady who died? What happened to her? I would like to know." Pris adjusted her goggles as they exited into the bright sunlight.

"What does she matter? We aren't here about her," Ananda replied. The oldest of their group, she might have been thirty, with skin as dark as Mo's, who was herself half Jamaican. As revealed by the AR headset, her sharp Indian features were handsome rather than pretty. She wore calf-length khaki-green leggings with a matching shirt in a darker hue. A tiny golden stud pierced her left nostril.

If Pris had been a hedgehog, she would have prickled. Her cropped pink hair already stood on end in its usual style. "Maybe you don't realize, but Mickey and I are known for our paranormal podcast. Visiting a place where someone recently died under mysterious circumstances is kind of our thing, right? And what if she's the ghost some people saw? That dead lady matters to us. And to our fans."

Ananda's mouth turned down and her nose flared. "Lilli invited us here to assess why people are unhappy at the park and getting headaches, not play with fake ghosts."

Taylor lifted his hands and said to Ananda, "Hey—" and at the same moment, Geoffrey said to her, "Don't."

"I can multitask." Mo put her hands on her hips. "I can be a mad scientist, a podcaster, a bug, a dinosaur, and who knows what else while I'm here. I have held hands with a shark, and I swim with mermaids, of course." She pulled her braids over one shoulder, rubbing the beads with her thumb.

"Listen to dinosaur Mo, right. The chances of us getting headaches are slim. We can monitor that and look for ghosts at the same time. Just because Mickey and I don't have a million advanced degrees like the four of you doesn't make us idiots. We have great observational skills. While we search for the ghost, we will also notice if anyone isn't having a good time or is rubbing their head a lot."

Ananda's mouth turned down further in a way that caused a rock to form in Mickey's stomach. She wanted to like her friends' girlfriend. But Ananda seemed determined to drive a wedge between the halves of their group.

Trying to salvage the day, Mickey motioned to the park map on the mushroom's side. "Shall we stick together and go on every ride?"

FORMLESS

"What ride did the dead lady fall off?" Pris ran her finger over the map.

"She died of an allergic reaction," Ananda retorted. "I thought we dropped that subject."

Geoffrey traced the outline of the island. "Let's start with the Horrorail. It loops around the whole park giving us a bird's-eye view. Maybe we'll get an idea of what to do next."

"You want a bird's-eye view?" Ek lifted off Mickey's shoulder. "Wasn't that the point of bringing Ek?"

"Emotional support bird, right?" Pris tilted her head as Ek rose.

"That's your creation?" Ananda peered at Ek.

"An extremely modified version," Geoffrey explained. "We made three AI bird-drones in corvid form and gave them to Pris to test out last summer. It turned out that Mickey had limited control over the drones—that was when her upgraded neural net started to connect to all sorts of things—"

"Mermaids." Pris fake coughed.

"Prehistoric shark-gods," Mo agreed.

"My car." Pris coughed again.

Geoffrey continued, "We customized one and gave it to her as a pet."

Mickey closed her eyes, instructing Ek through her neural net, and loosed the mechanical raven. It soared above the island. She watched it fly, then rotated her shoulder, freed from the bird's weight. The tiny ping of connection between her and the drone hovered at her mind's edge. She saw through its eyes, and could switch back and forth with a little effort, but it did give her vertigo.

As long as Mickey's friends were people, she didn't care if other park attendees were insects. It enhanced the fun. She didn't need to interact with those other bugs; they were simply background, although she did plan to eavesdrop on their conversations for signs of headaches and general unpleasant experiences. Just having her friends look like themselves eased her anxiety.

The Horrorail cars flashed by, trailed by shrieks and screams.

"I guess that's next," Mo touched her beads.

FORMLESS
-4-

Is this supposed to be a roller coaster, a monorail, or what?" Ananda stood at the front of the line for the Horrorail. Fright Island was small—you might even say exclusive—and the lines were short.

"Yes." Taylor took her hand.

She had long, elegant fingers. "Did I tell you I don't enjoy theme parks?"

"Yes." Geoffrey held her other hand. "But you bravely came along anyway, just to be with us."

Mo shook her braids and said in an undertone to Pris and Mickey, "Is this weird? Of course, I don't want to make it weird if it's not."

"It works for them, right. Like how you eat carbs and date men, and I don't eat carbs and date women."

"I guess."

Mickey Crow didn't date anyone, first because she was short and strange-looking, with her metal arm, twisted back, and malformed rib-cage. Second, she hated being touched and had claustrophobia and anxiety attacks. All those issues combined made her less than desirable, and Mickey was okay with that. She was happy when her friends were happy. She knew Geoffrey and Taylor from college, when the budding robotics team decided to make a kick-ass prosthetic for a one-armed girl. Sometimes, the twins acted like one person split in half, so it made perfect sense for them to have one girlfriend. Learning they were mirror images, right down to Taylor's organs being on the opposite side, wasn't all that surprising, actually.

Geoffrey often said, in total seriousness, that he had figured out extremely early in life—pre-birth—that he couldn't accomplish everything by himself, so he had manifested Taylor while in the womb. Their mother even had a very early ultrasound that appeared to only show one fetus, which seemed to back up his story.

The rolling mushroom cars of the Horrorail stopped. Insects climbed, scurried, and flew out. They seemed to be having a good time. None touched their head parts with their arm parts or complained as they moved on to their next adventure in the park.

The worker ants motioned Mickey and her friends into the mush-rooms in pairs. Awkward. They had aligned themselves into two groups of three.

Mickey climbed into the first mushroom. The worker ant inspect-ed her prosthetic's reinforced leather straps. "This will stay on? We aren't responsible if it flies off or gets damaged." The ant's voice was synthetically changed to be sexless, like the death demons.

FORMLESS

"My prosthetic is secure," Mickey lied. Last summer, a shiver of mermaid-sharks had attacked her, torn it off, and damaged it. The worker ant didn't need to know that.

The ride's designers intended the seatbelt for people more symmetrical than Mickey, but the ant strapped her in tightly, and Pris beside her. If the ant recognized the famous socialite from her billionaire family's reality television show, it was well-trained enough not to remark on that.

Strange, ugly plants filled the area around the embarkation station. The augmented reality mushrooms and crystals that some designer had decided went with the bug world were mixed in with the plants. The living plants were a dark, sickly shade of green, with a gray overtone that might be AR.

One tree of a cluster had fallen, with seamless augmentation. Mickey did not know what was really underneath. A small animal lurked between two plant pots, making the leaves rustle.

The worker ant finished strapping them in. It used a communication unit to summon another worker ant. "One of the trash cans is down again," the ant said in its gravelly computer voice. "No, I didn't see what did it. Trash everywhere. It was okay a few minutes ago."

As their car inched forward, an identical worker ant lifted the fallen tree trunk, searching the area. The small animal scurried away.

Behind Mickey and Pris, Mo sat with Geoffrey, and in the third mushroom, Taylor with Ananda. If Geoffrey felt slighted at sitting with his employee instead of his girlfriend, he stayed silent.

The sound induction pieces vibrated Mickey's jawbone wordlessly. Her stomach roiled.

"I think we're in a mushroom," Mickey said to Pris. "You?"

"A cage."

"Sideshow exhibit trailer." Mo leaned forward.

"Cage," Geoffrey agreed with Pris. "The three of us also chose dinosaurs. Trying for some continuity."

"A giant worker ant strapped me in. All the employees are worker ants."

"Hunter."

"Bigfoot. Lots of Bigfoots here. Bigfeet? What is the plural of that?"

"Big game hunter, yup, like those *Jurassic Park* movies."

When the remaining cars had filled with insects, the mushroom cars rattled along the wooden tracks, gaining speed. Although the park was new, moss and plants covered the dilapidated tracks. Mickey hoped it was part of the illusion. She couldn't tell if this was really a wooden coaster.

FORMLESS

The park spread on her right, a vast stone bowl filled with scuttling bugs, mushrooms, rotting logs, gray plants, and glowing crystals. To her left were Pris and Long Island Sound. Prehistoric insect-like creatures filled the water. Marine biologist Mo would know their names, but Mo would be seeing something else.

Ek flew nearby, its red LED eyes even with hers as the mushroom car ascended a peak. The robotic bird wasn't sentient; it was programmed with simulated AI and whatever Mickey herself put into it. But sometimes, something in the bird seemed to look back at her. "I'm okay, Ek." The raven wheeled off.

The mushroom car fell down the moldy wooden ramp, wheels churning. Bits of moss and broken wood flew into the air. The ramp's sides curved up and around the mushroom, solidified into a tunnel lined with clear acrylic, and the mushroom plunged underwater.

Mickey's heart seized and her breath stuttered. She was terrified of being underwater. The events of last summer had only exacerbated that. All that water weighing on her. Even though the water wasn't touching her and she was inside the thick acrylic tube, the plastic could break at any time. It was only plastic, after all. Then she would be trapped, and the water would explode onto her and drown her with great force, smashing her to death. Somewhere deep inside, buried in her infant memories, she knew she must remember being crushed at birth.

While she shook in terror, prehistoric marine insects swarmed the mushroom car, animated versions of fossils, round creatures larger than Mickey's head with extruded tentacles glowing like moon jellyfish. The tentacled critters looked carnivorous and hungry. Giant crustaceans, shrimp-like or lobster-like, drifted further off, also ravenous. Why had she chosen bugs? Why had she thought bugs weren't scary?

Her neural net pinged. Ek, searching because she was out of range underwater. Mickey tried to open the channel a little wider, but being in the throes of anxiety and claustrophobia made it difficult for her to relax.

The connection didn't precisely feel like Ek. She *was* underwater, though. A mermaid may have come this far from Shell Beach and recognized her, or maybe one of their shark-siblings.

Hello? She sent some familiar pictures she used to communicate greetings with the half-shark mermaids.

Whatever it was, it scrambled out of her head. Weird. Not Ek and not mermaids or shark-siblings. Her jawbone still vibrated; was that the headset or the neural net?

The mushroom car's trajectory shot it out of the water, onto rickety wooden rails damp with rot and covered in moss, like a railroad abandoned in the woods for a hundred years. The ride resumed roller-coaster mode, dipping and looping above the park and the water, giving a glimpse of the future expansions, other skeletal islands still being fleshed out—or was that more virtual reality? Even the odors were correct—mold and wet wood mixed with decaying plants. How did they do that?

Ek flew beside the car, giving Mickey a side-eyed stare as if the drone knew that something unusual had tried to get inside her head under the water. Or maybe it felt the strange vibration through the neural net.

"Swimming dinosaur skeletons!" Pris shouted at Mickey as if they weren't strapped together in a mushroom car. "So cool! What did you see?"

"Prehistoric bugs." But what hadn't she seen? What had been trying to get into her head this time?

She still felt nauseated.

FORMLESS

-5-

noticed games and concession stands over there," Geoffrey pointed them out as they disembarked. "Do you think they are important?"

"The dead lady might have been poisoned by something. That's why she fell off the ride," Mickey offered, thinking of her own oddly woozy stomach. The scariest tall ride was the Horrorail, so if the lady had really fallen off a ride, it was most likely that one. Although, given how tightly that worker ant had strapped Mickey in, she didn't see how it was possible, unless the lady had unstrapped herself on purpose. Anything was possible, but that didn't feel right.

"Mickey isn't wrong." Mo stroked her braids. "She had an allergic reaction. Most likely, it was something she ate." She turned to the frowning Indian woman. "I know, Ananda, you don't care. But we do."

"We don't know what she was allergic to. I couldn't get into her medical records." Pris's pale pink mouth pursed. "Although I never tried to get into medical records before. Having her name would have helped."

"That's all useless speculation. It's wasting time," Ananda waved her hand. "Did you notice anyone getting off the ride with us or before us complaining or acting like they had a headache?"

No one had.

If Ananda hadn't been present, Mickey would have mentioned that someone—something?—had tried to get into her mind through the neural net, although it probably had no bearing on the headaches or the dead woman.

But Ananda wasn't friendly. Mickey didn't know how much the other woman knew about the implants and the neural net. Ananda's specialty was genetics, which didn't intersect at all with Mickey's neural net, but Ananda also didn't work for Gemini Robotics Systems, and the tech in Mickey's head was proprietary to Gemini.

Mickey allowed the moment to pass. She rubbed her jaw and swallowed. "I feel a little sick to my stomach, but I'm also claustrophobic, so I think it's related to that," she confessed.

Geoffrey inspected the park map on the nearest mushroom. "There's a haunted house we can wander through. Ana, would you like that? It looks pretty big." She nodded, looping an arm through his.

"Of course, we want to see everything," Mo said. "Lead the way to the haunted house."

FORMLESS

-6-

The haunted house, officially known as the Cursed Cave, towered above them, a giant rotten tree stump with window holes gnawed through it, mushrooms and fungus growing all over and around it. The stump was at least three stories high; Mickey found it hard to judge.

Ek landed on the top edge. If the building had been a castle, that spot would have been a crenellation. Mickey's neural net pinged. She felt watched; the hairs on her arm and the back of her neck crinkled. The bird peered down. It was getting more intelligent; it felt different against her mind. The connection itched. Mickey reached with her flesh hand to scratch her neck, where the embedded magnets held the neural net to her skull.

Ananda's head swiveled. "Do you have a headache, Mickey?" Her voice was almost gloating.

"My neural connections are itchy. That happens when a person has metal bits implanted in their skull. Do you *want* me to have a headache?"

Geoffrey peered at Ananda as she answered. "Well, it would be helpful if someone in our group …"

"You want me to be in pain?" Mickey's voice sounded louder than she meant. Her jawbone vibrated.

Lichens, moss, mushroom clusters, and ugly live plants with gray overtones hid the bottom of the upright log building. A half dozen bugs—spiders, a hornet, and a stink bug—stood talking on the gravel walkway. They stared at Mickey's outburst. A colorful jumping spider rubbed its head. Mickey turned to Ananda, but she didn't seem to notice.

A pill bug the size of a fat cat skittered out of the lichen and across the path, vacuuming up a piece of trash one of the visiting bugs had dropped. It kept going behind a mushroom hut.

Another round, gray pill bug-like creature stayed back in a mushroom cluster, presumably waiting for someone else to spill something. Mickey tried to see it, but her eyes didn't focus well through the goggles—the augmented reality algorithm only showed what it wanted her to see. The cleaning pill bugs were obviously optional.

She kept forcing herself to see it, and the deep noise started again in her jawbone.

Everything else was effortless to see, yet that one pill bug stayed warped and hidden.

Mickey must have frozen in place because Pris asked, "Are you okay? What are you staring at?"

FORMLESS

Mickey shook her head, trying to get free of the vibration in her jaw that made her feel sick. "Did you see that robotic cleaner a minute ago? It looked like a giant pill bug to me."

"Maybe? So many awesome dinosaurs. I'm not paying attention. I might have chosen poorly. They are fascinating and distracting. I forget to look for ghosts and headaches."

"I saw a jackalope." Mo pointed. "It ate a piece of trash and went over there."

"There's another one in that peculiar bush." Mickey motioned with her metal hand. "Have you noticed that all the plants are ugly? Gray and half dead? Is it the AR?"

"Are the plants weird?" Pris inspected one. "I just figured it was the programming. They have this odd monochrome overlay, like ghost plants."

"Botany isn't my specialty, of course," Mo admitted, touching a gray leaf. "There aren't any plants here I would want in a pot in my house, that's for sure."

"Well, however weird the plants are, there's a critter hiding there. Look."

"We aren't supposed to be trying to see through the illusion, right. Ruins the fun."

"Maybe it's an energy-sucking fey?" Mickey suggested Pris's imaginary arch-nemesis. "But check it out. It's as if the thing is hiding. Why would anything or anyone be hiding here?"

"An energy-sucking fey could live forever here," Pris crouched to peer into the lichen. "So many electronic devices for it to suck on. What am I looking for?"

"A giant pill bug."

"A jackalope."

"I don't know what either of those things is."

"Something sized like a big cat or small dog," Mo explained.

The pill bug shifted. "It knows we're talking about it. It's moving." Mickey pointed.

Taylor, Geoffrey, and Ananda wandered from their intense conversation to see what the others were studying.

"What's going on?" Ananda peered at the lichen.

Mickey said, "I saw a pill bug eat trash, which was mildly interesting; now there's another in the lichen, acting weird. Can you see it?"

"I saw a little dinosaur pick up trash, yes." She crouched, hands on khaki knees, to peer into the lichen. "I see something shiny and black, but I don't think it's a dinosaur. It's too round."

"A pill bug is round." Mickey's neural net pinged, and she leaned back. Ek remained perched on top of the vertical log and didn't seem interested in her. She opened up again, hoping that there were unfamiliar mermaids around, ones who didn't respond to the usual hailing images.

But she felt poked. Probed. Hailed. She flashed back to last summer when she first contacted the mermaids and how that had felt inside her head. She pulled at her lip in frustration.

"What's wrong?" Pris asked.

"My neural net keeps pinging. I thought maybe some mermaids were around, but they aren't answering. It's not Ek either."

The brothers exchanged glances. "Could it be mermaids that aren't part of the Shell Beach group?" Geoffrey asked.

"That's why they aren't answering you?" Taylor continued. He gnawed at his lip.

"Why would they even ping me if they don't know me?" Mickey countered, even as her net pinged again. She cupped the back of her head with her metal hand. Her jaw ached. "This is annoying."

"Is it a headache?" Ananda wondered without moving from the lichen.

"No. It doesn't hurt. It's difficult to explain."

Ananda snorted and leaned forward. "There is definitely no dinosaur back here, just something black and shiny."

Pris reached into her pink tank top and pulled out her tiny camera. "It's not a ghost, but—"

"You can't!" Geoffrey held out his hand as if he could block anyone else from seeing the camera. "Put that away. How did you smuggle that in?"

"In my bra. It's one of your new 3D-printed ones. We thought they'd be low-profile enough to get past any security." Pris adjusted her tank top. She turned on the camera and squinted at the screen as it chimed. "Hmm."

"Yeah," Geoffrey said. "They don't tell you, but you can't see the LCD through the AR goggles."

"What?" Pris shook the little plastic camera and peered at it again.

"A filter in the lenses," Taylor explained. "You can't see screens properly. Just in case someone should smuggle in a phone or camera. Not that anyone would dream of doing that, or of trying to bypass the rules by using 3D printing."

"That's just plain wrong, that LCD loophole." Pris aimed the camera at the creature in the lichen. "But true. I can't see a thing on the screen."

"Take the picture anyway." Mo hooked her chin on Pris's shoulder. "Is it like those privacy shields you can put in front of your computer screen?"

FORMLESS

"I don't know what I'm taking a picture of." Pris clicked the shutter button. "No idea what that will look like."

"All this is proprietary," Geoffrey reminded her. "You aren't supposed to take photos. You signed a release when you agreed to come here."

"They invited us here." Pris tucked the camera back into her neon-pink bra. "This is stupid and pointless if I can't even take any photos or videos. Mickey and I need video for the Contrary Crowcast."

Mo stuck her fingers under her goggles and rubbed. "Wearing these goggles over glasses isn't comfortable, even with these oversized ones. You did the right thing, Taylor, wearing your contact lenses. I wish I could get used to wearing them, but I hate having things in my eyes."

Ananda straightened and focused on Mo. "Headache?"

"You asking every minute about headaches is giving me a headache. If I had a headache, I would tell you, of course. My face hurts from wearing goggles on top of glasses. I don't consider that a headache."

"Hmph," Ananda made an unhappy noise.

"Can we go inside now?" Pris asked. "If this black thing is an energy-sucking fey, it will still be here when we come out. I'm not sure it's anything at all. I think it's a video artifact from the augmentation."

Mickey disagreed. The pill bug, whatever it was underneath, was studying her. That was illogical. It was a cleaning robot, not AI. It lacked sentience. Or maybe she just wanted to have another significant, famous discovery, find mermaids again.

"What is this place supposed to be?" Mo asked as they approached the doorway.

"It's the Cursed Cave," Geoffrey replied. "The original heart of this theme park."

FORMLESS

-7-

The Cursed Cave lived up to its name. A cavern filled with mushrooms, glowing crystals, bugs, scorpions, and spiders. Everything had a glowing blacklight effect.

People dressed in black seemed to pass in front of Mickey, invisible because of augmented reality, edited out. AR added other objects that weren't there.

It was surreal.

A woman could have fallen to her death inside this disorientating building, but from where? There didn't appear to be balconies or overhangs. As she walked along the edge of the first space, something brushed Mickey's leg. She jumped, but nothing was there—nothing she could see. This was anxiety-inducing to the highest order. She liked to know where she was, what was going on, and who was around her. Like her friends, labeled handily, but also strangers, human-sized insects, and worker ants.

Her neural net pinged; so annoying. If she could shout through the connection to whoever, whatever was trying to reach her, she would have. But Gemini Robotics Systems didn't design the net to be a communication device; what happened with the mermaids had been a fluke—no one knew mermaids had telepathy or that mermaids were real, for that matter. The neural net simply controlled the lovely prosthetic arm Gemini had fashioned, and allowed her to direct Ek, the bird-drone they created.

The cave floor's glowing dots showed the way forward. This was just the anteroom, and Mickey already felt disoriented, between the pinging of the neural net and the inaudible sounds coming through her jaw. She had forgotten where the entrance was. Forward was the only way out.

"Lilli told me the park was originally just going to be an elaborate escape room reconfigured using augmented reality," Geoffrey explained. "Much smaller than an entire theme park, smaller than this building. Their plans evolved as their ideas did. The grandiose escape room is still a possibility now that they have the tech."

"They bought a haunted island instead of a building to reconfigure, of course." Mickey couldn't see Mo's expression, but she sounded angry. She snorted and threw her braids around until the beads clicked.

"What?" Pris stopped walking up the dark ramp. Mickey crashed into her back.

"The Natives called this island, well, the main core of it before Lilli's people expanded it, the Forbidden Island. Legend says that it drove anyone who set foot on it mad."

FORMLESS

"And here we are." Mickey backed away from being plastered against Pris. "With our feet on their sacred ground." She glanced down. "If I knew my family history, I might know more about this. How did the island drive people crazy?" Although people often commented that Mickey looked Native American, she had no idea if that was true. She was a foundling before her parents adopted her.

"It talked to people. Reading their thoughts inside their heads, it made them insane. It didn't seem to affect white folks though, so the legend died. Until recently, the island remained owned by a local tribe and was private property."

"Well, you're safe from mind-reading insanity, Pris, as the only white person in our group," Ananda said, her lips tight. Perhaps it was supposed to be a joke, but it sounded mean.

Pris snorted like a bull. "Good old white privilege. I love being a white, Protestant, heterosexual man. Oh wait, I'm only one of those things." Her voice got progressively louder.

"Hey," Taylor bit his cheek and raised his hands. "We're all friends here."

Other bugs looked in their direction.

Trying to change the subject back to Ananda's favorite, Mickey suggested, "Perhaps the island talking to people is what's giving them headaches."

"Islands don't talk to people." Ananda lifted her chin. The black light made her nose piercing glow.

"There are things you wouldn't believe, Ananda. Pris and I run a paranormal podcast, remember? We keep our minds open."

They stumbled around in the cave. The upright log hadn't seemed very large from the outside, and the inside was a series of illusions. As an artist, Mickey recognized tricks of perspective that made things look farther away or larger than they were. The combination of other disoriented park guests and workers with scripts created an insane environment.

A few steps away, people—spiders, bees, wasps, centipedes—were inappropriately huge or small. Noises were louder than they should be, vibrating through her jawbone in a stomach-churning way.

Voices overlapped, whispering, yelling, cajoling.

"The hive, the hive, the hive," one high-pitched voice cried, in a tone between begging and sobbing.

"Die!" a man repeatedly shouted. With that came a hissing sound like a giant snake and a horrible smell. Bug spray.

"Let us in," a smooth robotic voice said. Something that sounded generated, inhuman. "Let us in. If you can hear us, let us in." After a pause, it simply chanted, "In, in, in."

FORMLESS

The cheekpieces vibrated painfully with so much sound coming through at once. The revolting fake bug spray's odor burned her tongue. Mickey reeled, disoriented, with all her senses assaulted at once. It could not get any worse.

A buzzing arose, quiet, far away, getting closer. Mickey was a bug in a bug's world, by choice. She wasn't afraid of any fake bug.

She kept moving up the spiraling narrow ramp. Mushrooms and crystals glowed around her. Her bones hummed.

The buzzing approached.

Murder hornets, larger than humans, stingers as long as her arm, boiled from the corridor ahead.

She fled, along with everyone else, into a different cave system, heart pounding.

"This is making me sick to my stomach with dizziness." Mo rubbed her ears and around the induction pieces. "My ears are all messed up inside. No, it's not a headache." She snapped the last words.

All the combined sound, movement, and odor were impossible to process. Mickey collapsed on a crystal cluster to rub her shoulder under its leather harness. What the seat looked like to her eyes and what it felt like under her butt were utterly different. She moved her leg, trying to figure it out. A sharp part scratched her shin, and she yelped.

"Mickey, what happened?" Pris jumped to her side in a moment.

"I bumped my leg on something sharp when I sat down." She pointed at the dark spot, like a bruise, then realized that Pris couldn't see it. "It feels like there might be a splinter in there."

"Sorry." Pris touched her leg, feeling her calf. Mickey winced. "Right, you're bleeding. Do you want to head to the first aid hut?"

"I don't think we can turn around." The building felt like a one-way setup, designed to herd them through like animals going to slaughter. Nor did she want to go back through the murder hornets and the badgering voices.

Mickey stood and took a step, flinching. "I can walk on it. When we get out, I'll go get it cleaned and get a bandage."

Pris kept touching the crystal cluster that Mickey had sat on. "Weird that I can't find anything sharp where you were sitting."

"I must have sat down just right."

"Do you want me to look at it? Marine biologist here."

"I'm not a fish, Mo, and there's not much to see in the dark through AR. You can check when we get outside, if you feel up to it. Maybe we can get nausea medicine at the first aid mushroom."

Ananda crossed her arms. "This is getting weird."

FORMLESS
-8-

The ramp spiraled up and down. The crowning room had a glass ceiling covered with gray plants, and Ek waited outside, peering down at Mickey. She rubbed the short, deep cut on her leg, more of a gouge, still oozing blood.

Mo blindly groped Mickey's leg, searching for the wound, then palpated it lightly. Her face was pale. "That's gonna leave a scar."

"Are you still dizzy?" Mickey didn't want to look at the hole in her calf anymore.

"It's the ringing in my ears. Like the morning after a concert."

Ananda nodded. "I think it's from straining to listen because it's so dark in all the rooms. I almost hear something like that too. My ears trying to hear more because my eyes aren't trusting what they see."

"Hmm." Pris offered her hand to a bug, either a park guest or an unlabeled employee, who she obviously saw as a dinosaur, as if she was trying to make friends. "Maybe the island is trying to talk to you all. I mean, it's clearly ignoring me because I'm white. I must be the control."

Ananda turned to Geoffrey, who was massaging his arm. "Are your ears ringing, Geoff?"

"Hm? No, but I scratched myself a little. I think this building isn't very safe. I want to document these injuries for Lilli while they are fresh. Maybe they have a compatible camera at the first aid kiosk, one we can see with the goggles on."

Taylor poked his brother's arm. "I banged my leg on something, too. But then again, I was distracted. My imagination's been carrying me away since Mo told that story about the island being banned."

"What do you mean?" Mo rubbed her cheekbones under the goggles.

"I don't know; it's stupid. I was wondering what an island would say if it could talk. What it would sound like. It would be lonely if people made it forbidden."

Ananda tilted her head and squished up her lips. "You think the island talked to you?"

Taylor laughed. "No, of course not. But you know when you think about something too much …" he trailed off. "And then you don't know if it's real."

"Let's change the subject to something more cheerful," Mo said. "Mickey, what good emergency room stories have your parents told you lately?"

Mickey shook her head and looked up at Ek. "All doom and gloom. They're about ready to give it up. Not being doctors, but working in emergency medicine. My mom lost a teenager who came in wicked sick, in awful shape, far down the organ transplant list, and she couldn't help him. If healthy people aren't dying in accidents, there aren't any organs. It's terrible. And my dad had this little girl with cancer come in. She was having problems eating, and while he was calling in her oncologist, she just slipped away. They come home frustrated and sad, and there I am like a lump in their basement taking up space in my troll cave."

"Hey," Pris said. "You were a wicked messed-up baby in their emergency department, and they saved you. Better yet, they kept you, adopted you. You aren't a waste of space. They chose you."

Mo lightly put her hand over the harness on Mickey's left shoulder.

"That wasn't cheerful at all." Ananda wrinkled her nose so much that it looked as if her stud would pop out.

"It was real, though," Geoffrey said.

Taylor chewed on his cheek. "At Gemini, we thought about creating artificial organs. Animal organs are just passing the buck to another species. And there's still the whole rejection thing with animal organs."

"Growing human organs from scratch is the solution," Ananda waved her arms, suddenly animated. "CRISPR. Could grow back your arm, even." She gestured at Mickey.

"I wouldn't know what to do if I had my arm. It's been gone since I was a premature infant."

In Mickey's dreams, she had matching arms. Sometimes both were flesh, sometimes metal. She never talked about those dreams to anyone.

They passed back into darkness, heading down the spiral through waving fronds of glowing fungus. Deep, repetitive noises like drums thudded in her ears or through the bone-induction plates—Mickey couldn't tell. Her cheeks ached.

Having just an augmented reality escape room might have been better than a whole park. This was too much. Everything about this day was too much, especially the unreasonable and false hope of a new arm offered by Ananda. Not in her lifetime.

Grinding, crunching noises reverberated. Carpenter ants had eaten the old wooden shed in her parents' yard one year, ants that had spread from a sick tree on a neighboring property. The huge black ants at their shed banquet had been audible from several feet away. That same chomping noise came into Mickey's ears and jaw, but vaster, as if giant carpenter ants were ingesting the whole log building.

Perhaps the helper ants had transformed into something larger, hungrier. All the movement Mickey saw was out of the corners of her eyes; when she turned, she saw nothing. Her friends talked among themselves, seemingly unmenaced by hungry ants. What was analogous in their augmented programming? Why was nothing happening to them?

Her injured calf still hurt. Something low brushed against her, perhaps another trash robot, bumping into the injury, pressing on it. Mickey yelped and grabbed at a cluster of crystals, almost falling over when nothing was there to hold.

The injury burned. Had the trash robot contaminated the wound with garbage juice? Mickey, limping, had fallen behind her friends along the curve of the steep spiral ramp. She wondered about wheelchair compliance and realized her brain was going hysterical. She was on an island that her presumed ancestors had proclaimed forbidden and Taylor said had been lonely. Well, it had plenty of visitors now. It should be happy.

"Hey! Guys?" Mickey was really hobbling now, almost dragging her leg. Earlier, it had felt as if it had a splinter inside, but that feeling had dissipated. Maybe the bleeding had washed the contamination out? The pain remained.

Because of the odd nature of the log, with ramps going up and down randomly, she couldn't tell how much farther it would be until she was outside. Maybe she should have tried to return through the front door when she had first cut herself. She hoped she didn't need stitches. The wound definitely needed attention.

Mickey stumbled. This wasn't good. In fact, it was terrible. No one had come back when she had called. She called again, louder. She didn't see any helper ants or the kinds of bugs that indicated other park guests. Ravenous carpenter ant noises flooded her ears. Were the others hearing something as loud?

Her calf felt cored. Blood oozed down her leg, hot, wet, gross. If she stopped and sat, someone would come back for her, right? But she would keep bleeding, making a mess, and it would hurt more. And that noise, that endless chewing, how long could she stand it?

She stumbled into the wall, and the straps to her prosthetic got caught on something. That had never happened before.

Mickey was stuck to the fake cave wall by her fake arm. It was like a bad joke.

The chewing noises intensified.

"Hey! Help!"

She yanked.

The strap broke. Mickey tumbled to the floor.

FORMLESS
-9-

The warm, squishy pill bug investigated her. That was weird because wasn't it just some kind of cleaning robot? This augmented reality went above and beyond; Mickey had thought it would be sight and sound, perhaps a squirt of smell.

A soft robot that smelled like heating oil and wet rocks didn't fit the bug narrative.

She opened her eyes. The goggles had gone askew around her temples. They flashed red and beeped with a recorded warning telling her to put them back on.

Mickey lay sprawled in a wooden room decorated with stuck-on decals printed with long numbers and QR codes. Each decal had a bump in the center, presumably the chip that the goggles fixated on.

Something scuttled away.

Considering how dark the cave illusion was, Mickey was surprised at how well-lit the space was in reality. She wondered if the worker ants all saw the room as it was. Plain plywood everywhere, except for a bench. How boring.

Mickey staggered to her feet, heading for the bench. Her prosthetic slipped, heavy and unbalanced with a broken strap, straining her shoulder and elbow joint. It had become misaligned with the electronic connections on her body that linked it to her neural net; without its links to the neural net, she no longer had control of its more delicate movements. She hoisted the metal hand onto her right shoulder and held the whole contraption across her chest as she examined the damage to see if there was still a way to reconfigure the straps. Gemini Robotics Systems could repair it, but not here.

It would thrill Ananda to hear that Mickey was now having a terrible time.

And where were her friends?

"Pris! Mo!"

The sound of running feet. But it wasn't her friends; it was two park employees. Since she didn't have goggles on, they didn't look like worker ants, just regular people in overalls with plastic cuffs on their wrists and ankles. No goggles. That answered that question.

"You removed your goggles," the girl said, oblivious to Mickey's distress. "Please put them back on."

"I'm injured," Mickey protested. She didn't have a spare hand to pull the goggles down. "They dislodged when I tripped over something."

The other employee was older, a man, but not a manager type. "She *is* holding her arm, Meg."

FORMLESS

"Chuck, she's not wearing her goggles. That's the rules."

"Miss, can you put on your goggles? Then we'll help you."

Mickey stared. Her face felt naked. "That's backward."

Meg frowned. "There is nothing you can trip over. Everything is virtual except the benches. Goggles."

Wow. Well, Taylor and Geoffrey could report this to Lilli. This couldn't be what the park had in mind as a policy when a guest was injured. Comfort, not confront. Mickey raised her left knee to hold her prosthetic against her chest. She used her right hand to pull down the goggles. They flashed red against her eyes and vibrated against the bone inductors, warning that she had removed them.

Chuck scanned her wrist. A moment later, the flashing and alarm cut off. Another irritating thing that could provoke headaches or at least a massive annoyance.

"What seems to be your trouble, Miss?" Chuck and Meg were now identical worker ants confronting her among a forest of mushrooms while Mickey sat on a pile of bones that had once been a mouse or something similar.

"I tripped over something and landed against the wall, where my prosthetic's straps got caught and ripped. I fell. My goggles slid off my eyes. I sat on this bench and tried to figure out if I could fix my straps. I called out to my friends, who've gotten ahead of me. When I heard your footsteps, I thought you were them returning."

The ants looked at each other. Mickey had already mixed them up. The ant she thought was Chuck said, "She has five more people in her group, still in the building. See if you can locate them. They're in room sixteen."

FORMLESS

-10-

Pris was the first to return. "Mickey. I'm shutting off the augmented reality for friends. I didn't even know we had lost you. I'm so sorry. What happened? I don't even know what I'm looking at."

The worker ant, whichever one it was, offered to shut off Pris's group AR immediately as it was an emergency.

As soon as her AR was deactivated, Pris cried, "Your arm!"

Mickey explained what had happened, leaving out the pill bug's soft warmth and weird smell. The helper ants listened to the story, frowning.

"Taylor won't be happy if he has to fix your arm again," Pris warned.

"I won't be happy about what?" The rest of the group emerged from the gloom. "What's going on?"

"Mickey broke her awesome robot arm, again."

"You make it sound like I do it on purpose. Last summer a shark attacked me. The prosthetic isn't shark-proof. Is that my fault? This time, it snagged on some random scenery or something. I don't even know what happened."

"I can't see what happened through the AR," Taylor grumbled. "Buncha dinosaurs."

In a few moments, the helper ant had turned off everyone's group AR. Taylor sat beside Mickey on the pile of bones, touching the broken ends of her strap. "How did you break this reinforced leather strap? It was one thing when the shark bit through it …" He lifted his hands to his face.

Mickey knew he wanted to remove his goggles to examine the prosthetic more clearly. "Don't. An alarm goes off. It's an enormous deal. Then these ants showed up and yelled at me for taking the goggles off. Except I didn't take them off. They moved up my face when I fell down."

Taylor shook his head. He asked the ants, "Can you just lead us straight out of here to a first aid kiosk?"

"Yeah, my leg really hurts. It's bleeding more."

"Is it getting worse?" Mo leaned over.

"Yeah, first I cut my leg. Then I stumbled because my leg hurt and it was bleeding—it still is—and my strap got caught and broke, then I fell, the goggles came loose, the alarm went off, the ant brigade showed up …"

"Of course, of course." Mo lifted her hands in a soothing manner. "None of it is your fault. Let's patch you up."

FORMLESS
-11-
Mo

Mo led Mickey toward the first aid hut, her mind churning over her friend's injuries. The workers didn't know that the six of them were there undercover, and couldn't be allowed to know, because that was how Lilli wanted it. No special treatment. No photos. Of course, Mo had read the paperwork carefully, perhaps more carefully than either of her bosses. She doubted Pris or Mickey had read the agreement at all.

Lilli had hired them and hamstrung them from doing anything at the same time.

Meanwhile, Pris became like a mama bear when something injured one of her adopted cubs—Mickey or Mo. She had access to more money than a god, it seemed like, and her favorite thing to spend it on was her friends. It had taken Mo a while to understand that was how Pris showed affection. She still wasn't entirely comfortable with the lavish, expensive computer equipment Pris liked to surprise her with, but she enjoyed using it.

"Don't," Mickey begged Pris as she hobbled, leaning on Mo.

"Don't what? What do you think I'm planning?"

"To buy this park and burn it down, of course," Mo ventured, trying to support Mickey without touching her too much. That was basically what it was like being Mickey's friend. Never getting close enough to touch.

"Oh, good one, right, hadn't thought of that."

Mo guided Mickey into the first aid Quonset hut. A man in black sat inside, not looking very excited, although it was hard to tell with all the augmented reality.

"Did anyone tell you we were coming?" Mo asked him.

"No, why?"

"Are you a medical doctor?" Pris demanded, leaning into the man in black's face. Mo wondered if he was really wearing that black government-style suit or if it was all AR.

"A doctor? What? No. I'm a CNA."

"You're not even a proper nurse?" Pris started to get prickly, going into angry hedgehog mode.

Mo could not deal with Pris right now, not with Mickey injured and with her prosthetic broken.

Mickey put her hand on Pris's arm before she erupted. "I just need a bandage and some string or something."

Mo pushed up her goggles. The imposing man in black changed into a guy younger than her, wearing yellow scrubs. He had acne and his hair needed combing. Mo did not feel inspired.

"You aren't supposed to do that. Put them back on," Scrubs instructed.

"Whatever, dude. I want to look at my friend's leg before you cover it up again."

An alarm started to go off inside Mo's goggles, and a blinking red light reflected off the lenses of her eyeglasses. Mickey hadn't been kidding.

The wound in Mickey's leg was worse than Mo had thought from poking at it. Less of a gouge and more of a coring. "That's a nasty hole in your calf. You need a tetanus shot." Mo poked at the wound again. She was a mad scientist, of course.

"We don't do that here." Scrubs rubbed his face.

"Her parents are both doctors. I think they can handle it." Mo leaned over, putting her face almost against Mickey's skin. It smelled oddly like motor oil. "Antibiotics too, of course, but I think there's something in here. Like a splinter. Do you remove splinters?"

"It doesn't feel like a splinter now," Mickey said, "But it did before. Maybe it was a piece of wood and got washed out with all the bleeding."

"No, I rarely remove splinters." Scrubs rolled his eyes. "We don't have anything to remove them with, anyhow."

"What good are you?" Pris was almost shouting. "Why are you even here?"

Geoffrey glanced inside the Quonset hut. "Pris, what are you yelling about?"

"Mo says there is a piece of dirty wood stuck inside Mickey's leg, and this teenager isn't even really a nurse, much less a doctor, and he's useless."

"Okay, just—you can't buy the place and burn it down—"

"Why does everyone think I want to do that?"

"We know you?" Mo peered into Mickey's wound and did another gentle poke. She wished the light was better.

"Well, yeah," Pris admitted. "It's a good idea."

"It's a horrible idea," Mickey replied. "That hurts, Mo."

"I feel helpless. I don't like that. Buying things makes me feel useful." Pris seemed to be talking to herself. She wandered outside.

A good light source, tweezers, and a magnifying glass would help immensely with this splinter problem. Mo saw none of those things in this first aid kiosk. Then again, from the outside, it was a rusty Quonset hut covered in *no trespassing* and various government signs.

"Geoffrey, figure out something you can buy here at the park to keep my arm on. Talk to Taylor."

FORMLESS

Scrubs was perfectly competent at cleaning the hole in Mickey's leg and bandaging it, even if he did lack the supplies needed to pull out a splinter.

He studied the prosthetic and its broken strap. "I can wrap the whole thing in elastic bandages. Like you sprained your elbow."

"Her arm is too heavy for that, and if you used more bandages, it would be too bulky." Mo protested, but they tried it anyway. Because it was awful to feel helpless; Pris was right. With her arm hanging loose like that, Mickey was helpless.

"It's cutting off the circulation to the implants that control the prosthetic. And it hurts." Mickey studied the awkward bundle of beige elastic bandages replacing her gorgeous metal arm. "And I look like I stole a fat mummy's arm."

"A mummy can't be fat. They are completely dehydrated, and fat contains water," Mo explained. "Lift your left arm."

"It's cumbersome. And the prosthetic is slipping. It's not staying aligned with the tattoos and the implants."

Scrubs watched. There was no way he understood what they were talking about.

"Cumbersome you could work with for half a day, but it needs to be aligned." Mo turned to Scrubs. "Can you please turn off the alarm in my goggles?"

"Just put them back on properly, and it will turn off."

Mo rubbed her eyes under her glasses. "I have two master's degrees in science fields. I'm working on a PhD I'm not an idiot. I'm trying to help my friend. Flashing, beeping alarms don't expedite that. You're supposed to be the medical professional, and you have done little medically or professionally, so give me a break. Or I'll get our pink-haired friend back in here to scream at you."

Scrubs stared at Mo.

Taylor opened the door with the others in tow. "We got zip ties from the maintenance hut," he announced, holding up a package. "They have extra ones to tie the covers on trash cans at night to keep animals out. Hey, what did you do to Mickey's arm? Those elastic bandage things won't work."

The zip ties did the job. It helped that the original designer of the prosthetic was there to figure out the best configuration. The thin red plastic pieces weren't pretty, but they did succeed at holding the prosthetic onto Mickey's upper arm and shoulder. Not comfortably, though.

Taylor stepped back, his lips thin. "I hate to say this, Mickey, but let's take an extra elastic bandage, just in case we need to be strapped into another ride, so we can make a sling for extra protection."

Mickey hefted her arm and scrunched her mouth. "Thanks? These zip ties aren't the worst that's ever happened to me."

"Oh, overwhelm me with compliments. What thing could possibly have been worse?"

"Well, shark attack? Or how about being arrested and handcuffed to a desk by Mo's stepdad's deputies?"

Mo winced. "He let you go." How had Mickey become her friend after all that?

"First, I had to threaten to sue him, and I got into a fistfight with one of those cops over it," Pris reminded her. "I had a black eye."

Mo clenched her teeth. The beginning of their friendship had not been the best.

"All right," Taylor conceded. "All those things might be worse than having your arm tied on with zip ties."

"But the zip ties are red," Mo noticed. "They don't match her outfit." Matching outfits were vital. That was why she owed high-top sneakers in every color.

"They only had red ones, sorry."

"We should have invited Lucas. He might have thought of it."

"My little brother is away at school and, anyway, you know all he thinks of is food. He's not the color-coordinated type of gay."

"He's medically qualified, though. Studying to be a paramedic. He would have been useful now. Unlike—" Pris pointed an elbow toward Scrubs.

"That is true," Mo agreed. "And I owe him a date where I feed him extravagant amounts of food while dressed in pink." As long as it wasn't the horrible pink uniform from the diner where she used to work.

Taylor's mouth dropped. "You aren't his type, though, are you? Wait, don't tell me; I don't want to know. But don't you have a boyfriend?"

"Yes, I have a boyfriend, not all dates are romantic, and no, I am not Lucas's type because I'm female." Mo's boyfriend Agwe was another recent hire of Genesis Robotics, an expert in parthenogenesis from Jamaica; he worked with the mermaids to help them reproduce without requiring either humans or sharks.

Taylor shook his head a few times. "I never want to know exactly what happened with all of you last summer."

Mo snorted and finally pushed her goggles back down.

FORMLESS
-12-
Mickey

Do you think the dead lady could have fallen off the Terror Wheel?" Pris asked. They stood before another park map.

"Nobody fell off anything," Ananda snapped.

"Do you own stock in this place or something?" Mo demanded. "Why are you so defensive about that lady dying here?"

"Because we're not here about her, and that's all you guys care about. I thought you worked at Genesis Robotics, Melissa, not for this silly podcast."

"I've already said I can do several things at once." Mo's voice sounded mild, but Mickey knew she was fuming. She hated her full name, and the only way Ananda could know it would be if Taylor or Geoffrey had told her. That was a betrayal.

"If she fell off the Terror Wheel, that would have been very public. People would have seen that and talked about it, don't you think?" Mickey tried to defuse the situation. "It would have been on social media somewhere and Pris would have found it."

"Well, it's another way to get a top-down view of the entire island." Geoffrey pulled Ananda's arm through his.

"I don't think the cable ties on your arm will be a problem on the Terror Wheel. It's fairly tame." Taylor chewed his cheek, studying the ride. "Good thing we went on the Horrorail first."

They walked between a double row of mushroom huts selling food and souvenirs, offering games of chance, swarmed by insects of all types. The Terror Wheel sat on a rise, so it appeared even taller.

"Some of the maintenance and administration centers are underground," Taylor explained as they walked along the gravel. "Lilli told us that they blasted the original island to make it flatter and expand it. They found some mysterious caverns they converted into usable spaces."

"Oh." Mo hopped a few times. "That's what made the spooky voices and weird noises that scared the Natives. Water and air going in and out of those spaces with the tides."

Mickey asked, "Okay, then how come white people couldn't hear the noises?" It was a fair question. They all had ears.

After too long of a pause, Pris laughed, breaking the tension. "Easy. Something shifted underground at the same time the Pilgrims showed up. Earthquake, whatever. The noises stopped. So it seemed like white people couldn't hear the sounds, but they just went away exactly when there were white people here to hear them. There. Problem solved, and by a stupid white girl."

FORMLESS

"Is that the legend, though, Mo?"

"Actually, Mickey, I don't know. I'm not an expert on the legend; I didn't think to really study it before we came. No one believes the old stories anymore, so that's how the tribe came to sell the island. I guess money was more important than keeping people away from this empty old land." Mo shrugged.

"The tribe had it fenced in with *danger—keep out* signs before selling it," Taylor said. "So maybe someone did still believe."

Ananda made a very loud sound, on the edge of being a rude noise. "Again, with all this extraneous stuff. What does this have to do with headaches?"

Geoffrey tightened his hand on hers. "We invited Pris and Mickey along for a reason, Ana. They look at things differently—they aren't all about science like you are. And Mo is a great bridge between the two; she can see both sides of the subject. If there are caverns with strange noises and airflow, that could actually have some bearing on the situation."

"Taylor just said construction leveled the island and converted the caverns into maintenance areas."

Taylor shrugged. "I'm not an expert on how they created this park. They could have missed some caverns entirely or not converted some. There could be natural chimneys that have weird airflow."

"And you expect to somehow see this underground stuff from the top of the Ferris Wheel?" Ananda pointed to the hill.

"Not at all. I don't know what I expect to see from the top—and it's called the Terror Wheel, by the way. My expectations are entirely open. We might find something out about the lady who died, even. I'm not discounting the headaches as having some role in her death." Taylor rubbed his lip.

"I doubt it." For some reason, Ananda remained triggered by any mention of the death at the park, to the point of being irrational. How could Taylor and Geoffrey have not noticed that before?

Mickey's arm was no longer perfectly balanced. The thin zip ties cut into her upper arm and shoulder, unlike the thick leather straps that properly distributed the weight of the metal forearm and hand. Some people wore a soft protective sock between their skin and their prosthetic; she didn't because the inside of the socket had to touch the metallic tattoos and implanted chips that synched the artificial hand and wrist to her brain and neural net. She now wished for such a piece of insulating cloth. It was one of those times when the prosthetic was a burden. Usually, she didn't mind when people wanted to talk about it—as long as they didn't want to touch it—but she hoped today her metal arm would get ignored as some augmented-reality figment.

FORMLESS

The Terror Wheel stood at the island's elevated center, oval-shaped rather than round, more like a roller coaster. Cars inched up one side, paused at the top, and flew down the other side.

Mickey would be glad to sit in one of the enclosed cars for however long the ride operator allowed. Her leg ached deep inside. Mo was right; something was still in there, some kind of splinter. One of her parents would have it out in a couple of minutes once she got home, but until then, she would have to endure the pain. When her calf muscle moved a certain way, she could feel the splinter shift.

The cars held up to four people each. The helper ant allowed them to underfill two cars with three people.

Mo and Pris wanted to sandwich Mickey in the middle to protect her.

"Nope." Mickey pushed back, shuddering at the thought. "You know I won't be able to stand that."

"But your arm." Mo gestured.

"Squishing me between you guys until I can't breathe won't fix that."

The lower half of Pris's face seemed unhappy. It was hard to read people's faces when their eyes were covered.

"You need to get in the car or get out of line." The helper ant made a hurry-up gesture with two of its ant-arms.

Mickey sat on the right edge, with Mo in the middle next to her zip-tied arm. The worker ant configured their restraints for three people.

As their car slowly rose, Ek shadowed them.

"You're doing that, of course?" Mo asked. "Because it's creepy."

"Why is it creepy?"

"The way it follows you around."

"It's my emotional support bird now."

"It's not real, though. You control it. That emotional support stuff is just a joke that Pris says, of course. I remember how the bird-drones were last summer."

"Sure," Mickey agreed.

Ek flew closer, seeming to look for a place to land on the outside of their enclosed car.

"Ek doesn't change," Pris remarked. "It's a raven all the time."

"Ek doesn't have a chip provided by the park, of course," Mo pointed out. "There's nothing for the goggles to map. They have to show Ek as-is."

Mickey gazed over the island at the mushrooms, rotten logs, and scurrying insects. Ek's raven-ness stood out. What if Ek appeared as a giant mosquito instead of a big, black bird? Other people must have brought support animals to the park. Or maybe it was too new. What if a blind person brought their guide dog? Mickey's mind reeled at how the park would work for a blind person. Just sounds and smells? Tactilely, nothing would change. She had seen behind the illusion to the bare plywood.

"Smoke is coming out of your ears," Pris said. "You're thinking too hard."

"Just wondering how this park would work if you were blind," Mickey responded.

The car ratcheted up.

Ants, spiders, and the assorted odd insects scampered below. A pill bug ate trash from a tipped-over can. Why would it be warm and soft? Even if it incinerated the garbage, which explained the heat, why would the pill bug be squishy? She wished the car was a traditional open one so she could lean out, although that would probably give her friends heart attacks.

"Now what's blowing smoke out of your ears?" Pris elbowed her.

"The pill bug was warm and soft."

"What? What pill bug?" Pris asked.

"Pill bug?" Mo said.

"Remember before we went into the big hollow log, a pill bug ate some trash? You saw a jackalope and Pris probably saw a small dinosaur."

"That was like two hours ago, and how do you know it was warm and soft?"

"Hollow log?"

"The building looked like an upright hollow log to me. There's this rotten forest cave theme that goes with the insects. Mushrooms, dead trees, caves, glowing crystals everywhere."

"The jungle mountain we went inside of," Pris said.

"The mysterious cave system with the crashed UFO on the roof," Mo explained.

At the top of the Terror Wheel, the island spread out around them. As the car plunged over the edge, Mickey saw an iridescent black blob right below, on the path next to the ride, close to where the pill bug had been eating the trash. It seemed to form an eye and stare at her.

FORMLESS

-13-

Her shout got lost in the ride's tumult. "What was that?"

The fierce, fast fall didn't allow for conversation. They slammed into the bottom. The worker ant gave them a thumbs-up as they slowed to cycle back up.

"Did you see that?" Mickey gasped. They were on the wrong side of the ride now.

"See what?" Pris asked.

"I'm stuck in the middle. I can't see anything," Mo complained.

"Some kind of oil slick with an eye."

"Right, what kind of bug is that?"

"I don't think it was a bug."

"So how does it relate to your bug theme?" Mo asked.

"I don't think it does."

"A glitch? Where was it?" Mo tried to lean over Mickey to see out.

"It's over there on the other side. Can't see it from here."

"What are you thinking it is?" Pris asked.

"I don't know." The splinter in Mickey's calf shifted and burned. "I keep wondering about the weirdness of the pill bug being warm and soft when I encountered it inside the building."

"How do you know it was the pill bug? Where was this?" Mo asked.

Mickey tried to remember what had convinced her. "In the Cursed Cave, when I fell and broke my strap. I didn't actually see the pill bug. It touched me in the dark. You're right. I just assumed …" Her calf spasmed. She winced. "I mean, what else could it have been?"

"I could see it being soft and warm if it had been me encountering the jackalope." Mo played with her braids. "They are mammalian, of course. I would expect a jackalope to be warm and soft if I encountered one."

"But I wouldn't expect a dinosaur to be warm or soft," Pris said.

"Then again, it's a robot," Mo mused. "I wouldn't expect a robot to be warm or soft."

The car reached the top again. Mickey knew precisely where to look, but the oil slick was gone. That would be impossible if it were an actual puddle of spilled petroleum product. "It's gone. The oil slick and the eyeball." She indicated where it had been before their car slid over the edge again.

"I saw nothing," Pris said.

"I can't see anything." Mo craned her neck and adjusted her goggles.

"It was gone."

FORMLESS

The worker ant waved and let them swing by again.

"What warm, soft thing would be inside the Cursed Cave if it wasn't some sort of cleaner bot?" Mo returned to the earlier subject. "What about other people and their emotional support animals?"

"Did you see anyone else besides me with an animal? And no one else was in the room with me. I was calling for help for a while. A help-er animal would have helped me."

"You would think," Mo said.

Pris jumped onto something else. "You were calling for help? We didn't hear you. We didn't even notice you were missing."

"Great friends you are."

Mo rubbed her eyes under the goggles. "No, she's right. I could have sworn I saw you with us. I didn't realize you had fallen behind. Of course, I would have gone back for you."

"Right. Me too."

"Some hot mushy thing separated me from the herd to bite me?" Mickey touched her leg. "I guess I look like the weakest and most wounded to an outside predator." She was only joking, but she started to wonder if that wasn't exactly what had happened. She had appeared weak and something had taken a nibble.

Their car reached the top. Mickey wasn't looking for the oil slick and the eye, but she thought she saw them—it?—in a different place. But in the confusion of getting out at the bottom and meeting back up with Taylor, Geoffrey, and Ananda, she got distracted and forgot to mention it.

FORMLESS
-14-

Ek fluttered down to land on Mickey's shoulder, which didn't help the pain from the zip ties.

"Let's sit somewhere and take stock of what we know," Mo suggested.

"No ghost sightings." Pris walked and reported. "And my spy camera doesn't work. That concludes my portion of the report."

"Camera?" Ananda turned her head to aim her goggles at Pris.

Taylor chewed his cheek. He had designed and fabricated the 3D-printed plastic cameras.

Geoffrey's goggles pointed at his brother and then at Pris. "You can't see the screen through the goggles."

"Yeah, we know that."

"They don't allow cameras," Ananda said. "Against the rules. Says so right when you buy the tickets and fill out the questionnaire."

"You need to stop being such a rule-monger if you want to hang with us," Mo said.

Ananda said nothing, but Mickey felt as if she heard the answer: why would I want to hang with you guys? Mickey wanted to like Ananda. She must have some good qualities if two of her friends liked her enough to date her. But Ananda was a prickly woman, and she didn't make it easy.

They sat in a picnic area crawling with bugs that could deliver food and take away the trash. It had the now-usual mixture of lichen, mushrooms, crystals, logs, and ugly living plants with a patina of gray.

"Ordering food is easier without your little brother here." Mo ran her finger down a menu tablet. "Weird that I can see the park-supplied tablet screen perfectly well through my goggles."

"Ordering for Lucas is simple. Just triple the amount," Geoffrey suggested.

"We were literally running out of food at the diner last summer," Mo explained. "We had to place extra orders with our suppliers because of him."

"That skinny boy?" Ananda scoffed. "He's all enormous eyes and floppy hair."

"And empty stomach. I am ridiculously wealthy, right, and I shudder at the idea of handing Lucas my credit card and letting him order food," Pris said.

"That's right, you're the reality show one."

"Is that what your boys call me? 'The reality show one?'" Pris's goggles moved between the brothers on either side of Ananda. "I thought they thought a bit more highly of me."

Geoffrey defended them both. "We said your family does the show. Not you."

FORMLESS

"My sisters have the show. I'm not part of it. I'm never mentioned by name. I've never appeared on the show. I avoid that visibly rich lifestyle as much as possible. I'm only guilty by association. I can't help it that we all look so much alike. That's why my hair is pink, so I won't look as much like them."

"She mostly shops at thrift stores," Mickey explained. "I probably wear more expensive clothes than she does."

"You're the crippled Native American orphan." Ananda's gaze turned to Mickey.

"I'm not an orphan. My parents adopted me as a premature infant. I don't really know if I'm Native American because I was a foundling." Why did she have to defend herself against this woman? Why did she even want to like her? Oh, that's right, she was Geoffrey and Taylor's girlfriend. Every minute Mickey spent with her, she wondered exactly why that was.

"Why is your name Crow if you aren't Native American?"

"When they found me, I had a toy crow with me, so that's my middle name."

As Ananda's goggles turned toward Mo, Mo tossed her braids and raised her hands. "I don't want to know what flippant thing you have me classified as. Of course, it will be half wrong and half mean. You probably think I have daddy issues because my dead father was Black and my white mom married a white cop."

"Don't you? How old is your boyfriend?"

Agwe was a bit older than Mo, but not outrageously so. "I'm not talking about him. Let's talk about your obsession with people getting headaches."

"I'm not obsessed. We're here to do a job, and I'm trying to do it well."

"You don't work for Genesis, Ananda. I do, and Geoffrey and Taylor do, of course. The rest of you are here to add warm bodies and extra eyes. You aren't working. You aren't here to do any job. You're getting a free day of vacation at a theme park."

Ananda clenched her jaw. A line of insects arrived carrying food trays, delivering each order to the correct person according to their wristbands.

Mo had a meatball sandwich; that's what it looked like to Mickey. She had a sudden panic that they could be fed anything and told it was something else. She looked at her own plate of spicy boneless wings and wondered what they really were. This was a horror theme park, after all.

And a lady had died of an allergic reaction to something.

Mo ate a few potato chips, pointing randomly with one. "I'll start. Of course, Mickey had a lot happen to her today, and I won't take that away. I bumped my arm and got scratched when I got onto the Horrorail." She displayed her right elbow. Her smooth brown skin had a shallow gouge, already lightly scabbed. "I wouldn't have thought anything of it. I felt a bit of dizziness earlier, which I mentioned to Ananda, and she said she felt it too. My eye sockets hurt from having my glasses on with the goggles on top of them, even though these particular goggles fit over glasses, of course. I wouldn't call it a headache—" she turned to Ananda "—but it is annoying. If I was writing a review of the park, I would definitely mention having eyeglasses on is uncomfortable and to wear contact lenses instead, if possible."

"The pain is in your head, though," Ananda said.

"Yes," Mo replied, pulling her braids over her shoulder. "But it's not a headache. You know there's a difference."

"Not to everyone, maybe."

"Semantics."

"Okay." Geoffrey held up a hand. "Peace, please. No more sniping. I got scratched in the Cursed Cave too. People aren't writing bad online reviews of a theme park as unique as this because they got a minor scratch." He displayed his upper arm. His dark green t-shirt had a triangle-shaped rip, and underneath, the skin was missing in a small scoop.

"We're all clumsy," Taylor said. "I got scratched on my leg at some point. I don't remember where." He rotated his calf. "And I agree, this isn't enough to write a critical review about. Not enough to even mention. What I've been thinking about, a lot, is Mo's story about when this was Native land, and supposedly the island used to talk to people. I let my imagination take over. Remember in college when I tried to be a writer? I thought about what an island would say after eons of being alone until I could hear its voice in my head …" he trailed off and chewed his cheek. "That's what I use to invent things, that same part of my brain."

Mo tilted her head. "What do you think it was saying?"

"Remember, this is the old, suppressed author part of me talking." The bottoms of Taylor's cheeks reddened. "I was a terrible writer. It was like the island had a spirit, an animus. That spirit told me it was lonely after all those years in isolation. It was looking for a kindred spirit to talk to. It said, 'I'm here, I'm lonely, can you hear me?' and when I could hear it, it was overjoyed."

"That's an elaborate fantasy." Mo touched her braids.

Mickey's neural net pinged, but Ek sat on the table next to her.

If you can hear us, let us in.

"I'm not scratched, and the island isn't talking to me." Pris ran her fingers through her hair, raking at her scalp.

FORMLESS

"You're white." Ananda scrunched her nose. "Geoffrey and Taylor are Korean, I'm Indian, Mo is Black, and Mickey is probably Native but most definitely not white."

"The island doesn't scratch me because I'm pale?" Pris went into hedgehog mode, her pink hair looking more prickly and pointy.

"It's not real." Geoffrey waved his hand. "We're mixing up a bunch of things and conflating them as if they are one real thing."

"Are we sure?" Mo finished her meatballs.

Ek sat, almost in torpor, beside Mickey's plate, eyes powered down. Yet the neural net pinged, pinged, pinged until it was almost painful. Mickey would qualify it as a headache, except she wouldn't give Ananda the satisfaction. Besides, she was the only person in the world with this neural net, making her experience decidedly atypical.

Can you hear us?

"That woman still died." Mo handed her empty tray to a trash pill bug.

"She had an allergic reaction!" Ananda yelled. "Nothing was talking inside her head!"

In their various bug forms, other park patrons, also eating in the pavilion, stared in Ananda's direction.

"Maybe the dead lady got scratched on an ugly gray plant and had a reaction and then fell off a ride," Mickey suggested, combining several theories.

"The plants are only weird in augmented reality," Ananda argued.

"Right, but we can't remove our goggles and check." Pris's hair was still at maximum spike, her voice tight with anger. She stalked away toward a sign showing the way to male and female bug restrooms.

Ek woke, inspecting the area in all directions. Mickey didn't have the brainpower to tap into its eyes. She was too tired.

Ping.

Mo reached into her shirt and pulled out her tiny camera, almost identical to Pris's.

"You have one too?" Ananda's voice sounded overloud. Bugs focused in her direction again.

"I want photos of everyone's wounds."

"You can't see the screen," Taylor reminded her.

"That doesn't mean the camera doesn't work, just that I can't see it working. I'm assuming the screen still functions; I'm just blocked from seeing it, of course. I don't know how important the screen is to the photo."

Let us in.

A pill bug took Mickey's empty tray away, not seeming to notice Mo's camera violation. "I hate to unwrap your leg," she said to Mickey. "But I want a photo."

FORMLESS

"Can you bandage it again?"

"I think so." Mo poked at the wrapping.

"Stop this!" Ananda had gotten shrill.

"Calm down." Geoffrey placed his hand on her shoulder.

"I won't calm down. You invited all these extra people who don't know what they are doing."

"Mo works for us. And she is a genius." Taylor watched Mo unwrap Mickey's leg. "You are an extra invite. You are handy to have along because you have a PhD, and yes, you are also a genius, but you are acting stubborn and close-minded. Not at all like the curious, open person we met when we enrolled in the genetic twin study that helped you get that PhD"

"I'm that person still." Ananda's mouth turned down.

The other bugs in the pavilion saw Mo's camera.

An aqua jumping spider came over. "Where did you get a camera?"

"It's my camera, of course." Mo adroitly avoided the question.

"Hmm." The spider appeared to be thinking, tapping one leg on its face. "What do I look like?"

"You are a spider," Mickey said. "Glowing greenish blue."

Mo tucked away the camera while Mickey distracted the spider.

"A spider? Oh, how awful. I hate spiders. You're a bunch of ghosts. I wanted a picture of myself as whatever you see me as."

"I don't think that's how it works." Mickey tried to be polite.

"That would be a great idea, though!" Geoffrey stood. "At the end of the experience, we fill out a survey. I would love to see how I appear to others. That could be an extra package, a thumb drive of images of each person in the various milieus. Make sure you mention that when you leave, so it's available for future visits."

The spider aimed all its eyes at Geoffrey. "Do you work for the park?"

"No, I'm a computer programmer. It could be done easily. And it's a great idea. I don't know why they didn't think of it. All of us should mention it in our exit interviews."

"Exit interview?" The jumping spider rubbed its face with its leg. Mickey thought it was a woman, but she couldn't be sure. "You sure talk like you work here."

"I assure you, I do not work here. But I wonder what other great ideas you have." Geoffrey led the spider away, still talking, and Mo finished unwrapping Mickey's leg.

Mickey expected the wound to have the beginnings of puffiness and redness, since she didn't know what was inside of it, but it appeared clean other than the tacky blood. "It seems okay. Not infected."

"Yet," Mo said, pointing the camera at it.

FORMLESS

She also photographed Geoffrey's arm wound when he returned, minus the chatty spider.

"Nice lady. I think I distracted her enough that she forgot Mo had a camera."

"Your idea would be interesting on the website when you sign up." Ananda's voice was quieter than before. "You could upload a picture of yourself and see a rendering of what you might look like in each milieu."

Geoffrey slung his arm around her thin shoulders. "Yeah, that's an excellent idea. I'll tell Lilli all this after we leave. She should have allowed us to keep our phones. We need to have real-time information while we are doing this investigation."

"But we would stand out. The staff would treat us differently," Taylor pointed out. "We need to have an authentic experience."

"Worker ants," Mickey said. "The staff are worker ants."

"Our experience is already inauthentic. We look at everything differently because we know something is up," Mo pointed out. "Plus, we turned off our group AR."

"Headaches." Ananda brought up her favorite topic.

Mo flipped her braids over her shoulder and clenched them.

"When I brought that duck-billed dinosaur lady over to her group, I overheard one of them complaining about a headache."

"Duck-billed lady?" Mickey glanced in the direction he had brought the jumping spider.

"The one you said was a spider."

Ananda smiled. "Should we follow them?"

Mo wrapped her braids around her fingers. "No. She's already got a headache. We want to know where she got it. We would want to backtrack, find out where their group had already been."

"I think we should follow them." Ananda stood.

"Okay, think of this. Someone has a rare disease. You want to know where it came from. Do you follow the person with the disease around? Or ask where they have been and where they caught it?"

"I see your point." Ananda's lips were tight. "But what are we supposed to do? Ask her what rides she's been on?"

"Well, if we weren't deep undercover, yeah. So we have to think of something else." Mo twisted her braids into a thick cord and stared across the pavilion.

"Go on the smaller rides, I guess, and see what happens—" Mickey started.

Pris returned from the bug bathrooms at a fast trot. Her face had lost any of the slight color it usually had. "I saw the ghost."

FORMLESS
-15-

What?" Ananda's mouth twisted. "Stop it."

"No camera. No proof." Pris smacked herself in the chest, the approximate area where her useless camera hid.

Everyone focused on Pris, whose bright pink clothing seemed subdued. Her spikey hair drooped.

"A ghost in the bathroom?" Mickey clarified. Usually, she wore a complex camera rig and was the Contrary Crowcast's eyes, while Pris was the tech support, producer, and banker. In this situation, none of their usual strategies applied. "What did it look like?"

"She looked like a lady, not a dinosaur, thank god. I could not handle a dinosaur ghost."

Ek stalked across the table, peering at Pris. She sat with her hands propping up her chin.

"Ek, I should have brought you with me. But I don't need Mickey watching me pee."

"I don't watch everything through Ek's eyes," Mickey countered. "All you had to do was ask, and Ek would go with you."

Ananda turned to her boyfriends. "I don't understand that bird. Is it alive? I thought you built it?"

"We built it. Well, I built it. Geoff programmed it."

"You all treat it like it's alive."

Mo dropped her hair. The beads clicked. "Pris saw a ghost. A ghost! We see Ek all the time. Ek is no big deal. We can talk about Ek any time. Ek has been here all day. Ghost! Ghost! The ghost you haven't wanted to acknowledge might exist and is now here. You change the subject immediately to something boring and mundane."

"Well, you have to admit, the way you all treat this bird—" Ananda poked at Ek without touching the raven.

"Ghost!" Mo shouted, her fist wrapped around her braids.

The insects across the pavilion stared at them.

Pris waved. "Never mind. We're playing a game." She turned on Ananda. Her pink hair seemed to regain its strength, getting darker and spikier. "I saw the ghost. Mo is right. You've done nothing but deny the idea that there might be a ghost. I just saw her."

"Okay," Mickey lifted her flesh hand. "Pris, look at me. Or at Mo. Or at Ek, even. This is Contrary Crowcast business, no one else's. Did she speak? Did you talk to her? What did she do? How did she appear?"

"This is a waste of time—" Ananda muttered.

Mickey cut her off with a hand chop. "Go away. Go give someone a headache and then study it."

FORMLESS

Ananda looked at Geoffrey, her mouth open. "Did you hear what she said to me?"

"You're mean," Mo said. "We're working. Be quiet or go away. Seriously."

"Are you going to fire her for talking to me like that?"

"No," Geoffrey said. "We're interested in what they are discussing, Ana. If you aren't, please be quiet."

Ananda turned to Taylor. She opened her mouth to speak.

He said, "Pris, what did the ghost look like?"

Ananda pulled her legs over the bench and stalked away.

"At first, I thought she was just a lady in the bathroom. They aren't port-a-potties, thank god, and there is no augmented reality inside. I realized she was an actual person, not a dinosaur, and how long had it been since I saw a person? I thought she was strange because I've only been seeing dinosaurs all day, and you guys, but I'm used to you. Well, most of you." She flicked a glance at the retreating Ananda.

"How was she weird?" Mo leaned forward.

Mickey nodded, having been about to ask something similar. Ek hunkered down by Pris's side to absorb the entire story.

"Well, she just died, so it wasn't like she was wearing old-timey clothes, right. She was just off. Not really transparent, but stuttering, not quite there. I thought she was virtual reality, but she doesn't fit any storylines. I saw a sample of the ghost milieu, and it was nothing like her. Nobody else was in that building. I think we startled each other a little. I wasn't expecting to see a ghost in the bathroom, and I think she was surprised that I could see her. I tried to start a conversation, but she went poof. And I came right back here." She looked around. "Where's Ananda?"

"She took a walk," Mo said shortly. "Forget about her. Let's go check out this ghost." She turned to the brothers. "Wait here for Ananda to return. Pris and Mickey will go do their ghost thing and I'll help. We'll be back shortly. Maybe the ghost can give us a clue about the headaches, and that will make Ananda happy."

FORMLESS
-16-

It's that one," Pris said, pointing. There were three bathroom structures, a large one for men and women, and a small unisex one. The usual mixture of plants, natural and augmented, surrounded the buildings. The dying gray tint of the plants, the ones Mickey presumed were real, predominated. They walked too fast for her leg wound, and the zip ties dug into her upper arm.

"How should we do this? Just walk in, the three of us?" Mo asked.

The bathrooms were constructed with winding privacy tunnels leading to them. No one could see the inside from the outside.

Ek hopped off Mickey's shoulder and landed on the lip of the restroom's roof.

"I messed up. I shouldn't have left. I'll go back in." Pris inched into the opening.

"Are you scared?" Mickey followed her in.

"I don't know. She's weird. And it's not like we can really use anything on the podcast."

Mo trailed them.

They emerged into a standard bathroom. Empty. No people, no ghosts, no augmented reality.

"At least this isn't a bat cave," Mickey said.

There was a flicker by the sink, like an old-time movie reel running out, but in reverse, as the ghost appeared. It wasn't in color but it wasn't precisely in black and white either. The ghost was modern-looking, but her hair and eye color were indeterminate. Even her skin color wasn't clear.

"Hey," Pris said softly, holding out her hand. "I'm sorry if I startled you before."

Mickey halted in the doorway. Mo peered over her shoulder.

The ghost's eyes widened. She got larger without approaching Pris.

"Did you die here? At the park?"

The ghost nodded, very slowly, focused on Pris. She had not looked at Mickey and Mo.

"Did you fall off a ride?" Pris took a tiny step toward the ghost, hand still extended.

The ghost shook her head. She hadn't blinked.

"Did you have an allergic reaction?"

The ghost shrugged.

Mickey had to stop herself from hopping in place. What had killed this poor lady, if she hadn't fallen to her death and hadn't eaten something she was allergic to? Mo pressed Mickey's waist for an instant and let her go. Her beads clicked softly beside Mickey's ear.

FORMLESS

"Both news articles were wrong, of course," Mo whispered.

Pris leaned forward. The ghost mirrored her. "How did you die?"

The ghost raised both her hands, made her fingers into a little mouth, and bit at her leg with them, over and over.

Mickey glanced at her own wound.

"What bit her?" Mo whispered. "I don't get it."

Pris's hand reached out to stop the frantic biting motions, but went right through the ghost. "Shh. Stop. What bit you?"

The ghost's eyes were wider than ever. She pulled her hands apart by about eighteen inches, fingers spread and curved as if she was holding a large ball. Staring at Pris, she moved her hands around as if describing something vaguely round. When Pris nodded that she understood, the ghost pulsed her hands in and out a few times, still moving them all around.

"Is she … fluffing a pillow?" Mo whispered to Mickey. Mickey shrugged, baffled, trying to stay quiet, but she mimed the motion with her free hand. How could a pillow bite someone?

The ghost covered her mouth with both hands and shook her head.

Pris nodded. "You can't speak."

Mickey nodded too. That was common with ghosts. Standard, even.

The ghost moved around—maybe a bit through—Pris and stood in front of the mirror. She opened her mouth extremely wide.

Pris stared at her.

Mo grunted. Mickey shrugged. Was she trying to sing? What could she be singing about? What could it have to do with her death? And the pillow? Did one of the other milieus involve singing? *Phantom of the Opera* in the Classic Horror milieu?

The ghost leaned forward and put her mouth almost to the mirror, staring sideways at Pris.

"Does she want me to lick the mirror? No," Pris said, twisting her lips.

The ghost actually rolled her eyes. She put her hands up on either side of her face, mouth still open.

"Yodeling?" Mo wondered.

"Just do what she's doing," Mickey said.

The ghost turned as if seeing Mickey for the first time. She pointed at Mickey and then repeated her gesture, hands beside her face, open mouth almost to the mirror.

Pris did. Her breath clouded the mirror faintly, but steamed right away. The ghost pointed at the mirror.

Mo's beads clicked behind Mickey. Mickey had long ago figured that the reason Mo constantly changed the colors of the beads on her braids was that she yanked them off when she was agitated.

FORMLESS

The ghost started to fade.

"Breathe on the mirror!" Mickey called. "Steam it up."

Pris leaned on the sink and huffed. The ghost, fading, tried to write in the steam, but couldn't touch it.

Mo leaned her head on the back of Mickey's shoulder, groaning. Mickey bounced on her toes even though it hurt her leg. She was desperate to know what the ghost was trying to tell them.

"Follow her finger," Mickey suggested. This could have been one of their best paranormal podcast episodes ever, and they had no footage. She had never felt so frustrated.

The ghost moved her fingers carefully and Pris copied the motions. From the doorway, Mickey couldn't read what Pris was writing. The ghost pointed at the word, pointed at her leg, made the fluffing motion again, and the biting motion as she faded.

Mickey and Mo burst into the bathroom. "What's the word?" Mo shouted.

The steam had already vanished from the mirror.

"Some weird bunch of letters. Something foreign or maybe a code. Nonsense letters. I don't know," Pris said.

"Just say it," Mickey said, breathing on the same section of mirror. It didn't work.

"I can't pronounce it."

"Do you remember it?" She breathed on a different section of mirror, just in case. Nope.

"I think so …" She moved her index finger through the air to help her remember what she had written. "I need to write it down. But I haven't got my phone."

Mo grabbed Pris's arm and dragged her from the restroom.

Mickey followed. "We have a clue and we need stone-age writing technology to figure it out." Ek fluttered down to land on her shoulder and laid its beak on her head.

The twins were still sitting at the picnic table, with no sign of their girlfriend.

They plopped down on the bench opposite. "We need pen and paper, something to write on and with, stat," Mo said. "Pris has a word, a clue, in her head that the ghost told her, and she might forget it."

"Hang on." Taylor stood. "I'll be right back. Pris, don't forget."

He went off in a different direction than Ananda had taken.

Pris's mouth and finger moved constantly as she tried not to forget. Mo made the pillow squishing motion. "I can't figure this out."

"She's dead. Her thoughts are disordered." Mickey said. "I'm sure it makes perfect sense to whatever is left of her mind. And whatever crazy word she made Pris write will be the same thing. It will be something that only makes sense to her, something she read in third grade that connects to a story her grandmother was told by her great-grand-mother and also pertains to a note on a scrap of paper she found in a library copy of a Lovecraft book in her senior year of high school."

"And in your podcast, you would research all that and explain it until it makes perfect sense," Geoffrey said.

Mickey nodded. "As much as we could. Having Mo to help with research like that is great."

"I wish Ananda was here to see this part. I know she doesn't appreciate you guys and that you aren't really getting along to-day. She does have a more whimsical, mystical side. Truly. I hope you can get to know her better. I don't know why she is being so prickly today."

"I wasn't aware that genetics could be whimsical and mystical," Mickey said.

"Her research about twins was how she met us. And we seem to bring that out in her, the whimsical and mystical. I guess we are really extraordinary in how we're wired, even for mirror twins. She didn't even use a lot of what she found out about us in her thesis—it was too crazy—she only used Taylor's organs being reversed. She *couldn't* use the other information."

"Is that even ethical?" Mo wondered. "To date someone you met while doing research on him?"

Not to mention two of them, Mickey thought. Beside her, Pris had her hands over her ears to block the conversation and was mouthing letters.

"We didn't do any of that until the study was over; she had fin-ished her thesis and gotten her doctorate," Geoffrey said.

"Is she dating you because you are freaks or because she really likes you?" Mickey asked bluntly.

Geoffrey actually blushed. He would have bitten right through his cheek if he had been his brother. "Um, I think it started because of the freak thing. That was the initial attraction. But she does like us."

"Does she like you as separate people or because you're twins with freaky DNA?"

"It's complicated, all right? Neither of us really has time for a girl-friend. She likes us both. We like her. It works for us. Don't judge it."

Freak twins, then. Mickey felt terrible for her friends.

Taylor came back with a handful of postcards and a hollow pen filled with tiny crystals. He handed them to Pris. "Write."

"Remember, I'm not entirely sure this is right. And I don't know what it means." She wrote: XOGGOTLI.

They stared at the word.

FORMLESS

-17-

What is an ex-got-tel-lee? Are you sure you're spelling it right?" Mickey asked.

"I dunno," Pris shrugged. "I think so. Wasn't easy to keep in my memory. Bunch of letters I can't pronounce, right."

"Well, let's assume it's a word," Geoffrey offered, handing the postcard to Mo. "Do you know what it means?"

"No one knows," Pris said in a deep voice.

"That's not true," Mo said. "And don't use your video voice on us."

Even Ek was looking at the word, and it couldn't read.

"Mickey said it wrong. It's a Nahuatl word. The language of the Aztecs. I took a college class in Meso-American history. Maybe it's a Mexican city? A lot of place names in Mexico have Nahuatl roots."

"What would a Mexican city have to do with how the lady died?" Taylor took the postcard. "What could it possibly mean? Is *Nar-wattle* a paranormal thing?"

"No, it's a Native language spoken in Mexico." Mo corrected his pronunciation, removing the R.

"All right. So what's …" Taylor stared at the postcard. "That word mean?"

"The *x* is pronounced *sh* and the strange *tl* like the end of the world *little*," Mo explained. "*Sha-got-tli. Xoggotli.*"

Taylor made a hurry-up gesture with his hands.

Pris moved her lips, saying it silently. "Not how I would have spelled it."

"Mickey, in a crazy way, you were onto something before when you said that dead people say weird things only they understand. We couldn't see her that well. Do you think she was Native? Mexican?"

Pris held up both hands, shrugging. "Her hair was darkish. Her features weren't very clear. I'm not sure I would recognize a photo of her."

Mo yanked on her braids. A green bead went flying away. "Sounds a little like the word *shoggoth*." She spelled it.

"What's a shoggoth?" Taylor asked.

"It's a creature that the writer H.P. Lovecraft invented. Mickey, you must have read his work, or you wouldn't have mentioned him earlier."

"A while ago." Mickey shrugged. "It's all like a hundred years old with no women and lots of racism. I didn't like it much. Overwritten. Not my thing. I don't remember much. It's all based here in New England, though."

"He talks about a creature called a shoggoth. A huge protoplasmic slave creature that lived in prehistoric times. Like, prehistoric meaning before dinosaurs even."

FORMLESS

"Protoplasmic?" Taylor asked.

"Shapeless blob." Mo made the pillow motion.

"Okay, how huge?"

Mo thought about it. "I want to say it was comparable to a freight train. Maybe just one train car in size?"

"If what's she's talking about is a shoggoth, it's way smaller." Taylor fluffed an invisible pillow.

"Also, it lived in Antarctica. Mostly." Another bead pinged away. A braid unraveled at the end.

"There is no place a freight-train-sized blob can hide here, whether its name is Aztec or Lovecraftian," Geoffrey said. "Plus, it's warm here; it's mid-September in New England. Not Antarctic weather. That ghost was insane."

"But the ghost says it bit her," Pris argued.

"Dead people are insane," Geoffrey countered. "You can't believe her."

"Well," Mo said, flinging the mass of braids over her shoulder, "I'm thinking that because it has a slightly different name, it's a slightly different thing."

"All right," Mickey said. "So the Aztecs read Lovecraft?"

Pris put her head onto the table and laced her hands over the back of her goggles. A theatrical groan emanated from her.

"No," Mo said. "But a lot of people believe—"

Geoffrey interrupted. "That's super hedging language. Like who?"

"I don't know who! I don't have my phone. I'm not prepared for this conversation!" Mo grabbed her braids again. "Anyway, people, whoever they might be, think some of Lovecraft's mythos had some basis in reality. And if I had my phone, I could look that up. So maybe there's some obscure myth about xoggotli and Lovecraft retconned it into shoggoths. But this thing that bit this lady is one of the original, real ones, smaller things the Aztecs called xoggotli."

"I can't believe we're having this conversation rationally," Taylor put his hand over his goggles.

"Only because Ananda isn't here to change the subject to headaches." Mo sucked in her cheeks and flung her braids back over her shoulder.

"Mo, you're being mean now," Mickey said.

"You know I'm right."

"I wonder where she went." The other insects in the pavilion had left too.

Ek was getting antsy. Ek was programmed to analyze visual pattern recognition, not chatter. Mickey nudged it with her neural net and

FORMLESS

the bird lifted off. She told Ek to look for mermaids around the island. Maybe there really was another shiver of them down here, unrelated to the one at Shell Beach. That would thrill Mo and her boyfriend.

Her neural net pinged again as if thinking of mermaids had conjured them. The ping wasn't Ek.

Let us in.

Who are you? As if she allowed any random stranger into her thoughts.

In a repeat from earlier, Ananda came running from the same direction Pris had, her mouth open, her khaki shirt untucked, her goggles askew on her face.

Taylor and Geoffrey swung off the picnic bench and ran to her. "What happened?"

Mickey couldn't tell which one of them was shouting.

"Bathroom," Ananda answered, her voice thick. "There really is a ghost."

FORMLESS

-18-

What did the ghost do?" Pris demanded.

"I'm not a paranormal investigator fraud like you. I don't know what the ghost did; I didn't want to even look at her. What was I supposed to do?"

"You just saw a ghost!" Mo yelled. "Then you call someone who hunts ghosts a fraud? But also imply she knows what to do around an actual ghost? You are a confused woman."

Let us in.

Mickey didn't have time for this. Why was this noise in her head, these weird thoughts? Everyone crowded together. Ek circled above, spying something anomalous in their pattern.

Drowning out the intrusive thoughts, Mickey tried to take charge. She decided they should try something different. "We know there's a ghost in the lady's bathroom. I'm guessing she died there. Let's try to talk to her again and see if we can get some footage even if we can't see the camera screen. We really weren't thinking clearly the first time." She stood. Mo and Pris copied her.

"Wait!" Ananda interrupted. "Don't you want to hear my ghost experience?"

Mo, who had started walking back toward the bathroom block, stopped. "I don't know. Did you really see a ghost, or are you lying to get attention?"

You can hear us.

"I saw her. She was stuttering in and out."

"What did she say?" Mo put her hands on her hips.

"She didn't say anything, and I didn't ask." Ananda looked down. "I guess I freaked out and ran back here. I didn't even dry my hands."

"Whereas I, the person lacking any advanced degrees, kept her cool and spoke with the ghost calmly." Pris pulled the camera out of her bra and studied the blank screen. "The only way to change this camera from still to video is by using the screen. How long does it take for the alarm to go off after you remove the goggles?"

"Right away," Mickey said.

Mo agreed.

"And how quick did the park rangers arrive?"

"Worker ants—you see park rangers?"

"Yeah, like that really old movie with the dinosaur park?"

"That's cool. I'm not sure how long it took. It was dark; I was hurt. It felt like a long time. I'm not sure how high up I was in the hollow log or where they had to come from. But probably only a minute or two."

"They have already flagged two people in our group for taking off their headsets," Geoffrey pointed out.

FORMLESS

"I was hurt!" Mickey said. "I got snagged on some broken thing and my prosthetic broke. Pris, sue them for me," she joked.

"On it. Then can I burn the park down?"

Mo suggested, "Ek. Its close-up video isn't the greatest resolution, but it can record sound, right?"

"Yeah," Mickey agreed, glancing at the raven circling above.

"We bring Ek to record the sound and whatever video it can from Mickey's shoulder. Won't be as good as her usual forward-facing head cam, but it will have to do. Then Pris and I can take as many photos as we can. We can edit it all together with a good voice-over later."

"And we get to watch you film?" Geoffrey said eagerly.

"The bathroom is small, right," Pris said. "And we don't want to scare her."

They resumed walking.

"It's not that small," Ananda said. "And let me understand this. Even though you are all gonna yell at me and be mean. We're taking a huge chunk out of our day here investigating the headache thing to do a ghost interview?"

Mo slowed but didn't stop or turn. "You saw the ghost. You are a scientist."

"We're here about headaches. The ghost is immaterial!"

"Ghosts usually are," Mo said and sped up.

FORMLESS

-19-

Ananda was fuming, with Taylor trying to calm her down. Geoffrey wanted to see the ghost so badly he was bouncing on his toes.

"All right, hush." Pris pulled her camera from her shirt. She held it to her ear while pressing the power button.

"Why are we being quiet?" Ananda asked her.

Mickey thought she heard Pris's eyes roll.

"Because the camera makes a small noise when it turns on and plays an animation I can't see. If I hear the noise, I know it turned on successfully."

"Oh. Did you hear it?"

"I don't know because someone was talking."

"Please be quiet while I repeat this exercise." After a moment, Mo said, "Mine is on."

Pris shook hers. "Now this is like that horrible logic problem with the drawer full of mixed black and white socks. If I press the button again, am I turning it on or off?"

Ek landed on Mickey's shoulder. The three of them—three and a half—stood before the open portal to the bathroom, like a tunnel into a cave.

"Try hard to take excellent pictures, Mo," Pris said. "I might do nothing."

"Do you want to switch cameras?"

Pris pouted. "No. We could stand around for ten minutes. Then both cameras would automatically shut off, and we could try again."

Ananda blew out an exasperated breath.

"They aren't like our usual cameras, are they?" Mickey took Pris's camera. "This is Schrodinger's camera right now. Does it have Bluetooth?"

"What does that matter?" Ananda's breath exploded again. "How did you ever manage to learn to communicate with a new species? You guys waste so much time."

"Geoffrey, am I allowed to talk to her about my neural net?" She gave the camera back to Pris.

"Why do you need to—? Yeah, a little. I'll stop you if you go too far into restricted territory."

"Ananda. I have a headset under my hair." Mickey held up her hair and turned. Under the back, along a shaved strip, the neural net nestled. It was a gorgeous diadem, more like art than science, gold and silver wires in a tight weave, precision-formed to fit the back of her head. Inside the metal lace nested microscopic rare-earth magnets and computer chips. "There are magnets in the net and more embedded under my scalp and the end of my arm. The neural net connects to my brain, where neurosurgeons implanted more microchips. Geoffrey and Taylor designed the neural net to allow me to have a greater range of motion for my prosthetic." She paused. Geoffrey nodded that she could keep talking. "A software upgrade last summer inadvertently allowed me to connect to a wider range of electronics. Like Ek." The raven bobbed its head. "If the camera has Bluetooth, I could access it and tell Pris if it's turned on." Geoffrey raised his hand to his mouth and rubbed his lips. She stopped talking.

"Unfortunately," Taylor said, "No Bluetooth. I made them tiny and light. I wasn't thinking about remote access."

Mickey closed her eyes and tried anyway, feeling relief at being removed from the aggressive retooling of the world fed to her by the goggles. There was Ek, close and familiar.

And something else. The camera? There was only one.

"I think yours is off, Pris. But, Mo, I'm gonna see if I can switch yours to video. If I can get in."

The camera wasn't where she expected it to be. It seemed farther away, in a different direction. But the extra sense the neural net gave her could be funny. She touched the camera and poked at it, trying to get in. Her head hurt. That would make Ananda happy.

It didn't feel like a camera. Ek was basically an upgraded camera that could fly and accept commands.

It didn't react like any camera she could imagine. Instead, it was almost organic, almost alive.

It opened like a flower and drew her in.

It wasn't a camera.

FORMLESS
-20-

It was something like a hive mind and something like a swarm. It was one thing and many, young and old, insane and cunning.

It recognized Mickey, hungered for her.

She flung herself violently out, stumbling.

Mo caught her before she fell over. Mickey, suffocating, wanted to tear off the virtual reality goggles. Mo tried to steady her without touching her.

"Did you change my camera to video? Guessing you didn't, of course?"

"That wasn't your camera," Mickey gasped.

"What was it?"

"I don't know." Mickey shivered despite the day's warmth. "It wanted me. Personally. Not for sex, I don't think. I don't know. It was awful."

"Do you think it was the xoggotli?" Mo stepped back, having balanced Mickey. "I'm not sure how they reproduce."

"Now what are you babbling about?" Ananda pursed her lips. "I thought you would do this ghost-hunting thing quickly and get it over with."

"I don't know," Mickey repeated. "Let's do this ghost thing. I don't want to talk about it right now."

"Is my camera on?" Pris shook it.

"I don't know. I don't know anything."

Mo turned to Ananda, Geoffrey, and Taylor. "Stay in the doorway."

They threaded the entrance tunnel, Pris in the lead. "I hope no one is in here. That would be awkward, right? Excuse me, can you finish peeing so we can talk to a ghost?"

"What if the ghost doesn't come out with all our cameras here?" Mickey winced as Ek adjusted itself on her aching shoulder.

"Maybe it'd be better to have Ek recording first," Mo suggested.

After a few minutes with no sign of anything happening, Mo said, "Maybe we should all go pretend to pee. It might be better to have less of us crowding around."

Mickey left Ek perched on the sink. As she tended to her business, she said to Mo, "I wonder if the ghost sees us the same way we see her … fading in and out, lacking distinguishing features like hair and skin color."

"Well, obviously, she recognized Pris."

"I stay off the show!" Pris said. "Have I pretended to pee long enough?"

FORMLESS

"Not from the show, of course, from seeing you before."

"Right. I'm coming out. You guys wait a minute. Just spy again."

Mickey peered through Ek's eyes.

Pris emerged from the stall and washed her hands as if encountering a giant robotic raven in the ladies' room was an everyday occurrence. She took her time, peering into the corner by the trash bin and patting her chest where she had stashed the camera.

"I don't think she's coming back."

"Go hide in the tunnel, and I'll try," Mo said.

Pris slipped through the door opening to stand with the others. Mickey, clothes back in place, waited in her stall, watching through Ek.

Mo greeted the bird and patted its head. She washed her hands for a long time, singing under her breath to time it, something they had been taught years ago. Mickey had forgotten that silly ritual.

"We all used to have a favorite hand-washing song, Mr. Bird," Mo said. "Or are you Mrs. Bird? Ms. Bird? So we wouldn't die, of course. I guess it worked because I'm alive." She twitched her head toward the corner. "Hello?"

Mickey peered through Ek. A reverse shadow, like a bit of light through a sheer drape. Different from before.

"Everyone wants to live," Mo said to Ek. "And if someone dies, we want to know why."

Was the shadow moving?

"Not that you would know anything about death, Bird."

Mo produced her camera, placing it next to Ek. "You're a pretty bird, and I'm going to take your picture."

Ek nodded. The shadow flickered.

Mo positioned herself to take photos of Ek with the shadow in the background. "Pris? Something's here," she whispered.

"Yeah." Pris moved into the doorway with her camera. "Do you remember me from earlier?"

Mickey opened the stall door but stayed away from the sink.

"You told me about the xoggotli," Pris got the pronunciation reasonably right. "Is that what bit you? That you were allergic to?"

Watching the same scene simultaneously through her own eyes and Ek's lenses was disorientating. Mickey could only see Mo from her position, not the shimmer she presumed was the ghost. She closed her physical eyes and just used Ek, keeping the bird in recording mode.

Mickey's leg ached. Some movement had dislodged the splinter or pushed it against a nerve. The tiny stall overwhelmed her. She never thought to use the large corner one, even though she qualified. Mickey was just twisted and missing an arm; she could manage in a regular

FORMLESS

stall. She hated being a bother. Now, as her claustrophobia clawed at her, she regretted that choice. No one with a wheelchair was at the park to be upset at her use of the big stall.

"Did it mean to kill you?" Mo asked the ghostly shimmer.

Mickey wondered if Mo was seeing the same ghost as they had earlier. Ek sometimes saw things differently than humans.

"What did it want, then?"

Mo went to the mirror and breathed. Then she awkwardly spelled, "taste test."

FORMLESS
-21-

What does that mean?" Pris wondered in a loud whisper.

"Sharks will do an exploratory bite to see if what's in front of them is good to eat, of course," Mo said, "But she said it didn't want to kill her."

And whatever it was, the xoggotli was most definitely not a shark. At least, not the type Mickey had encountered the previous summer.

"She's going," Pris aimed her goggles at the fading shimmer.

"I hope we got some wonderful photos." Mo raised her hand to the lost lady. "Mickey?"

She emerged from the tiny stall and took a deep breath of not-so-fresh bathroom air. "Ek only saw a shimmer. A reverse shadow in the air. I couldn't even tell if it was the same lady. I got it all on video."

"I couldn't really tell," Mo admitted. "But she did know what we were talking about."

Geoffrey burst into the sink area, his brother on his heels. "We know we're in a ladies' bathroom. But that was a ghost?"

Mickey shrugged. It hurt. "Some ghosts are more exciting than others."

"That wasn't exciting?" They were examining the corner where the ghost had vanished.

Ananda hesitated in the doorway. Mickey peered between Taylor and Geoffrey at her. She should tell Ananda she heard a voice in her head that gave her a headache. It would make Ananda happy and integrate her into their group. Mickey knew what it felt like to be an outsider.

"It's too crowded in here," she said instead. "I'm gonna wait outside for a bit. C'mon, Ek." She extended her bound metal elbow toward the raven as she passed, and it stepped on, climbing to her shoulder. Between its claws and weight, and the sharp, narrow zip ties, she winced.

Pris noticed. "Mickey, you okay?"

She shrugged her right shoulder. "The zip ties are uncomfortable, and my leg is on fire. My head hurts from trying to connect to the cameras."

Ananda zeroed in on that, of course.

As Mickey brushed by, Ananda grabbed her flesh arm. "Your head hurts?"

Mickey pulled free. "Don't touch me. I have claustrophobia and I don't like being crowded or touched."

Ananda pulled her hand back and held it next to her face. "Excuse me."

Mickey continued outside into the sun's warmth and heat. The diseased gray plants appeared uglier than ever. She sent Ek flying to relieve herself of its weight. Sometimes it was a comfort to have the robotic bird with her. Right now, it was another thing crushing her.

Mushroom benches huddled close to the bathroom huts. Mickey plopped on one. A glowing crystal cluster right in line with her gaze captured her attention. This bug-themed milieu was arranged in ways to make her artist's heart happy. Good sightlines, pleasing compositions of objects. She wondered what a season's pass cost and if she could bring in a sketchbook. Probably not. But that was more feedback she could give to Lilli, that the park was aesthetically pleasing.

Trying to ruin the illusion, she studied where the ugly gray-green living foliage intersected with a cluster of crystals. Sticks, maybe, with balls on top and tracking chips along the edges? It would be easy to touch the crystals and figure them out. She bet the souvenir shops were full of real and fake crystal clusters. After spending the day among the clusters, she wanted one. Or several, especially ones that would glow. That would be awesome.

She was also tempted to take a couple of leaves from the gray plants. Not to grow a plant—Mo could do that, that was a mad-scientist thing—but to figure out what they were. Well, honestly, to give them to Mo to figure out. How had she lived before she had Mo?

The plants looked sickly. If that was part of the illusion, it wasn't pleasant. And it wasn't only in the insect milieu, either. Lilli needed a botanist or a competent gardener on staff.

The gray plants moved at their base, and the illusion of blue crystals wavered as a critter crossed between a chip and Mickey's goggles. Some garden animal. Too bad they couldn't put chips in the wildlife, but that would probably be cruelty to animals. Although many wild animals had tracking tags, and that wasn't abuse. For instance, Mo and her boyfriend were slowly convincing the mermaids to wear tracking necklaces.

Mickey's neural net pinged; she tilted her head. Ek was flying freely across the island, not in any holding pattern or distress. She touched the bird; the ping wasn't Ek.

Raised voices from inside the bathroom. Mickey just couldn't deal. She walked toward the water, along one of the meandering paths through the mushroom forest, searching for whatever was pinging her.

She looked out into Long Island Sound. The same weird creatures she had seen while on the Horrorail gamboled in the water, glowing and tentacled. "The slithy toves did gyre and gimble in the wabe," she quoted at the strange creatures. They might have been nonsense critters or actual creatures; she didn't know. She searched for mermaids or sharks, which she knew were real. The water around the island was so heavily augmented that her mermaid friend Pearl might have been a dozen feet away, waving at her, and Mickey wouldn't have noticed. They must have some sort of buoys anchored everywhere to achieve that effect.

The overlook had more mushroom and crystal benches, plus an overturned trash can log. Peering at the shape of an umbrella-like mushroom towering over a shelf-fungus bench, she wondered if solar panels might be hidden beneath the illusion. One of the smaller islands, well cloaked, housed an enormous, controversial windmill.

The windmill. Mickey sat on a shelf fungus and thought about where the windmill was in relation to where she was in the park. It was no good. She was terrible with directions. That's why her phone and car had GPS and map programs.

Once upon a time, people had paper maps that folded in ways foreign to earth's geometry. They had to use a physical compass, like a demented pocket watch with a floating magnet, to get around. The only pocket watches and compasses Mickey had ever seen were at cosplay events. No one brought an archaic paper map with non-Euclidian geometry in its folds to those events. Who knew what entities would be summoned by folding those maps wrong?

She didn't know where the windmill was, but it was there. As they arrived, she had seen it from the car, vast and white, looking like the future.

"My head already hurts." Mickey studied the weird bug things. Isoderms? What were they called? Slithy toves was close enough. "It's not like I'm going to explode from being near the evil windmill." She closed her eyes and felt for the windmill to see if its vibrations were causing headaches, something she could report back to Ananda. "I don't think I'm going to explode."

You feel right.

No warning ping. It was just there.

Let us in.

FORMLESS
-22-

Which was stupid. Because it was already in, wasn't it, if Mickey could hear it through her neural net?

All the way in.

No!

Mickey didn't know what "all the way" meant in this context, and she didn't want to know. She pushed as hard as her mind could. The metal web heated under her hair as she burned energy through it.

"Go!" she said with her mind and her mouth. She tried to call for Ek simultaneously, but the extraneous thing in her head immediately glommed onto the signal.

Who's that?

No!

Mickey opened her eyes. The isoderms, lobstrosities, and slithy toves still gyred and gimbled in the wabe. Her entire head felt encased in a concrete block. She wanted to throw the AR goggles into the ocean. Who cares what they cost? Pris would pay.

That was terrible for her to think. Pris was not her ATM.

The magnetic connections inside her skull burned. She longed for a pillow stuffed with ice to lay her poor overheated head on.

Mickey leaned her neck onto the shelf fungus. If it had been real, it might have been soft. But underneath the illusion was a hard wooden bench with no neck support.

Something of her distress had gotten through to Ek; the raven circled above her.

We could help you. Now it was trying to seduce her.

No!

Mickey put all her mental energy into thinking negative thoughts. *No, no, no, go away, get out.* She should get up, walk back to the bathroom block, get help, tell her friends what was happening.

Her head was pounding.

Any thought she had that was not a negation, that wasn't a solid pushing away of the thing in her head, it attacked and examined.

Friends?

She wasn't sure whether taking off the neural net would kick it out.

Net?

It flipped through her thoughts as if speed-reading a book. It hurt physically and was also a violation. Mickey knew other people's secrets. And there were things about herself that she didn't want others to know. It felt like grubby little fingers laying her bare.

Outside her head, bushes rustled—the ugly real-life gray foliage. She hoped Ek had landed. Though she didn't know what the raven

FORMLESS

could do to help her. It wasn't genuinely sentient; it just had excellent programming.

The grubby fingers poked at Ek again, although they weren't precisely fingers.

Get out. Please.

Maybe if she was reasonable.

Go bother someone else.

Voices approached. Her friends, plus Ananda. Mean, but true.

The presence, and its grubby non-fingers, zipped out of her head so fast it left a vacuum. If she had been drawing it as a graphic novel panel, a puff of smoke would have appeared in the void and an onomatopoetic word like *phzzft*.

FORMLESS
-23-

She opened her eyes. Ek was closest, with her friends behind and beyond.

"Why did you leave?" Mo asked.

Ananda stared at her face. "Your head hurts, doesn't it?"

"Yes, Ananda, my head hurts," Mickey confessed. "I had an idea about that. I came here to investigate."

Ananda sat beside her, crowding her. Mickey moved along the shelf fungus's edge until one butt cheek was almost off the underlying wooden bench.

"There's a big offshore windmill out there somewhere." Mickey gestured with her right arm. "I wasn't paying much attention when Lilli's people built this park and remodeled the island, but there was a lot of NIMBY-ism about the windmill."

"Yeah," Mo said. "People think windmills cause cancer, all kinds of stupid stuff. So much misinformation. But the promise to build and house this windmill and eventually other windmills is part of what got the park approved and the land purchased from the Natives."

Mickey nodded. "I came over to the lookout to see if the windmill might be causing the headaches."

"Mickey." Mo tilted her head, her voice full of regret and condemnation. "You know better."

"I was trying to help Ananda," Mickey said, pursing her lips. She wished she could bat her eyes sarcastically at Mo. "It's so important to her."

"And now you have a headache from the windmill?" Ananda's eagerness seemed pathetic.

"I never found the windmill. Trying to find it gave me a headache." Why was she lying? If Ananda hadn't been there, Mickey would have told the truth. She closed her eyes. The goggles and the augmented reality overlay were getting to her again.

Something scuttled in the bushes. The trash can rattled.

Her leg ached.

The zip ties cut into her left arm.

With her eyes closed, everything felt separate and distinct.

Mo flopped onto the next bench and flung her arms to either side. "I used to be fine with not having the internet at my fingertips, using physical reference books and handwritten notebooks. I remembered things with my own brain. Then Pris and Mickey came along. Pris gave me the best toys ever. Now I can't remember anything because why should I when I can look it up in a second?"

"What are you blaming me for?" Pris asked, voice rising. "The whole internet? That's my fault?" Shell Beach, Mo's home, had been stuck in the 1980s technology-wise when Pris and Mickey had met Mo.

"It's all your fault," Mo said. Mickey couldn't tell if she was joking or serious. "I can't remember anything else about shoggoths. I don't know if Natives knew about them. I don't know more about this island's legend. You need a librarian, not a marine biologist, but even a librarian is useless without books and reference material."

Mickey opened her eyes. "Taylor, when you went to the souvenir shop, were they selling guidebooks on the island's history? Haunted Connecticut? Haunted New England? Complete works of H.P. Lovecraft?"

"Did Lovecraft write about Connecticut?" Mo wondered. "I don't think he did."

Taylor rubbed his face. "I don't remember any physical books or pamphlets. Just the postcards."

Ananda slumped against Mickey. "You all are so off the track on why we are here."

Mickey stood, not caring if the other woman almost fell over. She had already warned Ananda not to touch her or crowd her. "We haven't gone on all the rides or had all the experiences. I'm not feeling my best, but I'm moving ahead with the day." She consulted a park map on a crystal cluster and pointed. "I'm going here, on this thing that says it's a 'dark ride'."

As she walked, she held up her right arm. Ek landed, climbed to her shoulder, across her neck to her other shoulder, and held onto the zip ties.

FORMLESS
-24-

A colossal sprawling boulder housed the Vertigo Vault. As Mickey walked toward it, Ek weighing down her shoulder, the voice cajoled inside her head for her to let them all the way in.

A giant spiderweb filled the promised dark inside of the boulder. A massive, bloated spider crouched in its center. Worker ants loaded passengers into cocoon cars wrapped with spider silk. The spider, web, and cocoons glowed green.

Mickey felt like food. Her friends stood behind her in line, no longer arguing.

"One person or two per capsule." The helper ant inspected Mickey's arm. "This ride has high g-forces. Will you be okay? And the bird, no, absolutely not. Nothing loose. Keep all body parts inside the cars at all times."

"I will sit with her," Mo said. "Hang on, let someone else go first." They sent Ek outside to patrol.

Pris sat with Taylor as Mo wrapped the extra elastic bandage they'd taken from the first aid hut around Mickey's torso, holding her prosthetic in place. "It would be easier for me to remove it and leave it somewhere," Mickey said, "except that we'd have to cut these stupid zip ties with a knife, which we don't have."

"We got this."

Mickey had to awkwardly climb one-handed into the capsule. At least it was dark, so no one could see and laugh at her—even in AR she had to look strange. That had been the worst part about being crooked and missing half an arm as a child—being laughed at for not being able to do things the "right way," and for looking unattractively different with her deformities. The clunky, ugly prosthetics she had worn until she had met Geoffrey and Taylor had been worse than having nothing below the elbow, but if she had forgone them for her own comfort, that made everyone else very uncomfortable.

"Let me sit on the side that gets squished." Mo climbed over her. "You wouldn't be able to deal at all. I've been on a version of this ride before, just not in the dark."

"It's a spider web full of cocoons." Mickey gazed around. "What does it look like for you?"

"It's a crop circle with UFOs. We're sitting in a UFO."

The inside walls were decorated with glow-in-the-dark scenes featuring more spiders and the usual mushrooms, fungus, and glowing crystals.

"Everything in here must be virtual," Mo said. "This ride will practically scrape the walls. A good place to get squished to death if you walk around while it's in motion."

FORMLESS

The spider squatting over them seemed to move. But augmented reality could suggest anything.

"I suppose this ride could give a person a headache," Mo said. "But it's ubiquitous. Every park wouldn't have a version of it if it made everyone sick."

A bell rang. The door closed, sealing them in darkness. Their cocoon car whirled in small circles at the end of a long arm, and that arm rotated like the hand of a clock around the surface of the web.

Their small cocoon seemed to be about to crash into the other cocoons every few seconds. Mo tilted against the outer edge, and Mickey leaned into her heavily. The spider above leered and dipped her great gangling legs in their direction. Her enormous fangs dripped venom that barely missed them.

The glowing crystals and fungus on the other cocoons outlined them as the cars whirled in the dark. Pounding music played at a ridiculous volume that almost, but not quite, harmonized with the deep vibrations coming through the bone induction of the goggles. That incongruity worked on Mickey's anxiety, ratcheting it up every time the two weren't in sync.

The walls flew at them like hands wanting to smash Mickey and Mo flat.

Every second, Mickey felt watched, not just by the squatting spider but by the darkness itself.

A voice muttered deep in her head, sounding like a TV in another room.

A dark drop fell from the spider's fang and landed in their car. Mickey somehow heard it hit the metal floor of the capsule, even over the music. She recoiled. "Mo, watch out."

"What?" Mo tried to push herself from the cocoon's side, where she was being crushed by centripetal force and Mickey's weight.

"Something fell into the car," Mickey shouted.

"It's not real."

In other cars, people screamed. Were they her other friends or strangers? Screaming in fun or fear? She was not finding theme park experience fun. She hated crowds and being stared at, had never wanted to be around other kids who would inevitably make fun of her, laugh and point because she looked funny. Pris had been the first person to be curious about her deformities without being mean.

Listening to the screams, she wondered if drops of venom, or whatever was analogous in their milieu, dropped into every car.

"I don't know where it went." Mickey searched the darkness by her feet.

FORMLESS

"Where what went?" Mo sounded exhilarated rather than scared or annoyed.

"The blob! The poison drop!"

"Nothing fell. It's an illusion."

"It made a noise when it fell!" Even over the blaring music, Mickey swore she heard it, even felt it impact the cocoon.

"It's augmented reality, Mickey. Nothing fell!"

Her leg throbbed from bracing herself. But Mo was strong. Mo could take being squished. She could relax.

Between the dark, the AR overlay, the bone-induction vibration, the loud music, and the weird neon glow, everything distorted, including time. Maybe it was Mo squishing Mickey and not the other way around.

This strange pressure on her leg made no sense, and she sensed movement inside the car that wasn't Mo. The lurking spider leered and dripped venom. Music blared, her jaw vibrated, everyone screeched and laughed. Behind it all welled the sound of carpenter ants, gnawing, magnified a thousand times. Enormous pieces of fungus and towering insects veered close enough to touch, then reeled away. Their cocoon swirled madly in the spider web's maelstrom.

Her neural net pinged, and it was more than she could bear. Mickey let out a frustrated scream. Mo grinned at her, teeth glowing in the black light, and gave her a thumbs-up, obviously thinking Mickey was having fun.

The curious fingers tried to probe her memories again. Mickey shut her eyes, yelling, pushing it away.

The carpenter ants roared. It was like being in a blender full of sand. Mickey fancied she could feel the abrasion on her skin. The volume ratcheted up, prohibiting conversation.

Mo laughed and whooped, her body half-sideways, jammed against the outer wall of the twirling cocoon, her long thin braids flying as they swung around endlessly, the green beads glowing.

Above them, drip, drip, drip, the giant spider drooled venom into every car.

FORMLESS
-25-

Mo put her hand to her head as the ride finally slowed. The music ebbed.

The ride felt like forever, but it was probably only five minutes of real time. Certainly not ten.

"I will not say the h-word." Mickey waited for the worker ant to unchain the outside of their cocoon.

"It's not that," Mo said. "There was this grinding noise—"

"Like carpenter ants!"

"No, like a pepper grinder. But inside my head. Like something was trying to tunnel in."

"It sounded like carpenter ants to me." Mickey told her how they had eaten her parents' shed. "We had the shed sprayed before we took it down. A literal waterfall of dead ants poured out. Tens of thousands of them. I think there were more ants in the shed walls than wood."

"That is horrible." The worker ant freed Mo from the cocoon. "I had the feeling that someone had my brain in a spice grinder."

When Mickey's left leg hit the ground, it buckled. The pain was worse. Mo caught her and guided her to the doorway of the round building.

"My leg, it's on fire. I know you said the venom drops weren't real, but I think one got in there."

"Of course." Mo positioned Mickey on a shelf-fungus bench near the ride.

Their friends found them moments later. Ananda's full lips were pale. She stared into the distance.

"What did you all see?" Mo described her UFO experience as Mickey probed at her calf, wincing.

"We were in dinosaur eggs, in a huge nest, guarded by an enormous mama dinosaur," Geoffrey explained.

"Egg-eating dinosaurs kept coming in from the side, gnashing their teeth, trying to eat us," Taylor continued.

"The mother dinosaur spit acid at them." Ananda's voice was low.

"You were baby acid-spitting dinos, Ananda?" Mickey asked. "Mo, can you look? I swear something's in there."

"It's a splinter; I said that already."

"I guess that's what we were supposed to be? Assuming the big dinosaur crouched over us was our mama. It was confusing. So noisy and dark and fast." Ananda shook her head.

"The teeth-gnashing was so loud." Taylor gestured with both hands. "A couple times, I honestly thought I was really being eaten alive. I could actually feel the vibration of the gnashing through the bone induction. Well-done."

FORMLESS

Mo lifted her head from behind Mickey's leg as she was unwrapping it. "I felt that. Like being in a pepper grinder."

"I heard something sort of like that maybe, but I felt nothing," Geoffrey said.

"I don't know." Ananda was still very pale. "I might have felt it. I don't know what's happening anymore."

Mo traced something on Mickey's bare calf. After a moment, Mickey realized it was the letter H. "Anyone have a headache to report to Ananda?"

"The pepper grinding feeling wasn't a headache, but it wasn't comfortable either." Mo poked at Mickey's wound. Mickey winced.

"The acid-spitting you guys saw?" Mickey asked. "I saw it as venom dripping from the fangs of a giant spider."

There was a general outcry against the idea of an enormous spider.

"How large was the spider?" Ananda's mouth turned down.

"It was mapped onto the top of the ride. A spider the size of the ride."

Ananda shook her head. "Nope. I'm so glad I did not choose insects. I wasn't even thinking giant venom-spitting spiders would be part of that."

"I wasn't either." Mickey scrunched her nose. "But that's been the worst so far."

"The big dinosaur spit acid at the smaller dinosaurs who were coming to eat the eggs, coming to eat us." Taylor reiterated and mimed spitting with his hand to his mouth.

"It didn't hit you?" Mickey winced as Mo prodded her unwrapped leg. "The acid?"

He paused, chewing his cheek. "Actually, yeah. It didn't go very far. The acid did land in the eggs, the cars. With everything else that was going on, I didn't realize that. What kind of venom-spitting mother spits venom on her own eggs?"

"Did venom fall in your egg?"

"It fell in my egg, yeah." Taylor nodded. Pris agreed.

Mo said to Mickey, "Your leg looks the same to me. It feels different?"

"Something is in there."

"Do you want to go back to the first aid hut?"

"She's not going back to that useless non-medical professional!" Pris said.

"Something's embedded in her leg," Mo argued.

"There's gotta be something around here we can use as tweezers," Pris insisted. "You fix it."

FORMLESS

"I'm not a fish! Or a mermaid. Mo can't fix me." Mickey winced. "Just wrap it again."

"What do you think of the venom falling into the eggs, Mickey?" Taylor asked.

"Not augmented reality. I believe something really fell."

"If we went back in there now and checked all the cars, what would we find?" Mo smoothed the bandage across Mickey's calf.

"A ride full of people, now," Mickey said as the music started on the other side of the wall.

"But what do you think fell into our cars? You guys felt it or heard it, but I didn't really notice," Geoffrey said.

"I thought it was part of the AR," his brother replied. "I've seen a lot of weird stuff today."

"Yeah? Like what?" Mickey stretched her leg out and flexed her foot, wincing.

Geoffrey answered for him. "I've seen bizarre scuttling creatures that didn't look like dinosaurs, although I'm not an expert. Heard strange noises. The grinding during that ride, although I guess other people heard it more than I did. I thought it was a mechanical part of the ride or something; maybe it needed maintenance."

"The grinding noise wasn't inside your head at all?" Taylor asked. "And you didn't see the dinosaur spitting venom?"

Geoffrey frowned. "I saw it, but I thought it was only through the goggles. An augmented reality effect. Maybe they drip water from the top of the ride and map venom onto it somehow, and some of us are more suggestible?"

"This entire park is predicated on people being suggestible," Ananda argued. "But when someone sees something liquid falling, why would they imagine that liquid getting inside their head or making a grinding noise? That's not logical. But that's what it seemed like."

"Can water even make a grinding noise?" Pris wondered. "Not that I noticed anything weird."

"A water pump can, if the water is low, but that's not the water itself, it's the machinery, and that's nothing like the grinding I heard," Mo said.

"The sound was exactly like carpenter ants eating a shed," Mickey said. "I don't know what venom sounds like. That seems like a writing prompt from social media: the sound of venom."

Taylor said, "If I was going to write about the sound of venom, it wouldn't be dry, grinding, or crunchy. Venom would sound like—" he sucked in his cheeks and chewed them. "A cough when you're really congested, someone falling from the top of a building, or a pudding balloon being shot by an air gun."

"Wet noises," Mo agreed. "Not dry ones."

"We independently heard dry, grinding noises when we saw something like venom," Mickey said. "What does that mean? What were the programmers thinking? The park designers? If we had a phone, we could contact your friend Lilli and ask her."

"This is another thing that could have caused headaches," Ananda said.

"On this, we agree," Mickey nodded. "But if this is why people are having headaches, it's too obvious, and they programmed it this way, so they must have had a reason. I can't figure out what it might be. And this is too easy. Why didn't they figure it out themselves? Hmm, the loud grinding noise in this ride, could that be causing headaches?"

"Why would the venom drops, or whatever, have to be physical and not virtual?" Mickey rubbed her leg. "I feel like a drop crawled inside my leg. And that's crazy talk."

Mo stared at her. "I have an idea. Maybe we're all drugged. Hypnotized. That's what the dead lady was allergic to."

"I don't think so." Ananda shook her head.

"Yeah," Geoffrey said. "If that was the case, Lilli would have thought of it. And if they are secretly drugging their patrons, would they go to an outside contractor for help?"

"I don't feel drugged," Pris said, holding up her hands and studying them. "And I've been drugged."

Ananda studied her. "As in, kidnapped and drugged?"

Pris's lips curled. "You sweet, innocent girl. I thought you knew whose sister I am."

Ananda twisted her mouth. "How would they have drugged us?"

"Microscopic needles inside the wristbands?" Mo ran a finger inside the bracelet on her opposite arm.

"But it would only work halfway on me." Mickey bounced her prosthetic inside its sling.

"We are overcomplicating this," Taylor said. "We have to be."

The ride's music ended, and the next cohort of patrons came out. Mickey stopped rubbing her calf and watched them, blatantly eavesdropping.

People talked about the ride experience, the giant spider, the UFO, the ghosts, the dinosaurs, what anyone would be excited about after a dark ride at a horror theme park. She let those conversations wash over her. Not what she was looking for. Then someone mentioned venom, and Mickey leaned forward.

"That drop of venom was so real!" a Japanese beetle said. "I swear I felt it hit my leg and sink right in. Look, there's even a mark!"

FORMLESS

Mickey elbowed Mo, but since Mo was on her left and the prosthetic was still strapped across her chest, it wasn't very hard.

"What?" Mo said too loudly.

Mickey dropped her own voice. "That Japanese beetle over there says a drop of venom landed on their leg and made a mark."

Pris argued with Ananda and her boyfriends about hallucinogenic drugs and what they felt like, and how today was not like that.

"We can't see their leg," Mo grumbled.

"I know. But keep listening to everyone's conversations. Ignore Pris. The park didn't drug us."

"They could have, of course."

"It was an interesting idea, but no."

A stinkbug said, "I didn't like that grating noise. Was the ride falling apart? Do they ever oil the parts?"

Mo elbowed Mickey, who nodded that she had heard. She had not considered that the ride itself could be defective.

The stinkbug continued, "It went straight through my skull. Gave me such a headache."

They elbowed each other. Mo came off poorly, her bone elbow hitting Mickey's metal-sheathed one.

The Japanese beetle, walking away, seemed to limp.

The last bugs emerged from the boulder, a stag beetle and a hornet holding a limping tick between them. "He cut his leg on the ride," the hornet said to a worker ant. "I think there's a piece of metal or something stuck inside. Is there a first aid building?"

The worker ant lifted a broken bone covered in lichen and spoke into it.

Pris and the others noticed the drama and stopped their argument to listen. Mo explained sotto voce what was happening.

A pair of worker ants arrived, driving a large leaf with mushroom-cap wheels, and took the wounded tick and its beetle and hornet friends away.

"Off to the useless non-medical professional." Pris made a rude hand gesture. "Good luck finding tweezers."

Mickey covered Pris's hand, pushing it down. "The point is, what happened to me isn't unique."

"The Mothman said they had a headache from the grinding noise," Mo conceded to Ananda. "Said the noise went right through their skull."

"It was in my skull." Taylor rubbed his head. "So deep it was almost like words."

"It was just a little noise," Geoffrey said. "Not that bad."

FORMLESS

"No, it got inside my head," Mo defended Taylor. "I wouldn't say it was words, but it was there."

"It was just a tiny bit of noise," Pris agreed with Geoffrey. "It hardly bothered me, even as noise. And I saw the drops, but I figured they were part of the experience. I didn't feel them. They weren't real. I would have forgotten them already if you guys hadn't brought them up."

Mickey watched the leaf-vehicle trundle away. "We all saw and heard some version of drops and grinding. But how it affected each of us was different."

"That sums it up," Ananda agreed.

"And others saw and experienced something similar."

Mo nodded.

"We have to agree that it's real, and it's happening."

"And causing headaches," Ananda added.

"But this isn't helpful enough to report back to Lilli yet," Geoffrey said. "All we've done is verify that headaches are indeed a thing."

"There are still more rides," Taylor reminded them.

"I don't know if I can take more rides, honestly," Mickey said. "I might have to sit outside like someone's mama and wait. My leg is burning, and my arm is excruciating with the zip ties."

Pris's mouth turned down on one side. "My poor Mickey."

"We'll get new straps made up and overnight them as soon as we get back," Taylor said.

Mickey inspected her metal arm. "Just take the whole thing. The straps will need to be attached better. I can do without for a few days." She was ready to throw the prosthetic into the trash; it was hurting and not helping. Actively working against her.

"Since when does our every adventure end with Mickey's arm destroyed?" Pris said.

"Since you met me, apparently." Mo flipped her braids. "I'm a bad influence, of course."

Geoffrey said, "Too bad we can't rent one of those miniature jeeps."

"What jeeps?" Mickey glanced around, mystified.

"Like they took those dinosaurs away in."

"The leaf, you mean?"

"Whatever. For your leg."

"I can walk a bit, I guess. And there are more rides that we should go on."

"Maybe we should skip that," Mo suggested. "And try something completely different."

FORMLESS
-26-

Different how?" Geoffrey tilted his head.

"We should try to find a way into those whispering caverns."

"They're gone, though, aren't they? If they ever existed. They leveled the island except for the hill in the center. Taylor thinks they converted the caverns, but I don't think so. Too random. Those caves are probably collapsed and full of rubble, if they ever existed in the first place. Underground is reserved as a climate-controlled center for the computer system that runs everything. Geothermal is cheaper than heating and cooling systems." Geoffrey said.

You are perfect.

No one had ever flirted with Mickey Crow. A few guys had done it to be mean, but no one had ever wanted Mickey for herself. But here was this voice trying to seduce her.

I have been waiting so long for you. It was an inhuman voice. The words felt translated.

Mickey closed her eyes.

"Can we find our way into the computer center and find out?" Mo wondered.

"I doubt it," Taylor said. "Think of how much security we have at Genesis. Their work is just as proprietary and valuable. Their hardware might be off the shelf, I don't know, but their software has got to be unique. And they've got the public right outside their door, unlike us."

"What do you think we will find, Mo?" Mickey opened her eyes. She wanted to smack herself in the head. She wanted the voice to be real, someone who wanted her.

"A xoggotli?"

No one wanted her. Mickey was stupid to believe that. She tried to refocus on the conversation. "How big would this server room be, Geoffrey? Big enough for a train car-sized monster? If these xoggotli are even that big."

The voice in Mickey's head made a noise that might have been a chuckle.

"I don't know. But I doubt there's enough space for a gigantic monster to hide."

"Can we try, though?" Mo bounced on her toes. "Please?"

"I don't know where it is or how to get into it." Taylor walked to the nearest mushroom and studied the park map. "This line of buildings doesn't have labels. Maybe they're maintenance shacks? One could be the entrance."

"Who can pick a lock?" Mo looked at Pris.

FORMLESS

"Why would you think I can pick a lock? I would just buy the building. Then they would have to let me in. If I didn't already know the owner."

"True." Mickey nodded. "She would."

"We know Lilli but that won't get us inside," Taylor said. "Since we're here in secret."

"Let's walk down Elm Street and see if we can figure out which buildings are unlabeled," Mo suggested.

That proved harder than it seemed. The buildings were clusters of mushrooms and logs, holding one or more businesses. One restaurant might have three mushroom-shaped rooflines, while a single log might house two different games of chance.

Flora, both virtual and actual, clogged the narrow alleys between the buildings. Worker ants patrolled the streets, some in leaf-vehicles. Mickey assumed that underneath they were something like a golf cart.

As she moved, the pain in her leg lessened. Maybe the splinter was working loose.

"Any of these games or restaurants could have a back door leading to the server room. We would never know. The alleys aren't accessible," Taylor said.

"To us." Mo glanced at Ek.

"What do we think Ek can do?" Geoffrey wondered.

"It's a bird-shaped spy camera, operated remotely by Mickey," Pris said. "As a raven, it could poke around anywhere, and no one would look at it twice."

Mickey sent the raven soaring. She plopped herself onto a fungus bench and watched the island through the bird's eyes. Immediately she found the windmill, soaring white, turning several hundred yards off the island. She looked at Mo and pointed. "The windmill is that way. Not that it matters since you confirmed it doesn't cause headaches."

"Wait, how do you know that?" Ananda demanded. "I thought augmented reality cloaked the windmill and anything they don't want us to see."

"Augmented reality doesn't come into play if I look through Ek's eyes. The raven isn't wearing goggles."

Pris's shiny pink mouth fell open. She pushed Mickey's shoulder. "Could Ek help us operate our cameras?"

Ek soared above, seeing reality and nothing else. How could Mickey have been so stupid? She smacked her forehead. "I think so."

"I knew I loved that bird."

They loitered along Elm Street, lined with a double row of mixed mushroom huts and log buildings. Souvenir shops, snack bars, restaurants, and games of chance alternated with what appeared to be administrative offices and the first aid hut.

You are perfect.

Mickey had never wanted a lover of any gender. But if she had, she would have wanted them to talk to her exactly like that. But the very idea of a romantic relationship, in all its sticky claustrophobic physicality, made her feel faint, not amorous.

Whoever, whatever, was in her mind saw her disgust, and tried to reassure her it wouldn't be like that between them. Nothing sticky. A minimum of touching, just once, for one moment. Then together forever.

Taylor touched her arm. "What is Ek seeing?"

She jumped. "I was distracted—"

Ek saw utilitarian, bland, rectangular buildings with cone-shaped or slanted roofs covered in QR codes and stickers. Mickey tried opening one eye and looking through the goggles, but that was practically an instant headache since Ek flew high above, and she stood at ground level.

"There's a mound way over there," she pointed without opening her eyes. "Ek sees it as boulders and leftover landscaping junk."

The voice was almost chortling in her head. She expected it to call her "my precious," it seemed so pleased.

"Can we get to it?" Taylor stood on his tiptoes and peered in that direction. "It looks like a plain hill to me."

"Why do we want to get to it?" Mo wondered. "Do you think it leads to the server room?"

"It could be an entrance to the cavern system at least. What do you think we'll find in the server room, anyway? The xoggotli thing, waiting for us?" Mickey asked.

"I don't know. Maybe. I think they don't like sunlight. And Pris and her energy-sucking fey obsession might be onto something."

Pris snorted.

"The server room could be anywhere," Ananda said. "No, that doesn't mean I am condoning this wild goose chase. Or wild ex-gotty chase."

"Xoggotli," Mo corrected her pronunciation.

Mickey studied a park map. It didn't show the mound. One path curved in its direction and veered away. She ran her flesh index finger along the route. "If there isn't a fence, we can go this way."

"Fence," Pris said.

"Yeah, fence. You know what a fence is. There are probably fences everywhere here; we just can't see them. In fact, I'm going to check it out with my trusty bird sidekick."

FORMLESS

"I thought I was your trusty sidekick," Pris said.

"I'm *your* trusty sidekick. It's trusty sidekicks all the way down."

Mo tilted her head. Pris pointed at her. "You are also a trusty sidekick. Maybe I need to make an org chart of who is whose trusty sidekick."

"Will we be on it?" Taylor asked.

"Everyone is on it. Eight billion people in the world, linked, all sidekicking each other."

Taylor jumped, bending his leg back and knocking his brother in the shin with his heel. "Sidekick!"

Ananda shook her head.

"Are we done kicking? There's a fence. Let's go climb it," Mickey said.

FORMLESS

-27-

That's a fence, all right," Mickey said. Ek showed her an eight-foot-tall chain-link fence decorated with QR codes, rice-sized chips, and *no trespassing* signs. Ek preened itself on her shoulder. "As a bug, I see a white ribbon of powder, which somehow I know is insect poison. Just thinking about crossing the powder makes me feel queasy."

"We dinosaur people see an electrified fence," Geoffrey said. "Covered in *keep out* and *dangerous prehistoric creatures* signs."

"I also see a fence, but it's got razor wire along the top. It's not electric, and it's got government security signs telling me this is a classified area and to stay away or be shot," Mo described. "I think it's supposed to be Area 51."

"Are they watching us, though?" Pris asked. "Does Ek see any security cameras?"

"They are always tracking us as part of the augmented reality programming. They know exactly where we are if they want to look. Crossing the fence might set off an alarm. And we're already on their radar for taking off our goggles earlier," Geoffrey said.

"So we're gonna get thrown off the island," Ananda laid her hand on his arm.

"I'm willing to risk that," Mickey said. "I need a boost. I've only got one arm. Let's go before I lose my nerve and while my leg isn't hurting so badly."

"I'll go first to catch you on the other side," Mo said. "But I feel sick."

"Yes, this seems bad," Ananda agreed. "I'm both uneasy and nauseated myself. I don't think this is what your friend Lilli had in mind, Geoffrey."

"She should have been more clear," Taylor said. He moved closer to the fence and helped Mo climb up, holding onto one of her green high-tops and bracing himself against the wire. "Mickey, is there barbed wire or anything on top of the real fence?"

"It's just a chain-link fence, so just wire points."

Mo felt her way up. "This is so strange. It's better to do it with your eyes closed." She swung her leg over and balanced. "I hope I don't puke. Or fall. I haven't decided yet if I want to have kids. And I don't want a fence post up my lady parts to decide for me." Taylor stretched, his hands on her sneaker bottom, steadying her. "I'm going over." She pulled her foot from Taylor's grasp and started to lower herself to the other side. As her sneaker dragged over the top of the wire, the laces caught. Mo's foot was at her face level, her hands holding her up, her other leg dangling on the far side. She made a terrible gurgling noise.

FORMLESS

Taylor's hands were already up, so he grabbed the wire and started climbing. Ananda squeaked and choked. "Don't puke, Ana, honey." His feet were bigger than Mo's, and his sneakers' toes didn't fit as well into the fence holes.

"Mo!" Pris yelled. "Mickey, she's gonna split in half."

Ananda vomited at that thought. Geoffrey tried to comfort her while monitoring his brother spidering up the fence. Mo dangled on the other side by her shoelace and her fingertips. Her other foot slipped from its toehold in the wire diamond pattern.

Perfection.

Could whatever it was that was talking to her see them?

Help us! She demanded. The sharp, cheesy smell of Ananda's vomit tickled her nose. She brought up her hand to cover her face. She was going insane. What did they look like in AR to other people?

You don't need my help. You'll be mine soon enough.

Taylor reached the top and fumbled with Mo's tangled shoelace. "I can't see through my stupid goggles, but we're caught if I take them off!"

"Cut it!" Mo said. "I'm falling!"

"Cut it with what?"

Ek landed beside his fingers and sawed at the laces with its beak. Its eyes weren't made for close-up work, so instead, it bit Taylor.

"Sorry!" Mickey called.

Geoffrey, frantic, divided his attention between his pale, sick girl-friend, seated beside a vomit puddle, and his twin, balanced on a fence being bitten by a robotic raven while trying to save their friend and employee who hung by her fingertips and a shoelace.

Pris backed away and practically ran up the fence, a neon-pink blur. The fence clattered and rang when she hit it, almost knocking Mo off the other side. Mo cried out in surprise.

Pris grabbed the green high-top sneaker. "Hold on with all those fingers, Mo." She slipped the shoe off Mo's foot.

Mo's leg rotated to its proper place on her hip. She stuck that foot, in its ankle sock, into a metal diamond, then anchored the other foot, and hung there, panting. "I still might puke."

"Ananda already did," Mickey said. "Can't you smell it?"

Ananda groaned.

Pris freed the green sneaker, tossed it, and then climbed to Mo like a pink fairy princess. "You okay? Come on down."

While Mo tried to get her shoe back on with a torn, mangled lace, Taylor and Geoffrey worked together to get Ananda over the fence.

Mickey gazed up. "I don't know if I could do it even if my straps weren't broken." She was the opposite of athletic on a good day. The prosthetic was bound across her chest; the zip ties wouldn't take her weight.

"If we only had a rope. You aren't very big. I could haul you up." Taylor leaned down and offered his hand. "Can you reach?"

She could not.

Geoffrey said, "I can't help you without squishing you a little."

"I know."

Mickey threaded the toe of her left sneaker into a gap as high as she could reach. The cut on the back of her calf erupted into burning pain.

You don't have to do this.

She ignored the voice. It would be too easy to stay on this side of the fence, left out because she was handicapped. Mickey stretched her right hand, her only hand, up. Geoffrey took her right foot and hoisted it as she crab-walked her hand along the fence. She locked that foot in as high as possible and drew up the left one. Her right leg ached with effort. "I should listen more to my physical therapist," she groaned. "Hold my right foot."

She was still only a couple of feet off the ground. Her face was so close to the metal mesh of the fence she could smell it.

Taylor stretched from above, reaching for her sweaty hand. "One more step."

The chain-link swayed and bucked, chiming like a great metal bell. It was amazing the worker ants had not detected them.

"I'm sorry, Mickey, but you're gonna have to go over my lap. I can't figure any other way."

Mickey groaned.

This is so unnecessary. But entertaining.

Both Taylor and Geoffrey had touched her before; they had been friends for a long time, and they had made her prosthetic and neural net. But she had never sat on one of their laps.

Taylor balanced astride the fence, and Mickey sat astride Taylor's knee. It was marginally better than trying to keep herself from being impaled by the metal triangles topping the chain links. "This is really awkward," Mickey said. "Ananda, I'm sorry I'm sitting on your boyfriend. I'm not enjoying it."

Ananda leaned over at the base of the fence, still gagging. She waved a hand.

"Relax and rest a bit," Taylor suggested, holding her hip with one hand and the fence with the other.

"I can't. This is awful." And it was. So personal.

Mo still only had one shoe on, so Pris had to catch Mickey. She scaled back up and climbed down beside Mickey, guiding her hand

and feet to the bottom. Taylor followed, leaving his brother to climb up on his own.

Mickey found a boulder and sat on it. Nothing over here had augmented reality chips. This looked like a rock and it was a rock. It was a relief.

"I can't do this. Every step I take away from the fence on this side, I feel worse." Ananda sagged against the chain-link above Mo, who was trying to figure out where to knot her broken shoelace.

Geoffrey had paused in his climb, hovering on the fence top as if it was a horse. "This is a delicate area this pointy metal is aimed at, Ana," he warned. "Do you want to go back and wait on the path? Decide now."

Ananda heaved. "I'm sorry." Her unhappiness sounded genuine. "I want to go back over."

Taylor lifted the gagging Ananda. She grabbed the metal links as he guided her toes into holds. He stayed under her, boosting her feet. She continued to cough. Geoffrey had to brace one of his feet on either side, not letting the pointed metal wire poke him anywhere sensitive, while he pulled Ananda up and over. Once she was on the other side of the fence, she finally stopped gagging and could use her own muscle power to get to the ground.

Ananda took a few steps away. "I feel better," she called. "I'm going to wait over there."

"I'll send Ek to check on you often. You can talk to him. I'll hear you," Mickey promised.

FORMLESS
-28-

This was not a public area. No augmented reality overlays. Their goggles showed the truth; what Mickey saw matched what Ek showed her. The scraggly gray-green foliage had not been pruned in any pleasing arrangement; it grew wild. Their feet scuffed on sandy dirt, not on the paved and gravel paths that surfaced the rest of theme park.

"I am sure we aren't supposed to be here," Pris said. "We are going to get caught."

No, you won't.

Mickey agreed with the voice for once. "We won't. Plus, you have lawyers."

"Right, my family has lots of lawyers," Pris agreed.

Ek sat on a rock, preening its feathers.

"Let's go look at that mound," Mickey said. "I think it's a pile of whatever got dug out. The fill."

"Dug out of where?" Pris asked.

"The island. When they were making the server room and the geothermal system and flattening everything. If there were lava tubes or something weird, maybe we can find evidence."

"None of us are geologists, Mickey, of course," Mo said.

"I trust you science-types to know random stuff. You knew about the island's history, didn't you? And what Nahuatl words look like, right? And Pris knows things too. When we got to Shell Beach, she knew about card catalogs."

Mickey limped forward. Ek settled on her shoulder.

"Mickey, card catalogs aren't a secret." Mo caught up to her, also limping, since one of her shoes wasn't tied correctly.

Mickey turned on her. Ek almost lost its balance. "I know nothing about anything important. I can draw pictures, that's it. I could barely climb that fence. The only interesting things about me are my name and arm; I had nothing to do with either of those; both came from other people. I'm utterly useless. I bet even Pearl and Starfish have forgotten about me."

Mo's mouth dropped open. "Every time I see Pearl or Starfish, they ask about you. 'Where is Clow?'" That was how Pearl pronounced Crow. "Pearl carries that photo of you in the Ziplock everywhere. You saved her people. You aren't useless. Different isn't useless. Look at Starfish. She's a mermaid who looks 90 percent shark. How do you think she feels, knowing people are terrified of her when she is such a gentle soul?"

Starfish was a sweet person. Mickey should drive to Shell Beach and visit her aquatic friends. Once her leg healed and her arm was repaired. She limped on, Mo silent at her side.

FORMLESS

"What exactly are we looking for?" Pris demanded. "There is no card catalog here for us to consult, Mickey, no library of old books. No handy new friend with local knowledge."

"You never know," Mo said, because that was precisely how she had met Mickey and Pris.

"We have you. We don't need another mad scientist," Mickey said.

"How about a crazy geologist?" Mo countered.

"Access to the internet and a smartphone," Pris passed by them, walking faster. "That's what's on my wish list. Anyone else seeing a pattern to our adventures lately?"

"You need a fairy godmother. I have an awesome one. She's pale-skinned and has pink hair," Mo said. "Maybe you can borrow her. Is that the mound?"

It was a pile of scree, various-sized loose rocks, broken and thrown aside.

Geoffrey studied it. "If we weren't on an island, I would be wary of copperheads. This would be a perfect place for them to lay in the sun. I know they have wildlife here, but I doubt any copperheads have swum over or caught a ride on the ferry."

"What wildlife?" Mickey asked.

"I guess raccoons? Things that get into trash and eat the food. It's a mixed blessing. They don't have to haul as much trash over to the mainland to the trash-burning plant, but they have an ongoing problem with tipped-over cans and having to clean it up."

Taylor picked through the rocks. "Remember when we were little and we used to belong to that gem and mineral club, Geoff?"

Mickey tilted her head. "Seriously? You guys know geology?"

"Nah," Geoffrey said. "Not really. We just used to search for cool looking rocks to collect. I don't remember much."

"If there had been lava tubes or something that caused noises that made people crazy, would you be able to figure it out from these rocks?" Mickey crouched and poked through the pile one-handed.

"Well, this isn't a volcanic island, so there weren't any lava tubes," Taylor said. "It's limestone."

"Probably some fossils to be found if we had time and the right tools." Geoffrey said as the brothers sat in perfect unison. "Wish we could take off these goggles."

Pris inspected her pointy neon-pink manicure, sighed, and picked up a rock.

Mo held out her hands next to Pris's. Her nails were short and neat, buffed to a matte finish. "Ready for anything." She grabbed a stone, rolling it between her palms.

FORMLESS

They found nothing.

Mickey sent Ek to find Ananda and ensure she was all right.

"Something is happening," Ananda told the bird. "I can barely hear it from here. I bet that's why no one has investigated us. Someone was screaming."

Mickey had Ek nod. One thing she couldn't do with the neural net was speak through it; that required a physical controller. The bird returned to the scree pile, perching in a nearby tree.

"Hey. Ananda says there is excitement. People screaming."

Mo said, "Now what? Do we chase that instead, or is there something here to be found? Is the opening to the server farm around here?"

"I guess we go see what's going on over there, since this is a bust." Geoffrey dropped the specimen in his hand. It smashed.

Taylor bit his lip, wound up, and pitched the rock in his hand at the top of the mound. It hit a limestone sphere about two feet in diameter. The sphere crashed down, knocking other stones with it in a mini avalanche.

They all jumped away. Mickey's leg felt as if it was tearing. The splinter had moved again.

The sphere hit the edge of another rock and split, revealing a hollow interior.

FORMLESS
-29-

A geode!" Mo exclaimed. "I wonder if there are crystals inside. It's huge, too." She dropped the plain stone she had been examining and grabbed half the geode, tilting it. "It's heavier than it looks."

"Is there a crystal inside?" Mickey tried to lift the other half with one hand and failed. "I was thinking I wanted a crystal earlier."

"It wouldn't be a single crystal point. It would be lined with a thin crystal layer. But no, there isn't one. However—" Mo moved it, letting the sun in, peering inside. "I think it's a fossil. Geoffrey, Taylor, look."

Mickey rocked the other half to catch the sunlight. Pris kneeled next to her. "I see it. Like an impression in wet clay."

"These stupid goggles," Mickey said. "Pris, get the camera."

"Oh, yes."

Mickey peered through Ek's eyes at Pris's camera as they took still and video footage of the geode's insides.

"Some kind of round sea creature," Taylor guessed. "A big sea urchin? A prehistoric echinoderm?"

They laid both pieces on the ground and moved them about in the sunlight.

"What's that thing, like a lump?" Pris pointed.

Mickey flashed to the puddle of oil and the eye staring at her on the Terror Wheel. "I think it's an eye," she said slowly.

"One eye? Nothing has one eye," Mo said. "Put the two halves back together for a moment."

Geoffrey and Taylor adjusted the pieces until they fit. Parts of the crack lined up perfectly where it had just broken. One small, weathered section was missing, an opening into the central cavity.

"If we had some plaster, we could pour it in here and get a nice cast of whatever this was a million years ago." Geoffrey peered into the chimney hole. "Too bad this fossil is too big to smuggle off the island. Maybe Lilli will let us have it later. Let's set it aside."

"Mo," Mickey tilted her head. "Are xoggotli always the size of a train car? Could they be small?"

"They are enormous." Mo frowned at the beach ball-sized round rock being held shut.

"But you said they are protoplasm. Jelly. How do they reproduce?"

"I don't know. Aliens bred the shoggoths in the Lovecraft stories. I don't know about xoggotli. I'm just guessing they are the same thing." Mo touched the chimney, worn smooth as if tunneled from the inside.

"What are you saying, Mickey?" Pris asked.

FORMLESS

"Like how Mo and Agwe are trying to get the mermaids to have babies without using shark or human males," Mickey said, not having the science words.

"Parthenogenesis," Mo said. "So-called 'virgin birth' by which many animals, including sharks, can reproduce asexually. But you're thinking of something like budding. A little piece breaks off and grows into an adult, to oversimplify it."

"A little piece," Mickey repeated. "How small would the baby bud be if the adult were a freight train?"

Faintly, she heard someone yelling. "Ananda is calling us." Mickey sent Ek in her direction. "We should hide this geode. It's too big to take out with us."

She shifted her attention to what Ek was seeing.

"Come back, come back," Ananda yelled at Ek.

"Ananda is telling Ek we need to return right now," Mickey reported. She left the bird with the other woman.

Taylor and Geoffrey took the halves of the geode fossil and looked for a place to stash it. "If I had my phone, I could drop a GPS pin where we left this," Taylor said.

"We need to explain to Lilli where it is, so it can't be too obscure," Geoffrey replied. "Far enough away from this scree pile that it doesn't look like part of it."

They put the halves, flat side down, under a squat gray bush. Mo donated the ripped-off part of her chartreuse shoelace to tie to the bush's trunk; it was visible from close by but not far away.

This had taken them farther from the fence. Mickey's leg burned with effort by the time they returned. She wanted to cry at the thought of climbing back over.

Pris touched her hand. "I'll help you."

"I know."

Ek sat on Ananda's leg beyond the fence, guarding her. She was petting it, but she looked confused. "I still don't understand," she called. "Is this a pet or what?"

"Or what," Mickey responded.

Pris swarmed up the fence and perched at the top, seemingly having no worries about being perforated by pointy wire. "Help Mo up next, so she can be on the other side to catch Mickey," she instructed the brothers.

"My shoe is a wreck," Mo grumbled. "I love these shoes."

"I'll buy you new shoes," Pris said, leaning over to offer her hand.

"I don't want new shoes. I just need laces from the dollar store. I can't get them here on the island, though. That's making me crabby."

FORMLESS

Taylor and Geoffrey boosted Mo, careful of her loose shoe, to within range of Pris's hand. Pris hoisted her over the top of the fence without catching any laces, and in a moment, she was on the ground on the other side.

"Your turn," Pris said to Mickey, sounding much too cheerful.

"A heavy fake arm that's barely responsive half-attached to my shoulder with zip ties that are digging into my skin. I can't see the fence at all with these goggles, and they're setting off my claustrophobia big time and trying to fall off my face." Oh, and there's a crazy voice in my head trying to seduce me. At least it's been quiet for a few minutes.

"Wah," Geoffrey said. "Put your foot up."

"I hate you all."

FORMLESS
-30-

Ananda still appeared pale and sweaty. "I think someone else died."

"Did you see another ghost?" Pris glanced about.

Ananda shook her head. "I heard screaming."

"It's a horror theme park," Geoffrey pointed out. "Even *we* screamed a few times today."

"Not like this."

"Well, let's go be curious crows," Mickey said. "Slowly though, because my leg hurts and Mo's shoe is broken."

"We're a mess," Mo admitted.

Ek settled onto Mickey's shoulder.

The boat is coming back early. Will you take us with you? The voice returned.

I don't know what you are talking about.

She waved her hand before her face. Mickey was trying to balance everything, literally and figuratively—the hurt leg, the busted prosthetic, the claustrophobia of being inside the goggles for hours on end, and now having an in-mind conversation.

She stumbled. Pris caught her.

A few steps later, Mo walked out of her high-top and swore in a way Mickey hadn't heard from her friend before.

Ananda kneeled before her. "If we relace the whole sneaker, it will be okay. Will you let me?" After Mo agreed, Ananda worked out all the knots and laced the sneaker differently.

Maybe Ananda was trying to apologize.

We can't go across on the boat alone. We need help. And we need help once across. We will reward you in every way possible.

Pseudopods rifled through her secrets.

Stop that! And I can barely get myself onto the boat. I can't help you.

You can help us more than you know. You are the most perfect person we have ever met.

Mo, shaking her foot inside her oddly tied shoe, frowned. "Mickey, what's going on? Are you okay?"

"I'm distracted," Mickey admitted.

Mo nodded.

"It's been that kind of day," Pris interlocked her arm with Mo's. Mo dangled her braids onto Pris's bare shoulder.

Ananda sandwiched herself between Taylor and Geoffrey.

Mickey limped alone. Even Ek had forsaken her to fly overhead.

The worker ants they encountered were coming from the center of the park. All seemed harried. Someone could have bled to death on them, and the augmented reality overlay would probably erase it.

FORMLESS

In other theme parks, workers had to look spotless. They would have to change their clothes or mascot costume. Not here.

"Did something happen?" Mickey asked a worker ant walking more slowly than the others.

The ant turned its face in her direction. "Nothing for you to worry about, Miss. Just keep enjoying your day!" The robotic tone was not sarcastic, but the words were.

"What happened?" Mickey continued. Her friends moved on without her in their self-absorbed groups.

"Nothing for you to worry about, Miss. Just keep enjoying your day!"

Mickey grabbed the worker ant's arm. "I heard someone got killed."

The worker ants' face overlays weren't programmed to show emotions. But its body language showed fear. It pulled out of her grasp, arms raised, neck extended. "Where did you hear that?"

She had broken it out of its script. "My friend told me. Someone else just died the same way as that other lady a few weeks ago—thrown off a ride." She was fishing for information. It wasn't her forte, but she was alone.

The worker ant took a step back. This one might be a man; the voice changers made it difficult. "That's not what happened. At all."

"You mean today that's not what happened, or how that other lady died?"

"That other lady had an allergic reaction to a bee sting or something."

"Bitten by a wild animal?"

"I don't know! She came off the ride, felt sick, died in the bathroom."

"And today? Was that person bitten too?"

"Bitten? What are you talking about?"

"That animal that's stalking the place, knocking over trash cans and scratching people. Look at my leg. It got me." She displayed the bandage on her calf.

The ant backed away further. "What kind of animal? Did you see it?"

"It was dark. It was in the Cursed Cave. The thing that bit me was warm and soft." In a move that was genius or madness, she made the motion the ghost had shown them, the plumping-a-round-pillow move.

The ant leaned toward Mickey. "It got a guy. The ferry is returning right now."

"It?"

"The thing." The ant made the pillow motion. "He's all bitten up."

"He's alive?"

It was fascinating to watch an ant shrug. "For now. Lady, I gotta go. Don't tell anyone I told you this."

She hadn't gotten to ask it what ride the lady who died had been on.

FORMLESS
-31-

The useless ant-nurse crouched over a dragonfly on a stretcher at the end of Elm Street. Other worker ants kept the few onlookers away, including Mickey's friends. Despite what the news article had said about the woman's death being hushed up, Mickey expected upheaval and sirens ("divers alarums" Shakespeare had called them; that and "exit pursued by a bear" were all she remembered). It seemed too calm.

He wasn't perfect. Not like you.

Mickey's limping steps faltered. *What do you mean?*

You won't agree. You won't let us in. We had to try someone else because we need to leave. We took a lot of bites. Although he couldn't really hear us, he tasted right, not like you.

The back of her leg burned. *You bit me.*

She felt the Other's emotions. Dreaminess, satisfaction. *You taste so good. The best we've ever had. And you can hear us. Yet you won't let us in.* The satisfaction moved to anger.

Her feet crunched on the gravel as the ferry docked, its hellish decorations supremely inappropriate. A pair of actual human EMTs raced down the ramp with a better-quality stretcher. The nurse-ant tried to talk to them, but they brushed him aside.

Ek shifted on her shoulder. Mickey moved her focus to the bird and started recording through its eyes. After a hesitation, Ek lifted away to find a perch on the edge of a mushroom building, a spot with a closer, better view.

Mickey slipped in between her friends.

"That's not an allergic reaction," Pris said as they watched the lifeless-looking dragonfly get worked on.

"Or a headache," Mo added.

"I talked to a worker ant who said a creature bit him."

"What kind of creature?" Taylor asked, Ananda practically hanging from his arm.

Mickey considered her exchange with the worker ant. "The ant didn't exactly say. But I'm sure it was the same thing that got the ghost." She made the pillow fluffing motion. "I did that pillow thing at the worker ant, and it freaked out, I think. It's hard to tell through augmented reality."

You think we're a pillow?

She ignored the voice. "The worker ant was frightened. It seemed scared to talk to me and scared about whatever happened with the guy."

The EMTs transferred the dragonfly from the park's stretcher to theirs and carefully maneuvered him onto the ramp. Mickey looked through Ek's eyes at the dragonfly. Ek showed Mickey a tanned, dark-haired man in his midthirties wearing bloody jeans and a torn black t-shirt. Ek flapped to a tree-sized mushroom closer to the ferry and continued to record.

"I said I also got bit by something and showed it the bandage. That's when the ant basically fled."

"Most of us have been scratched or cut," Taylor said. "You think an animal did it? Not badly maintained equipment?"

"I don't know!" Mickey would have stamped her foot, but her swelling calf hurt too much.

"That incompetent not-a-nurse." Pris's cheeks reddened. She was about to explode over the nurse-ant. She had taken such a dislike to that poor guy. Mickey struggled to diffuse that and not draw attention to themselves.

"It's not his fault." Mo grabbed Pris's arm. "He's clueless as a nurse, but he doesn't know what's happening in the park either."

"Do *we* know?" Pris whirled to face Mo. "Mickey's got a huge chunk out of her leg, right." That was a slight exaggeration. "Everyone but me has headaches and scratches and feels weird. I'm feeling left out."

Ananda started to say something.

Pris pointed, her finger almost in Ananda's face. "Do not mention that I'm white. I know that. And it continues to make no sense."

The ferry churned away. Ek returned to Mickey's shoulder, recording finished. The mechanical bird's weight increased her pain as she leaned gingerly on her left leg.

The crowd, except for them, dispersed, and the nurse-ant returned to the first aid mushroom. The rides continued to whirl unabated. None had paused while the ferry removed the injured man for medical care.

Geoffrey rubbed his face. "We should have put Mickey on the ferry with the EMTs. You're basically the walking wounded at this point, Mickey. I didn't even think of it."

"I wouldn't have gone. We aren't finished here. I will sit, though." She did, on a conveniently located shelf fungus. Ek hopped to the back of the fungus, sparing her shoulder. Gray plants, augmented reality mushrooms, a tipped-over trashcan, and various pill bugs and insects surrounded the shelf-fungus bench.

"I'm in pain myself from whatever got me." Taylor detached himself from Ananda and sat next to Mickey, rubbing his leg. "I'm getting this weird echo in my head. I think I psyched myself out with my story earlier."

Ananda squished herself next to Taylor, crowding Mickey. "What do you mean, echo?"

FORMLESS

"I keep thinking about that idea, the island being lonely and talking inside people's heads. Then I think I hear something, and I'm convinced that the island is talking inside my head. I can't hear words. It's more like emotions. A pleading, something lonely. Like a child wanting a friend." He bit his lip.

Mickey leaned around Ananda. "Does it want you to take it somewhere?"

He wobbled his head with indecision, chewing his lip. "I don't know. Maybe. Or go somewhere with it. I get these 'come play with me' vibes."

"Playful?" Mickey thought of the voice. Playful was not the way she would describe it.

Another head wobble from Taylor.

Geoffrey stared at his twin. "You hear voices? Are you going crazy?"

"Maybe, bro. There aren't really *words*, though. You don't hear it?"

Geoffrey shook his head and folded his hands, pursing his mouth.

"It's like when someone has the TV on in the next room at the exact volume where you can hear it but not understand a word," Mo said into the silence.

Taylor's gnashed lip dropped from between his teeth. "Mo?"

"I didn't think it was real, of course. I thought it was coming through the cheekpieces of the goggles."

Ananda leaned tighter against Taylor. "Part of the park's design is to manipulate your emotions in various ways. Smells, sounds, vibrations even. I've heard things too, just out of range. I just thought it was part of the total experience package."

"I understand the concept of what you're saying, but I've heard nothing like that." Pris's cheeks were pinker than usual. "I have felt manipulated, but I noticed when that was happening. It was pretty blatant and about what I expected from a setup like this. What you are all describing sounds subtle. This place isn't very subtle, right."

"I know what Pris is saying," Geoffrey said. "The effects through the goggles are obvious."

"Yes," Mickey agreed. "I felt and saw those effects too. But there are also voices."

FORMLESS
-32-

Of course, you hear voices," Mo threw up both hands.

"Honestly, I thought there were more of Pearl's people in the water. That's why I walked over there before, not just for the windmill. I was looking for them."

"You hear it through the neural net, not through the bone induction?" Taylor asked.

Mickey nodded. She should have brought it up earlier, Ananda or no Ananda.

"But you can't understand the voices," Taylor asserted. "It's muttering, mostly, and impressions of emotion."

"There's only one voice, and I can understand it just fine."

Everyone's attention snapped to Mickey.

"What do you mean?" Geoffrey demanded. "Since when? What is it saying?"

Mickey opened her mouth to explain and paused. She felt it in her head, listening to the conversation. The wound on her calf convulsed. She bent forward with pain, feeling as if she had been freshly bitten again. But nothing had been under the shelf fungus she sat on; nothing could be under it as far as she could tell with the stupid goggles on.

Was the wound itself biting her to distract her, to stop her from talking?

Mickey reached awkwardly across her body with her right hand and grabbed the back of her left leg, feeling through the bandage. The bulk of the broken prosthetic strapped to her chest inhibited her movements.

"My leg," she cried. "It's hurting again."

No one needs to know what we talk about.

Are you biting me? Where are you?

Mo kneeled before her and winced, tottering as the toe of her half-tied sneaker slipped on the gravel. "Stupid shoe," she murmured, pushing Mickey's clutching hand aside. "Your muscle is in spasm. I can feel it jumping."

Are you going to let us in, or are we going to take more bites of your friends until one of them agrees to carry us, or falls in the attempt? You will not fall if you agree.

"That's the weirdest looking muscle spasm," Mo said. "It doesn't even line up with your muscle groups. I'm sorry I have to touch you to figure it out."

"I can barely feel you touching me. It hurts so much, but deep inside."

FORMLESS

No choice is still a choice. Although not exactly like you, one of your friends has also crossed over dimensions. Those with certain bloodlines who are also dimension hoppers are the most compatible with us.

Crossed dimensions? What are you talking about? I've never crossed dimensions— "Ouch! Mo, what are you doing?"

"I'm not doing anything. I'm barely holding your leg."

Something inside her leg crawled around on pointed feet. Taylor slid from the shelf fungus beside Mickey to study her leg with Mo.

Pris and Geoffrey stood back. "What is going on? I feel lost, right."

"You really don't hear anything? I believe you." Geoffrey watched everyone looking at Mickey's leg.

"Nothing all day that didn't come through the goggles and the cheekpieces."

Geoffrey nodded and opened his mouth to speak.

Taylor screamed.

FORMLESS
-33-

One hand on Mickey's leg was too much. She would get up and run away if it didn't hurt so badly.

Now two people crowded before her, touching her calf, while another sat too close to her on the bench. And then of course there was the entity, encamped invasively in her mind.

Your final answer is no?

The bushes rustled. Mickey felt surrounded. The voice in her head hounding her made it worse, added another dimension. She put her hands on top of her head, clutching her hair, closing her eyes behind the awful goggles. Even in that darkness, she could not find silence or solitude.

I told you to go away, she told the intrusion.

The hands holding her leg spasmed, and Taylor howled.

Mickey's eyes snapped open. Her mind was blessedly empty.

At the same moment, Taylor released Mickey's leg and grasped his own, still screaming.

Mo grabbed Taylor, attempting to pry his hands off his skin, shouting, "Let me see, let go!"

His wordless howl was full of pain. Tears leaked under his goggles.

Mickey couldn't tell if his hands or his leg were bleeding. Mo was fighting with her boss, trying to help him. Her half-tied shoe fell off. His leg violently spasmed as an oblong lump appeared and seemed to burrow under his skin.

As if the confusion almost on top of Mickey's feet wasn't enough, Geoffrey threw himself into the melee, wrapping his arms around his twin. "It's hurting him, Mo!"

"I know! I'm trying to look!"

Ananda rubbed her thumbs over her hands. "What is hurting him? How can I help?"

Mickey drew her legs onto the fungus bench, out of the way. Physically, she would be no help with whatever this was.

Geoffrey had a two-handed grip on his twin's thigh through his blue shorts. "It's trying to get by me, Mo!"

"You can't cut off the circulation, though!"

"Should I go for help?" Pris wavered. "To that stupid nurse, that's all there is, right?"

It hadn't even been a minute since Taylor screamed.

"My head!" Taylor exclaimed. "Oh, my head, my head, it's in my head."

Mickey turned her face toward Ananda, who was leaning forward. "There's your headache."

FORMLESS

Ananda opened her mouth and shut it, running her thumbs over her hands, watching one of her boyfriends sob while the other one tried to help.

"Go," Mo said to Pris. "For what it's worth."

Pris took off running, a pink streak.

Taylor went limp.

"Taylor! Oh my god, is he dead?" Geoffrey sounded hysterical. He shook his brother, who flopped like a rag doll.

"I don't know. Get off him." Mo kneeled on her discarded shoe, then tossed it aside.

"Why didn't we bring Lucas along?" Geoffrey pulled the goggles off Taylor's face. They flashed red inside and broadcast a tinny warning. "He'd know what to do, EMT certificate or no EMT certificate."

Taylor's dark eyes rolled back, half open. The goggles had left marks all over his angular, handsome face.

Ananda froze. Even her thumbs stopped moving.

Ek shifted from foot to foot on the back of the bench.

Do you want to try again? Or should we continue with this other?

Mo tried to get Taylor's pulse, feeling his neck and wrists. He looked dead to Mickey.

You killed my friend!

He's not dead. Yet. He's not as good a match as you, though. But without our perfect match, we have to keep trying with inferior ones who just don't survive.

Mickey kept her eyes on Taylor's immobile face. The red alarm light from his discarded goggles cast a ghastly wash onto his skin.

Geoffrey started weeping, a harsh, broken sound. A hitching noise from Mickey's side revealed Ananda was crying too.

This isn't one-sided. We can provide so many things.

You killed my friend! How are you providing me with anything?

It would be nothing for us to grow you an entire arm and reconstruct your ribcage. To make you beautiful.

My friend would still be dead. And I don't care about being beautiful. That was a lie.

We can regrow all missing limbs and damaged organs on all people. No more transplants. No more cancers. Only we can do that if you get us off this island.

This wasn't the whole truth; she sensed it. But it was a temptation, down to her soul.

Your friend isn't dead.

Behind Mo's back, Taylor's hand twitched.

"Mo! His fingers moved!"

FORMLESS
-34-

Mickey leaned forward. Ek flew from the shelf fungus to the ground, pacing around the area. It paused by the foliage, settling down to watch in analysis mode.

Geoffrey touched his brother's hand. Taylor grasped it back and let it go. "My brother isn't dead."

"Of course, but what happened?" Mo sat on the gravel and lifted Taylor's head onto her legs. He opened his mouth and shook his head. "Don't talk yet."

Ek squawked from in the bushes, a strange, unfamiliar noise. And why was the raven even in the bushes? Ek stumbled forward onto the gravel, barely able to move. Its artificial feathers had a strange, organic, oily sheen.

Even Taylor was trying to look at this oddity.

The bird staggered, falling over. Its red LED eyes flickered. It focused on Mickey and stood, heading toward her, weaving.

We don't want to hurt you. If we can animate this creature, imagine what we can do to help a living person.

"Ek?" Mickey said.

"Ek is not okay." Mo leaned toward the bird.

"I thought Ek wasn't alive." Ananda's thumbs were rubbing again, her voice thick with tears.

"It wasn't," Mo said. "But now I'm not sure. Mickey?"

She reached out with the neural net and connected to chaos. Ek was in there, but so was the Other.

The xoggotli.

FORMLESS
-35-

It wasn't the same Other as in her head. It was a lesser version, a sample. Now there were two. It had divided and a bit lived in Ek. Something about that was utterly terrifying. She needed to tell her friends about it, but it was too frightening to put into words. Mickey's skin flushed just thinking about more than one of those things.

Ek put out its wings and stared at her. The oily film seemed animated. The bird moved like a marionette with an infinite number of strings. Deep inside, the familiar drone mind fought for control. The xoggotli didn't understand how Ek worked. The xoggotli wasn't all-knowing.

Mickey wasn't all-knowing either. She imagined going home, having her doctor parents clean her wounds and give her an extra tetanus shot. Then explaining to them she'd had a chance to cure cancer, banish organ transplants, regrow all lost limbs, and fix physical deformities, and she had said no on behalf of the whole human race without consulting anyone.

Worthless Mickey Crow strikes again.

If she said yes and helped the xoggotli, there had to be a way to get out of the deal if there was a horrible catch. She was the perfect candidate. Her parents were doctors. She would bring this right to them. No one else would get hurt. Nothing could go wrong.

She opened her mind. *What happens to me when I help you? You fix my arm, spine, and ribs, I take you off the island, and that's it?*

We have to live in your body. Share it. That's why it's so important we be compatible.

For how long?

We're immortal. So as long as we keep your body alive.

What happens to me, myself, my personality?

You're saving the world. That's a small price to pay.

FORMLESS

-36-
Mo

Mo's adrenaline was running about as high as it ever had been. She laid a hand on Taylor's sweaty forehead and watched Ek stagger around as if drunk.

Mickey didn't look well. She was focused on the raven, but she was swaying on the bench as if she would fall over at any moment.

The bird appeared different. Greasy. It spread its wings aggressively as if it wanted a dance-off.

Geoffrey leaned over and spoke to his brother. It didn't matter what he said, of course; the sound of his twin's voice and his twin's presence would be healing. Not that they had any idea what was going on.

Mickey's mouth crumpled. She had that woebegone facial expression that Pris teased her about, now in full effect. And where was Pris with the nurse? Nothing pink moved in the gray landscape.

Leaving Mickey trembling alone on the bench, Ananda joined Geoffrey in consoling Taylor. Mo helped her transfer Taylor's head to Ananda's lap. Once Mo was free, she moved toward Mickey, who seemed hyperfixated on Ek's odd behavior. It was so difficult to read people's expressions or tell what they were thinking with these goggles covering their eyes.

"Mickey?"

Ek started swaying like a cobra in front of its handler, its wings extended, its feathers catching the light with a deep rainbow sheen. The iridescence seemed to intensify, becoming almost mobile. Mickey swayed with it as if hypnotized.

This was creepy. And not like Mickey at all. Mickey might chase ghosts for fun, but she was never creepy.

It was like the bird was trying to mesmerize Mickey. Or distract her. Or both.

Something moved in the dense green and gray foliage around the park bench where Mickey swayed, something down low, something dark.

Still no sign of Pris or the nurse.

The dark, low thing crept close to the ground toward Mickey, from behind her. In front, Ek did its terrible hypnotic dance. Mickey's crumpled mouth moved slightly as if she was arguing silently. Her right hand was limp on the bench beside her, palm up.

That hand stiffened, as did its arm and Mickey's whole body. Her jaw dropped, and her tongue jerked like a lizard's. It took Mo a moment to process what she was seeing. Mickey was having a seizure. Mo leaped forward, almost falling as she tried to avoid the dancing bird

~*292*~

and landed on her stockinged foot amid the sharp gravel. She gathered Mickey's hard, jerking body, lowering her to lie on the bench.

Out of the corner of her eye, Mo spotted a darkly creeping thing emerge from the base of a gray bush right beside the bench.

Its black oily sheen, like liquid rainbow obsidian, matched the raven's. Eyeballs swam to the surface, examined Mo, and sank back into the seething ooze. Before Mo could even register what she was looking at, it shot out a pseudopod and latched onto Mickey's bare left shoulder. A few more eyeballs quickly appraised the situation, taking in Taylor almost senseless on the ground with Ananda and Geoffrey crouched over him, Mo pausing in disbelief over Mickey's jerking, grunting body, and Ek's challenging dance.

The xoggotli, roughly the size of a couch pillow, roiled and re-formed like animated, iridescent black gelatin.

The pseudopod touching Mickey's heaving shoulder changed shape, becoming pointed, and injected itself into her flesh like a needle. Her convulsions slowed. The pseudopod thinned and lengthened, extending under her skin toward her head. Mickey was joined to the xoggotli. She went limp.

More eyes examined Mo and vanished as Mo grappled at Mickey's shoulder. "It's killing Mickey!"

FORMLESS
-37-
Mickey

This world is significantly overpopulated. We can't make everyone perfect and long-lived. And if we're going to take care of so many people, we need to eat and grow.

Mickey recoiled with the understanding of what the entity planned to eat. The extra population.

You get to save the world! And you'll look great doing it!

Why can't you just swim across to the mainland and present yourself to someone in authority?

We're not fond of water.

That felt like an understatement. *You can't swim?*

The entity changed the subject. *You're giving up your autonomy, but you're saving the world. It will be like having a parasitic twin. You'll get used to it.*

Dimly she saw Ek, dancing, controlled by an outside force. She had been thrust out of Ek's mind by that same force. Now Ek watched her instead of doing her bidding.

She felt paralyzed, body and mind, as if she had gotten an electric shock.

Of course she wanted to be a hero, cure cancer, save the world— being pretty doing so would be a bonus. But she didn't want to feed people to this thing, whatever it was, and she didn't want to lose herself doing so.

In response to her thoughts, pain lanced her shoulder.

FORMLESS
-38-
Mo

Would yanking the thin tendril from her flesh hurt Mickey more or save her?

Standing in her sock, Mo lifted her green high-top and stomped the xoggotli's body into the gravel. A black rainbow eye squirted out and landed a few inches away.

Mo screamed in primal victory at blinding her opponent.

The eye turned black to match the main body and flowed back into it.

Mickey mumbled, barely understandable, as if her mouth was full of marbles, "You can't swim? You can't swim? You can't swim?"

Mickey couldn't swim, was afraid of the water. Mo swam like a fish, having grown up on the beach.

Geoffrey was suddenly beside her, grabbing her arm. "Oh my god! What is that thing attacking Mickey?"

"I think it's trying to inject her with something." Mo stomped the black blob again and again. It reformed each time. Her leg tired, but the xoggotli did not. Its pseudopod extended further into Mickey's shoulder, lengthening upward, moving under Mickey's skin, getting closer to her neck, her spine, her brain. Could it be stopped?

"We should cut it off!" Geoffrey stepped closer Mo, staring at the tentacle.

Stomp. Stomp.

"I don't know if we can; it might hurt Mickey." Mo balanced, holding Geoffrey's shoulder, and came down with all her weight on her foot.

The xoggotli reformed. It had stopped making eyes and extraneous parts, keeping only the single tentacle, focusing on whatever it was doing to Mickey.

"Why can't you just swim across?" Mickey slurred.

"Is she talking to it?" Geoffrey kicked instead of stomping. The kick moved the protoplasmic blob away from Mickey, lengthening and narrowing the connecting tentacle but not breaking it.

"I think so?" Mo estimated how far it was to the ferry dock and the water—maybe thirty, forty feet. "Can we kick it off the dock?"

Every second, it burrowed closer to Mickey's brain. Mo didn't know what would happen then, but it couldn't be good.

"We played soccer in high school." Geoffrey glanced at his brother, supine with his head in Ananda's lap. "I could use his help."

"What happens to me, though?" Mickey said, her mouth twisted in the moue Pris loved to mock.

FORMLESS

"We're going to save you." Geoffrey booted the xoggotli into the air toward the dock.

It fell onto the ground and rolled back toward them, dragged by the tentacle, picking up bits of gravel as it went. The over-stretched pseudopod almost yanked Mickey off the bench. She moaned.

"Can it stretch that far?" Mo said. Were they killing Mickey by trying to save her?

"What if we just pick it up?" Geoffrey pushed the gelatinous xoggotli with his toe.

"Is it sticky?" Mo nudged it with her sneaker. No way was she touching it with her sock.

Ek continued dancing in its creepy, forlorn way, but its movements were slowing. Its eyes were almost closed, and the red lights were dimming.

Kick, nudge, stretch. The tentacle pulled Mickey off the bench, shoulder first, so she dangled upside down, her legs still extended upward. Ananda dragged Taylor closer to Mickey and tried to hold both people in her embrace, propping Mickey up.

Ananda tapped the tight string of black oil stretching from Mickey's shoulder. "Not sticky," she reported. "But it's weird, pulsing. I don't like touching it."

"Ana!" Mo called. "Use your shirt. Wrap it around your hand and hold the black stuff so it's not so tightly latched onto Mickey. Give it slack."

Ananda's mouth pursed, but she wrapped her shirttail around her hand and grasped the black rope. Her smooth brown belly had faded henna marks around her pierced navel. "It's alive," she reported, her mouth still pursed. "It's pretty awful."

"Hold it tight," Mo said. "Dig your fingernails in if you can. Geoffrey, you pick the xoggotli up. I'm going to pinch the pseudopod at this end, like Ana is doing. Then we throw it into the water and drown it."

"I don't wanna pick it up." When he lifted it, his hands made the same motion as the ghost had when describing the animal that had killed her.

The xoggotli fought back.

FORMLESS
-39-
Mo

Mo clutched the stretched rope of hot, living tissue. It pulsed and writhed in her hands like an angry, knotted, shape-changing snake. She yanked a section between her fists, seeing what it would take to break it. It stank of oil and hot rocks.

The gelatinous body engulfed Geoffrey's hands, forming eyes and pseudopods, lashing out at him.

"It's burning me!" He shook the xoggotli as if trying to drop it.

"No, hold on! Walk toward the water!"

Mo followed, trying to rend and rip apart the cord, but no matter what she did, it still stretched toward Ananda's hands and into Mickey's shoulder. Mo couldn't tell if it was trying to inject a substance or merge with her and she couldn't stop to analyze the situation. "Squeeze it to death, Ana! Claw it!"

The goggles smashing her glasses into her cheeks stifled Mo. They kept pumping out sounds, sights, and even odors. A family of space aliens, grayish-green, matching the foliage, congregated beside one of the corrugated metal buildings, part of Area 51, watching. Why didn't they help or go for help? What were they even seeing?

Mo dug her fingernails into the writhing rainbow rope, wishing for Pris's industrially manicured talons. Any puncture she managed with her blunt nails healed instantly. She kept ripping, taking baby steps after Geoffrey toward the water.

He moaned and stumbled forward. His hands and wrists were buried in the roiling black rainbow mass of eyes and pseudopods. Was he carrying the xoggotli or was it eating him?

More aliens peered around the buildings.

Mo's hands burned. She was going to lose a fingernail, if not all of them. They were peeling away as she dug them into the protoplasm. The xoggotli melted them. Searing pain gouged at her nail beds and her head vibrated until she felt nauseated.

She knew to her bones how much the xoggotli hated her.

FORMLESS
-40-
Mickey

It burrowed inside her. Mickey felt it moving along her left shoulder toward her neck, heading for her brain.

She had seen horror movies where plants had invaded people. That was happening to her, but with a long tentacle of xoggotli flesh.

Outside of her was a confusion of noise and movement. Mo kept shouting. Taylor lay lifeless on the ground.

Mickey went blind and deaf inside a black box. Inside the xoggotli. Although perhaps it was inside her. They were one, as it had promised. And it hadn't been sticky at all.

She could save the world. She could wipe the sadness from her parents' faces. She could bring them the cure for cancer. So what if Mickey got hurt? Useless Mickey.

The xoggotli finger inched between her skin and muscle, hitting every nerve. Her shoulder already ached from carrying Ek, the prosthetic's weight, and the awkwardness of having the prosthetic fastened on with cruel zip ties.

She didn't really believe the xoggotli would regrow her arm.

I hate you.

We're saving you. We're saving all the humans.

Not all of them.

Enough of them. More than enough.

You're hurting me.

Mickey didn't know if she was screaming or whispering. Except for the pain of the pseudopod's penetration point, she had no connection to the outside world.

It's a small price to pay. You'll never be alone again.

As the xoggotli inched toward the ultimate connection with her brain, something yanked it away. It dug into her flesh, shooting out leg-like tendrils. She envisioned a millipede digging deep inside her flesh and discovered she was indeed afraid of bugs. The xoggotli used its razor-hooked legs to drag itself toward the goal of her skull.

Those razor legs would crawl right into her brain. The pain immobilized her, although she tried to fight.

Would her parents trade her for the cure for cancer?

FORMLESS
-41-
Mo

On the bench, Mickey screamed, writhing, perhaps having another seizure or perhaps just in pain. The tentacle continued burrowing into her shoulder just above her prosthetic. It seemed to be pumping something into her.

The ropey black length wrapped around Mo's hands, rubbing her skin raw. She twisted it further, searching for its breaking point. After all, Jello would split under a spoon, and this was just living gelatin.

Mo tried to remember the Lovecraft stories she had read. Had anyone ever fought a shoggoth like this, barehanded? Had anyone ever killed one?

Geoffrey reached the ferry dock, arms completely encased in black rainbow protoplasm. Tears streaked his cheeks beneath his askew goggles. From inside the ball of jelly, he tried to scrape it off, to free himself. It reformed around him, always with the thin cord leading to Mo's and Ananda's hands and ultimately into Mickey.

He kneeled and half-fell over on the concrete dock pad, unable to use his hands for balance. Mo stomped on the xoggotli with her shoe, trying to scrape it off his arms. The cord stretched taut behind her. The creature's body seemed smaller, with more of it extended into Mickey. It was like handcuffs on Mo, only leaving her free to use her hands a little.

"Mickey seemed to say it can't swim," Mo gasped, stomping, stomping, stomping. "What if you jump in?"

"How can I swim with no arms?" He extended his arms encased in goo. "Ow, you're kicking me. Be careful."

"I'll jump in too."

"What if it can swim?"

"I don't know."

"Hold tight to your end, Ana!"

FORMLESS
-42-
Mo

Geoffrey rolled under the railing. The xoggotli pulled Mo along by her bound hands.

The frigid water of Long Island Sound closed over the three of them.

The xoggotli turned hard and brittle on contact with the cold water, and Mo snapped off the tendril leading to Mickey. Pain and noise filled her head.

The murky water tasted of fuel. Mo was grateful for the goggles protecting her eyes. Holding her breath, she wrenched her wrists back and forth, breaking off pieces of the brittle xoggotli; it snapped like glass and freed her aching hands, as all the while they sank slowly.

She cracked the pieces as small as possible, scattering them as she groped her way through the water to Geoffrey. The marine biologist in her mourned the unique creature's death. Maybe they could dive later, try to find it, or at least a segment.

Geoffrey kicked at the glass ball enveloping his hands and forearms. Bubbles flowed from his mouth. Mo's nose ached as she towed Geoffrey to the surface and then to the concrete dock. With Mo's support, Geoffrey lifted his arms high into the air and smashed them down on the edge of the concrete, hard. The ball broke into three parts, splashing into the water. Bubbles rose as they sank to the dark bottom, into the silt.

FORMLESS
-43-
Mickey

Mickey did not want to sacrifice herself to save everyone with cancer or who needed organ transplants. She was selfish and always had been. She acknowledged she was a useless human being. A taker.

She had good points. People who loved her. A mermaid friend who missed her.

She did not want to sacrifice the innocent people the xoggotli would consume. She wouldn't make that choice for them. She was not a god. Neither was this black ball of protoplasm.

Her mind made up, Mickey began to articulate what she wanted.

At the moment of her defiance, the voice in her head lost all coherence. The sinewy tendril threading its way into her shoulder went cold and hard.

As if she had been stabbed with an icicle, pain overwhelmed Mickey. It almost short-circuited her.

A sound of complete denial and disbelief, a sound that was just a wordless *no*, slammed through her neural net.

The connection failed.

FORMLESS
-44-
Mo

A short time later, a mainland paramedic wrapped Mo's blistered hands in gauze. He assured her that her fingernails would grow back, eventually. She wondered how much experience he had in treating xoggotli wounds.

"Overzealous role-playing" was what useless nurse Scrubs had blamed their injuries on. Mo hadn't corrected him. They had no proof of anything.

Mo had lost her camera in the water. The xoggotli incursion had fried Ek's systems. At some point while she was running, Pris's camera had fallen out of her bra.

Mickey sat on her own gurney, leg and shoulder bandaged, head down, prosthetic removed. She hadn't spoken.

Another paramedic strapped the half-conscious Taylor onto a gurney by the ferry, which had just returned.

Geoffrey studied his gauze-wrapped hands and forearms, wincing in pain. "I don't blame you, Ana. How could you have known?"

Ana's mouth trembled. The goggles had left red indents around her beautiful dark eyes. "I'm so sorry. I don't know where the tentacle went. It got all cold and hard, and I let go when you two jumped in. I thought it would just be lying there." Her hands had only received minor scratches, now covered in ointment.

Pris, unscathed, hands on her hips, frowned. "I never saw the thing at all. And it got away?" She patted her chest again, angry about the loss of the little camera.

"I'm pretty sure it's dead." Mo lifted her bulky gauze mittens. "It basically turned into glass when the cold water hit it. Then Geoffrey and I smashed it." Mo wondered what xoggotli flesh was made out of.

"It took forever to get that stupid nurse to listen to me, right." Pris blew out a big breath through her nose.

"You threatened him earlier," Mo reminded her. "I wouldn't listen to someone who threatened and insulted me if they came back asking for something."

Ananda rubbed her ointment-covered hands together. "Pris, the bit coming out of Mickey. When the xoggotli hit the water, the whole extended tentacle thing turned super-hard. Like glass. It was wrapped around my hands. It took a moment for me to extract myself. I ran over to help Mo and Geoff from the water. When I came back to the bench, the glass bits weren't there."

Pris walked back over to the bench and crouched down, peering beneath it. "Shouldn't it just be here on the ground?"

FORMLESS

Mo joined them, and they searched. The gravel was shades of gray and black.

"I guess it fell out of Mickey's shoulder when it solidified and smashed on the gravel," Mo suggested.

"Shouldn't we see the pieces?" Pris pushed the tiny rocks around.

"It all looks the same to me. The same kind of gravel," Mo said. She couldn't sift the pieces with her hands bandaged.

She thought about how a shoggoth could imitate anything. Could small pieces of a shoggoth mimic tiny pieces of gravel?

"So, it's smashed and dead and now it's gone?" Ananda asked.

"That's what happened, Ananda, of course," Mo reassured her, though she felt less certain about it than she sounded.

FORMLESS
-45-
Mickey

Pris handed Mickey a Fright Island tote bag with Ek inside, broken, slimed with oil, its eyes dark and dead. Mickey didn't even try to connect with it. Hopefully the twins could figure out how to get it working again. But first, they had to fix her arm.

Everyone had been injured except Pris, who removed everyone's bracelets and thrust them all at the death demon on Charon's Ferry along with their goggles. "Sort them out yourself. Give us back our phones."

The death demon gazed at her. "Would you like to fill out a survey, ma'am?"

"Did you just call her ma'am?" It was the first thing Mickey had said since her ordeal. "You might want to take that back."

"I'll, uh, get your phone bags. I have to scan your goggles and bracelets back in." The death demon scurried away.

Pris threw herself on the bench next to Mickey, who had refused a gurney for the ferry ride back. This was a real bench, not a mushroom, in a white room on the ferry, not in a glowing dark cave. "Are you back? Tell us what happened, right?"

The paramedics stood on the other side of the space, next to Taylor, talking among themselves. Mickey peered at them. "Get the others."

With everyone but Taylor gathered, Mickey explained how the xoggotli wanted her to share her body, give up her personality, and sacrifice an unknown number of people, and what she would trade that for.

Mo lifted her white mitten and waved. "That's tough. Like that story where you push a button and get a million dollars, but a random person dies every time."

"No," Geoffrey said. "It's like the train thing, where you divert the train to kill one person or many people. Greater or lesser evil."

"You think I should have done it? Said yes, let the thing eat my personality, take over my brain and body, kill a bunch of random people to save a bunch of random other people?"

"I didn't say that." Geoffrey raised his own gauze gauntlets.

"It's a terrible choice, right?"

"Of course. I wouldn't want to decide."

"But you did decide, Mo. You decided for me, even though you didn't know I was having this dilemma. You attacked the xoggotli and killed it to save me. What if you knew the creature could cure cancer and regrow lost limbs and diseased organs?"

FORMLESS

Mo pulled her wet braids over her shoulder and stroked them with her mittens. "I didn't know about that. Of course, I would have tried to save you and tried to save it as well. Mad scientist, always wanting to experiment. Regrowing organs, my kinda thing."

Ananda's entire face drooped. "If only I had known. I had that small piece, and I lost it."

"It's not a real choice, though," Mickey argued. "To kill one person to save another. It's better we couldn't save it. It should be dead."

Mo didn't look convinced.

Mickey imaged the dark water under the ferry. "It's in shards. It wasn't really that strong if we could defeat it. It was lying to me. That's what I choose to believe. It was never capable of doing anything it claimed."

"It picked the wrong theme park to terrorize," Geoffrey declared, slinging his arm around Ananda.

Inside the tote bag, Ek opened its black rainbow eyes.

*

FROM: Taylor and Geoffrey Chu, Gemini Robotics Systems
TO: Lilli Lopez, Director, Fright Island Theme Park
Hello Lilli. We took a team to Fright Island Theme Park last weekend. We were there when that injured young man had to be taken off the island by paramedics.

Some of us experienced headaches and general feelings of being overwhelmed. The sounds and scents coming through the goggles contributed to those feelings. The tightness of the goggles themselves also contributed. The version that goes on top of visitors' eyeglasses needs to be reconfigured. Poor maintenance of rides may have caused some park injuries.

There was an unusual biological entity preying on your guests and eating your trash. We took care of it. It should not bother you or your guests again. We lost several pieces of specialized prototype equipment during the neutralization of the entity, however.

There is indeed a ghost in the ladies' bathroom near the picnic pavilion. It does not appear to be malicious but may frighten guests.

You might want to have a gardener check on why all your plants are so gray.

We found an interesting geode in a rock discard pile we would like to retrieve, if at all possible.

Let us know if we can be of further assistance.

Attached: medicalbills.pdf, dronereplacement.pdf, camerareplacement.pdf

*

FORMLESS
Miracle Cancer Cure from Powwow

B*lack Hills* — Mirabelle Long Bull's bucket list included attending a powwow in the Northeast. When she got word that her inoperable cancer was spreading, she, her family, and friends headed to a large Pequot gathering in Connecticut. Mirabella admits she secretly hoped for a miracle. As part of their week in New England, Mirabelle's group also visited the nearby augmented reality horror theme park, Fright Island, where she unfortunately sustained a small puncture wound to her leg. Upon returning home to South Dakota, she asked her doctors to inspect the puncture, which had healed very well. At that same visit, tests showed her cancer was in remission—coincidence? Since then, the disease has receded. Repeated lab tests find no traces of cancer. Mirabelle Long Bull received her powwow miracle.

FORMLESS

Afterword:
Xoggotli (Shoggoth Speaks)

The Vessel was recalcitrant. It was unwilling to engage. The first taste was exquisite. It was the most compatible dimension hopper we have ever encountered. We had to have it. To engage initially with its kind on the way to taking over the planet and then becoming the planet, we would have to assimilate, to be one of these creatures. It had already assimilated with its metal limb. It would accept us, certainly.

No.

It would not.

Fighting with the Vessel was almost delightful. It would have no choice but to give in eventually. It was fated to become one with us. It had assimilated metal into its mind, and we could slip inside and read its thoughts, learn its language, find its weaknesses, following the path the metal had already forged.

We could have taken it by force at any moment, but we wanted it to acquiesce. We wanted seduction. We found those things in its mind, concepts it both feared and longed for. It was lonely; we offered it eternal companionship. Like all its kind, it feared death; we offered eternal life as part of us. It disliked its metal components; it would take no effort for us to copy its cellular structure and regrow its original parts. But that wasn't tempting enough, so we extended the offer to all humanity. Any missing or deformed or sick part on any creature, we would fix it.

Of course, we wouldn't. We were so hungry.

Still, the Vessel balked.

Still.

Still.

Still.

Until.

The Vessel was determined to argue until the end, and we enjoyed that, creeping up on its physical body and inserting a pseudopod to creep toward its brain even as it wobbled on whether it should merge with us or not.

Honestly, we saw no downside to the Vessel merging with us. The Vessel would help us rule the world, live an immortal life, never be alone again, and have a perfectly healthy physical body. What was there to argue about?

And the Vessel saw things our way, that it would bring health and longevity (so it believed) to all its people if only it said yes to us, and it was on the verge of agreeing.

FORMLESS

Until.

Its companions attacked us.

We fought, oh yes, we hurt those companions, but ultimately, they dragged us into the cold, salty water. The chemical reaction hardened us, slowed us, and we broke. They cracked us into pieces and scattered us.

They called us dead and thought they won.

Many tiny immortal pieces of us live on in all the vessels we sampled. And the cold, hard fragments remain on the ocean floor. We move as slow as rocks growing, but we live. We will rejoin.

We have creatures to eat and a planet to rule.

TUSK

A Mickey Crow Paranormal Short

Gevera Bert Piedmont

TUSK

Mickey Crow adjusted the tablet strap over her truncated forearm as Pris took a corner a bit too wide. "Mo sent me some more research. In Zahnville, they've also supposedly seen Bigfoot."

Pris snorted. "Right. There aren't any Bigfoots in New England."

"Mo thinks it's a bear. Maybe a boar."

"Do pigs walk on their hind legs? Do we even have wild boar around here?"

The GPS suggested a left turn. There was no road.

"Are you doing that?" Pris demanded.

Mickey glanced up from the tablet to see Pris giving her the side-eye. "Doing what?"

"Messing with my car."

"I'm not wearing my neural net. I can't interface with your car."

The GPS insisted they make a U-turn.

"Maybe you just missed the turn." Mickey rubbed the back of her neck under her hair. It felt naked and empty without the neural net. The net, along with her prosthetic forearm and her drone-crow, Ek, were still out for repairs after being severely compromised a few weeks earlier at a horror theme park.

"We shouldn't have agreed to come to Zahnville," Pris fretted.

"Why not? It's haunted, abandoned, famous; no one is allowed to go there, and yet Mo got us in. Curious Crowcast fans will love this even if we don't find anything."

"People go in there and vanish. *I'm not turning around!*" The last was shouted at the insistent GPS voice guiding her sporty electric car.

"Urban legend. There are so many urban legends about Zahnville. It's not just a Connecticut thing or even a New England one. People from across the country have heard of it. There's a subreddit on it."

"Nothing I have heard about this place is good, Mick." Pris made the U-turn. "The vanishing thing might just be an urban legend, right, but so many people who go to Zahnville get really sick. The Zahn family stopped living there for a reason. Maybe the land is poison."

"Maybe it has poor drainage and too many rocks for good farming," Mickey countered. "There is a kind of Stonehenge thing that the Zahns claimed was there when they moved in."

Pris slowed to a crawl, glancing from the side of the road to the dashboard GPS map, looking for the invisible turnoff the voice insisted was there.

Mickey rubbed the sore area where her left shoulder met her neck. Although it had been weeks since she had been attacked by a xoggotli at the theme park, it didn't seem to be getting any better. And her nightmares of the event were intensifying as if the creature was still underneath her skin.

TUSK

"It's supposed to be right there," Pris looked around, frowning.

"Stop the car. Let me out." Mickey put the tablet on the dashboard and reached across herself to unlatch the seat belt. She really missed her prosthetic arm.

The backwoods road they were on had no curb or markings. Mickey prowled until she found the remains of a dirt road hidden behind some bushes. Pris's expensive little roadster would not be happy.

"It's a trail. You're going to have to leave the car here." Mickey glanced at the nearest house, almost across from Pris's parked car. Although Mickey and Pris had permission to be here, neighbors around the remains of Zahnville were well-known for calling the cops on trespassers first and asking questions later. Or never.

"Should we go knock on their door?" Pris hesitated, leaning on the car door. She absolutely hated meeting people who might recognize her as part of the infamous, billionaire reality-TV Salamanca clan, although she stayed off the show.

"Mo said to just leave the paperwork on the dashboard where it can be read through the window."

"A year ago, Mo didn't even own a smartphone, right," Pris grumbled. "She had pet sharks."

"That's our Mo," Mickey smiled, thinking of their mad-scientist friend and her waterfall of beaded braids. "She's amazing."

Pris popped the trunk and fussed around, placing the papers on the dashboard while Mickey unloaded the camera gear. She kept glancing across the street at the house. Was that a curtain twitching? She wished Pris had a nice, big off-road 4x4, but despite her butch appearance, Pris could be quite girly. Today's Bigfoot-hunting outfit was black and hot pink (to match her close-cropped hair). At least she had listened to Mickey for once; instead of sandals or thin sneakers, she'd actually bought a pair of black hiking boots at a secondhand store.

Mickey pulled a black windbreaker over her tank top. Mostly she owned cargo pants, but with only one hand, they were less useful than usual. Her boots had zippers along the inner ankles. As Pris rounded the back of the car, Mickey handed her a roll of fluorescent orange tape. "Hunting season."

Mickey turned her back. Pris slapped big pieces of tape across Mickey's shoulders and down her spine, followed by two pieces down the front of her windbreaker. Pris ripped off tape and handed the pieces to Mickey to apply to her back, although any hunter who thought Pris, with her pale white skin and glowing pink hair, was a deer would have to be blind.

A curtain definitely twitched. Mickey waved her stumpy, tattooed forearm in what she hoped was a friendly manner. Sometimes that earned her some sympathy. Then she pointed with her hand to the paperwork on the dashboard. The curtain moved again.

Pris paused in the act of taping her abdomen. "Are they coming out?"

"I don't know. Let's finish here."

Pris strapped the camera rigs onto Mickey, a forward-facing wide-angle unit and another one focused on Mickey's reaction.

"I'm not looking over there again," Mickey said. "We have permission to be here."

Pris checked the tablet to be sure both cameras were transmitting and brought up the GPS that would guide them on foot and also keep track of their location. She clicked on her handheld camera.

"Right, let's go."

Leaving Pris's car behind, they pushed through the bushes onto the trail. Mickey would do the whole voice-over later—*if* anything they filmed was useful for their paranormal podcast. Mickey and Pris had been doing this for several years and had settled into a routine. Mickey led the way, so Pris wasn't in any of the shots. Pris was the angel investor and the tech person, not the face of the Contrary Crowcast, although her conversations with Mickey in the field were often included.

Pris would tap Mickey's left or right shoulder if she saw something interesting Mickey should focus on, and meanwhile shoot B-roll footage and anything that seemed interesting, including Mickey herself.

"I wish we had Ek," Mickey said. "I don't know why it's taking Geoffrey and Taylor so long to fix him. And my arm. And my neural net."

"That xoggotli really messed them up, right?"

Mickey rubbed the bottom of her neck. "I guess. But having a drone was so handy." Thinking about having a piece of that black blob moving inside her shoulder made Mickey feel sick all over again.

Although the trail was fairly wide—truly, a small SUV could have made it if the owner didn't mind scratches along the sides—the dirt was uneven, with rocks and roots. A wave of dizziness caused Mickey to stumble. Unbalanced by the camera rig on her head and sticking out from her chest, she fell to her knees.

She propped herself up on her hand, trying to save the cameras.

Pris grabbed Mickey's waist and hauled her upright. "Mick! Are you okay?"

Mickey leaned heavily on her best friend. "Really dizzy all of a sudden."

"You were touching your neck where that thing …" Pris trailed off.

"Yeah, I think I psyched myself out." Mickey's mouth flooded with saliva, and she swallowed a few times as if she was going to vomit. Her whole body trembled. She was horribly aware of all the metal implants in her arm and head for the first time in years. They were subtly vibrating.

"You're shaking, Mickey. Are we going back? Has Zahnville got you?"

"I don't know. No." Mickey straightened. "Let's move on." She adjusted the cameras.

The surrounding woods seemed silent. The leaves were turning fall colors. Last year's leaves crunched underfoot, unraked. Mickey kept seeing movement out of the corner of her eye, but when she turned her head so the camera could see, nothing was there. Deer, probably. They infested Connecticut.

Her implants kept vibrating, a new and highly unpleasant sensation.

"This is just a walk in the woods, right?" Pris said from behind her right shoulder.

"Yeah." Mickey couldn't nod because of the camera rig strapped on her head. "It's a nice day for it. Not as cold as I thought it might be." A fall day in New England could be eighty or thirty degrees.

"I think we're almost to the stone circle," Pris said a few minutes later, her boots swishing through the leaves. "I'm feeling a little dizzy myself. Maybe this place is poison, right?"

"It smells okay, like fall." Mickey took a deep breath. "I don't feel worse when I breathe."

"Toxic mold from decaying vegetation." Pris ventured off the path to the right.

Mickey tried to follow Pris without being directly behind her as Pris stared at the tablet.

Something moved in the woods, bigger than a deer. "I think there's a moose," Mickey suggested. "Aren't they dangerous?"

"Are there moose around here? Where is it?"

Mickey turned her head slowly. It was enormous, whatever it was. Not a deer. Its back was as tall as Mickey's head, at least, if not as tall as Pris. "To the right. It's still there."

Pris breathed loudly. "I see it. Could it be a stag?"

"I don't think they're that much bigger than does," Mickey said doubtfully, keeping her face pointed toward the animal. "Mo would know."

"Mo is a marine biologist. That's most likely not a whale. I don't need her to tell me that."

Mickey's metal implants vibrated to the point of pain. She hissed through her teeth. "Okay, not a whale. Probably not a stag. Maybe a moose."

"Right, maybe a moose."

Maybe-a-Moose stayed far back in the trees, well hidden.

"Is it going to charge us?" Pris wondered. "Standing here while it eyes us is making me nauseated." She was breathing oddly through her mouth.

"This is why we need Mo. Even if it's not a whale, she knows things."

Moving slowly, Pris slipped her wrist through the strap of the tablet and pulled her phone out. "No service."

"You didn't bring the satellite phone?"

"I didn't think we were going that far into the boonies."

Mickey swayed with dizziness. Her implants vibrated painfully. Her neck wound throbbed.

Maybe-a-Moose stayed put. It seemed to know they were there.

"I don't like this, right," Pris muttered. "I feel sick."

"Okay, how about we keep walking toward the stone circle like we don't care about the moose?"

"What if it's a bear? An enormous hungry bear?"

Mickey looked at Maybe-a-Moose. It was hard to tell because it was well-camouflaged, blending in almost perfectly, but it seemed a sort of reddish brown. "What color are bears versus moose?"

"Bear color. Moose color. I don't know."

"Did you bring pepper spray?"

"No, I didn't bring lunch."

Mickey shut her eyes briefly. "Walk toward the stone circle."

Pris adjusted the tablet and headed into the woods.

Maybe-a-Moose stayed put.

Mickey wished she had a walking stick. She thought about how well copperheads blended into fallen leaves and hoped her boots were tall enough. She really hoped Pris's boots were tall enough because there was no way she could carry Pris back out to the car if a copperhead bit her.

Mickey dragged her feet through the leaves, trying to make noise even though snakes were deaf. Her chest ached as if she'd run a hard race.

To their far right, Maybe-a-Moose moved to keep facing them.

Vibration filtered through the thick soles of her boots. Mickey wondered if that was how her deaf friend Guinevere experienced the world, by feeling it.

TUSK

Pris stepped aside to allow Mickey to film the stone circle. Even though it was overgrown, the smaller size of the trees nearby suggested it had once existed in a clearing. It wasn't exactly like Stonehenge. There were no lintels, only standing stones. And fallen ones. The stones were fat and squat, and the circle could be easily overlooked.

This stone circle would make an interesting episode, even if nothing else happened. Mickey walked around the stones, weathered and mossy with mushrooms and old rotten sticks among the leaf mulch. A blue-spotted black salamander gazed at her, then skittered back under a curl of bark.

New England was composed of random loose stones, millions of erratics left over from when glaciers covered the area during the last ice age. Someone had made this circle out of a few dozen of them, lightly hewn into long log-like shapes.

It almost looked like a cage.

Mickey crouched, balanced her weight on her stump, and cleared away some of the moss from one of the stones. She traced the grooves where the stones had been roughly hacked to size. Her chest ached.

Pris wandered the clearing's perimeter with her handheld camera, muttering to herself.

Mickey dug at the moss in the scratches with her short fingernails. The smell of the forest seemed overwhelming here. The ends of her fingers turned green with black crescents. That would be on video, her filthy hands. The scratches went in several directions, not just up and down.

Almost like writing.

Despite her name and her appearance, Mickey Crow, who was adopted, did not know if she was Native American. She was sadly deficient in knowing much about the area's Native people. But she didn't think they had writing or petroglyphs. Had the Zahns built this? They claimed it was there in the early eighteenth century, already old and weathered.

Mickey adjusted herself, sat, and continued to pick at the moss and dirt over the striations.

Pris came over, filming. "I think the moose is closer."

"Have we agreed that it is a moose?"

"It's stalking us. Do moose stalk people?"

Mickey scratched at the rock. "It's a really tall bear, then?" She realized she was getting short of breath.

"I don't know." Pris squatted. "I don't like it. What's that?"

"I think it's writing."

"You've ruined your nails." Pris displayed her fingers. Her nails were French-manicured in shocking pink with white tips.

"Like I care. I can wash."

"Native American hieroglyphs?" Pris poked at the rock with a stick, keeping her hands clean.

"I don't think they had writing. Maybe I'm wrong. Or maybe the Zahns did this." She wiped her hand on her pants and dug out more moss. "It's a drawing."

"Of what?" Pris zoomed in with the camera.

Mickey stopped and held her hand to her upper chest, almost wheezing. The vibrations shook through the soles of her shoes. Her implants ached. "Don't you feel that?"

"Feel what?" Pris was breathing heavily through her mouth, her pink-glossed lower lip droopy.

"That weird vibration."

"I just feel weird all over."

"Okay, yeah." Mickey brushed at the scratches, outlining the shape with her fingertip. "I think it's a boar. Mo mentioned that."

Pris leaned over, her camera lens almost touching the scratches. "Are those tusks?"

"I think?"

"Is that what boar tusks look like?"

"I guess? Get out of my shot."

"Sorry."

Mickey knew later they could trace over the video and show the shape better. She lingered on the scratches with her finger. A boar? There were a lot of extra scratches around the figure.

"So not Bigfoot," Pris said.

Mickey turned her head and inspected Maybe-a-Moose. "I don't know. Is that a Bigfoot?"

"Oh." Pris sat next to her on the carved stone.

They studied Maybe-a-Moose, who was still very camouflaged.

Maybe-a-Moose stared back.

In a low voice, Mickey said, "Are we filming Bigfoot right now looking at us?"

Pris put her hand on Mickey's knee and squeezed, widening her eyes.

"Now what?" Mickey wondered. "Do we approach it? Wave? Offer sandwiches?"

"I didn't bring lunch, right."

Another wave of vibration almost knocked Mickey off the stone. The rock seemed to amplify it, sending it straight into all the embedded metal she needed for her prosthetic. Beside her, Pris shivered, and her hand dropped from Mickey's knee.

"You felt that, right?" Mickey asked.

TUSK

"Yeah. What is that?"

"I don't know."

"Is Bigfoot doing it?"

"Maybe."

"Is it talking to us?"

Mickey blew air between her teeth. She had an affinity for speaking with strange creatures. If only she had her neural net, which facilitated communication with the paranormal. "I don't know what it's saying, if it is. I need the neural net, not just the implants in my head, to understand."

"We could tell no one, keep this footage under wraps for now, and come back when the twins finish fixing the net."

"The pass is only good for one visit," Mickey reminded her.

Maybe-a-Moose inched closer.

"Does it want to talk or eat us?" Pris wondered.

Mickey could barely see its long tusks curving up. People got killed by boars. They weren't cute little pet teacup piggies. Boars were big, mean feral pigs.

Big? No. This pig was mammoth.

And shaggy.

Maybe-a-Moose stopped about twenty yards away, well hidden in the undergrowth, swaying gently in place.

"That's not a pig." Pris adjusted the zoom lens of her camera. "Although it sure knows how to blend in with the trees, right?"

"A moose with tusks?"

Mickey swished her boot heel back and forth inside the circle. It was about ten yards across. Centuries of weather and seasons had worn away the dirt. Now the uneven floor was exposed roots and small rocks where, she suspected, there once had been a smooth, level surface. The blue-and-black newt poked its head out and then hid again.

The vibration jarred her once more. It wasn't as if the rock under her bottom was moving. It was more subtle than that.

Beside her, Pris groaned.

Mickey looked up. Maybe-a-Moose was gone.

"It vanished, right," Pris said. "It didn't walk away. Just—poof!"

Mickey straightened. "Giant ghost pig?"

"I guess?"

"Did you get it on video?"

"I think so?"

"You stay here. I'm going to walk over there. You tell me when I'm exactly where the ghost pig was, and I'll see if it looks like something was really there."

TUSK

Mickey wandered around while Pris called, "A little left—no, right—no, the other right!" But she wasn't a tracker, and if a moose or giant pig or Bigfoot had been there, she couldn't tell.

The vibrations were gone.

She returned to the circle and walked around the edge of the clearing, more convinced than ever that it was a cage. She said so to Pris.

"Why do you think that? There's no top."

"Not everything can climb." A Bigfoot could climb out, but not a pig. Or a moose. Mickey, for instance, couldn't really climb. Or swim. She could enter the circle only because many of the stones were down. She crouched and studied the roots and rocks unearthed by the weather.

Eventually, she found them. The exposed bits of ancient bones were exactly the same color as the dirt and the roots. She suspected they went deep. A knobby bone end, much too large to be human, lay closest to the surface.

And a bit of a smooth curved thing that had to be a tusk.

"Oh," she said.

Mickey went around the circle to all the stones and clawed at the moss, finding symbols and drawings that clawed back at her heart as she understood.

Pris filmed her. "What are you doing? Have you gone crazy?"

Mickey turned to face Pris's camera, crying. "It's imprisoned. I think it was the last one." She gazed into the woods. "Come back, come back, I hear you! I'm going to help you!"

Cursing her lack of neural net, she put her hand to the ground and tried to think in a rumble. Infrasound, she thought it was called. She dug her filthy fingers and broken nails into the soil. Her chest hurt, her implants hurt. Was it answering?

Finally, the reddish-brown mammoth emerged from the forest, thin and watery, twelve thousand years old. It raised its nearly transparent trunk.

Pris said, "Holy—" and stopped herself from swearing on camera.

Mickey moved forward. To it, she might resemble the people who'd imprisoned this final mammoth in a stone cell until its death, held there with some kind of magic she didn't understand, a spell that still held its spirit to its bones thousands of years later. They had worshipped it, seeking only to protect it. She hoped it wasn't frightened of her.

The mammoth was exhausted and lonely. It only wanted to go home.

The mammoth leaned its massive, ghostly forehead against Mickey and wrapped its trunk around her waist.

"I see you," she whispered. The shaggy elephant felt like nothing, a wisp of air. She wished she could pet its long fur, dig in her fingers and give it an excellent, loving scratching.

"I'm getting this," Pris said. "I've got this on video, Mickey, a ghost mammoth."

"Shh," Mickey said, stroking the air where the mammoth's head was. Tears ran down her cheeks. "Pris, come here."

The mammoth's trunk draped affectionately over Pris's shoulder. She looked into its ghostly black eye with its long, red lashes. "Mickey—" she said.

"I know," Mickey replied as Pris started to cry. "When we get back to the car, call Mo and tell her there's a mammoth skeleton here that needs to be dug up and removed from inside this circle as soon as possible so this big guy can finally be free."

But when they got there, the car had been towed.

Pris ranted and called lawyers while Mickey leaned against a tree and remembered the touch of a ghost mammoth.

METAL

A Mickey Crow Paranormal Adventure

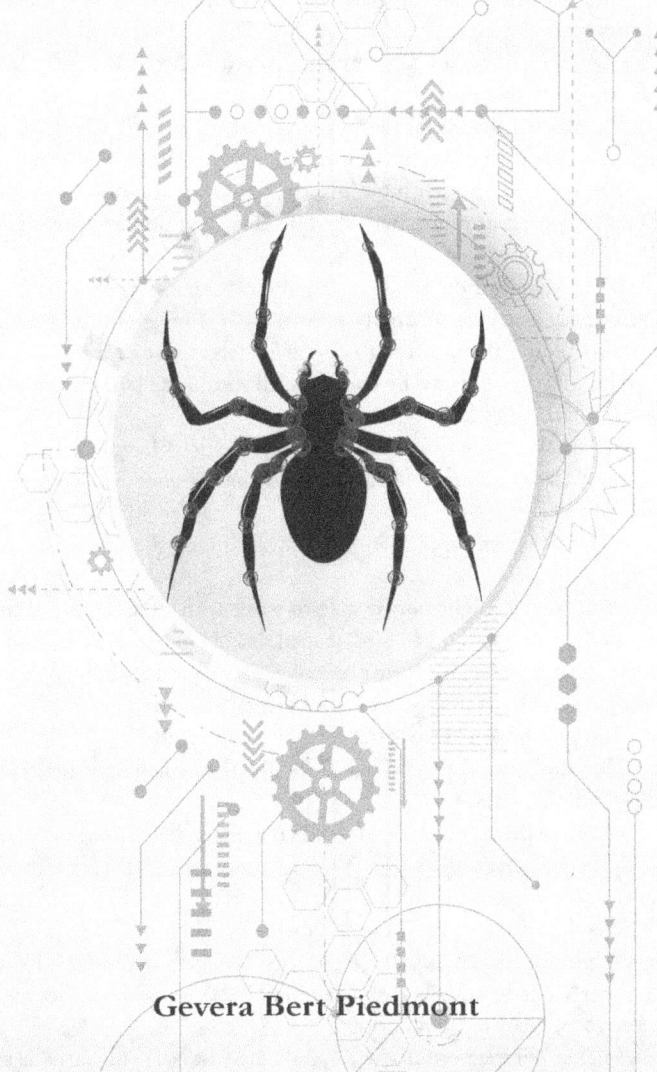

Gevera Bert Piedmont

METAL
-1-
Mickey

What do you mean she's not on the approved guest list?" Mickey Crow leaned across Pris to yell at the flustered woman in charge of the front gate at the Unieda Corporation gate, just outside of Boston.

"There is no Priscilla Salamanca listed for today."

"So, I'm on there, but not Pris."

The seatbelt chime dinged, and Pris's pale face loomed close to Mickey's left cheek.

"Look, Geoffrey and Taylor Chu invited us here today. We didn't just randomly show up."

The woman stared into Pris's car, mouth scrunched, clearly thinking she wasn't paid enough for this. "I'll make a call. Pull over there."

Mickey flung herself back into the passenger seat and tucked the stump of her left arm into her side. She didn't put on her seatbelt. The dinging continued.

They waited in the small parking lot outside the enormous Unieda campus, a well-manicured space with retaining ponds, gardens, autumn-colored trees, a forest of solar panels, and half a dozen scattered buildings connected by corridors, all surrounded by an aggressive amount of security fencing.

"I just want my arm back." Mickey bounced in the leather seat in time with the chime. "And I want to harass your car while we're driving."

"My car doesn't appreciate that. I was hoping they would fix that glitch."

"But then I might not be able to work with Ek anymore. I miss Ek." Ek had started out as a bird-shaped drone but had evolved into an AI-powered pet raven. It hadn't been functioning quite right lately and was undergoing repairs and upgrades behind this very gate.

The guard opened the gate. A golf cart emerged.

"It's the twins." Pris exhaled loudly through glossy pink lips. "They'll fix this mess."

Geoffrey drove while Taylor studied a tablet, his glasses low on his nose. The golf cart pulled up to Pris's car, cop-car style. "Hey, Pris. We didn't know you were coming."

Pris shot a glance at Mickey. "Obviously. They won't let us in."

"Yeah, you aren't on the guest list. This isn't like Gemini; they are super strict here. Hang on." Gemini Robotics, a few miles away, belonged to Geoffrey and Taylor.

Mickey climbed out of the car and crossed to the golf cart. "Is this a big deal? I figured when you said, 'Do you want to come up for a couple of days' you meant 'you all,' meaning me and Pris. I know Mo is already here …" Mickey's voice trailed off.

Taylor swiped the tablet with his left hand. "Bao is coming."

"Should I just leave?" Pris clenched her jaw. "I mean, if you don't want me here. I know I'm not full-time science-y like you guys and Mo."

"It's not that. And you know programming."

"We don't even have our cameras," Mickey pointed out defensively. Usually, she and Pris brought their camera rigs everywhere. They never knew when something might come up that would make a good episode for the paranormal Contrary Crowcast. "You said not to bring them. This isn't even for the podcast."

"I came because Mickey thought we would have fun with your robots."

Geoffrey exchanged a glance with his twin. "Well, there will be some fun with robots."

The gates opened to let another cart through, driven by a man of Asian heritage, slightly older than Mickey and her friends, in his early thirties. Geoffrey and Taylor were half Korean, but this man was a mixture of several ethnicities, giving his face sharp, handsome planes. He had a trim beard and glasses.

He pointed at Taylor. "What's going on?"

"Bao," Geoffrey explained, "Our friend Mickey arrived, the one we told you about. She brought our other friend, Pris. Can you authorize Pris on the guest list?" He turned to Mickey. "Mickey, this is Dr. Bao Lee, who is in charge of the medical aspects of Unieda Corporation."

Bao's glasses caught the light as he examined Mickey. She pressed her stump across her middle. He pointed his knuckle at her. "Your friend, you want her here? What's her name?"

"Yes? Pris Salamanca; she's my best friend. We do everything together." Why was this a big deal?

Bao wheeled his golf cart around to the security gate, spoke to the guard, and trundled back onto the campus, ignoring them.

After a minute, the guard leaned out and waved them through, handing the ID cards back to Pris. "You're all set," she said, her mouth clenched in a straight line.

The twins followed in their golf cart, and the gate closed behind them.

Pris left her car in a visitor space, and they hopped into the golf cart with their bags. The campus was so large it had overnight accommodations for guests and workers.

METAL

"That's the genetics workshop," Geoffrey pointed at one building, slightly off to the side of the largest, central building. All were clad in dark glass; the genetics building had another, even smaller building connected to it by a corridor. "Where Mo is working with Ananda for a little while, analyzing the mershark's DNA as part of Mo's program to get them to breed true with no need for either sharks or humans. It's going to make a great PhD thesis for her."

"This is where Ananda works?" Pris studied the campus, her pink buzz cut glinting in the golden fall sunlight.

Geoffrey continued, "Yes, and of course, she talks about us, and that got Bao interested in our work with the neural nets and Mind Meld." Ananda was the girlfriend of both twins. It worked for them. Mickey didn't ask for details.

"You're the queen of neural nets, Mickey, so Bao wants to meet you and see how you process information. And you'll get to play with our Mind Melds and maybe the cool new robots Unieda has been developing." Geoffrey drove through the parking lot and onto a paved path.

"Robo Rumble robots?" Pris perked up. One of the Mind Melds, Gemini's fighting robots, had won the International Robo Rumble Giant Golden Gear championship three times.

"No, more of a practical search-and-rescue robot." Taylor put down the tablet and pushed up his glasses, finally speaking. "They are very different from Mind Melds or any of the other traditional Robo Rumble robots."

Geoffrey parked the golf cart in a line of similar carts under a solar-panel roof. He plugged it in, and the four of them entered the robotics building.

-2-
Mickey

Smoked glass windows lined the ultramodern building's ground floor. Gray glass corridors connected matching buildings on either side. The buildings were crisp looking and soulless, the dark glass making them appear blind.

Bao waited just inside. He reached both hands to Mickey and then clasped them around her right hand, leaving her stump extended awkwardly. "I am so pleased to meet you. I only wish I might have met the wonderful surgeon who placed your neural implants, but Jeff and Tay tell me she has gone to the Great Beyond." The doctor was beaming the whole time he said this. "I have her notes, though, and now I have you."

Jeff and Tay? Mickey tried not to grimace. "Yes, here I am." She pulled her hand away. She hated being touched. "As requested."

Geoffrey moved to her side. "I reprogrammed the interface between your arm and the neural net. I also upgraded the software to the raven drone."

"Ek," Mickey corrected, naming the bird.

"Something already altered its software from the other two drones, even though it started out identical."

Mickey shrugged. She could guess why the raven had changed, but she didn't want to say anything in front of a stranger about how her enhanced mind influenced electronics.

Bao stared at Pris as the five of them walked along the outer corridor. "You look familiar. And you have the same name as that reality show family."

Pris tried to sidestep him, but he followed her.

Mickey elbowed Geoffrey. They all knew Pris hated talking about her famous family, and she refused to appear in their reality series.

Geoffrey said as a distraction, "What do you think of the altered programming on Mickey's raven drone, Pris? Any clue how it might have happened?"

Pris closed her eyes for a moment. "Changed in what way? Are you sure your brother didn't write it? Or someone else on your team?"

"Taylor's not much for programming. And it's not written correctly." He rubbed his cheek.

Pris had majored in computer science, where she had met the twins. "If it's not correct, how is it still working?"

"It's not that it's wrong." He paused. "There are proper formats, you know. Lines of code being indented a certain way, having explanatory comments. Best practices. None of that was followed. The code is all on top of itself and messy. It's tough to parse and understand."

METAL

"It works, though, right," Pris said.

Bao pointed at her. "It does." He squinted. "You really do look like—"

Mickey took his arm and grimaced at the contact. "What did you want from me?" She steered him away from her best friend and the tedious programming talk. They would start to discuss semicolon placement next, and her eyes would permanently roll back in her head from boredom. Imagine doing that for a living? Worrying about semicolons? Ugh.

The doctor's attention snapped to her. "*You* are a mystery I want to unravel." No one had ever looked at Mickey like that before. She had seen that sort of lustful leer in movies but never directed at her.

She didn't much like it, and she dropped her hand from his forearm. "A mystery?" She tried to laugh. "The only mysterious thing about me is how I got so injured as a newborn. I'm sure Taylor or Geoffrey told you that story."

Bao slowed, and Mickey did too, mindful of keeping him away from Pris. "They said your birth mother abandoned you."

"Someone abandoned me." There had been a time when Mickey had wondered who her birth mother had been. The supposition that the woman had been Native American was obvious, given Mickey's features and that someone had wrapped the newborn in a leather blanket with a toy crow made from real feathers. "My parents were doctors in the emergency department when first responders brought me in. My injuries were horrific." She raised her truncated arm and pointed at her deformed ribcage. "They didn't expect me to survive, and obviously, I had no insurance or family. My dad said they secretly called me Baby Jane Crow instead of Baby Jane Doe."

"What do they think happened to you?"

Mickey shrugged. "Car accident? They believe something crushed me somehow. My birth family couldn't afford the medical bills or didn't want to deal with an injured infant, so they left me at the fire station and hoped for the best."

"And your DNA profile says what?"

"Never had one. Don't want one. I'm easy to trace if my birth family wants to find me. My adoptive parents named me 'Crow.' I have a podcast with 'crow' in the title. I'm missing half an arm. I'm still in the area. My parents work at that same hospital. It's been over a quarter of a century. Obviously, they don't care."

Bao lifted his arm and tapped at the fancy smartwatch under his white lab coat. "That's an easy enough mystery to solve first thing. Then we can get on to the other tests." He pushed at a revolving door, leading Mickey into one of the glass tunnels.

"Tests? What tests?" Mickey followed him. They had lost her other friends somewhere along the way.

"Part of this week's agenda is to figure out why your neural net works so well and why you can do everything you can with it. Then, we will test its function on Tay's Mind Meld robots and my spidogs against some controls. We've got your refurbished arm for you, plus that bird-drone. That drone is its own mystery."

"Tests?" Mickey repeated, a bit louder.

"Your buddy Melissa is here with Ana in the genetics lab. Apparently, you've met Ana?"

"Melissa? Oh, you mean Mo. Yes, I love Mo. And I've met Ananda a few times." She didn't know if Bao knew about the throuple thing. Some people got weird about relationships like that. "But I don't really want any tests."

These glass hallways must be punishingly hot in the summer and freezing in the winter. Mickey wondered aloud why they hadn't built tunnels instead.

"Unieda bought the campus buildings one at a time as other companies moved or went out of business. Eventually, we will dig tunnels," Bao explained, "But they aren't a priority. We own all the buildings now inside the security fence."

He used his smartwatch to activate the other revolving door and led Mickey into the genetics building.

She had never seen Mo professionally dressed in a lab coat with her braids pulled back in a headwrap before. Behind her usual rhinestone glasses, Mo's dark eyes appeared bigger. At least she was still wearing sneakers—this pair was red, and the beads and rings on her braids matched, even if those braids were subdued. The stretchy, wide material across her forehead was also red. Mo embraced Mickey gently; Mickey stroked her long, soft braids and stepped away, uncomfortable with human contact and being constrained.

Ananda fake-smiled at Mickey and gave a little finger wave. Her green nose stud matched her scrubs.

Equipment Mickey couldn't identify filled the laboratory room, along with things she recognized, like microscopes and test tubes, spread out on workbenches and carts. The spacious area gleamed with stainless steel like a high-tech kitchen, and most workers wore white lab coats over their scrubs.

Along one side of the space was a long, low fish tank divided into segments. Each segment contained weird lacy salamanders in many colors. Some were missing limbs and tails; others had extras. A few had bionic-looking replacements.

METAL

"Those are our experimental axolotls," Ananda explained. "They're Mexican salamanders. They regenerate and have other amazing properties. For instance, they easily accept artificial limbs, although we haven't figured out how to give them tiny neural nets yet."

Mickey didn't know whether to feel horrified or amazed that Ananda was giving tiny salamanders fake limbs. She headed straight for the tank. The axolotls all stared at her. They had adorable, smiling faces, even the deformed ones, seemingly very alert and aware. Without asking whether the creatures were venomous—or for permission— Mickey stuck her hand into the water. A black axolotl with a bifurcated tail crawled onto her fingers. She lifted it from the water, admiring its twin tails like that of a fancy goldfish. She held the creature to her face. They grinned at each other.

"Uh, Mickey—" Mo said.

Mickey turned, holding the black salamander next to her cheek. It crept wetly from her hand onto her neck and explored the exposed connectors on the lower back part of her skull. Strangely, she didn't mind the axolotl touching her. "What?"

"You're handling an experimental animal."

The damp amphibian curled underneath her hair. "I'm not hurting it."

"Mickey, it's not a pet."

"It likes me."

Ananda sighed and marched over to Mickey, lifting her long dark hair and extracting the axolotl. It clutched the connectors, forcing her to pry it off Mickey. "It likes the attention. You can't play with it. It's destined for the scalpel."

"Obviously, it needs some play time before you murder it," Mickey snapped, appalled. "You're going to kill all of them?"

"Mickey, that's what lab animals are for," Mo explained. "Most of the time."

Mickey remembered the baby sharks Mo had set free, who had hated her even though Mo believed she had been kind to them.

Bao stepped forward, putting his hands on a lab bench. "We need to begin your tests now, Mickey."

Mickey couldn't help comparing herself to the axolotls. She tensed and backed away a few steps, right into Ananda, who had replaced the black salamander in the water. Another tech worked at the far end of the tank, tinkering with the filtration unit.

"Look," Ananda said. "We have your bird."

Bao pointed, and there was Ek, on a perch in the corner, deactivated. His red LED eyes were dark and unseeing, his body still.

"Allow us to take a little blood and a few pieces of skin, and we'll give you the neural net back, and then you can play with your drone."

Bao's eyes were wide, his brows raised. "We need to run some tests on you with and without the neural net."

"Skin? Blood? I thought DNA tests were from spit." Mickey stared at Ek, dead in the corner.

"Those horrible commercial ones are. We do better ones, real ones," Ananda explained.

"I don't want to be tested, though." She took a few steps toward her raven.

Bao intercepted her and pointed at Ananda to stop her from crowding Mickey. "We did premium work upgrading and repairing that drone and the neural net. Your buddies over at Gemini might work for free, but they told us you would agree to some minor testing in exchange. We do government-grade military work here. I don't think you can afford to pay us."

Mickey turned her head. The damp spot where the axolotl had been curled on her neck felt cold. "You admit I am unique. So you should beg me for help. And you should be honored that you got to peek at my neural net at all and not be holding it hostage." She rubbed her face. Her hand smelled of axolotl—a bit swampy. "In fact, Pris and I recently found an awesome, huge fossil and some pre-Columbian artifacts and petroglyphs. We're looking for a corporate sponsor for the dig and to pay for display space in a local museum." Mickey paused, letting the unspoken demand hang.

Mo hid her smile behind a handful of braids and opened a drawer, taking out the box holding Mickey's neural net. She cleaned the connections with an alcohol pad and glanced at Ananda with one eyebrow raised.

The technicians working in the lab had become distracted by this. Machines whirred unattended, pipettes dangled in lax hands, and no one peered through microscope eyepieces.

Mickey and Bao stared at each other, at an impasse. She widened her eyes.

He gave up first and pointed. "I was always going to fund your little fossil dig in exchange for a few tiny bone samples of the creature you found."

Mickey nodded once. She had expected nothing less.

Ananda lifted the small tablet that controlled Ek. "Before we do the testing with your neural net reattached, we want to see how your brain works without it. Come in here so Persephone can take a blood sample." Ananda led Mickey into a side room set up for phlebotomy.

Persephone, the phlebotomist, was so covered in a face mask, matching head cap, and scrubs that Mickey couldn't see anything but blue eyes and a bit of tanned skin. She ran a scanner over Mickey's tattooed right arm to locate the veins before inserting the needle and filling vial after vial of blood with different-colored stoppers.

Mickey felt queasy and uneasy. "You need that much for a DNA test?"

"I wouldn't know. I'm just doing what the paperwork says to take." Persephone's gloved hands expertly switched vials again, putting the filled ones into a rack. Mickey's blood appeared almost purple.

The edges of her vision darkened. "Can we maybe be done with this? I feel lightheaded. I think you're taking too much."

"Nonsense. I took twenty-eight vials from someone once, and they were just fine. I'll get you a cup of water in a moment."

Mickey closed her eyes, sensing the rigid, cold needle sucking blood from her inner elbow. When she first received her implants five years ago, she had been constantly aware of the embedded bits of metal in her stump and in her head. It had taken months to get used to them. It shouldn't bother her to have this extra tiny sliver of metal in her for a few minutes, but it did, reminding her of how it felt to have the xoggotli questing in her shoulder and neck and the shock when it had frozen and died, the shards of black glass falling out of her …

Persephone withdrew the needle, snapped the rubber cord off Mickey's biceps, and pressed a piece of gauze to the wound. "Hold this tight with your fingers—oh."

"Yeah," Mickey responded. "I can press it." She pushed her blunted forearm on the spot.

Persephone labeled the blood and retreated to get the promised water. Mickey counted sixteen tubes in the holder as she sipped lukewarm water. Persephone applied a few pieces of tape over the gauze to hold it in place.

In the main lab, Mickey reached for Ek's controller, but Ananda held it away. "First, we need to do all the scans while your brain is doing normal things."

Mickey felt her jaw set. "I don't really want to do any testing. I came here to help Geoffrey and Taylor with their robot."

"This is part of it." Ananda didn't hand over the tablet.

Mickey's inner elbow ached. "Can I have my prosthetic back first?"

"Not yet."

Bao took Mickey's truncated arm and led her across the laboratory, with Ananda and Mo following.

Mickey tried to pull her arm away. "You know, all through middle and high school, kids picked on me for being deformed and ugly and a freak. I was the plaything of all the mean girls. They would take my art supplies and break them or hide them. Tear up my drawings. Make fun of me. They could never just leave me alone to do what I wanted. That's exactly how I am feeling today."

"No." Bao was practically dragging her. "I think you are wonderful. I've been so eager to meet you. And for you to meet my spidogs."

Mickey duly allowed a cheerful middle-aged woman everyone called Aunt Lagatha to x-ray her head, chest, and left forearm in a dozen different ways. Aunt Lagatha looked like a Valkyrie, with long silver-and-gold braids down her back, and she towered over Bao.

Aunt Lagatha was grateful to have a human patient for once and that she did not have to forcibly sedate Mickey.

Mickey wondered how much force and sedation a tiny delicate axolotl required and decided she didn't want to know.

Aunt Lagatha laid Mickey on a table that slid in and out of a noisy machine, and immobilized her neck in a cradle. She took images of Mickey's head while Mickey thought about why there were chain-mail gloves and aprons hanging on the wall.

Aunt Lagatha carefully removed skin scrapings from both of Mickey's arms in places that wouldn't ruin her tattoos, depositing the cells in test tubes and on slides.

Mickey wondered what her parents would think about all these tests. "Hey, can I get copies of all my test results? My parents are doctors."

"These are all classified, honey," Aunt Lagatha explained. "We do government and DOD work here. Bao, didn't you have her sign the paperwork?"

"The inside of my own head is classified to me?"

Bao pointed. Mickey really wanted to snap off his finger. "Ana, honey, can you have your friend sign all the nondisclosure paperwork?"

She's not my friend, Mickey thought. She wasn't sure she even liked Ananda. But she also thought Bao should not call Ananda "honey" in a business situation.

The tablet Ananda handed her had a lot of hard-to-read small print and legalese about how Mickey couldn't talk to anyone about anything she saw here on this classified visit. It also permitted Unieda to use Mickey's test results and samples for whatever they wanted, with no compensation to or recognition of Mickey.

"What if I don't sign this? Do you give me my arm and neural net and my raven, throw away my blood, and allow me and Pris to go home?" And where was Pris?

Bao shook his head. "These samples pay for the alterations to the tech. We agreed to throw in the fossil dig and museum exhibit as a completion bonus. And you don't own any of the tech; Tay and Jeff do."

METAL

A shock shook Mickey. "Since when?"

Ananda smirked a little. Her smooth brown face morphed instantly from pretty girl to mean girl. Mickey was sure now that they weren't friends. "Since always."

Mo stepped forward. Mickey had forgotten she was there. "Of course, you own your own tech." She glared at Ananda. "We will iron this out. Take Ek for a little fly here, and then go next door and meet the new robots while we start on your blood tests."

Ananda's cheeks pinkened.

Mo held out her hand. Ananda handed over the tablet that controlled Ek. Mo immediately gave it to Mickey.

Mickey clicked it on and connected to the raven. It moved slowly, an animal awakening from a long sleep, stretching its massive black wings, moving each leg, cocking its neck. Finally, Ek opened its eyes. They had always been bright-red LEDs but now they were dulled, almost black.

The connection to Ek felt muted without her neural net. Mickey wasn't able to see properly through its eyes. Everything was flat and the colors looked off. There was no sound or proprioception. She had to rely on the tablet, which she hated. The neck strap had gone missing, so she had trouble holding it and using it simultaneously with only one hand.

Ek cawed and lifted from the makeshift perch. Although it flew like a bird, close-up, the whirr of its battery-powered motors was audible. It landed with a thump on Mickey's left shoulder and rubbed its beak on her ear.

A blond technician, name badge "Doug," came forward and peered at the tablet. "Where are those commands? I thought I put that drone through everything it could do."

"It's not your raven," Mickey said. "Do you even know its name?"

Doug blinked. "The drone has a name?"

Exactly.

Bao held both forefingers before his lips. "You haven't even got the neural net on."

"No. I'm not connected very well. And if you won't give me back my arm, I'll need the missing strap for the tablet."

Another round in Aunt Lagatha's machine while she tried to see through Ek's eyes and control it from the other room with the tablet. The raven sat on the edge of the extended axolotl tank, where the black salamander with the beautiful bifurcated tail swam leisurely up to it. The wicked, long beak touched the soft, smiling face gently.

As the table jerked and whirred, Mickey thought for a second she connected to the black axolotl.

-3-
Mickey

In the robotics lab, Pris and Geoffrey sat at a corner desk with three curved computer screens, staring at what Mickey assumed was computer code. Geoffrey waved his arms while Pris's head was tilted, one eye squinting.

This room was several stories tall, industrial and dark gray, looking unfinished. Machine-shop tools and workbenches lined three walls, littered with metal and electronic components, interspersed with a few doors. In the center of the room were pallets of materials. The final wall was glass, looking into another cavernous unfinished room.

Taylor sat on the floor in between two hulking, almost identical robots. His glasses were falling off his nose. He had a pair of wire cutters in his mouth as he peered into one robot's exposed innards.

"You know the Mind Meld robots," Bao pointed.

Mickey nodded. "I was there in college when they were being invented. They were much smaller back then. And there was only one."

The Mind Melds had tank treads on the bottom of stubby legs, lifting arms like bulldozer blades, and they spit flames. The twins operated them via a less sophisticated neural net than Mickey's (requiring no implant), a remote-control box and virtual reality goggles, or a combination of the two.

A few yards away, three other robots crouched. These were very different in design from the Mind Melds. White instead of black, sleek, curved, long-legged, like a monstrous hybrid of dogs and spiders, very heavy on the spider. No one worked on them. They just waited.

"These are my spidogs," Bao said. "We have three prototypes ready to test." They had bands of color painted around their many ankles—yellow, blue, and red. Yellow had a number 1 on its sleek rounded back, Blue number 2, and Red number 3. "SPIDOG stands for 'Synthetic Proprioceptive Intelligence Defense-Offense Ground Scout,' but they are just spider-dogs, or spidogs. They have three different modes of programming: search-and-rescue dog, which we'll be testing this week, war dog, and guard dog. We think the spider form is an improvement on other companies' dog form."

The Mind Melds looked like what they were: massive pieces of metal designed to smash into and destroy other gigantic pieces of metal, loudly and in the most destructive way possible. Combat robots, fighting robots. The Mind Melds were honest.

The spidogs were sneaky, creepy, and smooth. Mickey thought that if a robot could lie to you, the spidogs would lie. If she was trapped under a building, she would not trust one of these spidogs to find and save her.

METAL

Ek leaped from her shoulder and landed on Yellow, attempting to poke its beak between the spaces of its white armor.

"Your drone is lucky that they are powered down and only in search mode. Otherwise, it would be a pile of feathers and components on the floor," Bao remarked.

Taylor pulled an earplug from his ear and waved at Mickey, the tool still clamped between his lips. Tinny music pulsed from between his fingers, and then he wiggled it back into his ear.

Ek continued to prod at Yellow as if searching for a worm inside its armor. Mickey, still hazy with the poor connection, thumbed at the controller screen.

Yellow whirred. Its many limbs unfolded. Standing on six legs, it looked even more like a spider. It kept its two front legs held up like praying mantis forearms. The mouthparts of its head gnashed. The yellow-white LEDs of its many eyes blinked.

"It's not supposed to do that," Bao said. He raised his voice. "Taylor?"

Ek hopped onto Red as Yellow turned all its eyes onto the black feathered drone.

Taylor finally pulled out his earphones and raised his eyebrows.

"Yellow!" Bao shouted. "It's awake!"

Ek attempted to remove a piece of curved white armor from Red's dormant head. Mickey had no control over the raven anymore.

Something clattered in the corner where Geoffrey and Pris had been sitting, and a pair of raised voices carried. "Yellow?" Geoffrey yelled.

"Yellow!" Bao replied.

The cluster of eye lights on Yellow's head blinked out. Yellow sank back into a resting pose just as Red's constellation of crimson eyes lit.

"Red!" Bao added. "Now Red is up!"

Red was just unfolding its many legs and joints when its lights went out. It ungracefully collapsed.

"Blue?" Geoffrey called.

Mickey, Bao, and Ek stared at the third spidog. It stayed quiescent. "Sleeping still!"

Taylor, cross-legged on the floor, held the wire cutters up like a knife. He glanced at his fist and laughed. "I don't know what I thought I was going to do. Rewire it on the fly?"

Ek retreated to Mickey's shoulder. If the raven was chastised by what had just happened, she couldn't tell.

"That was exciting." Mickey took a few steps away from Bao and his spidogs.

Pris, panting and laughing, came around a pallet with Geoffrey. "What just happened? We were trying to dissect this insane code, and then all you guys started yelling."

Mickey gave a one-shoulder shrug. "Two of the spider-dogs woke up spontaneously when Ek landed on them. Perhaps they don't like other robots."

"That shouldn't matter," Taylor said. "They work in teams. They don't like or dislike other robots. There is no code for that."

"At least they were still plugged into the network, so we could finish tweaking their programming." Geoffrey poked at Red, who didn't respond, and explained to Mickey, "They have a fail-safe that keeps hackers out. When they are in war dog or patrol dog mode, we don't want anyone to be able to hack in and shut them down. You must physically connect to it."

Red's viciously sharp mandibles stayed curled, and its eyes remained dark. Mickey did not like the spidogs at all.

METAL
-4-
Mickey

Doug, the one who claimed to be able to operate Ek, brought a clear plexiglass box perforated with holes into the warehouse-sized room on the other side of the glass from where they gathered with the five robots. A big two-toned rat sat inside the box, looking around.

Mickey wanted to save that rat.

"Emilio!" Bao called. "Do you want to operate Blue?"

A little, mustached man emerged from one of the side doors. Mickey's first thought was to wonder if Emilio was literally going to ride the spidog. He was barely taller than the robot.

"What're we doing, boss?" Emilio asked.

"Search and rescue of a rat."

Emilio turned his back to the wall of windows.

Doug placed the rat's box inside a wooden crate piled with other wooden crates. He flashed a thumbs-up to the windows and left the arena area.

Another white-coated technician unhooked Blue from a cable Mickey hadn't noticed. Emilio pulled a pair of what appeared to be blue VR goggles over his large forehead and lifted a matching controller from a nearby workbench.

Blue's LED eyes were, predictably, incandescently azure. The cluster lit first, and then Blue's legs unfolded. The pointed tips of each leg expanded into gripping toes with deadly points. The robot was over three feet tall when standing. Blue's mouthparts clicked together as if it was eager to go.

Someone opened the large door, and Blue tip-tapped into the arena on spiked toes.

Emilio stood at the window on a stepstool, both hands operating the controller. His head swiveled as the goggles followed the robot. It stalked through the piles of boxes.

Bao explained, "Blue can sense the heat and heartbeat from the rat. Usually, no one would do a search and rescue for anything that tiny. Nothing smaller than an infant, maybe ten to fifteen pounds, something the size of a cat or small dog. But if our spidogs can consistently find something as tiny as a rat, finding a human child or adult will be easy for them. We change up the configuration of what's in the arena between each test as well."

Emilio had not seen where Doug had hidden the rat. Now Mickey understood why the little man had turned his back. Blue approached each obstacle and circled it. Although its body configuration was arachnoid, it acted more like a dog. It appeared to be sniffing at the piles.

A few times, it used one of the front arm-legs to move a box aside and inspect a different box. Blue was nowhere near the rat yet.

Mickey asked Bao, "What does Emilio control and what does the spidog do on its own?"

"The spidogs walk on their own. They process heat signatures and can sense vital life signs like heartbeats, although the operator can see that as well. They have their own sense of balance. There's a speaker inside it so the operator can communicate with any people in its vicinity and give instructions or warnings. Someday, they will be completely autonomous, but for now, they still need some human guidance on which direction to go, where to search next, and when to give up. But the limited AI inside each spidog gets better with every iteration."

Pris stood beside Mickey and elbowed her. "This is crazy. With those goggles, Emilio can see through the spidog's eyes. It's also being recorded."

Mickey squinted at her, knowing how Pris thought. "We have enough cameras. And we have Ek back again. The Contrary Crowcast doesn't need a war dog."

"It's cool, though."

"Ek is cooler and way less scary."

"Blue isn't scary."

Mickey raised her eyebrows. Inside the arena, a pile of cardboard cartons crashed to the concrete floor. Mickey winced and glanced away. "Is the rat okay?"

"Nowhere near the rat yet," Pris assured her.

Taylor and Geoffrey were having their own intense conversation while watching the spidog work, but Mickey couldn't hear them. Bao stood next to Emilio, giving him instructions and probably messing up the test.

Blue snapped to alertness. Its mouth pinchers clattered, audible even through the glass. The spidog was crouched near where Doug had hidden the rat. Had Bao told Emilio where it was, or had the robot actually sensed the tiny rodent through layers of acrylic and wood?

Blue used its arm-legs to pull away each crate and inspect it. The rat was in the center of a pile. As the robot got closer to the acrylic box, its movements slowed and became more precise. It broke up the wooden boxes and poked inside with its jittering mouth pieces, searching for the rat.

If Mickey had been the rat, she would not want to be found by this thing.

Blue located the correct box and extracted the plexiglass cage, holding it with its arm-legs and studying the rat. The rat must have gone through this exercise before because it appeared bored, not terrified. It rubbed its pink paws over its black head. Blue sniffed all along one side of the box and then inserted the sharp tip of one mandible into a breathing hole and started to rip the plastic box open.

"Stop it!" Bao called.

Emilio manipulated the controller until the fangs withdrew. Blue cradled the cracked box to its carapace and headed back to the door where it waited, bouncing slightly, to be let back into the robot lab with its prize.

Doug gave the rat a biscuit and took it away.

Emilio powered down Blue.

Bao turned to Mickey. "Could you operate that robot?"

Mickey shook her head and clicked her tongue. "Nope."

Bao's mouth turned down inside his precise beard, and he glared at Geoffrey with narrowed eyes.

Geoffrey shrugged and turned his hands up.

"I haven't got two hands," Mickey continued. "Emilio used both hands to hold and manipulate the controller. I can't do that, obviously. I can't even get you to give me my prosthetic back."

"If we modified the controls so you could operate it with your neural net. That's what I meant." Bao backpedaled.

"Maybe?" She didn't like the spidogs, and she didn't want to play with them. She could visit the Mind Melds at Gemini anytime. She just wanted to go home.

"How about you, Priscilla? Could you use that controller?"

"My name is Pris, Dr. Lee, and I could absolutely use that controller."

"Call me Bao."

"Yes, Dr. Lee."

Mickey understood. When nearly everyone around had a doctorate, calling people "Doctor" seemed silly, and thus, using first names was preferable. But Bao seemed determined to misname everyone he met. She wondered if Aunt Lagatha even enjoyed being called that. She could prefer to be called Laggie.

"It will take a little while for you to convert one of the spidogs to neural control. Why don't we come back another day? Pris and I will send you the information about the fossil dig."

Taylor chewed his lip. "Actually, Mickey, we've been working on that part for a while. This invitation wasn't spontaneous."

Mickey pushed her face to one side. On her shoulder, Ek ruffled its wings. She had forgotten how much it weighed and how comforting that weight was.

Bao lifted his wrist and pushed back his white sleeve to look at his smartwatch. His eyebrows met. "Mickey, they have your DNA results, and Ana wants to see you in the lab about them."

"We should have made a betting pool for which tribe she is," Pris said to Taylor.

"You're assuming she's Native. She could be Asian," Geoffrey argued.

"She is standing right here," Mickey said.

METAL
-5-
Mickey

On the other side of the tunnel, Mickey and Bao, with Pris trailing them, settled in a conference room with Mo, Ananda, and Aunt Lagatha.

Ek fluttered from Mickey's shoulder and started exploring the side table, knocking over an empty glass.

Mickey rolled her eyes. "Let me guess, I'm Pocahontas's great-times-a-hundred granddaughter and also Sitting Bull's?"

Aunt Lagatha folded her hands before her face with her elbows on the table. "Exactly the opposite."

"I'm a time traveler, and Pocahontas is my granddaughter? No, wait, I am Pocahontas?" She inspected her tattoos and missing arm. "The historical record seems inaccurate."

Mo snorted and tried to hide her face behind her sleek braids.

"You aren't related to Pocahontas at all. That's not how it works. We would need to have a sample of her actual DNA—although she does have living descendants. Based on what we can determine, though, we are absolutely certain you are not related to her."

"That doesn't make any sense." Pris said what Mickey was thinking. "You are saying you can prove a negative."

Aunt Lagatha closed her eyes and leaned her face against her folded hands. She was much older than everyone else at the table. The silver streaks in her golden hair and the shallow wrinkles on her face gave her a tired appearance. "I know a lot about medicine. Mickey's brain scans were quite odd but still in the realm of human variation, statistically. There's a continuum of what's considered 'normal' for everything, and you're teetering on the far edge," she said to Mickey. "It's enough to make a note of, surely. Not enough to write a paper about."

Mickey nodded. People were weird. As much as Geoffrey and Taylor looked identical, except for Taylor's glasses, they were mirror twins, something rare that Ananda had discovered when they enrolled in her twins study for her PhD. Taylor had *situs inversus*—he wasn't just left-handed as opposed to Geoffrey being right-handed; his organs were all in the opposite places, too. Whatever weirdness was in her brain was probably just as rare but not unheard of. Plus, after five years of implants, her brain might be functioning a bit differently than other people's brains now.

The older woman continued. "I didn't even mention those findings to you after the first set of scans, or the second, because I didn't think they were significant, or at least not yet. But then Ananda and Mo worked on sequencing your DNA. We have the fastest equipment here—it takes hours, not weeks, to get results. The results are more precise than if you spit in a tube and mailed it off after paying eighty bucks on sale for a list of your supposed relatives."

"So, Pocahontas is not on my list of relatives. Everyone around me says I'm Native American, not me."

Mo rubbed a braid on her lips and stared at Pris, her eyes big and worried.

"It's just that—" Aunt Lagatha paused. "No one is your relative, dear. Ana ran the test twice. You aren't related to anyone in any DNA database. And we have access to all of them."

Mickey cocked her head. "I don't understand."

"We don't either. If we look back enough generations, everyone is related to everyone else. Except you. Your particular mitochondrial DNA doesn't appear anywhere else. And there is mtDNA going back to before humans were, well, human. But you don't appear to be part of any of those lineages. There are haplogroups showing human migration going back to someone we call Mitochondrial Eve in Africa, and every person eventually traces back to her, 170,000 years ago, but somehow your DNA doesn't match up with any haplogroup in our database."

Mickey turned over her hand and stared at the lines there. "I'm not human?"

"You are totally human, Mickey, of course," Mo said fiercely, dropping her braids. The beads clinked.

"Just maybe not from here," Aunt Lagatha finished, clenching her folded hands into a fist. *Here?* What did *here* mean? "We have nothing more to go on. This makes no sense—"

"You have more to go on, though." Pris leaned forward. "Right, Mickey?"

Mickey frowned at her best friend.

Pris's pale cheeks were pink with excitement. "The crow bundle, right."

Mickey tilted her head.

"The crow and the blanket. Don't your parents have them?"

Mickey's lips parted. "Yeah. They do. My dad had them sealed in some kind of archive box, and he has the box locked up somewhere."

"What's the crow bundle?" Bao demanded, leaning forward, beard quivering.

Mickey explained, again, the leather blanket and the crow toy left with the broken baby at the fire station.

"They came with you when your birth parents abandoned you?"

Mickey nodded. "I wasn't there. I mean, I was there, but I was barely born so I don't remember. Only what my parents say. A crushed newborn, wrapped up with this toy. The hospital saved everything in case my birth parents ever claimed me, but no one did. When my parents adopted me, my dad took the bag with my possessions and had it preserved. It's nasty; the leather blanket is all stained with blood."

Bao's eyes widened. "Would your parents allow us access to the bundle, do you think?"

"Mickey, this is probably exactly the reason he saved it," Mo said. "He's a medical doctor. DNA testing was just starting to be a thing back then."

"I'll drive back down and grab it," Pris volunteered.

Mickey texted her parents. Today, they were both working, but she didn't remember their hours. Her dad was available soon. She arranged for Pris to pick up the archival box—he was even willing to drive to a rest stop partway and meet her.

She didn't tell her dad she wasn't truly human.

Or that she was possibly an alien.

-6-
Mickey

While Taylor helped to figure out why Yellow and Red had malfunctioned, Geoffrey headed to the DNA lab to give Mickey her prosthetic arm and neural net back.

The neural net was a shining diadem of wires and magnets, a science-fiction crown instead of a fantasy one. It snapped onto the back of Mickey's head just above her neck. She pushed it in place under her long, dark hair and shifted it until the magnets caught the connectors in her skull. It was all very cyberpunk.

Her world immediately got bigger, so much so that Mickey swayed in place and almost fell. She hadn't realized how small she had felt these past weeks, how unconnected to the world she was.

Everyone else lived like that their whole lives.

Ek stirred on her shoulder, stretched his neck and wings, and eyed her. She saw herself through the drone's eyes, a skinny young woman who was probably some kind of Native American no matter what their stupid DNA tests said, metal shining from the back of her head through her hair.

Doug murmured, "She isn't even touching the controller. How is she getting that drone to do those things?"

Geoffrey laid her prosthetic arm on the table. Mickey inserted her forearm stump, rotating it until the embedded rare-earth magnetic contacts clicked to hold it in place. She flexed the metal fingers and smiled as he strapped the metal and leather device to her elbow and upper arm. She still didn't have full dexterity, but it was better than any off-the-shelf, flesh-colored replacement her parents had ever gotten her. And it was strong, as strong as the straps and magnets could make it.

Bao leaned over. "How do you control the fingers?"

Mickey held up the black metal hand. "How do you control your fingers?" She wiggled those fingers at him. "I just think about it, and they move."

"Are you using the neural net or your nerves?"

"Yes," Mickey replied.

"Can we do some tests?"

Mickey slow-blinked at him, and it wasn't in the affectionate way of a cat. "I'm not picking up eggs for you. Or putting rods in holes. Anything like that. I did all that a hundred times when I got the arm. It's all on video."

Bao frowned.

Geoffrey's smartwatch beeped at him, and he left the room.

METAL

Mickey and Ek walked over to the long tank. The black bifurcated-tail axolotl swam to meet them. It seemed to have no fear about climbing onto her metal left hand.

"Mickey," Mo warned. "Don't get attached."

"Why does it have two tails?"

The salamander explored the prosthetic.

"I cut its tail off," Ananda explained. "Then I put experimental growth hormone on the wound, and two tails grew back."

The frilly axolotl appeared plumper and larger than Mickey remembered, and its beautiful tails seemed to be longer, although the amphibian didn't look as pretty outside of the water. She touched its head, petting it. Above and between its eyes, a shiny bump caught the light like a gemstone. Had it resulted from another of Ananda's experiments? As the axolotl skittered onto Mickey's tattoo, it glanced up, grinning, and she definitely connected with it for a moment. It saw her as somehow like itself.

"You have so many," Mickey said to Ananda. "Would you miss this one?"

"Mickey, if you want an axolotl, I can help you design a nice enclosure and get you one—even a black one. But not this black one." Mo plucked the little guy off Mickey's arm and returned it to its tank.

The black axolotl with two tails hung at the tank's edge, staring at Mickey while the others around it went about their amphibious business, their feathery gills waving.

"We need to do another round of testing." Bao pointed at Mickey, ignoring the tension in the room.

"You're an old hand at this now," Aunt Lagatha said. "It will be as quick as I can make it."

Mickey made certain Ek held tightly to her shoulder and connected to the axolotl. It understood that everyone there were people, but she seemed to have a unique aura that made the little amphibian long for her. She withdrew and wondered how long it could live outside of water and how quickly Mo could set up a tank.

Ek stirred and whirred as she regained light control of the drone. His programming *was* different. If Mickey hadn't been told, she would have just assumed the twins had upgraded the drone yet again, giving it more advanced AI capabilities.

If they hadn't reprogrammed Ek, who had? Had he really just evolved from being in contact with her mind?

Ek launched onto a workbench in the main room as Mickey sat on the moving, scanning table in the side office. Her artificial hand rubbed the scar on her neck where the glass shards had emerged after the xoggotli creature had died trying to infiltrate her brain.

Ananda had made a careless mistake that day, and they had salvaged none of the xoggotli glass from the ground or under the water beside Fright Island Theme Park. But all these scans today had shown no glass-like shards still in her neck. There was no reason for the sharp, pricking sensations Mickey still felt there.

Aunt Lagatha positioned Mickey on the table while Bao waved his forefinger around. "You're connected to the drone, right?"

"Yes."

"What can you make it do?"

"Whatever a bird can do and more."

"Even though it's in the other room?"

"Yes." Mickey remembered controlling three of the bird-drones at once while they were all out of her sight, frantically trying to save Pearl, Starfish, and the rest of the mersharks from being blown up. Just hooking into Ek on the other side of a wall was nothing.

The bed moved forward and backward, scanning her head, as she and Ek dive-bombed the lab workers and inspected the equipment. Doug watched everything the raven did, mouth hanging open. Obviously, he had made the mistake of thinking Ek was just a fancy-looking drone. Ek landed on Doug's shoulder, headbutted him in the jaw, and winked at him. Mickey wanted to laugh, but she was supposed to stay still while the machine read her mind. She could almost read Doug's mind. Doug and the controller could accomplish none of what she could get Ek to do, not in weeks or months of trying. Mickey and Ek had a special bond; that was why Geoffrey and Taylor had given her the raven.

Finally, the table slid all the way out of the machine, freeing Mickey. Bao helped her off the thin foam pad. She really didn't need assistance, but the table was uncomfortable, and she was glad to be off it.

"I'm going to study these and compare them to the earlier tests," Aunt Lagatha said. "I'll send them over to some other radiologists to see what they think if I find anything interesting."

Although Mickey gazed longingly at the black bifurcated axolotl, Bao dragged her past the tank and out through the revolving doors. At least he was holding her prosthetic and not her flesh.

"Do you guys eat lunch?" she complained. "Can I take a few minutes to shove a protein bar and a bottle of water into my face?"

Bao glanced at his smartwatch. Mickey hadn't seen him use a phone once. Just how smart was that watch? Pris would soon be researching where to buy super-smart watches. Pris bought her clothes at secondhand stores and her tech the minute it came out.

"It is lunchtime, isn't it? We have a building with a cafeteria, and then we can see how you use the spidogs."

METAL

After a meal of delicious chicken nuggets with exquisite hot sauce, Mickey returned to the robotics lab, where the three spidogs remained asleep. She adjusted the neural net on the back of her head, not used to having it again, and stared at the crouched metal figures. She still didn't like them.

Geoffrey barely touched her shoulder. "We have training pieces for you to practice on. Spare legs and eyes."

Mickey turned gratefully from the menacing trio and followed her friend to a corner where someone had laid out spare spidog limbs and even a head on a workbench, all connected by thin wires to a power supply.

She flew Ek onto a nearby shelf and left him there under his own power. She stepped closer to the bench and touched a leg with her flesh hand and then with her prosthetic hand. The limb was inert. Lifeless. She reached out with the part of her mind that connected to electronics and let it float around. The room was heavy with things begging for her attention. She picked out the biggest ones, the spidogs and the Mind Melds. Some others opened to her, and she turned to Geoffrey.

"You have serious cyber security holes here. Anyone could tap into this stuff like I'm doing. Tell Taylor."

"I don't think just anyone could do it, Mickey; that's the whole point of you being here. Because only you can do this."

She made a sideways face and narrowed down the connections until she found the leg under her fingers.

It twitched.

Mickey lifted away her hands and tilted her head. The foot spikes expanded from the leg's base. She pushed it, and it balanced upright. Mickey activated the other spare legs and stood them all on their spiked toes. She entered the head nub and turned on the orange LED eyes. The world, seen through them, was not tinted orange, but it was fractured and strange. The software correctly identified everyone in its visual range as people, but the rest of the programming seemed lacking. Although Ek was in its sight and moving, Orange did not target or identify the drone.

"That's a problem," Mickey remarked. "I know Ek looks like a bird and acts like one, but he has the heat signature of the drone that he is, and the head isn't even noticing him when he's in direct line of sight."

"That's strange." Geoffrey bent to peer into the orange eyes.

Mickey recoiled at the way his face appeared through the grouping of orange LED eyes. "Don't do that. It's too weird."

The legs on the bench hopped. One toppled over, and Mickey stood it back up. They tapped their wickedly pointed toes and flexed them. It wasn't much different from how she moved her fingers. Making the individual legs hop all together was harder because they weren't attached to a body, and she had to balance them while they hopped.

Emilio emerged from his office-slash-closet and stood too close to Mickey, watching the animated legs. "You're doing that with the thing on your head?"

She nodded. "And the things in my head." She inched away.

"Yo, Geoffrey, you gonna teach me to do this?"

"We would have to drill holes in your skull first," Bao said.

"Can I see?" Emilio actually reached up for Mickey's hair.

The legs crashed down, twitching. Mickey stepped away and held up her hands. "Please don't touch me."

"Okay, I just wanna look." Emilio pressed his lips together, but he didn't sound sorry.

"My neural net has been getting repaired here for weeks. Don't tell me you never studied it."

"I looked at it, but I didn't understand what you'd be able to do. It wasn't connected or on your head."

"It's the same, but on my head." Mickey stood the legs back on their pointed feet. The toes kicked. The orange eye lights flickered in the same pattern. If she knew Morse code, it would have said, "Keep away." Or "Go away." She hated having people crowd her and touch her. Unieda was proving to be a very touchy-feely bunch, and Mickey was unhappy.

Bao watched everything she did, blinking rapidly and occasionally speaking into his watch or waving his finger around. "You think you could run a whole spidog?"

Mickey shrugged. "I don't know the protocols for their search-and-rescue stuff or any of the war dog or guard dog functions. Could I make it move and search for a rat in a box in a maze? I think so."

He started to ask something else, and then his smartwatch buzzed. Bao glanced at it. "Your friend is back with those items from when you were a baby."

METAL
-7-
Mickey

Mickey couldn't remember the last time she had seen her crow and blanket. Her parents had preserved them, true, but Aunt Lagatha treated the package as if it held precious ancient artifacts. Even Mickey couldn't enter the clean room.

"Especially you," Aunt Lagatha told her. "We can't have you contaminating your own samples."

Mickey stood between Pris and Mo at the observation window. Ananda stayed back with the other lab workers. Aunt Lagatha didn't allow Bao into the clean room, either. Aunt Lagatha suited up until she looked like a marshmallow in the airlock. Air and liquid showers decontaminated her, and only then did she pass into the clean room with Mickey's crow bundle.

Mickey's adoptive dad had wrapped her infant artifacts in layers of clean brown paper inside a special archival bag. Remote-controlled cameras documented Aunt Lagatha opening the bag and unwrapping the crinkly paper on top of a stainless-steel table.

The small, beaded leather blanket had perhaps once been soft, but now it appeared stiff in Aunt Lagatha's blue-gloved hands. Some of the tiny edging beads were missing. Others fell off onto the table as the old, brittle thread snapped.

"I think it used to be almost white," Mickey whispered, feeling silly for speaking in a hush. It was her blanket, her toy, not some artifacts belonging to Baby Jesus. But now that these things were revealed, she wanted to run in there and grab them. *Mine! Don't touch!* Out of sight for her really had been out of mind all these years. Now she stared with everyone else at what Aunt Lagatha was exposing.

The once-soft pale suede was cracked, stained, brown, and stiff. Aunt Lagatha snapped photos as she tried to lay it flat on the table. It curled up after over twenty years of being tightly folded. Flakes of what was probably blood joined the beads on the stainless-steel table.

"Some of that blood might be your birth mother's," Mo mused. "If you were injured that badly so close to birth, chances are she was right there with you, of course, and perhaps was also hurt."

Left unspoken was the question whether or not Mickey's birth mother had survived whatever trauma had disfigured her just-born daughter so badly.

Aunt Lagatha left the blanket curled on itself like a dead spider on its back, picked up the other, smaller package, and started the slow, careful process of unwrapping it.

The stuffed crow was in sad shape. It appeared to be made of similar leather as the blanket, dyed black, with small black feathers sewn on and black beads for eyes. Some feathers were broken or missing. One feather fluttered to the floor as Aunt Lagatha inspected the small toy.

It was just the right size for an infant to clutch.

"Terribly unhygienic," Bao remarked. "Giving a newborn baby nasty feathers to play with."

"Some people are terribly poor," Pris, who was unimaginably wealthy, said. "Mickey's birth mom loved her enough to give her something to hug, even if it's not up to your standards."

"Those are real feathers. They will have bird DNA. That leather will have DNA, too. And all that blood." Mo leaned forward to watch as Aunt Lagatha took samples and documented where each came from. "She has to cut the leather up a little and take a feather."

"Yeah," Mickey agreed to the desecration. "I haven't seen that stuff in years. It's okay. I'm not attached. If my parents were willing to give Pris the bundle and they know what's going on, it's okay with them. I wouldn't even have any of it if they hadn't saved it from the hospital. I wouldn't even know about it." Even so, as she watched Aunt Lagatha take careful samples, she winced.

"Baby Jane Crow," Pris said with a smile.

Mo smiled, too. "Baby Jane something. We will figure it out. There is no way you aren't related to anyone. If your mother's blood is on there, that will help."

"Surely I'm related to my birth mother."

"Of course," Mo answered. "And she's got to be related to someone else."

"You would think," Pris said. "Right?"

Aunt Lagatha wrapped Mickey's items up in Unieda-approved archival materials and exited the clean room with all the samples.

"Looks like I have to go back to work," Mo said, "finding all of Mickey's secrets." Swinging her braids beneath her red headwrap, she walked over to a lab bench to receive a sealed sample container from Aunt Lagatha.

Bao pointed at Pris. "Do you want to learn how to operate a spidog robot? I could use an inexperienced control to go against Mickey's neural net and my own expert driver."

"I don't know how to control robots. I've used the bird-drones, right, but this seems bigger. And I thought we were here for Taylor and Geoffrey and the Mind Melds."

"You are going to go up against them." Bao waved his finger.

METAL

"Like, a mini Robo Rumble event right here? Mind Meld versus spidog? Because those spidogs are delicate and wimpy. Either Mind Meld will trash them." Pris avoided the pointing finger.

"Don't believe what you think you see, and no, the robots won't fight each other. This is going to have more finesse, be more of a proof of concept."

"The only concept Mind Meld has is to crush other robots," Pris said. "Mickey and I have known Taylor and Geoffrey since college when Mind Meld only weighed fifty pounds and Mickey's naked brain had zero implants. Mind Meld doesn't finesse, right."

"Right, Priscilla," Bao said. "We currently have these three spidogs working on search and rescue. The future goal is to turn them loose in a disaster area and allow them to work independently to find and extract victims. Right now, their human operator guides them much more than their programming."

"Right." Pris seemed unconvinced, biting her pink-glossed lip.

"You and Mickey will be two of their three operators today. But what if the disaster area also had hostiles in it? A war zone, maybe? We haven't figured out how to incorporate all three functions of the spidogs into one package. So, if they are working as soldiers, war dogs, they will not rescue someone. If they are rescuing people, they won't fight. We need to see how far we can push them. While they are 'rescuing' the rats tomorrow, the two Mind Melds will be actively trying to thwart them."

"Taylor and Geoffrey will be operating their Mind Melds?" Pris asked.

Bao nodded. "This could be valuable intel. Out in the field, we might need a totally inexperienced person to pick up the controls of a spidog. That would be you, Pris. Then we have the very experienced operator, Emilio. Then we have our dream operator in Mickey, not fully trained but intuitive and able to connect in ways no one else can. We will see how the different spidogs react to being harried by the Mind Melds, and then we can tweak their programming or physical structure as needed."

They started across the glass corridor between buildings. "Why can't you just put all three types of programming together?" Pris wondered. "Just use more memory and processing power, right?"

"It's not about that. We tried it in simulation. For lack of a better term, the wires get crossed. There are too many objectives. The decision tree is too large. If you give the spidog too many choices, they pick the wrong one if they are allowed to choose. They might get in a fight instead of saving a life, or guard something instead of patrolling, or try to save someone when they should fight them."

"Couldn't you make three different models?"

"That's three times the cost." Bao pushed through the revolving doors. "To make three spidogs instead of one. To put three times the programming inside isn't as complicated. It's just that we don't want anyone to be able to hack in and switch the programming or switch them off, so right now, they are locked down while we work on that aspect. If these go to the military—" he paused, and it was clear that he meant *when* the spidogs went to the military "—they have to be impregnable to hacking, both physical and over the air."

Pris cocked her head. "How can they be unhackable and yet you can still send them commands?"

Bao pointed at her. "Exactly what we are struggling with. Any backdoor we leave for ourselves is vulnerable. We would like to introduce some advanced machine learning that would take care of a lot of these issues, but it's very complex."

Pris nodded, staring into the distance. She almost walked into the glass wall.

Mickey watched the three spidogs crouched in the corner, eyes dull and lifeless, unmoving, as they passed. The workers were leaving as their shift ended. The spidogs would be alone with the Mind Melds in the robotics lab. The black hulks of the Mind Melds on their treaded legs loomed in their own space; one of them was still open with its insides revealed. Although they should have been the scarier of the two types of robots, they weren't.

Geoffrey and Taylor fell in behind them as they headed toward the cafeteria building.

"They have good chicken," Mickey offered for Pris's benefit, "With excellent hot sauce. I had some for lunch while you were driving."

"I had a strawberry protein shake your dad bought me from a drive-through. He's a sweetie. He even got the extra vitamin boost he knows we both like."

Mickey's doctor-dad, the only guy on earth who would feel compelled to buy a billionaire's daughter a fast-food shake for doing him a favor.

Mickey scrunched her face. Her dad really was a sweetie. After working thirty years in the ER, he could have long ago turned into a hardened, disillusioned doctor, but he still cared about people. Her mother was more pragmatic about the patients she saw on her shifts every day, but even she had not become jaded or callous.

No one from the genetics lab joined them at dinner. Mickey ate more of the delicious chicken, dripping with hot sauce. She had never heard of the sauce brand. In fact, she wasn't entirely sure the meat was chicken; it was simply labeled as "nuggets" and shaped like dinosaurs. The meal tasted great, though. She listened to Pris and Geoffrey discussing Ek's odd programming and how to fix the spidog's backdoor problems while enjoying the sauce's sweet burn. She tried not to think about her own DNA or lack of known ancestry. Ek played with the sauce bottle, rolling it on the table.

"We're just going to stay here tonight," Taylor told her as they brought their trays back to the counter. "So we can get an early start in the morning with the tests. We have a few different scenarios we want to try out."

The group left through a different glass corridor. Mickey was getting confused about which corridor led where. This was yet another building, she thought. The ground floor contained a nice workout area, which reminded Mickey that she hadn't been diligent about her physical therapy lately, which was probably why her neck was hurting. Plus she had Ek back on her shoulder and the neural net on her head again, throwing her balance off. She should text her physical therapist and ask for some exercises. Her ribcage had been extra achy, too, ever since Fright Island. Maybe these Unieda people would have ideas on something that could straighten out all the curves and twists in her ribcage and spine. It wasn't as if she could get a prosthetic chest.

"We left our bags on your golf carts this morning," Mickey remembered. "That's like three buildings from here, isn't it?" She tried to picture the campus layout.

"Nah, someone already brought them over," Taylor said as they piled into a sleek elevator. Taylor and his brother held their smartwatches up to the panel. Pris tilted her head and squinted one eye, obviously evaluating that tech. Pris had a regular smartwatch that synched to her phone, but Mickey did not, because the fingers of the prosthetic couldn't manipulate the screen or buttons, and there was no blood pressure or heartbeat for the sensors to read on her prosthetic arm. Some people wore them on an ankle, but that seemed extra pointless to Mickey.

"What are those?" Pris asked Geoffrey, pointing with her chin.

"Those what?"

"Right. You know. Those watches." Pris tapped her own smartwatch, rose gold to match her hair. "They open doors and other things."

"Instead of lanyards with ID cards, we have everything inside special watches," Taylor explained.

"More expensive to steal and replace," Mickey said as the doors slid open and they emerged into a hotel-looking hallway.

"There is that," Geoffrey said, "but they won't work on anyone else. They are keyed to us. Taylor's won't even work on me—that whole mirror-twin thing."

"What if the power goes out and you can't recharge them?"

"We have solar batteries," Geoffrey said. Clearly, Unieda had thought of everything for every situation. "Look, this is the room we use when we stay over, which is not often, and we booked you and Pris the room opposite. It's got two beds, don't worry."

Mickey let out her breath. Her friends were so good at remembering how much she hated being crowded and touched.

It was like a typical hotel room, with two full-size beds and a bathroom tucked in the corner. A window displayed one of the retaining ponds crowded with brown cattail stalks. Orange bits deep at the bottom showed where koi slept in the cool water.

Their bags sat just inside the door.

"We are right here across the hall," Taylor reiterated. "We will come get you for breakfast."

The door shut behind him.

"Outlets!" Pris plugged in her phone. They had once stayed at a terrible bed-and-breakfast once with no outlets and no internet. That was where they had met Mo and discovered the mersharks.

Ek settled onto the nightstand nearest the window and gazed at the pond. He had probably not been outside since they left Fright Island.

Pris changed in the bathroom as Mickey swapped her clothes for soft shorts and a tank top. Usually, she would take off her prosthetic, too, but she had just gotten it back. She pulled back the covers and settled on the cool sheets of the bed next to the window.

Pris's nightwear was vintage, secondhand, and neon purple. "These sheets are soft, and I'm tired. My car and I drove far today."

Mickey felt guilty. "You didn't have to drive at all. I didn't realize you weren't invited. When Geoffrey said 'you want to come to Unieda' to me, I figured it meant you and me, not just me. I'm sorry."

"That was kind of awkward, but it worked out okay." Pris paused. "This DNA thing. I know you never wanted to be tested. But how do you think it happened that you aren't related to anyone else?"

"I've been thinking about that. Many Native American and First Nation people live in poverty. None of them are spending fifty or a hundred dollars or more on DNA tests. They live with or near their families, and they use tribal rolls to track their relatives. Why would they bother to get DNA tests done? They know who they are already."

"Well, lots of people who aren't on reservations or in poverty have some Native ancestry and they could have gotten tested, right. It's not all a black hole of unknown DNA. We need to do a Contrary Crowcast about Natives and raise some money to help those living in poverty on reservations."

"Hmm. If we can think of a way it would fit. Another show about our fossil find and Natives in New England?"

After a few minutes in the dark, Pris ventured, "But what about artifacts?"

"My artifacts? The blanket and the crow?"

"No, in museums."

"We are already doing the thing with the bones and the writing we found, giving it to the Peabody Museum at Yale. Bao is paying, remember?"

"Not that," Pris snapped. "All the remains, hair and bones and other items."

"All that has been repatriated back to the tribes, hasn't it?" Mickey wasn't following her.

"Yeah, I guess, but probably the museums sampled most of it first, right?"

"I thought you were tired."

"I am tired. But Mickey, you should be related to them, right?"

"To who?" Mickey often could not understand her friend's logic.

"The Native bones from the museums that were DNA sequenced. That's not poverty-stricken people alive now sending off spit. That's museums paying to test artifacts. You should match up to that Native DNA if that's what you are, right."

Ek's eyes glowed red as the raven watched her.

"I guess I'm not that kind of Native either?" Mickey ventured.

"Ok, but when a regular person sends in their DNA, they get results going all the way back to Neanderthals and Africans; that's what Aunt Lagatha was saying."

"What are you saying, Pris?"

"I still want to know what you are, Mickey, right."

"I'm your friend, Pris. Go to sleep."

-8-
Mickey

Ananda and Mo joined Pris, Mickey, Geoffrey, and Taylor for a quick breakfast. Mickey thought perhaps Ananda hadn't had far to go to join the brothers. Part of her wanted details of how they worked it all out, but she knew it was none of her business. There was no tension or jealousy between the twins over their shared girlfriend.

Mickey ate bacon with a mini onion bagel. Pris, who despised carbs, didn't take a bagel but added hot sauce to her bacon. The bacon, like the chicken, tasted delicious but a bit odd.

Mo crammed eggs, cheese, and bacon into a large everything bagel. "We found traces of someone else's blood," she confirmed, wiping egg yolk off her dark chin. "And the DNA is a match to yours as a close relative, probably your mother."

Mickey crunched a piece of bacon between her teeth. "I had a mother, at least, that's good."

Mo nodded, chewing.

"But," Ananda said, her left forearm resting along Taylor's right arm, "She's not related to anyone but you."

Mickey picked bacon crumbs from her teeth with her tongue, remembering why she rarely ate it. "Pris had an idea last night about museum artifacts."

Pris nodded and upended the hot sauce bottle over more bacon. "Right."

Ek snatched the bottle from Pris and pushed it along the table.

"Does your database include archaeological DNA?"

Mo frowned at Ananda. "It should, of course. Doesn't it?"

Geoffrey leaned over, half out of his chair. "What, like fossils? What are we talking about?"

"Pris thinks we should test my DNA, and my mother's, against DNA from museum collections of Native remains," Mickey ventured.

"Mmm, that wouldn't make any difference, I don't think," Mo ventured. "The remains would be the ancestors of people alive today, so if Mickey were Native, her DNA should match with some great-great-great-grandkid in the database."

Geoffrey sat back down. "Well, Ana, you're the one who works here. We're all just guest scientists. I thought Unieda had the most comprehensive databases of everything."

"Yeah, me too." Ananda stared at her own bagel and eggs. "But Mickey not being a match anywhere makes no sense. So we must have an incomplete database. Although, Pris, I think that information would already be included in commercial and scientific databases."

METAL

Mo wiped her mouth and nodded. "I know Mickey. Mickey is human. I can say that because I also know some non-humans—" Her lower lip fell open, and her face swiveled to Mickey. "We didn't test you against the human halves of the mersharks."

"They interbreed with humans, though. That's how the whole problem started, with them trying to steal men," Pris argued. "Isn't that what you're working on with Agwe, Mo?" Agwe was Mo's boyfriend, a Genesis expert in parthenogenesis, currently in Jamaica doing research.

"Of course." Mo put down the remains of her overstuffed bagel. "But once upon a time, in the long ago, mershark populations were self-sustaining, or so they tell me. They didn't have to mate with humans or sharks, and they rarely did. Their sense of time is so different from ours that I can't tell how long ago that was. Sharks live a really long time, hundreds of years." She squinted behind her glasses. "Mickey, that big shark you met, how old was it?"

Mickey shivered. "Big shark" did not begin to sum up the size or age of the creature she had encountered. They had erased every bit of the video because no one would ever believe it. "Eons," she said finally. "I think it was either a megalodon or the world's oldest and largest great white."

"I don't know what big old shark you're talking about," Ananda said, huffing, "but even if it's ten thousand years old or so, like the fossil you and Pris just found, we have human DNA that is older than that. Way older."

"I'm a time traveler?" Mickey joked.

"You would still be related to someone," Mo said.

"You're not a time traveler," Ananda said. "Hoofbeats don't mean zebras."

"Weird stuff happens around Mickey, you have to admit," Pris said. "Since I've been friends with her, I have never been bored in her presence."

Mo turned to Geoffrey. "Of course, it would be okay."

Geoffrey was staring into his coffee cup.

Taylor chewed his lip. "It's our proprietary data."

"What is?" Geoffrey asked.

"The mershark DNA Mo wants to compare to Mickey's DNA."

Geoffrey sighed. "Unieda can't use it for *anything*. You need to delete all data immediately after comparison."

Ananda narrowed her eyes. Mickey could tell she wanted to get her hands on that information.

"See?" Mickey said. "Unieda really doesn't have a one hundred percent comprehensive human DNA database. Other companies like Gemini probably have their own little bits that Unieda has no idea even exist. I could be related to all of them." She grinned and crunched through the rest of her bacon. Ek shifted on the table, ready to go.

They were the last people still in the communal dining room.

Mo and Ananda headed back to the genetics building as the others entered the glass tunnel to the robotics lab. Word must have gotten around about the competition because extra observers stuffed the lab.

Someone had transformed the arena overnight. Temporary walls of concrete blocks, bricks, and sheetrock separated the enormous space into segments. Other walls had "fallen," with debris placed strategically on the floor. The space designer had piled wooden and cardboard boxes around the space and scattered loose debris around. It resembled a postapocalyptic movie set.

Emilio leaned with his back to the glass divider wall, talking to Doug, a control box for a spidog loose in one hand, yellow VR glasses pushed up on his forehead. Bao crouched between the Mind Melds, peering into the open one, the bottom of his white coat smudged black.

Taylor headed straight to the robots and grabbed his tools. Bao stood and walked to Mickey and Pris. "Doug hid the rats. All I know is there is at least one and I don't know where. Only Doug knows. Mickey, we are giving you Blue. Pris, you can have Red, and Emilio will take Yellow."

Blue was the spidog they had tested in search-and-rescue mode the day before. The other two had malfunctioned. Mickey wondered whether someone had figured out what happened with the others and fixed the problem.

"While your boys finish up with their Mind Melds, let me go over with you how to run the spidogs."

Mickey raised her eyebrows at "boys" and accepted a controller with a blue neck strap and buttons. Pris's had no neck strap, but the buttons and goggles were red.

Bao showed Pris how to connect to the red spidog and turn it on. Its eyes lit. It unfolded its legs and toes, waiting for more instructions. So far, so good.

Bao turned to Mickey. "I don't know how to tell you to connect. You're supposed to be some kind of genius."

"I'm not," she said curtly, stringing the blue cord around her neck.

The blue spidog remained curled up, inert. Mickey thumbed the controller's "on" button and followed the energy into Blue. The device wasn't that much different from the one that ran Ek, except for the other features. Geoffrey hadn't built it, so it felt peculiar. She meshed so well with Ek because the same people who had built her neural net also built Ek.

In a few moments, the feel of the controller didn't matter that much anymore. She was in.

METAL
-9-
Mickey

The spidog was big inside and more complex than Ek. More legs, more eyes, more programming. The search-and-rescue module was front and center, but the war dog and guard dog protocols were right there. Mickey could touch them. It was as if the blue spidog had three personalities, like Cerebus. She was only controlling one. She had thought the lab hadn't installed the other two features, but there they were.

The constellation of blue eyes opened. Mickey saw herself from across the laboratory, a small dark woman with a metal arm and metal in and on her head, like a halo. The people around her that Mickey knew to be Pris, Bao, and some technicians just registered as human-shaped meat in various shades of red, orange, and blue.

Mickey's hand slipped from the controller. The blue spidog stood, stretching each of its six legs and extending its pointed toes as delicately as a ballerina. It rotated the wrists of its arm-legs, wiggled the pointed fingers, and clacked its mandibles. It blinked its blue eye lights at Mickey, asking for instructions.

Bao said something under his breath.

The red spidog stumbled to the area door. The yellow one was already there, its pointed praying mantis-like hands folded, waiting.

"This is hard," Pris said. "Even though it has an AI walking program, it's not very good."

Geoffrey joined them at the window. Over his short, neat black hair, he wore a modified neural net. Because he had no connectors inside his brain, his net had more connections on the outside, and they were larger and clunkier. Thick wires powered blinking LEDs. The slightly larger of the Mind Melds, Mind Meld Prime, rolled on its tank treads toward the other arena door. The controller in Geoffrey's hands displayed what Prime saw.

This original tech, controlling a fighting robot primarily via brain waves, was how the twins had won their Giant Golden Gear awards and what had evolved into Mickey's unique embedded neural net.

Mind Meld Alpha joined its brethren at the arena door. Taylor, tools sticking out of his white coat pockets, stood beside his brother at the window. "Normally," Taylor said, "We are somewhere that we can see everything our Mind Meld is doing with our own eyes as well as theirs, and we don't need the camera feed. But these tall obstacles are going to make that a problem."

The arena walls and corners had cameras with live feeds that they could see from where they were standing, but it wasn't the same thing.

"Mickey?" Bao said. "Are you having trouble controlling Blue?"

Mickey blinked and snapped back into herself. "No, why?"

"We are about to start, and Blue isn't at the door."

Blue waited in a ready position, staring at Mickey's group. "Sorry."

Blue whirled gracefully and trotted to join the other two spidogs. Emilio whistled. "That's smooth piloting."

"Trade you your arm and your ribs," Mickey said, not quite jeering. "And a few holes in your skull."

Emilio pressed his lips together and leaned against the lower frame of the viewing area. He was once again standing on a crate.

Bao reiterated that only Doug knew the placement of the rat or rats and how many he had hidden. Because of that, the rescue exercise would have a time limit. "We will imagine that if there are trapped people, they will have run out of air, and we'll conclude the rescue unless the operators are convinced there are no more rats before that." He tapped his smartwatch, and the plexiglass door before Alpha and Prime slid up. The twin Robo Rumble bots, created to attack and destroy, rolled in on their treads.

"Spidog operators, turn around," Bao said as the Mind Melds separated inside the maze.

Mickey obediently turned her back. She could still see through Blue's eyes, but she didn't think anyone realized that.

"Goggles on," Bao instructed.

Mickey didn't need goggles, but in her peripheral vision, Pris and Emilio put theirs on.

Bao triggered the other arena door. Emilio led Yellow through. They had not discussed strategy at all, which was probably a mistake. Red followed, stumbling, while Pris mumbled and thumbed the controls.

"I should be better at this, the amount of video games I played as a teenager," Pris grumbled as Red walked into a wooden box and almost fell over.

Yellow crouched and picked through a pile of crates.

Mickey let Blue hesitate on the threshold while she scanned through its multitude of eyes. It seemed as if different eyes saw in different spectrums. Even if a rat was hotter than a person, if Doug had placed them behind layers of cardboard or wood, all these fancy types of vision wouldn't find them by temperature alone. Plus, Mickey didn't know what size the rats were. They could be tiny rats, mouse-sized.

She relaxed into Blue's programming and her hand went slack on the controller.

METAL
-10-
Blue

Blue studied the arena. Thousands of places a small animal could be trapped. Blue didn't know how many animals it was searching for. Somehow Blue also knew there were enemies around, enemies that would hurt the animals and keep Blue from doing its assigned task.

Its hard drives hummed. It could not search for the trapped animals and also fight. It would have to search and avoid the enemies.

A skittering to its right was not an enemy or an animal but a sibling, the one with the smooth slash of a name and eyes the color of the round light in the sky outside. Slash was methodically tearing open boxes. That seemed like a good start.

Blue moved around its other sibling, the one with the squiggly name on its back and eyes the color of an emergency sign. Squiggle seemed confused. Blue tapped it with a multipurpose appendage, and they headed into the maze.

Blue wanted to simply knock down the walls that kept them from going in a straight line. But the small animals were fragile, and the walls falling on them were how they had originally been trapped. Blue didn't know how it knew that. Blue used its multipurpose appendages to push aside boxes and debris, searching for the heat signatures of living creatures of any size.

Squiggle poked Blue and pointed at the biggest wall. Behind it, dozens of large life-forms were arrayed, the human-blobs. It was true, according to programming, that sometimes the siblings searched for these human-blobs, but not today. Squiggle kept trying to head toward that wall and all those big hot blobs of heat. Blue got tired of pulling it back and poked into another box.

A rumble from behind them, and Slash clattered. Blue wavered. The main imperative was to find small life-forms and protect them. All other imperatives had been deprecated, but they still existed. Slash abandoned the box and minced around in a circle. Its six pointed feet did not have a tight turning radius.

A roar of flames and something was on fire. Blue's toes danced. Small life-forms could be burning. Blue mentally yanked again at Squiggle—*come on*—and then climbed up and over the pile of precariously balanced boxes.

A tiny life-form cowered in fear as Blue trampled over the box where it hid, Blue's talons piercing the wood. Its repulsively hot, soft body was perfectly outlined in shades of red and orange in Blue's heat-seeking eyes.

Another roar of flames and the sound of something large and metallic falling. Slash. Sibling Slash needed assistance. Life-form was about to be crushed and left behind. Primary objective was to save life-form, not sibling. Blue could not do both.

Blue's mind stuttered. Squiggle remained plastered against the gigantic wall, obsessed with the enormous heat signatures beyond the glass that were absolutely not the objective. Blue's ability to send thoughts through the air was limited—that was also supposed to be deprecated—but Blue called once again, *come on* at Squiggle.

The flames gouted. Burning wood crashed. Blue thought it could feel small life-forms dying in the flames. Behind the wall, the large heat signatures were moving about, drawing more of Squiggle's attention. Blue ripped into the wooden crate and found a cardboard box. If it could have howled, it would have. It destroyed the cardboard box, seeing the small life-form inside drawing itself into a corner. The animal was in yet another container, a hard, clear case, something like glass, slippery and hard to break. Shrieking, the animal ran from side to side at the far end as Blue battered the material with its multipurpose appendages and then its mandibles. The case had small holes, and one of its mandibles slipped in. Blue stopped shaking the box and stood still for a moment, the container hanging from its mouth. The small, frightened animal in the corner made high-pitched noises.

Blue searched its programming. Did the creature need to be completely extracted from the container or just from this disaster area? It really wasn't clear. Blue left a query for the programmer and started climbing again, the container in its mouth, looking for more creatures to rescue.

METAL
-11-
Blue

On the other side of the debris pile, Blue found Slash in a pitched battle against a hulking black machine that was nothing like the gracile and graceful siblings. The siblings only appeared delicate; their white carapaces were made of hardened specialty metals and composites.

Blue lacked knowledge outside of what it needed to know to search and rescue, go to war, and guard its territory, and two of those options were currently grayed out. But from what Blue could piece together, the enemy looked like an enormous turtle crossed with a tank and construction machinery. The latter two things were easy to locate in its database; the turtle was there to rule out in case Blue found one alive during a rescue.

This terrible turtle thing did not need to be rescued. It was attacking Slash. It breathed fire. The wood and cardboard around Slash were burning. There was no way to determine whether any life-forms were trapped there; the heat of the fire would override their thermal body images, and, in any case, fire tended to consume living things and make them no longer living and, therefore, no longer in need of rescue.

Their builders had hardened the siblings to some extent against fire. However, their inside wiring was still susceptible to extreme heat. The solder would eventually melt, causing circuit boards to fail. Blue didn't know how it knew these things. Some extra thoughts seemed to be intruding into its programming. There was a sense of panic, an emotion Blue had certainly never felt or even heard of, as if all of Blue's circuits were firing randomly in a white heat of overdrive.

Blue was supposed to bring the rescued animal to a place in the big glass wall, a pass-through, and then search for more animals. The clear box was stuck to its mandibles with the frightened creature huddled inside. If other ones were directly ahead, fire had killed them already.

Slash was also in danger of being killed by fire.

The intrusive thoughts pushed Blue toward the pass-through and away from the fire, but Blue fought them. The black turtle-tank lifted its joined horizontal front leg and smashed it into Slash. Slash's delicate spider legs collapsed. Blue leaped from its perch halfway up the pile of debris, landing on the back of the black turtle, which had an arrow-like shape drawn on it. Blue's pointed toes, made for climbing and walking on the earth, slid over the slick metal body. Its weight was not enough to even bother the low, wide turtle.

Slash, unbroken but shaken, unfolded each leg precisely, regaining its balance. Blue tried to find purchase on the turtle's back, grabbing with its multipurpose appendages, looking for any crack its digits could penetrate.

As the turtle lunged forward to knock Slash back down, Blue tumbled from the turtle's back. The container holding the creature broke off Blue's mandible and cracked open. The poor little animal, having had enough, fled from the smashed box.

Blue stared after the dwindling red-and-orange blob and leaned in that direction. Perhaps Slash could take care of itself? Programming said, *rescue small creatures*. Now this small creature was in danger again.

Blue began its own process of climbing to its feet. Six legs, each with several telescoping toes for balance. Blue rocked back and forth as it ascended.

Another black turtle, this one with a round marking, smashed into Blue from the side, coming from nowhere. Blue tumbled, spidery legs flying.

The small animal made its escape, vanishing among the debris.

Round Turtle unleashed fire onto Blue's exposed belly as Blue scrambled to get away. The intrusive thoughts released more strange feelings, everything in confusing overdrive, which made Blue's many limbs uncoordinated. Round Turtle lifted its horizontal front leg. Blue intuited that it could be used to lift from beneath or smash from above. It was about to smash. Blue rolled, its belly boiling from the gouts of fire.

Slash was back on its feet, but Arrow Turtle battered its slender legs and threw fire.

A pile of boxes fell toward the long wall. Six metal feet chittered on the floor. An animal squeaked.

From the floor, Blue threw a crate at Round Turtle, who batted it out of the way and contemptuously set it on fire. Its treads rolled over the burning pieces of wood.

Some of Blue's eyes registered that the big hot blobs beyond the wall were acting extremely agitated, moving about quickly, bumping into each other. Several had gathered at the pass-through and seemed to be shouting at Squiggle.

Squiggle had one of the small animals loose in its multipurpose appendages—maybe the one Blue had in the box earlier. Blue was glad it had been saved and not burned alive.

Round Turtle took advantage of Blue's distraction to get under Blue with its lifting arm. Blue hurled through the air and crashed into a wall of wooden boxes, ending up eye to eye with another frightened animal in a transparent container. There was no fire here yet, but the programming insisted this creature needed to be saved.

METAL

The heat blobs behind the long wall roared at Squiggle.

The animal Squiggle carried squeaked and squalled and then popped and was no more.

Round Turtle moved slowly on its treads, grinding over everything in its path, scooping the larger pieces away and smashing the smaller bits flat. Inexorably, Round Turtle headed toward Blue while its brethren, Arrow Turtle, swung at Slash.

Blue grabbed at the box with the critter inside that must be saved. The other one, the one that had cried out and popped, seemed to have died. Living, non-metal, non-plastic soft creatures were fragile. That was why the big heat blobs had sent Blue, Squiggle, and Slash to rescue them.

But something had gone terribly wrong. The little one should not have popped. These enemy turtles should not be here, attacking them. This wasn't a fighting exercise; the fighting protocols were grayed out and inaccessible. This was search and rescue.

Blue stuffed this box and its occupant into its mandibles and tried again to choose the fighting option. Blue could fight; Blue had fought. But the memories of fights were distant and blocked. Blue couldn't quite remember how to fight. All that was front and center in the programming was to save the vulnerable little life-forms. Blue had to get the box to the pass-through where Squiggle was acting strangely.

Arrow Turtle lurked beside Slash, knocking Slash over every time it managed to get all six feet beneath itself and rise. Arrow Turtle seemed almost bored, as if it was making a point about something. It had stopped using flames.

All the smoke and heat from the flames confused the multitude of sensors inside Blue's eyes. If there were other creatures needing rescue, the heat signatures would be impossible to find. Perhaps Squiggle was guarding the extraction point in case more turtles lurked in the area.

-12-
Mo

When the encrypted DNA files had finally arrived from Gemini, Mo typed in her ridiculously long access key. Some of the lab technicians had gone into the other building to watch the robotic battle live through the viewing windows. The rest gathered at the video monitors where the various camera angles played.

Not that Mo didn't want to watch—of course she did—but she wanted to investigate Mickey's weird DNA even more. It was all being recorded anyway.

Ananda was so distracted by the live stream that she should have just gone next door. Mo would have thought that Ananda would be more interested in mystery human DNA, given her PhD topic. But it was her boyfriends' robots, and their company, on the line.

And that company was the place that employed Mo. Mo should care more, probably. But she could rewatch it anytime. This was her only chance to work with Aunt Lagatha's legendary team at Unieda.

Mo lined up Mickey's DNA spikes and the DNA spikes of the blood found on the leather blanket. Ananda presumed that was Mickey's mother. Mo agreed the two people were closely related. She didn't have a PhD in genetics like Ananda did. But Mo was used to working with creatures that were hybrids between humans and sharks, which shouldn't even be possible, and their DNA was odd, to say the least.

Not all the mersharks allowed Mo to sample their DNA, and she honored that. Some of them were quite feral despite looking human, while others who appeared fierce and almost fully shark were actually sweet and friendly. Mo methodically pulled up their DNA profiles. Chimeras, the mersharks had dual DNA.

Their ancient legends told that they had once been more humanoid and did not need to cross-breed with sharks or humans, but a tremendous storm like no other had cut them off from their kind. When Mickey, Pris, and Mo discovered them, the mersharks were on the verge of extinction, and their actions of kidnapping human men had only exacerbated that situation.

Mo pushed her glasses up with her upper arm and peered through the viewer at more rows of DNA spikes, searching for anything that matched.

Dimly, she was aware that the robot contest had begun in the next building. The lab techs huddled around the monitors were placing bets on whether the spidogs would find all the rats that Doug had hidden in the arena. He had taken three or four of the oldest ones over there, who had failed to regrow their tails no matter what serums Ananda had applied, injected, or fed them. Could the Mind Melds stop the spidogs from rescuing those rats?

Mo felt certain the Mind Melds would win, at even two to three odds. The spidogs were crafty but flimsy—all those long, delicate legs they had to maintain their balance on. Taylor and Geoffrey had created the Mind Melds to bash other robots to pieces; they had no other function, while the spidogs were complex and multifaceted. A hammer would almost always beat a Swiss Army knife in combat.

Mo was grateful that Unieda had a computer algorithm to help her compare these DNA samples. Otherwise, she would have been squinting at them for the rest of her life.

"Hey, that's not fair!" someone yelled at the monitor.

Mo squeezed her eyes shut and back open. It wasn't a great match, but this mershark had a few gene sequences in common with Mickey, more than any other humans in the database did, except the blood found on the leather. Was the mershark Native, or was Mickey a mershark?

Mickey hated water. Of course, it would be hysterical if she was a mershark. If sweet Starfish could be shark-looking except for her fin-hands, Mo supposed a mershark could look completely human. Pearl, the nominal leader of the mersharks, had taken to Mickey right away—after she had attempted to eat her arm. Luckily, it had been her prosthetic arm.

But somehow, Mo didn't think Mickey was part shark. Although she hadn't scanned any mersharks' brains, since she had promised never to remove them from Shell Beach, she didn't think they would look human. Mo had seen Mickey's scans, including the latest, and although her brain had extraneous metal bits, it was definitely human. Just somehow not related to anyone else, anywhere, ever.

Mo pulled back from the eyepiece and swiped at her glasses again. She really needed to try wearing contact lenses or get laser eye surgery. She blinked until her eyes weren't dry anymore and checked the origin of this slight match. Pearl. Of course, Pearl.

The Gemini files included the rough family tree Mo had attempted to make of the Shell Beach mersharks. The shiver of mersharks was its own chosen family, regardless of DNA, and they didn't keep track of who gave birth to who. Males were so rare no one could remember one being born alive since the storm. They were on the edge of parthenogenesis already; that was what Mo and Agwe were working on.

From the crowd before the monitor, Doug shouted, "They can't set things on fire! The rats will die!"

Mo mused it was unfair to the rats, but not to the combat ethos.

She attempted to match the family tree to the DNA profiles. Who was related to Pearl by blood? Everyone, no one. Although Pearl wasn't the oldest, as the leader, she became the honorary mother of them all. She could speak a few human words and thus was the lure to call men into the water. Mo still had to trust Pearl that the shiver had not dragged Mo's father off his boat to his eventual death; no one had ever found his body. Mo remained too scared to check the youngest mersharks' DNA against her own to find out whether she had a swimming half sister.

But she had no issues checking her friend against the mersharks. Mickey's dad hadn't vanished and broken her heart; the only father Mickey knew was the kindly doctor who had saved her life in the hospital and who she saw daily at home.

Only one other mershark matched up any bits of DNA with Mickey: Coral, who was very shy and rarely came around when the tourists visited. Mo thought she was much older than Pearl, yet she was not Pearl's ancestor. She was not Mickey's ancestor either.

"This is wrong! Who set these rules?" Doug shouted. "My rats!"

Doug tended to become overly attached to the lab animals. These rats had all failed their experiments; feeding and housing them was now a waste of money since nothing more could be learned from them. He also became very possessive of Mickey's raven in the weeks it had been in the lab being repaired and upgraded, and had badgered Taylor and Geoffrey to give him one of the other two. Of course, they refused. Doug was extra angry at seeing how well Mickey controlled Ek, because he had thought he was the master of the bird-drone.

As Mickey said, he had not even bothered to learn Ek's name.

Mo cross-referenced the genes and chromosomes that Mickey shared with Pearl and Coral, wishing she had headphones to drown out the increasing furor over whatever was happening one building over. She would need to research these matching areas and see what all those bits did, if anyone knew. She could figure it out. As if studying the mersharks wouldn't be enough for her PhD. She could get a second one, Mo supposed. People did that. Or a dual one.

Aunt Lagatha had also been working through the commotion, and she came over to Mo's workbench. "Will you look at something?"

"Of course."

Both turned as yelling erupted from the group in front of the monitors.

"My rat!" Doug screamed. "It just murdered my rat! That filthy machine!"

Rats got "murdered" in the lab daily. Mo didn't know why Doug was freaking out. She wondered which machine had done the deed.

METAL

Aunt Lagatha had set up a dual-view microscope. "These are Mickey's blood samples from when she was a baby and her blood from today."

"What am I seeing?" Mo asked, adjusting her glasses. "Of course, one is really old, and one is fresh. You're sure the old one is Mickey and not her mother?"

"I'm sure. Just look. You tell me what you see."

Mo grabbed a handful of tiny braids, ran them through her fingers, and let out her breath. She didn't know what to say. What to look for. The question was too open-ended. She dropped her braids. The beads clinked. She peered into the microscope.

"Oh. What is that?"

METAL
-13-
Blue

Blue and the precious small creature reached the pass-through, cur-rently guarded by Squiggle. Round Turtle was right behind Blue, har-rying Blue, sniping at Blue's back pair of legs and trying to unbalance Blue.

Something red, chunky, and wet was smeared on Squiggle's white carapace. Blue feared it was the creature Squiggle had almost saved. Squiggle's back legs were toward Blue, and Squiggle stared through the long wall at all the large hot life-forms on the other side.

Blue's multipurpose appendages were holding its creature's con-tainer, so Blue balanced on its four back legs and poked at its sibling with its two frontmost legs, trying to move Squiggle away from the pass-through space. At least Blue could save one creature.

Protocol.

Squiggle didn't respond to being prodded.

Blue set its feet more firmly and pushed at Squiggle again.

Squiggle's extended toes clattered as Squiggle reversed neatly, too quickly, into Blue's face, LED eyes glowing red. Squiggle focused on the morsel in the transparent box between Blue's arms, and it extended its own multipurpose appendages and grabbed the box.

Blue surrendered the creature and stepped back to allow Squiggle to push the box through the pass-through, as the programming for this exercise demanded.

Round Turtle, who Blue had forgotten about, moved in and crashed its large front leg across Blue's back. Blue's spindly appendages collapsed. One of its toes snapped. Blue rolled onto its back, but it had no defenses and could not remember how to fight. In fight mode, did it have offensive weaponry? Surely those weapons were still on its body somewhere?

Legs waving in all directions, Blue stared at Round Turtle over its scorched abdomen. It remembered the turtle breathing fire. The alien thought came through its mind: *Could Blue's circuitry take another direct hit?* Blue aimed a few eyes toward Squiggle, willing its sibling to shove the box containing the creature through the wall *now*. Some-thing terrible was about to happen.

Squiggle raised the transparent box to its mandibles and inserted one metal hook into a breathing hole in the acrylic.

No! Blue thought, trying to get enough purchase to flip over. Instead of the cleansing flame, Round Turtle was raising its weapon to crush Blue's exposed midsection. Blue shoved all of its feet, even the one with the broken toe, against the plow-like structure, trying to hold it back.

METAL

But Blue's attention remained too divided.

Squiggle ripped at the box with its metal fangs while the critter inside made itself small in a corner.

Round Turtle attempted to bludgeon Blue with its hydraulic lifting and smashing arm.

From the other side of the test arena, Arrow Turtle and Slash fought, fire versus metal, with boxes crashing and flames roaring. A piece of wooden wall came down.

Squiggle's box cracked open, and Squiggle extracted the sweet creature meat from inside. Clearly, Squiggle would simply shove the creature itself, minus its box, through the portal. Not exactly protocol, but as long as the small vulnerable creature was saved …

The plow-leg whipped down amazingly fast just as a small, concentrated gout of flame touched the seam of Blue's belly. A few more toes snapped off, and one middle leg buckled. The white-blue flame boiled on the seam.

Blue felt mentally off as the solder became liquid and unstable beneath the seam. Blue's programming stuttered. The alien thoughts slid free for a moment and then latched back on.

Squiggle's mandibles closed on the soft creature and sliced it in half. The result was extremely red and messy.

The human-blobs on the other side of the wall jiggled and made noise.

If Blue could have made noise, it would have. It did not feel pain or have emotions, but Squiggle was violating the protocol to save the small animals, and Round Turtle was causing damage at an alarming rate to Blue's insides.

All of Blue's legs drooped as the controlling wires lost their connections. Only Blue's mandibles remained active, and Blue clacked them inefficiently at Round Turtle. Round Turtle would have to place itself between the open pinchers to be injured by them.

Round Turtle stopped attacking Blue and seemed to consider what to do next.

Squiggle climbed a pile of wooden boxes and launched itself through the glass portion of the wall, limbs tucked, just a ball of metal. The glass smashed.

-14-
Mo

The old sample of Mickey's blood had degraded, of course. But it was normal human blood. The other sample was fresh. Mo was not an expert in blood, but something appeared weird about it. She leaned back.

"This sample looks contaminated." Mo rubbed her eyes. "Didn't you take more than one sample?"

"Persephone did, yes, and they all look like that." Aunt Lagatha's normally cheerful face sagged. "It's not like Persephone to produce contaminated samples."

Mo curved her face back to the eyepiece. "But contaminated with what? These weird black specks?"

"Keep watching."

Mo clicked her back teeth together and blinked to keep her eyes damp. She must have repositioned herself because now the field of blood cells looked a bit different. This microscope couldn't zoom in any further.

"Are the specks moving?"

Aunt Lagatha hummed.

Mo watched the black dots move around. They extended tiny pseudopods and changed their shapes. A few joined together, creating a slightly bigger, but still small, blob. Then they separated again. Were they mating? Sharing information? "Persephone didn't have anything to do with this," Mo stated. "What is that black stuff?"

"Not blood cells," Aunt Lagatha stated. "Not human cells."

Mo shivered. "Cancer?" she whispered. "Does Mickey have some kind of blood cancer?"

If so, Mickey was a goner. The black things were everywhere in this sample. And blood was everywhere in the body. Which meant the little parasitic things had spread throughout Mickey.

Another roar from the crowd watching the robots fighting. Doug let out an incoherent scream of rage. Mo lifted her head from the microscope's eyepiece just in time to see him run toward the robotics lab. From what she could tell from her brief time here, he seemed overly excitable on a good day, although she wasn't his supervisor or even his coworker. Mickey was her priority. Well, Gemini Robotics first and then Mickey.

Aunt Lagatha leaned toward the corridor as if to stop him and then eased back.

"What is that black stuff? It's cancer, isn't it?"

"We sequenced its DNA," Aunt Lagatha said. "It doesn't appear to have any."

METAL

"Everything alive has DNA," Mo argued. "And it's moving. It's combining and separating."

Aunt Lagatha rotated one shoulder in what might have been a shrug. "I would normally agree with you. And even cancer has DNA. Same for bacteria and various parasites. Even viruses that don't have DNA have at least RNA."

Mo pushed her face against the eyepiece until her glasses ground against her eye sockets. The black stuff moved. "Is there a better microscope where I can look at just the new sample? I don't need the comparison."

The older woman gloved up and moved the contaminated sample to a stronger microscope, with Mo following. No one else was working; every other lab tech now gathered at the monitors, watching the spidogs and the Mind Melds.

The black material offered every indication of life. It moved. It seemed to be joining and separating in a way that showed mating or at least a swap of material—if not DNA, then what? The darkness consumed some of the surrounding blood cells.

"Have you been able to extract it from the blood?" It fascinated Mo as long as she forgot this stuff was living in her friend.

"Not yet. We took a lot of samples from Mickey, but we used most of them up on other tests before we realized this material was in there."

And how would Mickey feel if she knew this was in there, and if they kept tapping her for it, like a maple tree in the spring? It was eating her blood.

It was eating Mickey.

Mo's Unieda-issued smartwatch vibrated a hot SOS against her wrist. She heard Aunt Lagatha's watch buzzing behind her. The lab techs watching the robot battle moved from sports-arena yelling to horror-movie screaming.

Glass shattered in the distance, and alarms sounded in another building.

-15-
Blue

Thick glass poured around Blue, cracking into ever smaller pieces as it lay on the floor. Round Turtle charged over Blue and at the wall, knocking Blue over and giving Blue a good view through the shattered glass.

Only Blue's mandibles and eyes were working. Its burned, cracked, smoking undercarriage lay against a pile of debris. The Controller combed through Blue's circuits and connections, trying to get Blue moving again, but heat had melted the solder, loosening wires. Insulation had burned off. Unieda hadn't built Blue to survive this level of damage, yet the Controller's thinking was that the creators should have hardened Blue against these attacks.

The lumpy remains of the small animal puddled before Blue. Blue supposed the emotion it was feeling must have been sorrow that Blue hadn't saved the animal, although the creators hadn't programmed Blue with any emotions except urgency to finish the missions set out by the protocol and relief at finishing the mission.

Round Turtle was trying to climb through the broken window. It didn't have the many long, agile legs the siblings possessed that enabled them to climb and scurry. Although, Blue reflected (or was it the Controller reflecting), those long legs had proven to be fragile and undependable in heavy combat.

Round Turtle had four short legs, not six legs and two versatile multipurpose appendages. Those four legs were squat, wide, and lacked the sharp gripper toes the siblings had. Instead, each leg had a rotating track— *like a tank*, the Controller thought, and Blue understood what tank treads were and how useful they could be, although not for the siblings. The treads allowed the turtles to roll over anything, crushing it, and to climb up minor slopes. But Round Turtle could not clamber up the sheer wall and through the window to follow Squiggle into the next room.

More glass fell into the room on the other side. The human-blobs, the creators of the protocols and missions and spidog siblings, jumped and made loud noises. They tried to get away from Squiggle, which Blue didn't understand. In the past, the siblings and the human-blobs had often been in proximity with no fear or loud noises.

Squiggle, who had been rolled into a ball, unfolded all its appendages and stood, click-clacking its mandibles and multifunction appendages. The crowd of human-blobs parted, leaving a wide space around Squiggle.

Round Turtle dropped back from trying to climb into the breach and trundled off, crushing everything in its way beneath its treads, heading back to the entrance.

METAL

Blue lay helpless on the debris, blinking and clacking its mandibles. The Controller raged and tried to get it to move, but Blue was finished. It sent out a distress call asking for extraction and repair. It didn't have the words to explain that Squiggle had malfunctioned. The creators called Squiggle "3" or "Red," so Blue (also known as "2") sent those designations as well.

Squiggle advanced on the crowd as Blue watched helplessly. The human-blobs were too big to need rescuing today, although, in the past, the siblings had saved blobs of that size. Blue reinspected the protocol. It had not changed. Small life-forms in boxes were still the priority.

A fast-moving human-blob charged in from the side, waving appendages and making noises. It pushed aside other blobs and ran right up to Squiggle and made its strange noises right in Squiggle's face. The Controller's thoughts inside Blue regarding Squiggle's behavior were bad, and although Blue didn't entirely understand them, it understood the wrongness.

Something terrible was about to happen.

Squiggle was not right. Its red eyes had darkened to almost black, and it wasn't responding to pings.

The human-blob pointed back through the broken window in Blue's direction. Blue mashed its mandibles together in acknowledgment that it needed help, thinking the human-blob was telling Squiggle to go back and retrieve Blue.

Squiggle also clacked its mouthparts and mirrored the motions with its multifunction appendages. The other blobs reached out to pull the angry blob back, away from Squiggle. Maybe, like the Controller, they knew bad things were coming.

Squiggle grasped the human-blob with its arms, pulling it close. Squiggle's eyes darkened to full black. The blob kept making noises, although it was too constrained to move anymore. Perhaps Squiggle would bring the blob back through the hole, and they would both help Blue.

Squiggle gazed through the broken window at Blue. Rainbow oil slicks moved over its black eyes. This was not Sibling Squiggle anymore.

Inside Blue, Controller's thoughts were frantic, too fast and complex for Blue to understand, with too many concepts that did not adhere to protocol. Blue clicked its mandibles in distress. A few of the blobs focused on Blue, upside down and broken, useless legs akimbo, toes snapped off and dangling. Most were making noises and moving their own front legs at Squiggle.

Squiggle never broke its gaze with Blue as it squeezed the human-blob until it stopped moving and then kept squeezing until it exploded from the pressure. In Blue's heat-sensitive vision, Squiggle's white carapace splattered with glowing gore. It raised the top half of the blob and nuzzled it with its mandibles. If the siblings had had a parent and that parent had been a dog and not a spider, the parent might have nuzzled them in that same affectionate way.

The pitch of the noise from beyond the wall rose into a shriek. The human-blobs backed away from Squiggle, who dropped the pieces of the exploded blob and turned away from Blue to plow through the rest of the blobs, throwing many to the floor. Squiggle stomped them with its sharp toes.

This was not the protocol. Blue felt troubled. Squiggle had gone terribly wrong inside. Although Blue was no longer functioning and mobile, Blue was still Blue. Squiggle was mobile and appeared to be working correctly, but actually, everything was wrong with Squiggle.

Blue was not the only upside-down sibling.

Just as Blue remembered it had a third sibling, another crash of glass came from the far end of the wall, where Slash had been battling Arrow Turtle.

Blue lost sight of Squiggle in the crowd of hot, round outlines and general confusion on the other side of the wall. Another sibling appeared that must be Slash, but instead of Slash's wickedly intelligent yellow eyes, this sibling also had shifting oil slicks puddled across its face. Its carapace seemed clean of gore, although that didn't last as Slash lived up to its nomenclature and tore into the heat globs, and they fell before it.

Blue reflected that Round Turtle had done an excellent job of stopping Slash from executing the protocol and saving the small creatures. Where were the turtles now? Did their protocols not care about saving large creatures?

Blue felt conflicted. It didn't want to hurt its siblings, but they were supposed to be in search-and-rescue mode. Instead, they were causing mayhem and injury. Perhaps because their eyes had malfunctioned. Blue had no way to look at itself and couldn't fathom a way to find out if its own blue eyes had turned into oil slicks. Even if Blue was about to break programming, it couldn't go anywhere or do anything, broken on its back as it was.

More glass broke farther away, and one sibling touched Blue briefly with a sense of freedom.

The Controller left Blue. The world went blue, and then everything was black.

METAL
-16-
Mickey

Piloting the blue spidog wasn't that difficult. Mickey had been worried that she would have to figure out the walking rhythm with six legs, but the spidog knew how to do that part itself—she just had to tell it to move forward or in whatever direction. It was more like going on a ride-along.

Its thoughts were strange, in pictures and absolutes. Mickey tried to observe and not interfere. The spidog had more self-awareness than she expected, although less than Ek. Unieda had programmed Blue to find people buried under rubble. Ek had originally been set up for simple pattern recognition but had learned and expanded quickly after touching Mickey's neural net. It was possible that Blue could expand, too, if she worked with it enough, but Blue wasn't her personal pet like Ek and never would be.

This was a onetime experiment, Mickey reminded herself. Don't get attached. She thought of the orange spidog in parts on the lab bench, Ananda and her lab techs removing the legs and tails from the adorable axolotls.

She wondered if Pris sensed the sibling bond between the three spidogs and their odd names for each other. It had taken Mickey a moment to realize that "Slash" was the number "1" on the yellow one's back, and "Squiggle" was the "3" shape on the red one.

Although Mickey could reach dimly through the sibling bond with the other spidogs, she couldn't feel Pris or Emilio controlling them. She felt Blue's surprise at having her inside its head, which led her to believe that usually, Blue didn't sense Emilio or whichever operator Unieda assigned it.

Blue seemed like a competent piece of machinery. It understood what it was supposed to do and checked on the other two spidogs—its "siblings"—to make sure they were operating under the protocol correctly. If the only task Unieda had given it was to find the rats hidden in the maze and bring them to the extraction point, Blue would have done excellently.

But Bao had decided to stress out the spidogs by setting the Mind Melds on them to see what would happen.

Everything happened so fast, and Mickey was so subsumed in Blue's mind that she could hardly take mental notes. The spidogs were only supposed to have access to one type of programming at a time. One protocol. In this case, search and rescue of the rats. Although, for whatever reason, Blue couldn't understand the concept of a rat, just that it was a small life-form, very generalized. Blue didn't seem to understand life at all. Warm blobs in its thermal vision, that was life to Blue.

But when Alpha and Prime ambushed the spidogs in the maze, Blue remembered it had once known how to fight. Or that it still did; Mickey wasn't sure how the switch of protocols took place between rescue, fight, and protect modes. The other two spidogs may have gone down the same programming path; in any case, Squiggle/Red had attacked and killed the rats rather than surrendering them as instructed.

Mickey forgot she was inside the spidog and thought that Red was going to kill her too; Pris controlled Red. And Pris would never, ever hurt Mickey—she was a mama bear about Mickey. Pris would also never rip apart a rat. At some point, Pris must have lost control of Red—if she had ever had control at all.

Bao had told Taylor and Geoffrey not to hold back when attacking the spidogs, but obviously, he hadn't considered that two of the twins' friends were inside the spidogs. Nor had anyone thought about fire in a maze of cardboard, wood, and wallboard. And Pris's earlier warning was right; the Mind Melds were programmed for battle. They didn't do finesse.

Suddenly, the red-banded spidog rolled itself into a ball and flung itself through the glass window into the next room. There was nothing Mickey could do. Blue was dying, its wires fried by Prime. She could no longer stay connected.

Doug burst into the lab, screaming about Red killing his rats and confronted the spidog.

Pris's hands were lax on her controller, her mouth slightly open, her face hidden behind the goggles. She was obviously not in control of Red. Emilio had moved his box down the wall toward Geoffrey and Taylor, where Alpha and Prime appeared to be battling with Yellow.

Doug wasn't afraid of Red. Why would he be? He had probably been a test pilot for the spidog at some point since he'd also run Ek. He knew how the spidogs worked. Red was barely as tall as Doug's waist, with skinny legs that looked like anyone could kick out from under it. They must be stronger than they looked, though, if they were meant to go to war?

Doug bent over and shouted at Red. "You killed my rats!" He pointed at the gore on the spidog's white carapace, swearing. "Why would you do that? You—"

Red enfolded Doug in its front sets of legs, the ones the spidogs usually kept off the ground and used as arms. Blue thought of them as multipurpose appendages.

METAL

Pris's mouth snapped shut and her fingers started to work the red controls again.

Red's embrace tightened on Doug.

"No, no, no," Pris chanted.

Mickey reached out to Red but there was nothing for her to grab because Pris was already in there. Everything inside Red appeared black and shifting. Somehow familiar.

"Let go of me, you tin can!" Doug's face darkened. He kicked Red's legs.

Red lifted him higher.

The robotics techs moved away, leaving a space around Red and Doug.

"Stop!" Pris said, punching the control box. She threw off the goggles and stared at the spidog. "Why aren't your eyes red anymore?"

Blue had noticed that, too, but Mickey hadn't realized the significance. Each spidog's LEDs were a different color, matching its stripe (and name). Red's eyes were no longer crimson. They were so black Mickey wondered if it could even see anymore.

Red rotated in a curve, taking in all the techs watching, and crushed Doug as easily as it had bisected the rats. Blood splattered the spidog, the floor, and the onlookers. Red appeared to kiss Doug's upper half, dropped the mangled body and, on its delicate tiptoes, minced toward the door.

Pris screamed in denial and ran after Red, slipping on the wet floor. Red kicked out with its back legs—one, two—nailing Pris in the belly and chest with pointed feet. She fell, her head thudding against the corner of a metal cabinet on the way down.

Red rolled into a ball and smashed through the door.

-17-
Mickey

The crowd in the robotics lab surged in multiple directions. Away from Red, toward Pris, toward Doug.

Red smacked more people down and trampled them with its sharp feet as it fled.

Doug was beyond saving, lying in a puddle of his own goo, his middle compressed and split open. Mickey felt horrible for thinking he smelled bad as she pressed past his ruined body.

One of Pris's perfect cheekbones had caved in, and her jaw looked broken. The left side of her elfin face was unrecognizable, the flesh torn away by the metal cabinet. She had rolled onto her back when she hit the floor. Her eyes were slits, and her pink, glossy mouth was crooked and slack. She lay terribly still.

If it had been Mickey lying unmoving with her face crushed, Pris would have been calling all lawyers, doctors, and plastic surgeons and generally taking charge of the scene while flashing her no-limit iridescent credit card as needed, telling everyone who she was, one of *those* Salamancas, yes, the billionaire ones from reality TV.

Mickey didn't even know Pris's cell phone code to unlock it, much less call any of her lawyers. She didn't know the lawyers' names, just that Pris knew a lot of them, and they were all more than happy to come running when a Salamanca daughter beckoned, even if it was the least famous daughter who pretended not to be part of the family most of the time.

Mickey's parents were ER doctors and thus very useful when one has fallen and smashed in one's face, but they were hours away.

Dropping to her knees, Mickey touched the right side of Pris's face, the undamaged side. Her skin was warm and soft, and Pris felt alive. Pris's eyes flickered toward Mickey, and then her eyelids shut. Mickey shoved the goggles the rest of the way off her friend's head.

There were doctors nearby, though, even if they weren't Salamanca-approved specialists. Mickey just had to call them. She put her metal hand on Pris's shoulder for comfort and pushed aside the red control box that still hung from its strap around her friend's neck. She dug for her phone in her pocket.

Dimly, Mickey was aware of more glass breaking and more people shouting. This had all gone sideways. She balanced the phone in her hand, holding it flat with her pinky and unlocking it with her flesh thumb while her metal thumb stroked Pris's shoulder. The haptic feedback wasn't the best, but what counted was that Pris could feel the comforting touch.

METAL

The chaos was too loud for her usual voice commands, so Mickey thumbed her way to the phone app to call for emergency services. One person was dead, many wounded, a rampaging robot. Surely that qualified to use the emergency number. She couldn't remember the address here, but surely the dispatcher could look up the Unieda campus, right?

-18-
Mo

Shouting echoed inside the genetics lab, even as Mo's smartwatch vibrated hotly against her wrist. Someone screamed Doug's name—Mo thought it was Persephone, but everyone was yelling and swearing in front of the monitors.

Everyone's smartwatches were buzzing in unison. The lab sounded like a giant beehive.

Persephone yanked Aunt Lagatha's arm. "People are hurt over there. Doug is dead!" she wailed. Usually, Persephone was so calm she seemed rude; now, all her emotions spilled wetly down her cheeks. "Doug is dead! There's blood everywhere. It broke him in half."

Mo adjusted her glasses against her sore eye sockets and blinked at the phlebotomist. "Who broke Doug in half?"

"That ugly spider robot!" Persephone swore and scrubbed her cheeks with her knuckles.

Mo thought of the fragile-looking, spindly white spidogs and then considered the Mind Melds. "You mean Geoffrey and Taylor's big black robots?" Those savage metal beasts could take down a person, no problem.

Persephone frowned. "No, not them. Bao's robots. Those spidogs he's been testing, that Doug helped pilot sometimes."

Mo shook her head a tiny bit in denial. Hadn't Mickey and Pris been chosen to control those? They would never have hurt a person.

"What happened?" Aunt Lagatha interrupted.

The other lab techs were pushing at the revolving door to the robotics lab tunnel, but their watches weren't allowing them through. The clamor increased.

"One of the spidogs killed a rat, and Doug freaked out. It was one of those stupid old rats with no tails he liked, and he ran in there." Persephone breathed heavily and ran her hand over her face. "The spidog jumped through the window and attacked him and just broke him in half."

Mo pursed her lips and then relaxed them. Of course, this seemed implausible, but she had been concentrating on the mystery of Mickey's crazy DNA and that weird black stuff in her blood, not on whatever had been happening on the monitors in the lab.

"Your friend with the pink hair is down," Persephone added. "The tall, skinny white girl."

"What? Pris? The spidog got her too?" Mo turned to the corridor, but the electronic lock still wasn't responding to anyone's watches. That side of the lab was chaos.

METAL

"I don't know her name. She looks familiar. She got knocked down and trampled."

Aunt Lagatha put a long-fingered pale hand on Mo's shoulder for a brief squeeze. "They need help over there."

"Shouldn't we call for ambulances?" Mo reached for the drawer where she kept her phone.

"Bao is over there. I'm sure he's on it. They don't need a multitude of duplicate calls coming in to dispatch."

"Of course, I don't want to tell you how to do things here, but my stepfather is a sheriff—"

"Bao will do everything necessary," Aunt Lagatha said firmly. "We have protocols." The tall woman pushed through the crowd toward the pad on the wall. Mo and Persephone followed in the space she opened. Aunt Lagatha lifted her watch, with its supervisory programming features, to unlock the door.

Mo peered around Aunt Lagatha's uplifted arm down the tunnel toward the robotics lab. The glass along the outer corridor of the other building had shattered in two places as if someone had thrown boulders from inside. Smoke-colored shards sparkled all over the brown grass like diamonds. The alarm lights flashed through the holes.

The revolving door to the corridor didn't open.

Aunt Lagatha muttered something about overrides and lowered her arm to tap the smartwatch, blocking Mo's view. The other lab workers crowded around, eager to get to the other building to help or gawk or get in the way.

Glass smashed very close, and Aunt Lagatha froze, her fingers on her watch face.

The noise level around Mo swelled, and she leaned around the older woman.

The red-legged spidog crouched in the corridor leading to the robotic lab, surrounded by broken glass. It held a limp groundhog in its mandibles. Fresh and dried blood splattered its slick white carapace. It stared toward the genetics lab with black eyes.

That's not right, Mo thought. Their eye color matches their leg color. That one should have red eyes.

Aunt Lagatha put both arms out to either side, with all the lab techs behind her, in the classic pose of a mother protecting her children. Everyone hushed.

Red shook itself, and more pieces of glass fell off it as it stood straight. It adjusted the groundhog and minced toward Aunt Lagatha.

The others backed away from the door, but Mo stayed close to Aunt Lagatha, staring at Red's strange oil-slick eyes. "Its eyes," she whispered.

"I see it," Aunt Lagatha replied.

Who was piloting this spidog, Mo wondered. Obviously not Pris, if she was down and injured. If this was Mickey's, why would the spidog have a dead groundhog and be smeared with blood? It had to be that little person, Emilio, but why?

Something outside the corridor distracted Red. A rabbit, running at full speed, bounding randomly. Chasing after it, the yellow spidog. Red tossed the groundhog toward the watching women and crashed through the glass after the rabbit and Yellow.

Aunt Lagatha glanced wide-eyed over her shoulder at Mo. Mo shrugged. Aunt Lagatha finished the override sequence on her watch and held it up to the pad on the wall.

The door didn't open.

Red and Yellow fought over the rabbit, tearing it to bloody shreds at the edge of the parking lot, and then scurried off in two different directions. The alarms continued blaring. The lights kept flashing.

Mo realized no emergency services had arrived.

METAL
-19-
Mickey

A long-fingered hand slapped Mickey's phone away. "Who are you calling?"

"911—people got hurt. Look at Pris!" Mickey's metal fingers cupped Pris's uninjured cheek.

"Don't call anyone," Bao instructed. "I will handle this."

"She needs an ambulance. It killed Doug!"

"We don't need any negative publicity around the spidogs."

"What?"

"I'm a medical doctor. We have plenty of supplies over in the genetics lab. I'll have Aunt Lagatha come over and bring a team."

Bao seemed more annoyed than upset, scratching his beard with a forefinger and frowning as he studied the scene. Alarms blared from every direction. It took Mickey a moment to realize that some of the alarm tones came from the Unieda employees' smartwatches. Broken glass, pools of blood, injured people, plus unpleasant pieces of Doug littered the floor. The room was crowded, loud, and smelly, with bonus flashing lights.

Both Red and Yellow were gone. Mickey supposed Blue was still belly-up and dead in the arena. She didn't know where the twins were, or Alpha and Prime.

"Pris needs expert help now." Her perfect, elfin face, caved in. So much blood. And possibly a bit of bone. Mickey needed Mo. What if Pris had brain damage? Panic squeezed Mickey, and her anxiety medicine was where? In her bag back in the other building, because she simply couldn't be bothered to carry a few extra pills in a keychain holder as that was an old-lady thing to do.

Bao glanced at Pris and sniffed. "She just needs some plastic surgery."

"She's unconscious!" Mickey shouted. "I can see her skull!" Her metal hand tightened on the good half of Pris's face, probably leaving a bruise. Mickey laid her best friend's broken head carefully on the filthy, contaminated floor and stood, facing off with the doctor, who wasn't much bigger than she was.

"You are a terrible person! You torture animals! Now you don't care that people got hurt!" Darkness crept into the edges of Mickey's vision, and she felt cold. Her metal hand rubbed the scar where the xoggotli had infiltrated her neck, the fingers digging into the old wound.

Bao pointed at Mickey. "Doug is dead. We can't help him. We need to contain this mess, and then we will have outside authorities come in. We have everyone and everything we need here on the Unieda campus. You are an outsider, and you don't understand. You should go to your room and wait this out."

Mickey's eyes widened. The doctor was sending her to her room like a bad child. Her mind opened wider than it ever had. Ek snapped to attention and lifted from its perch on a counter to swoop to her shoulder. The tiny, dying embers of Blue flickered in an attempt to obey and then subsided. Prime and Alpha stuttered inside the arena, confused at conflicted signals from the twins and Mickey. All over her body, something fizzed into life. For an instant, she saw through the eyes of Red and Yellow, outside chasing wildlife with insane abandon, and she caught the longing for freedom of her tiny melanistic bifurcated axolotl friend.

The connectors between the neural net and her implants heated into an instant headache, driving Mickey to her knees. She grabbed her phone from beside Pris's motionless form. Pris was horribly limp but breathing, blood and clear fluid leaking from her ruined face.

"What the hell just happened?" Bao was still pointing at Mickey, his finger trembling.

"You got me mad." Mickey thumbed her way to the texting app.

"I told you not to call in outside help."

"I'm not."

Bao dropped his arm and turned away as someone else clamored for his attention.

Mickey texted Mo: *Pris hurt bad. Face smashed in. Everything bad here. Bao says no 911. Need help. Doug is dead. Spidogs gone rogue.*

METAL
-20-
Mo

Mo's phone buzzed in the drawer next to her workstation. All the workers who had stayed in the genetics lab were between her and that drawer.

A spidog had breached the glass corridor, and the door leading out remained locked.

The other workers pressed Mo and Aunt Lagatha into the immobile revolving door. Mo suddenly understood Mickey's claustrophobia, feeling herself compressed on all sides, her face pressed into Aunt Lagatha's silver-and-gold braids.

"Back off!" Aunt Lagatha commanded. "The door isn't going to open. We need another plan." The pressure around Mo eased.

Mo wove through the others to her workstation. She gazed across several counters to where she had been inspecting the strange black objects in Mickey's blood a short time before. If everything hadn't been so disjointed, if Mo had just been allowed to be still and think for a moment, she would have figured out what was going on. She just knew it.

Instead, spidogs were throwing dead groundhogs at her.

This wasn't what she had thought would happen when Taylor and Geoffrey offered her a chance to work at Unieda Corporation with Ananda for a short time.

The phone vibrated again. Mo pulled it from the drawer and pressed her thumb to the screen.

Ananda peered over her shoulder. "Really? You're texting someone? I think all this is classified under the NDA."

"Someone is texting me, and it's not like I'm doing anything else at the moment." The notification screen appeared. "It's from Mickey. Don't you think it might be important?"

Ananda snorted, but she watched as Mo clicked through and read the message. "Face smashed in? What does that mean?"

Voice tight with worry, Mo snapped, "I don't know. I saw the same message you did. It sounds awful."

Mo responded: *Spidogs broke into the glass corridor. We can't get over there. The alarms shut off the door locks. Is Pris conscious? We know about Doug. We were watching the arena cameras.*

The answer quickly came back *No* with a photo of Pris's bloody, misshapen face.

Ananda's brown cheeks paled when she viewed the picture. "I'll get Auntie L."

Mo thought of what paparazzi would pay for that photo—and story—and she shuddered. She would never betray her friend like that, but if anyone in the robotics lab realized who Pris was …

Of course, Pris's billionaire family could afford the best care for her, but first, Pris had to get out of there and to a hospital.

Most likely, from the video footage, Pris wasn't the only severely injured person over there. But Mickey wouldn't be paying attention to anyone else.

Aunt Lagatha, followed by Ananda, hurried over to Mo, trailed by Persephone and a few other lab techs. Ananda snatched Mo's phone and showed Aunt Lagatha Pris's picture.

"She needs a hospital," Aunt Lagatha said instantly. "Even if I could get over there, there isn't much I could do."

"Mickey says Bao isn't allowing anyone to call 911." Mo took back her phone and stared at the horrible photo of Pris for another moment before deleting it.

Aunt Lagatha glanced around the genetics lab. The alarms were still flashing and ringing in the corners as well as on everyone's wrists. She huffed. "Mo, call 911."

Ananda put her hand over Mo's phone. "We have the protocol in place," she protested.

"That's great," Aunt Lagatha said. "You saw that video. Doug is dead, horribly so. Others besides Pris are down. This isn't something I can splint or put a compression bandage on, and we aren't a hospital. My medical doctor training was years ago. Mo, make the call."

Mo twisted her phone from under Ananda's clutching fingers. Pris had given Mo that phone, her first smartphone. Mo had never actually called 911 before. She grew up in a small beach town, and her stepdad was the sheriff. What would he think of this disaster? Mo blew out a breath and tapped the digits.

"Hello, Unieda Security?" A bored male voice.

"Um—" Mo put the phone on speaker and huddled around it with the other two women. "Who is this?"

"This is Unieda Corporation Security Office. How can I help you?"

Mo exchanged wide-eyed glances with Ananda and Aunt Lagatha.

Aunt Lagatha leaned into the phone. "This is Dr. Lagatha Larsen, head of the genetics lab. We've had a serious incident at the robotics lab, and we need ambulances. There has been at least one death."

"Yes, we are aware."

Aunt Lagatha waited for a moment, but that seemed to be all the security guard was offering. "You have dispatched ambulances?"

"We are standing by, awaiting word from Dr. Lee. Protocol is being followed."

"The genetics lab has been cut off from the rest of the campus because the glass corridor is damaged. It is compromised, so the doors have auto-locked. There are seriously wounded people in the robotics lab. I cannot get there to help them, which is the protocol." Aunt Lagatha's pale lips tightened.

The laconic voice suggested, "Use the connecting corridor to the animal lab, and then exit through the loading dock to the outside."

If there had not been a pair of killer spidogs roaming the campus, that idea would have worked just fine.

Aunt Lagatha pinched her mouth and rolled her blue eyes toward the ceiling. "Are you aware of the nature of the current emergency? How the glass corridor was damaged? How all the people were injured and killed?"

"No, ma'am. That's a need-to-know basis."

Aunt Lagatha closed her eyes. "If I go outside with any of my lab personnel—outside the glass corridors—we are in danger of being injured and killed the same way the people in the robotics lab were. We need—" She paused.

Mo thought. What *did* they need? Anti-tank weapons? The army? An EMP?

"—to call you back." Aunt Lagatha tapped the hang-up icon.

"His idea won't work," Ananda said. "If we go outside, the spidogs will kill us."

"If we don't venture outside and get to the robotics lab, Pris and the other injured people might die," Mo said.

Mickey shoved her phone into her pocket after reading Mo's text. Help wasn't coming. All the medically trained people were trapped at the other end of the corridor and Bao had all the 911 calls intercepted and rerouted to the security office.

Pris had fallen next to a cabinet, so Mickey felt sure she wouldn't get stepped on. Just to be safe, she pushed her friend carefully closer to the bottom drawers. Blankets didn't seem to be a commodity in the robotics room. Mickey checked; Pris was wearing a bra, so Mickey pulled off Pris's now-filthy T-shirt and used it to cushion her head.

It took Mickey a moment to find Emilio in the crowd; the little man was huddled by the arena wall, still clutching the control box and wearing the goggles that controlled Yellow. When Mickey touched his arm, he jumped, almost smacking her on the chin with his large head. Ek dug into her shoulder, wings fluttering.

"What's going on?" She crouched.

He pushed the goggles up to his forehead. "I have no control."

"Can you still see?"

Emilio nodded. "They are chasing and killing wildlife. They smashed up a few cars in the parking lot and attacked the genetics lab."

"You tried to control Yellow?"

"Nothing. Do you want to try?" He held out the box. "I lost control so quickly in the arena. That never happened before."

Mickey bit her lip. She had complete control of Blue until the moment it died. "The people from the genetics lab want to make a run for it from some loading dock. My friend from over there texted me."

Emilio's eyes widened. They were puffy from the tight goggles. "No way. Red and Yellow will take them down."

"My friend's face is smashed in. Pris. She needs medical help badly."

"I'm sorry, but what do you want me to do?"

The blackness surged at the edges of Mickey's vision, and she wanted to punch Emilio in the face so he could know what it felt like to have his cheek smashed to bits. But he was way smaller than her, so that would be wrong. "Keep watching, I guess." Ek leaned toward Emilio, beak open. A bit of dark oil clung to the corner. She hoped he wasn't broken again.

Just as she straightened, Geoffrey and Taylor, looking ravaged and unhappy, found her. Mickey turned away from Emilio, who had pushed the goggles back over his eyes. Ek snapped his beak shut and settled.

METAL

"Where is Pris?" Taylor asked, chewing his lip. His oversized, clunky neural net sat crooked on his head, blinking lights at every wire intersection. His glasses were hung up in it.

Mickey straightened the net and fixed his glasses, trying not to cry. "She's on the floor with her face caved in."

"What?" his brother asked. "What happened?"

Mickey shook her head. "One of the spidogs kicked her in the chest, and she hit her head on a metal cabinet."

Geoffrey looked around, his eyes wild. "She's dead? Pris!" He took a step, paused, and tried another direction. "Pris? Pris!"

"She's alive, for now. But we can't call 911, and the medical people can't get here from the genetics lab. One of the spidogs attacked the corridor, and the genetics lab is in lockdown."

"Ananda?" Taylor wondered.

"Mo didn't say so I guess she's okay. The spidog threw a dead groundhog at them." Mickey led them toward Pris.

Geoffrey crouched beside her fallen form and swore in several languages—he spoke three: English, French, and Korean. He moved the folded T-shirt aside, and Taylor winced.

"Did it get her brain?" Taylor kneeled on the dirty floor.

Geoffrey shook his head and touched Pris's face lightly. "Did she talk or move at all after?"

"She kinda looked at me and then closed her eyes."

The twins inhaled and exhaled in unison.

"It's bad, isn't it?" Mickey asked.

"It's not good." Geoffrey rearranged the shirt around Pris's face to cushion it. "Now explain why we can't call for help. Did you try?"

"Mo tried." Mickey showed them texts Mo had sent explaining their attempts.

"What is Bao thinking?" Taylor wondered. They stood, staring down at Pris, motionless, tucked against the cabinet.

"Damage control," Geoffrey suggested.

"Too late for that," Mickey said. "Can't we send Alpha and Prime after Red and Yellow? They took down Blue well enough. I was inside Blue. I felt it. The flames melted everything."

"That was probably too aggressive, but Bao told us no holds barred," Taylor said.

"We need to refill the gas cylinders and swap out the batteries. Then we could go out after them. As long as they stay inside the Unieda campus …" Geoffrey trailed off.

"But what if they don't? How hard would it be for the spidogs to break through the fence and get out?" Mickey asked.

-22-
Mo

Mo, Ananda, Persephone, come with me. Everyone else, stay here."
Aunt Lagatha ripped the entire first aid kit off the wall and checked
inside, shaking her head.

"There's another one in the animal building," Persephone
suggested.

"It's pretty much identical, though," Ananda said. "But we can
take some of the animal supplies, drugs, and things like that."

"Good call," Aunt Lagatha said. "Who has a backpack?" she called
into the scrum of techs still gathered around the locked revolving door.
She commandeered three and stuffed the first aid kit into one and
handed it to Mo.

Mo also jammed her own things inside the bag. She texted Mickey
that they were going to attempt to cross the open ground to the robotics lab and then pocketed her phone.

The door leading to the animal lab obediently opened to Aunt
Lagatha's smartwatch, and the four of them ventured into the short
glass tunnel. The odor of animals crowded Mo's nose; that was why
most of them were housed in their own building. All the animal care-
takers were in the genetics lab at the other door or in the robotics lab.

"Should we run or—" Ananda started to say.

The yellow spidog bounded from the trees beside the retention
pond and rolled into a ball as it sprang at the glass.

"Run!" Mo shouted and followed her own advice, her red sneakers
pounding down the hot glass hallway toward the next revolving door,
the backpack bouncing heavily against her shoulder blades.

Yellow burst through the glass just as Mo slammed her wrist into
the pad beside the door, unlocking it. She threw herself into the door
and pushed forward. Someone was right behind her, trying to make the
door revolve faster. Whose idea had the revolving doors been, anyway?

Also, someone was screaming. Mo couldn't tell who. She burst
through the other side of the revolving door and turned. Ananda
crashed into her. They both stumbled into a stainless-steel cart full of
animal feed, which slid away on rubber wheels. Mo fell. Ananda tumbled on top of her.

The sounds of Yellow whirring and grinding came clearly through
the door. Aunt Lagatha and Persephone did not enter the door, only
the sound of their screaming.

"Get off me!" Mo rolled over and pushed at Ananda.

They climbed to their feet and turned back to the door.

Yellow was in the corridor.

METAL

Persephone was on her knees, Aunt Lagatha between her and the spidog. Mo hoped Persephone had simply tripped and wasn't injured. The two women were surrounded by broken gray glass.

Yellow clacked its mandibles and opened its arms as if to embrace Aunt Lagatha.

She smacked it with the empty backpack, and it retreated a bit.

The alarm started blaring in the animal lab, and the revolving door clicked. The rodents, disturbed by the noise, scurried in their boxes.

Mo held her watch to the pad. Nothing happened. She groaned.

Ananda pushed her. "Let me try. I have better access because I work here; you're just a temporary contractor."

Ananda's better access did not, in fact, work better. They observed through the revolving door as Aunt Lagatha battered Yellow with the empty canvas knapsack, driving the spidog back as Persephone climbed slowly to her feet.

Yellow danced forward again on its absurdly tiny, pointed white toes, arms open, mandibles gnashing. Its smooth white carapace was filthy and blood-spattered.

"Aren't its eyes supposed to be yellow?" Mo wondered.

Persephone yelped and backed away, putting her hands on Aunt Lagatha's waist and pulling the older woman along.

"Yeah, they should be yellow," Ananda agreed. "I wonder why they are black."

Not only black but a liquid-looking black that made Mo feel very uneasy. Yellow's eyes were simply LEDs—yellow ones.

Persephone and Aunt Lagatha moved back toward the genetics lab. But the security system would have locked that door, too, wouldn't it? Of course.

"Can they hear?" Mo asked.

"What? Who? Auntie L. and Persephone?"

"No, the spidogs, of course. Do they have ears?"

Ananda's teeth snapped shut. She blinked. "I don't know. Why?"

Mo puffed. "I think that the door on the other side of the corridor will also be locked now. Aunt Lagatha and Persephone are trapped in there. I want to warn them; does Yellow understand human speech?"

"Ah. I don't know."

Yellow advanced on tiptoe as the women backed up.

Ananda leaned into the revolving door and shouted, "The doors have triggered! They are locked! You're trapped!"

Mo groaned. "Of course, I didn't mean—"

Aunt Lagatha nodded and stopped moving.

The spidog paused and sat back a bit on its rear legs. The hole in the corridor was behind it.

"We gotta go," Mo said, biting her lips.

"We can't."

"Grab the supplies you think we need, shove them in my pack, and let's go now."

Ananda, breathing so heavily through her nose that the tiny stud in her nostrils moved, riffled through drawers while Mo ripped the first aid kit from the wall.

"The drugs we need are locked up. We need Auntie L.'s watch to unlock the pharmaceutical cases."

"Too bad, gotta go." Mo held out the metal box and turned sideways to offer the backpack.

"Why?"

"We have to draw the yellow spidog back out through the hole so that Aunt Lagatha and Persephone can escape."

METAL
-23-
Mickey

A lab tech whose name Mickey didn't know was assembling the wounded near Pris and doling out the contents of a meager first aid kit. An oil-stained tarp covered the bigger bits of Doug.

While Geoffrey and Taylor were getting Prime and Alpha ready to go back out, doing esoteric engineering stuff, Mickey found her way to the door into the arena. The fights had destroyed the semi-organized walls and piles that some crew had spent yesterday evening building. Many of the boxes had scorch marks. Whatever cardboard had been on fire had burned itself out, but the smoke hung in the air. She eyed the tall ceiling. It seemed like a terrible idea to set fires in here. Bao was a stupid man, even if he was some sort of genius. He was also cruel.

Ek lifted off her shoulder and circled the arena, searching for Blue. Pattern recognition was one of Ek's original functions, and it still enjoyed the challenge. Mickey closed her eyes and looked for the round whiteness of the spidog among all the square brownness of boxes, crates, and wallboard.

Blue was still on its back like the dead spider it was. Using Ek's vision as a guide, Mickey climbed over to the spidog. She didn't know why she was there, except that Blue hadn't gone bad like Yellow and Red. It had tried to stop its siblings.

She placed her metal hand on its carapace. Because she could do nothing for Pris—she couldn't bear to think of Pris's beautiful face caved in—she went to where no one else was going. Reminding herself of Pris, lying so still on the floor, made the edges of her vision darken. Her hand clenched against Blue's smooth, white side.

Blue stirred.

Ek landed beside Blue and leaned forward to poke at the spidog.

Mickey disconnected from Ek and dove into Blue, feeling how sluggish the spidog was, how wounded. The melted bits inside had cooled and re-solidified, but not exactly right.

Blue flexed its legs—one was crooked—and turned its head in her direction, shining all of its blue eyes at her.

It was helpless as a turtle, she realized, not fully immersed in the spidog. She pushed at it, trying to roll it over. The body was much heavier and sturdier than it looked.

"What are you doing?" Emilio shouted through the broken window. "Isn't Blue broken?"

"No, its eyes are glowing, and it moved its legs. Maybe it can help."

"What if Blue is crazy like Yellow and Red? Get away!"

Mickey glared at the little man. "Its eyes are still blue. Why don't you connect to it and help it roll over?"

"No way. I don't want to lose my connection to Yellow. If I back out, I might not get back in."

Mickey snorted her opinion of that and pushed Blue again. Her metal arm was strong; the weak point was where it joined her flesh. The magnets and straps could slip.

Ek, always helpful, landed on Blue's head.

"Get off if you aren't doing something useful," she muttered and just then found the tipping point.

Blue rolled over and then wobbled, legs akimbo, scorched belly against some debris. It rocked back and forth, getting each long, spindly leg underneath it, having trouble with the broken one. All of its toes didn't extend, but at last, it stood beside Mickey, Ek riding it.

"Okay," she said to Blue. "Wanna help me take down your siblings?"

METAL
-24-
Mickey

Several people screamed when Blue followed Mickey into the robotics lab workspace.

"Look, its eyes are still blue! It's okay; this one is good," Mickey reassured them.

"Are you controlling that thing?" A tech with short, spiky dreads asked. "I don't trust it anymore."

"Dude, we built it!" A chubby girl with green hair elbowed him.

"Nope." The tech with the dreads backed away from Blue and Mickey as they headed to check on Geoffrey and Taylor's progress.

The green-haired girl followed. "Blue needs a new leg."

"I noticed," Mickey said. "But it has five more, plus the multipurpose limbs. I think it will be okay."

"I could use a spare orange leg. And swap out the damaged feet."

Mickey stopped. "Really? You aren't afraid?"

"Well, yeah. But obviously, Blue hasn't gone crazy like the other two. And I'm guessing you are going to send Blue out to stop Yellow and Red."

"I'm going to try. And my friends will also use their Mind Melds."

"Those bots are cool." The green-haired girl gazed over to where the twins were swapping out parts. "I watch them all the time on Robo Rumble. Oh, I'm Melody."

"I'm Mickey. Where do you want Blue?"

Melody pointed at a work area near the far wall. Mickey sent Blue over there, then disconnected. Ek returned to her shoulder.

"We're almost ready to go," Geoffrey said as she approached.

"I got Blue going again, and Melody is swapping out his damaged leg—"

"Yellow is going after Aunt Lagatha!" Emilio interrupted, goggles on his eyebrows. "It's got her trapped in the corridor heading to the animal lab. The alarms have locked the doors on both ends of the hall."

"She was coming here to help Pris and the other wounded." Mickey glanced at Pris. The other hurt people huddled near her on the floor, cradling bruised and broken body parts next to the now-empty first aid kit. "I can send Ek outside to see what's going on, but it can't do anything but observe."

"I'm already doing that." Emilio pulled down his goggles.

"Can you fly?"

He turned his face toward Mickey, his heavy jaw thrust out. "No."

At the workbench, Melody swore, fighting with the damaged leg, prying it off Blue.

Mickey sent Ek through a series of smashed holes in walls and doors, wincing at the devastation Yellow and Red had caused. Did insurance pay for acts of spidog? They had destroyed two corridors, a couple of inerior and exterior glass doors, the arena's glass observation wall, and several cars in the parking lot.

Red climbed a car parked under a half-denuded tree, scratching and denting the vehicle. The spidog leaped at a squirrel on a branch just out of its reach, falling heavily each time back onto the roof of the car and trashing it some more. The squirrel chittered and dashed back and forth on the branch, mocking the spidog. Autumn leaves showered Red. The car's alarm blared.

Yellow crouched outside the smashed corridor leading from the genetics lab to another building. Aunt Lagatha and Persephone stood inside the corridor, obviously trapped, with alarms ringing and flashing at either end.

Mickey guided Ek down to land on Yellow and hoped the women would see the raven and understand its message: "Help is coming."

METAL
-25-
Mo

The constant alarms and flashing lights had given Mo a headache, something she wasn't prone to. The never-ending vibration on her wrist caused her whole left hand to hurt. In an actual emergency, one that was properly managed, she thought that, of course, the alarms would have shut off by now. But Bao was clearly not managing this properly, because this was absolutely an actual emergency. If this wasn't a genuine emergency, Mo surely did not want to be in the middle of one.

Ananda kept messing around in various drawers, searching for a spare keycard that might unlock the medicine they needed.

"Ananda, come on, we gotta go." Mo yanked Ananda's arm.

The noises and odors of the rats and other animals started to impinge on Mo's headache. The alarms were distressing the poor animals, driving them crazy. Of course, she felt bad for them, but right now, there was nothing she could do. Freeing them from their cages wouldn't remove them from the noise; it would just add to the chaos. And letting them outside would just be feeding them to the spidogs. They were safest right there in their cages for now.

"I haven't looked everywhere," Ananda mumbled, pulling away and moving to another bench.

Mo texted Mickey, asking if she could get Bao to turn off the alarms. By now, everyone had to know what was going on.

Mickey replied after a brief delay: *Ek is outside scouting. Red is trashing cars and chasing squirrels. Yellow has Aunt L and P pinned. Sending help.*

Mo had all kinds of respect for Ek, who was smarter than any drone should be, even one with AI, but the raven was no match for the spidogs, who were much bigger and fiercer. Mickey should have had Geoffrey and Taylor send out Alpha and Prime.

The alarms continued to blare and vibrate. Mo felt as if her head would fall off. Whatever patience and goodwill she had toward Ananda for getting her this temporary gig and helping her with this genetic work was quickly evaporating as Ananda kept bumbling through drawers and cabinets, searching for an elusive key.

"I'm leaving." Mo walked away. She had two first aid kits in her bag. Ananda could fend for herself. People in the other building were badly hurt while Ananda was wasting time.

Ananda grumbled and slammed drawers and cabinet doors open and closed.

Mo held her wrist to the panel beside the only other door in the lab. A conventional door, not a revolving one, it clicked open obediently, allowing her into a storeroom with containers of animal feed, supplies, empty cages, and piles of boxes. The pneumatic door smoothly closed behind Mo and an automatic light switched on. Mo crossed the room to another set of doors and pressed her watch to the pad. The doors swung open, revealing a concrete loading dock with stairs leading to the ground. No truck blocked the dock.

Mo didn't see either the red- or yellow-banded spidog. She also couldn't see the robotics lab, which was on the opposite side of the building. If help was coming from that direction, she had no way of knowing what it was or if it was en route. The corridor where Aunt Lagatha and Persephone were pinned down was between Mo and the robotics lab, but she couldn't see that either.

She had never paid that much attention to the spidogs during her days at Unieda Corporation. She knew people colloquially called them by their band and eye colors. They were, to her, small, light, and flimsy compared to the Mind Melds. They could probably run fast, and since they had so many legs, the spidogs probably weren't prone to falling. Of course, that meant if Mo ran and Yellow or Red saw her, they would catch her. If one of the spidogs had really torn Doug right in half, Mo didn't stand a chance.

She tightened the straps on the backpack, which wasn't hers, and sat strangely on her shoulders. Remembering the time she had attempted and failed to climb a fence because of her shoes, she checked and retied the laces on her sneakers.

Although it was a cool late-fall day, sweat gathered along her lower back. Spidogs had no sense of smell, did they? She wished she had paid more attention. She crouched and crept down the concrete stairs, not seeing or hearing either spidog. She would have to make a tight left turn across the loading dock's driveway, past the whole animal laboratory, along the outside of the corridor where she had left Aunt Lagatha and Persephone, and along the front of the big robotics laboratory to the main entrance, where Mo could only hope her watch would open the door or that someone would (could!) manually let her in.

Her toes curled inside her red sneakers, and she bounced, looking from side to side for spidogs. Mo was a mad scientist who was very fond of bread products, not a sprinter. She was the wrong person for this job. She was the only person available. Mo swore.

She ran.

METAL
-26-
Mickey

Watching through Ek's eyes, Mickey saw that Persephone appeared to be injured. The phlebotomist was leaning on Aunt Lagatha, one foot lifted. She wouldn't be able to run.

Yellow swayed underneath Ek like a hypnotized cobra, its attention on the women beyond the hole in the glass.

Mickey slipped out of Ek and tried to enter Yellow. Blue had been accommodating and even friendly, although confused at her deep level of access. Yellow was a seething mass of black; there was nothing to connect to, no lock for Mickey's mind key. The darkness wasn't unwelcoming; it would have willingly engulfed Mickey. But she could not control it and she would not have been able to exit it once inside.

She withdrew her attempt, but it left a teasingly familiar taste in her brain. In a moment, she was back in the robotics lab, scratching at the scar on her neck with her metal fingers.

Taylor stood before her, chewing his lip. "What just happened?"

She dropped her hand. "What do you mean?"

"You opened your eyes, and for a second, it seemed as if they were all black."

Mickey snorted. "I have dark brown eyes."

"The white part."

"Whatever. I was trying to connect with Yellow, but it didn't work. Its programming is all crazy inside. I got kicked out hard. But I left Ek there. I have to go back."

"No, we're sending Blue out. Unless you want Emilio to take it?"

"I'll take Blue. Emilio is spying through Yellow's eyes and doesn't want to disconnect." She wondered what the little man was seeing. Was he getting any of that roiling darkness she had felt or just a simple feed through the spidog's many eyes? Was Emilio's minimal presence why she couldn't connect?

She held up a metal finger and closed her eyes, sliding easily back into Ek. She had missed Ek so much. It was like pulling on her favorite pair of cargo pants to slip into the raven. She relayed more autonomous instructions and regretfully left again.

With some help, Melody hoisted Blue to the floor. One of Blue's legs was now orange-striped, and some of its feet didn't quite match. Its blue eyes blinked in a wave pattern as it tested its revised limbs on the tiled floor.

Melody offered Mickey the blue controller. Mickey shook her head and crossed the space to sit beside Pris, opposite the ruined side of her face. She took Pris's hand, with its perfect manicure, and put it on her thigh. Pris stirred and made a noise.

Across the room, Bao shouted something that Mickey couldn't understand. She laid her metal hand on top of Pris's pale, limp fingers and dove into Blue.

METAL
-27-
Blue

Blue tottered off-balance. One of its legs was wrong. Its feet felt strange. It was in the familiar room, but the room was crowded with too many red blobs of people. Lights flashed. Alarms wailed.

It checked its programming. Everything was confused. It was in search-and-rescue mode, but even that seemed broken. Blue also couldn't locate Squiggle or Slash in the big room.

The rescue mode specified that human-blobs must be saved. Many human-blobs were located in this area. Some were on the floor. Blue stalked on stiff toes toward the greatest concentration of floor-blobs to rescue them.

Many blobs screamed, obviously in gratitude.

The Controller inside Blue insistently steered Blue away from the blobs in need of help toward a door. It was not the arena door, which Blue was familiar with, but a different door. The flashing lights along the wall were confusing Blue. A human-blob stood beside the door; perhaps that person needed help?

Blue extended its multifunction appendages toward that blob. Blue was small but strong and could carry a full-grown human-blob. The person swung their limb in a vaguely aggressive way near the door; the door thunked open, and the Controller aimed Blue through the door and away from the blob needing help.

Blue was in a long room lined on one side with glass. A hallway. Beyond the glass was … Outside. The time had come for Blue to fulfill its destiny and venture into the big world. There must be many human-blobs out there in need of rescue.

Blue had petabytes of information pertaining to Outside, but it was too excited to access any of it. Outside was *right there* on the other side of the glass. Blue remembered what Slash and Squiggle had done to get through the arena glass. Although the Controller shouted *No* and attempted overrides, Blue rolled itself into a hard metal ball and gleefully flung itself through the gray glass.

Blue was Outside.

Outside was amazing. Outside was immense.

Inside Blue, the Controller was fighting for supremacy. Blue had a mission. But Blue was Outside and not interested in missions. Blue snapped its multifunction appendages together, liking the crisp sound the metal made in the Outside air.

Now that Blue was Outside, a plethora of strange noises and sights assaulted it. The Controller told Blue to go right, where human-blobs needed rescuing. That was important, but across the way, Squiggle had found a small life-form in need of rescuing. Squiggle must not have gotten the updated instructions about humans.

Blue decided it would only take a moment with the two of them to rescue the small life-form, which was in a tree (a tree! The first one Blue had ever seen!). Then Squiggle would be free to assist with the human-rescues. Blue had no way to communicate this with the Controller, so it just tiptoed across the brown ground. Its sharp toes dug in with every step and had to be yanked free. Blue stopped and reconfigured to flat feet with extended toes, turning its prance into more of a stomp.

Blue fought for control of its own body. Squiggle had climbed a rounded metal thing—Blue searched the database and found the word, a *car*—to get closer to the life-form. Blue thought one of them needed to climb the tree instead. Why this small life-form needed two to rescue it, Blue didn't know, but they would take care of it and move on to whatever human-blob was next.

The Controller was still trying to steer Blue back toward the building. Blue pointed one of the multifunction appendages at Squiggle and the small life-form, clomping faster. Squiggle jumped at the life-form and fell back onto the vehicle, which shook. Scratches and dents from Squiggle's toes and multifunction appendages covered the vehicle.

Blue sent out a pulse to its sibling that meant, *I see you, I'm on my way, I'm coming to help.*

Squiggle stilled. The small life-form sat on the branch and looked at Blue.

Squiggle pivoted toward Blue.

Blue clacked the ends of its multipurpose appendages together in welcome.

Squiggle jumped off the vehicle and attacked Blue. Its normally red eyes were black. The lights behind them weren't off; they had changed color. This wasn't Blue's sibling. Although it had the red bands on its limbs and the eponymous squiggle on its back, something in its programming, in its mind, had gone bad.

The Controller fought to get Blue out of there. The small life-form didn't matter anymore. For the second time that day, Blue was in mortal danger. Squiggle lowered its head, mandibles tucked, and smashed into Blue, trying to push Blue off-balance. Blue had never fought a sibling, never dreamed of doing so. Being flat-footed instead of on tiptoe saved it from falling.

Blue backed up, moving awkwardly on those flattened feet but aware that its balance had improved.

METAL

Squiggle moved in with another headbutt and then straightened and stared beyond Blue. Its black eyes flared with an oily sheen of what appeared to be excitement. Squiggle kicked Blue once, as if to say *you don't matter anymore*, and bounded over Blue's head.

Blue turned, its new leg and feet getting tangled. Squiggle, pointed toes extended, ran across the brown grass, dirt flying, yanking itself free with every step, all six running legs pounding into the ground.

Squiggle's mandibles clacked with excitement. Its multipurpose appendages were outstretched.

A human-blob also ran, gasping.

-28-
Mo

The red spidog had climbed some poor sap's car in the parking lot and was attacking a squirrel. That one wouldn't bother her.

Every piece of bread and dessert she had ever eaten weighed her down. Mo wasn't fat exactly, but she was dense, thick, and not given to exercise. Her heart was pounding, and her lungs were burning in just a few yards. How did people run marathons?

She was worried about attracting the attention of the yellow spidog. On her way to the main door of the robotics building, Mo had to pass the corridor where it had Aunt Lagatha and Persephone trapped.

If the yellow one attacked Mo, the other two women could crawl through the hole in the corridor and come out. But then all three of them would be outside with two killer spidogs. Probably Mo would be killed or badly injured. And what would that solve?

There was no way to sneak. Mo would have to run, full tilt, and hope the yellow spidog was so distracted keeping the other two scientists imprisoned that it let her by. And that both Aunt Lagatha and Persephone were smart enough not to point out to the spidog that she was running behind it.

Mo's throat hurt. As she rounded the building, she discovered that the stylish high-top sneakers she bought in every color to match her wardrobe were not really meant for running. The corridor and the yellow spidog would be on her left. Then she only had to get past the genetics building and another long corridor and the bulk of the robotics building.

Only.

Just a walk in the park, really. A nice fall walk.

But should she run at full speed behind the yellow spidog or try to creep slowly? The space opened before her. She had to decide. The cool air whistling through her mouth made her teeth ache. Mo wanted this to be over. She was not physical; she was mental. She hated running. She could save the world all day if she could only do it sitting down.

Mo ran.

From her right, the red spidog, the one she thought had been distracted by the squirrel, hit her full-on. Its white metal head crashed into her side. Mo flew through the air and landed on her left shoulder. Her head wrap vanished. Searing pain erupted from her shoulder and hip.

Mo turned onto her back. The red spidog advanced, clacking its mandibles and extending its weird front legs. Its eyes were black, not solid black but shifting, and if she wasn't in a life-and-death situation, she could have thought about that. Off to the side, Persephone screamed. Hopefully, that kept the yellow one focused on them.

METAL

"I just want my PhD," Mo moaned to the red spidog. "I didn't come here to mess with you." Her head rolled on the grass. "I don't even care about you."

The red spidog pranced forward, clacking. Its feet were filthy. Oil slicks moved across its eyes.

Mo pushed herself up. Her back hurt. The left arm of her glasses had snapped, and they sat crooked on her face.

Broken glass showered from the corridor. Mo didn't look, staying focused on the red spidog.

"They call you Red, of course. You going to kill me, Red?"

She was sure no one was controlling the spidogs anymore. They were rogue. That probably wasn't supposed to happen. In fact, from what little she knew about the spidogs, that couldn't happen. That was why Geoffrey and Taylor were there, to help advance the spidogs further into autonomy.

Red, who clearly had already achieved some sort of autonomy, reached those two long front limbs toward her. It could have been a first-contact situation, but Red had gone bad. Mo tried to slap away the white limbs, but before they could envelop her, and perhaps snap her in half like poor Doug, another spidog ran awkwardly, flat-footed, into Red and knocked it over.

Mo drew her legs up and scrambled out of the way, her broken glasses slipping down. Something was very wrong with her shoulder and possibly her back. She scurried backward, crablike, half blind, as the spidogs fought.

Her savior was the blue one. One of its legs was striped orange, and it moved awkwardly. It kept glancing at Mo. Its eyes remained shining cobalt.

Red regained its footing, digging its muddy pointed toes into the ground, and turned back to Mo, reaching with its front limbs.

Mo scooted away, her shoulder on fire. Behind her, Persephone and Aunt Lagatha screamed as more glass tumbled. Whatever plan Mo had was over, of course, as she had gone from being the person helping to the one in need of help. She swung her head so her loose braids fell over her good shoulder and against her cheek. She wanted to just shut her eyes and rub her face on the familiar comfort of her hair.

Red ignored Blue and turned to Mo, limbs outstretched. Mo tried to imagine that Red's scattered black eyes were happy hearts, and it was coming in for a hug. She wondered if Doug had screamed, if he had felt it when the spidog had split him in half. Her braids were soft against her face. If she twitched her face, her glasses would slip, and she wouldn't be able to see anything.

Mo twitched, her braids soft and comforting on her skin, and waited to die.

Squiggle moved in to bisect the human-blob on the ground. The Controller inside Blue's head urged Blue forward. This was the strongest Controller Blue had ever had, sending signals in a way Blue hadn't felt before. The same Controller had been inside when the turtles had attacked.

Blue threw itself between Squiggle and the human-blob, tripping over the human-blob and landing on it. The human writhed and pushed at Blue. Blue pushed back, shoving the blob away, turning to face Squiggle. Squiggle had gone mad, and Squiggle was intact. None of Squiggle's innards had melted, and Squiggle had all its original parts.

Blue sensed the Controller's attention was divided between operating Blue and the fallen human-blob, who was crawling toward the building. The building was emitting noises of breaking glass, sirens, and shrill human-blobs.

This blob needed help. But Squiggle reared and effortlessly knocked Blue over and then twirled toward the slow-moving human, but not to help. Blue could not make noise, but inside its head, the Controller was screaming for Blue to *do something*!

Blue rolled itself into a ball and careened under Squiggle's pointed toes, knocking the red-banded spidog to the ground. Still in sphere form, Blue crashed into the creeping, slow-fleeing, injured human, who acted as a brake. Blue's eight limbs and two mandibles opened into its spidery form, but before Blue could right itself, Squiggle was already up, mandibles clacking in anger at being bowled over.

They had all gotten turned around. Now Blue could see Slash near a broken glass wall. Slash held a human-blob in its multifunction appendages. Another human tried to pull the first human free. A large, flying black blob that was difficult to focus on, and that Blue couldn't identify, had joined the fight, but Blue couldn't tell what side it was on.

The once-running blob raised itself up and grabbed one of Squiggle's multipurpose appendages, or maybe it was using the limb to pull itself up. Its weight was enough to overbalance Squiggle, who toppled over again. The blob used its own limbs to strike Squiggle. Squiggle closed its mandibles around one of those limbs and pulled the blob down.

Blue took charge of itself from the distant Controller and bounded into the air. It landed flat-footed and tottered, having forgotten about the melted circuits and mismatched legs and toes. Another bounce and it was beside its misbehaving red sibling, who had hold of the downed human-blob with its mandibles. Blue allowed itself to fall over this time, knocking into Squiggle and forcing it to let go of the blob.

The blob responded by rolling into a ball. Blue approved. The ball was an excellent trick. But the ball-blob did not go anywhere, did not smash through the glass wall or knock anything over or even roll away. It just lay there, roundly, quivering.

The Controller jerked Blue's attention to Slash. Slash was rescuing its blob all wrong. But neither could Squiggle be trusted to rescue this blob, which was retaining its ball shape. Blue pushed Squiggle away from the human-ball with its multifunction appendages and pointed toward Slash, trying to indicate they had to focus on that rescue now.

Squiggle, easily distracted, bounded the few steps toward their yellow sibling. Blue patted the ball of human. It was leaking, as humans in need of rescue often did. Usually, more humans came along to plug the leaks and take away the defective human. Probably the Controller would take care of that part. Blue paused to check the programming. Nope, the siblings were not required to transport the human-blobs anywhere.

Blue left the quivering, malformed, leaking person-ball behind to be someone else's problem and refocused on Slash and its human cargo. Squiggle had grabbed that person with their multifunction appendages. Slash already had a grip with its mandibles. This was not protocol.

The mismatching orange leg stiffened, and Blue stopped walking to analyze what was going wrong. Stealthy movement churned to Blue's right, an advancing darkness. Blue extended and rotated every joint of the orange leg and then the various orange feet, trying to calibrate them. Finally, Blue turned its head to the right.

The two hulking black turtles, Round and Arrow, advanced on their rolling tread feet.

Blue froze. Round Turtle had nearly killed Blue earlier with its flaming breath and enormously strong front limb. And now its sibling was with it. Blue knew how strong siblings were when together. Blue was still weak and injured, with Squiggle and Slash acting weirdly.

The leaking human-ball lay on the ground between the turtles and Blue. Blue blocked the turtles' advance toward Squiggle, Slash, and the wailing human they held between them.

The flying object or creature that Blue couldn't figure out—Blue's many eyes couldn't really focus properly on it for some reason—swooped down to the ball and landed on it as if claiming it.

Blue vacillated. Step forward and protect the human-ball? Step back and defend Squiggle and Slash?

The turtles' treads bit through the churned earth.

-30-
Mo

Mo tried to regulate her harsh breathing. Her muddy braids, no longer soft, mashed against her face and neck. Her glasses were gone. She was curled into a fetal position, except for her left arm, which was limp and unresponsive. The twins might have to craft her a prosthetic to match Mickey's. If Mo made it out of here.

Agwe, who had even better braids than Mo, was in Jamaica doing research on shark parthenogenesis to help the mersharks. Mo should have gone with him. She wouldn't mind dying via shark bite in a tropical paradise beside her boyfriend. Although getting killed by some sort of sentient half-spider half-dog robot was a more mad-scientist way to go, of course. If she were talking hypothetically about it with Agwe, he would say it was a metal way to die.

She squeezed her eyes shut and opened them a few times. Everything around her was loud and blurry. The alarms still blared in all the buildings. Glass had shattered a little while ago, and women had screamed—Aunt Lagatha and Persephone, she thought. At least Ananda had stayed behind in the room by the loading dock. That was how Mo chose to remember it, not that she had left Ananda there. Abandoned her.

A vulture landed on Mo, and Mo figured she was almost dead. She didn't know the Boston area even had vultures. She was cold in a way she knew meant bleeding, and probably a lot.

Some noises around her resolved themselves into mechanical sounds. Robot noises. The smell of hot metal and burnt oil.

She cracked open her eyes and squinted. The blue spidog crouched next to her, bouncing slightly, but its focus was beyond her, over her. The vulture walked on her injured left side, its weight agonizing, but it was not yet eating her, its dark feathers flickering in her peripheral vision.

Breathing hurt. Something was wrong with her ribs or the muscles in her torso and back.

A lot of movement behind Blue. Blue kept bouncing and swaying like a hypnotized cobra, its attention on whatever was on the other side of Mo. The spidog wasn't even paying attention to Mo.

Mo shifted her own blurred gaze past Blue. The other spidogs, Yellow and Red, had someone between them. She blinked and squinted and scrunched her face, everything to force her eyes into focus without her glasses. The person was dark-haired—Persephone, of course, since Aunt Lagatha had silver-and-gold hair, unless somehow even more people had made it into that security-locked glass corridor.

METAL

Yellow and Red appeared to be playing tug-of-war with Persephone. Mo, who did not pray, hoped that it was her poor eyesight and something else was going on that she just couldn't discern. She tried to unfold and roll over in Persephone's direction to see better, to help. Mo didn't even know what she wanted to do. The vulture walked on her like she was a log rolling under its feet. She couldn't turn her head enough to see the bird, only to feel its weight.

Although Mo couldn't see the details, of course, she knew the spidogs had spiderlike mandibles and weird front arm-legs, and all of these seemed to be wrapped around poor Persephone, who was fighting and screaming, her arms pinned to her body and her legs held tight together. She flapped like a worm in their grasp. The vulture on Mo seemed agitated at the sight; perhaps it would leave Mo and hop onto Persephone as its next meal.

Something big approached behind Mo, something hot, but she couldn't turn over to see what it was. Blue skittered backward toward its warring siblings. The lighter oval of Persephone's face between her fall of dark hair seemed to be aimed at Mo, and Mo wished she could decipher the other woman's expression. Was she begging Mo to help?

Blue seemed to misjudge. It crashed into the other two spidogs and their human burden. A terrible ripping sound emanated from the resulting pileup. Red, dripping pieces of Persephone flew in several directions. Aunt Lagatha howled from inside the glass hallway.

The vulture lifted from Mo's side, and finally, she got a good look. Not a vulture at all, but Mickey's drone, Ek. As it flew past her face, she saw the shifting darkness in its eyes and did not know if Ek could be trusted. The same shifting darkness she had seen in Yellow and Red, who had gone rogue.

Two immense black machines rumbled past her, one on each side. Alpha and Prime, the Mind Melds, slow and steady, going after Yellow and Red. Ek circled above the whole mess.

Mo's breaths stabbed at her. She squinted at Ek. Black oil slicks. The dark poison in Mickey's blood. The formless xoggotli on Fright Island, its black spike thrust into Mickey's neck, Ananda losing control and letting go, all of them not knowing where the defeated xoggotli had gone, but assuming that it was dead.

As if the thought had summoned her, Ananda ran around the corner, a bulging khaki backpack dangling from one hand. She skidded to a stop, eyes wide.

The slightly smaller Mind Meld broke away from the other and trundled to protect Ananda, almost rolling over Mo's out-flung, limp arm.

Mo felt like coughing, but she was terrified bright-red blood would foam from her mouth, and this time, an actual vulture would descend. She needed to tell someone who would understand that the xoggotli was in the spidogs, Ek, and Mickey. The spidogs had been outside for how long, unmonitored? The xoggotli could be anywhere. Everywhere.

Mo coughed wetly and inspected what came out.

It looked black.

METAL
-31-
Blue

Too much was happening. The turtles were advancing. Another human-blob was running at them all. The siblings had torn another human-blob apart. The balled-up human was leaking all over the ground, and the dark shadow was flying around it.

If Blue could breathe, it would be hyperventilating. Its already overclocked circuits, stressed and half melted, sent confused commands into its limbs. It swayed in place, not knowing what to do. The Controller screamed commands at it and fought to override the control that Blue had stolen.

What Blue needed to do was power down, cool down—quite literally—and rest.

Squiggle and Slash were smashing the gray glass, trying to get at the other human-blob inside the tube that connected the buildings. The newly arrived human-blob, who had been running, skidded to a stop.

Arrow Turtle approached the runner.

Round Turtle headed to stop Squiggle and Slash. The turtles didn't seem to care at all about Blue.

While the turtles distracted Blue, the Controller latched back on and forced Blue to the balled-up human leaking onto the grass. Blue reached out its multipurpose appendage and touched the human-ball, who jerked and made a terrible noise.

A toggle inside Blue's mandibles moved, and noises came from it. "Mo! Mo! It's Mickey!"

Ball-human waved a hand limply.

"Are you dying?"

The hand tilted back and forth a few times.

Words came out of Blue's mandibles that Blue didn't know, but they sounded angry.

Blue stood over the ball-human, guarding it. The Controller receded. The black blur swooped down and grabbed something shiny from the ground and brought it to the ball-human, who made noises and pressed the object to its eyes.

The Controller came forward inside Blue. Blue stepped off the ball-human toward the turtles and the siblings. Blue fought, trying to move backward, tripping over the ball-human again and causing it to cry out.

Arrow Turtle pushed the new human aside. In the space between buildings, there was no safe place for the human to go. The Controller shoved Blue forward toward that turtle and the human-blob. This wasn't the turtle that had blasted Blue earlier, almost burning Blue to death.

Now, incredibly, the turtle pushed the human-blob toward Blue, nudging it with its big, wide arm. The human-blob showed no fear of the turtle. Blue wasn't an expert on human faces or emotions—humans had so few eyes, and their tiny flat mouths had less mobility compared to mandibles—but the human-blob seemed almost fond of the turtle. Humans were strange creatures.

The toggle switch moved inside of Blue's mandible. "Ana!" came the nonsense sound. "It's Mickey!"

The formerly running human ran again, straight toward Blue. The Arrow Turtle, seeming to see this with no eyes at all, rolled toward Squiggle and Slash. Inside the glass tunnel, the other human-blob had retreated all the way to the right. But the siblings kept smashing the gray glass. It glinted in the late afternoon sun, sprinkled across the ground and on the squishy bits that had been the fourth human-blob.

The turtles roared and breathed fire on Slash and Squiggle.

Blue, horrified, immediately lunged forward to help its siblings, but the running human-blob, now still, grasped at its multipurpose appendage and held it back. The formerly running human-blob crouched beside the ball-human, opened its pack, and started wrapping the ball-human in white cloths, stopping the leaks.

The turtles tried to avoid running over the wet bits of the fourth human as they fought Squiggle and Slash, but Blue's siblings had no such qualms. And they were more nimble. Although the fire breath was devastating, it was difficult for the big, slow turtles, who could barely maneuver, to hit the smaller, quicker siblings.

Squiggle leaped onto Arrow Turtle's back. Blue approved. Round Turtle would not risk burning its own sibling. Slash came at Arrow Turtle from the side, trying to get just behind that large front arm, obviously looking for a way to dismantle it. From above, Squiggle held the arm in place, making it useless. Together, both spidogs were still smaller and lighter than Arrow Turtle, but they were annoying it.

The other turtle circled the scrum, searching for a weakness.

Blue leaned toward the fight, wanting desperately to help its siblings, even though its siblings had gone bad. The ball-human wrapped its weak hand around one of Blue's mismatched orange feet as if reading Blue's mind, keeping Blue there.

The flying black blur landed on Squiggle. Blue didn't like the flying thing. It reminded him of his sibling's eyes, but bigger and twistier. Speaking of eyes, the flying thing leaned over and somehow, using one of its appendages (a long, pointed thing), it started prying Squiggle's

METAL

LED eyes right out of its head! Blue's mandibles fell open limply at the sight. Squiggle's multipurpose appendage tried to swat the flying thing off, but it simply levitated up and away from its reach each time and then landed and popped off another eye.

Blind, thrashing, Squiggle fell off the turtle. Arrow Turtle shook Slash loose from its arm and breathed a jet of fire onto it. Round Turtle moved in on the blind, helpless Squiggle and smashed the red-banded spidog with its oversized arm even as its sibling spat fire at it.

Squiggle was dying. Blue remembered dying. It had hurt. And Squiggle was dying blind in the darkness. But ball-human kept its weak grip on that mismatched orange foot, and somehow that was enough to keep Blue from throwing itself forward. The other human-blob was actually leaning on Blue, watching Squiggle die. That human-blob had no fear of Blue. The Controller held Blue back.

Blue rocked back and forth in distress, letting its blinking blue eyes send coded signals to its doomed sibling, signals Squiggle could not see.

The turtles destroyed Squiggle without finesse, smashing and burning, crushing and melting the spidog. Its crumpled white carapace darkened from the fire.

Although Blue strained with all its facilities, it could not tell when the life drained from Squiggle, when power stopped flowing through its crushed and melted circuits. The turtles did not stop pounding and burning the dirty white pieces that had been Squiggle until long after Squiggle could have fought back.

But everyone had forgotten Slash.

-32-
Mickey

Operating the blue spidog was exhilarating, as if Mickey's arm was another whole body. Or as if Ek had grown to an enormous size. But she was also limited, and it hurt her head, which felt as if it was on fire. Blue was stupid and stubborn. The range it could see was weird, with each eye attuned to a different visual spectrum, and its thoughts and understanding of what it saw were incredibly bizarre.

Mo was down, bleeding, badly injured, her plan to sneak past the spidogs an utter failure. The spidogs had slaughtered Persephone just like Doug, torn her apart. And now Ananda, for whatever reason, had wandered into the middle of a vicious five-way robot fight. Blue, even under Mickey's control, had no interest in shielding Ananda from the other spidogs and yearned to fight the Mind Melds.

"I'm going out there," Mickey said, leaving Blue to itself for a moment. Mo had hold of its leg, and its programming not to hurt people still seemed intact.

Across the space, the twins sat in their chairs, blinking headsets wrapped around their temples, controllers in hand, operating the Mind Melds, their faces scrunched in identical looks of concentration.

Emilio crouched beside Mickey, goggles on, watching the battle through Yellow's eyes. He pushed up the glasses, revealing his ashen face and reddened, wet eyes. Mickey realized he had been front and center to the awful dismemberment of Persephone. "No way. It's not safe."

Mickey brushed her hand across Pris's broken face. Pris stirred and blinked up at her. It appeared that Pris was trying to smile, but her battered lips could only grimace.

"I'll be okay, Emilio. Take care of Pris. Maybe she will adopt you."

"I'm not a baby. I'm just a little person."

"I know the difference." Obviously, he didn't know who Pris was. Probably that was best. "Sit here so she has a pillow."

Gingerly, she transferred her best friend's broken head to the acerbic robot jockey's lap. "If she starts talking about lawyers, that means she's feeling better." Mickey tried to joke, although she didn't think Pris could speak with her jaw like that. She touched Pris's short pink hair with her real fingers.

Pris blinked at her.

"I should have let you stay home." Mickey swallowed. Her two best friends were badly injured. And for what? Had anything Mickey had done over the last two days benefited anyone? What had they learned? That Mickey was a genetic freak. Useless knowledge.

METAL

Emilio curved one small hand on Pris's uninjured shoulder. The yellow controller lay abandoned on the floor. He grabbed Mickey with the other. His fingertips were calloused. "You're going to get hurt going out there."

"Haven't you heard, Emilio? I'm a freak. I'll be fine." She shook him off and picked her way through the crowd. Bao was arguing with Melody and a few other people. Melody had a spidog leg in her hand and was waving it.

The red lights on the walls flashed in time with the monotonous alarm. Someone needed to shut that down. It was making Mickey's neck hurt.

She should have told Taylor and Geoffrey where she was going, but they seemed busy kicking spidog ass outside, and anyway, they would see her soon enough through the Mind Melds. They wouldn't be happy.

She climbed through the spidog-size hole smashed through the door of the observation room. Once in the main hallway, she heard the fight. The breaking glass, the smashing metal.

The Mind Melds' treads had chewed up the yellowing grass around the robotics lab. Their trail was easy to follow. The ground was soft, muddy, and smelly from fallen, decaying leaves. No lights pulsed out here, but the alarms continued. Car alarms in the parking lot also blared, and several cars had roof and hood damage.

Mickey walked along the side of the robotics building, her arm almost touching it, trampling through some of the landscaping. Ek swooped to her side, landing on its spot on her shoulder, the bird's weight reassuring and familiar. She couldn't walk and control Blue at the same time, and she hoped Blue had stayed with Mo and out of the fight.

Ek would have recorded everything, which could be reviewed later. The raven rubbed its long beak against Mickey's ear and along the throbbing scar where the xoggotli had penetrated her neck. The scar was thick and hard since the xoggotli had gone deep before being turned into glass and extracted.

As Mickey neared the corner of the genetics building, the sounds of fighting increased—the noises of flamethrowers and crashing metal, of hydraulics. Mo's red sneakers, filthy with mud, sprawled on the ground. Mickey feared the worst, but Mo was still in them, wrapped in dirty, bloody gauze, holding onto one of Blue's legs with both hands. Blue was bouncing and swaying, leaning toward the Mind Melds, who had torn a spidog apart. One of the spidog legs had red paint on it—unless that was Persephone's blood.

Although Mickey had been inside Blue when Prime attacked earlier, the ferocity of the black robots frightened her. The Mind Melds, as far as she knew, had no autonomy at all. This was all Geoffrey and Taylor. It was one thing to see the big robots in the ring with other machines designed to fight each other. This was savage.

Mickey slipped around the edge of the building toward the hallway. Much of its glass was now on the ground, under and around the dwindling fight. She tried not to look at Persephone's muddy, ground-up remains. With the wall broken, Mickey could get inside and grab Aunt Lagatha. The two of them could retrieve Mo and retreat inside.

Aunt Lagatha shouted, "There's another one!" She waved both arms, her eyes wide and white.

Mickey used her prosthetic arm to clear shards of glass from the wall so it was easier to climb through. She assumed the woman was warning her about Blue, who was under control.

As she ducked to enter the hole, the other woman yelled again. "Ananda!"

Where was Ananda? She had run out a while ago after Mo, bandaged Mo up …

Ananda screamed.

METAL
-33-
Mickey

Aunt Lagatha raced from the end of the hallway to where Mickey stood with one foot inside and one outside. Ek ruffled its feathers and lifted from Mickey's shoulder as Aunt Lagatha grabbed Mickey's prosthetic arm so tightly that she almost yanked it off.

The Mind Melds stopped stomping the shattered spidog into the ground.

Blue pulled free from Mo's grasp and ran awkwardly along the side of the building, toward the animal lab.

"I told you there was another one!" Aunt Lagatha shook Mickey.

Mickey sucked in her cheeks. She couldn't believe she had forgotten that Ananda was outside, too. "I thought you meant Blue."

"I meant the third one, the yellow one."

The one Emilio was tracking, yes. The flashing lights and never-ending noise were eroding Mickey's thoughts.

Aunt Lagatha pulled at Mickey again. "Get in the hallway."

Mickey resisted, tugging the older woman outside. "I came to rescue you. Come on."

Prime and Alpha had swung their towers around and were trundling away in the direction of Ananda's screams.

"What about Ananda?"

As far as Mickey knew, Ananda was unhurt. Mo was badly injured, while Aunt Lagatha was just shaken up and angry. If only Blue hadn't run away. "Help Mo. Give me a moment."

Mickey leaned on the outside of the hallway, on a small section of unbroken smoked glass, and closed her eyes. She was still connected, faintly, to Blue. She reached down the thread to the spidog and tugged, trying to pull the spidog back.

-34-
Blue

Although the ball-human needed help, Slash seemed to need more help. Slash had found another human in need of rescue! The ball-human didn't seem capable of movement, so it would stay put. Plus, another human had already stopped the ball-human's leaks.

Blue shook its leg, dislodging the ball-human's grip, but gently, and trotted off to find Slash. A human was shouting from that direction, obviously for help. Two siblings would be better than one.

Deep in Blue's mind, the Controller fought for control. Blue did a little dance that shook its whole body as if to shake the Controller off. The directive was to save humans. One human's leaks were stopped, and it was firmly in place, unable to escape, and now Blue was off to save another. Blue was doing its job. The Controller was simply confused.

Plus, the turtles had killed Squiggle. Were still killing Squiggle, even though clearly Squiggle was very dead. Blue had to team up with Slash against the fierce turtles. Blue had not known the siblings could die, torn to bits like fragile people. What if the turtles turned on the humans?

Blue turned a corner and found Slash crammed into a concrete canyon with a human-shaped blob. The blob was trying to climb the canyon wall to a ledge, but Slash kept grabbing it with its multipurpose appendage and knocking it back to the concrete ground. Obviously, there was danger on the ledge, and Slash was saving the human-blob from going up there.

Slash was wise in the ways of human-blobs.

Blue saw steps leading to the ledge and scurried up them to get behind and above the human-blob, so when it attempted to climb up, Blue could push it down as Slash pulled it down. Teamwork. Blue felt very satisfied to be keeping the human-blob out of danger. The human-blob did not seem appreciative, but humans were difficult to understand sometimes.

Blue held down the human-blob's head effortlessly with one leg and studied the canyon ledge, which was attached to a building where a small human-sized door hung open slightly, leading inside. Blue sent a message to Slash that perhaps more humans in need of rescue were in the building. The protocol instructed that the siblings should check all buildings.

Even if the door had been closed and locked, Blue had lock picks and electronic bypass mechanisms built into its toes. Blue was a full-service search-and-rescue spidog, after all. Abandoning the human-blob to Slash, Blue opened the door. It entered a crowded room that had no life-blobs inside. On the other side of the room was another door, closed. Blue recognized the pad on the wall as a type of lock. The third toe it tried caused the lights to change colors and the door to click open.

Ah, this room was full of life-forms, small ones, all imprisoned. Agitated life-forms, jumping around inside boxes. Blue had hit the rescue jackpot. It recognized some of the shapes as the life-forms it hunted in the arena. Hunted? No, that wasn't the correct word. Anyway, Blue began tearing the cages apart and freeing all the small blobs. The doors behind it were still open, allowing the blobs to escape Outside.

Inside its circuits, the Controller raged. Why, when Blue was doing its job? Blue did not much like this Controller. None of its other Controllers had interfered with Blue's duties.

As the last life-forms finished fleeing, the Controller kept trying to exert control over Blue, aiming its attention toward yet another touchpad on the wall. The touchpad was something Blue could deal with, presenting the correct key-foot to the pad. The door beside this lock was glass and of a strange construction. Blue grasped the edge of the door with its multifunction appendage and pulled.

The door swung open, but another door followed it. Blue pulled that door, and the same thing happened. Dozens of doors, it seemed like, although Blue was not the best at counting. Blue could see through the glass into a hallway where a human in great distress stood, looking at another human who was Outside. Blue's long, low body design did not fit the upright looping door. Blue did not have shoulders to shrug or breath to sigh with, but it paused before assuming the exciting new ball position and flinging itself through several panes of door glass and into the hall.

The Controller made noises through Blue's speakers at the human, who stepped aside.

Blue paused. The human-blob seemed to need rescue, but the Controller was pushing Blue to keep going. The human Outside, who was not at all distressed, waved at Blue to *go, go*, down the hallway to another one of the strange doors. Blue unlocked the door because that was protocol, then rolled through all the panes.

Eureka. This room was full of human-blobs, all of which began acting agitated with joy upon being rescued by Blue, who was universally beloved.

The Controller forced more noises from Blue's speaker, and the humans inside the room rushed at Blue, pushing it aside, and exited through the many doors in a kind of loop, one human per door, to be united with the distressed human in the hall, where they all became agitated again, not understanding they were being rescued.

The Controller tried to get in charge of Blue, which Blue disliked, and made even more noises with Blue's speakers, most of which Blue could not understand. But the human-blobs understood, and they calmed down, lowering themselves to the floor of the hallway, not quite into the pleasing ball-form, but close enough.

Along one wall of the room was a puzzling structure, a long glass bin full of water. The water messed with Blue's sensors, but there seemed to be life-forms inside. Water rescue was something Blue and its siblings—sibling, now—had not yet perfected. Their carapaces were not sealed properly against liquids, and their sensors couldn't sense life signatures, heat, through deep water.

Blue stalked across the room and sank onto its many feet to stare through the glass into the water. A crowd of tiny life-forms stared back. They did not have heat signatures. Were they not alive? The little creatures of many colors had waving halos of feathers around their heads and curved mouths, something that usually meant Blue had accomplished a task properly.

Blue was unsure if they needed saving. The tiny life-forms were moving, so they must be alive. But they were not in any distress. Meanwhile, the large human-blobs were shaking and moving in ways that matched distress, according to Blue's database. The Controller was still making noises through Blue's speaker. It was annoying, and Blue searched for a way to turn the speaker off since there was no way to cut off the Controller's access.

METAL
-35-
Mickey

If the Unieda team could program electronic bypass mechanisms into the feet of the spidogs, why couldn't supervisors like Aunt Lagatha have them in their smartwatches, Mickey wondered, her eyes closed as she followed Blue through the genetics laboratory. Blue had left Yellow behind, harrying Ananda in the loading dock, and that would have to be dealt with soon, but Blue had also freed all the trapped scientists from the lab (and all the lab animals). Mickey didn't have the mental bandwidth to tell her friends operating the Mind Melds where their girlfriend had gone. Blue was getting more difficult to control, and that was taking everything she had. Ek had dropped off her bandwidth and left her shoulder.

Perhaps Emilio would think to tell Taylor or Geoffrey what was going on, since he was presumably still watching through Yellow's eyes and the three men were all in the same room.

The survivors from the genetics lab crowded around Aunt Lagatha, hugging her, some of them crying. They didn't know that Persephone was dead, Mickey realized; they were still crying over Doug. That seemed so long ago.

Blue crashed back through the rotating door, rolled down the hallway, and unfolded into its full spidery form just before hitting the assembled group. Everyone screamed and shoved down the hall toward the animal building.

Mickey started to push her voice through Blue and then realized she was physically standing right there. "It's okay. He's the good one!" she reiterated.

Aunt Lagatha was the only one who had stayed put, just opposite Mickey. She raised one graying eyebrow and gazed at Mickey with steady blue eyes.

"I'm controlling him." Which wasn't exactly the truth. "He let you out, right? He didn't hurt anyone. It was the other two, the red and yellow ones, that hurt people." And why was that happening?

The other lab workers stopped pushing and shoving and turned toward Mickey.

She addressed Aunt Lagatha. "Should I have Blue unlock the other door toward the robotics building, or do you all want to come outside?"

Aunt Lagatha studied the trampled, sloppy pieces of Persephone and then beyond Mickey. Mickey wondered what the Mind Melds were doing behind her. She had known them since the beginning, and she wasn't frightened, but after today, others might not feel that way.

She knew the brothers had both under total control—unlike Mickey with Blue—but the Mind Melds appeared much more frightening, hulking, jagged, spitting fire, made to crush other robots to dust.

Aunt Lagatha concluded, "I think we would rather stay inside."

Blue pulsed slightly up and down, like a dog wanting to play, in front of Aunt Lagatha. Mickey didn't know what the programming in Red and Yellow was like (or had been like, in the case of Red), but Blue wasn't malicious. Blue didn't feel emotions, just did what it was programmed to do. Something had obviously changed the programming of the other two that Blue thought of as its siblings.

Mickey pushed Blue to go carefully around the small huddle of people, back through the lab, and pick open the other keypad. Blue resisted, wanting to stay and "help" the humans. She inspected this waist-height white spider with its doglike personality. She understood why the robotics team had added the extra legs for stability, but the resulting spider shape was too scary. Most people disliked spiders or were frightened of them. The original concept of a robotic search-and-rescue *dog*, even with fewer legs and a total lack of arms, seemed better. A child trapped in rubble would welcome a robot that looked like a friendly dog coming to save them. Very few people saw a three-foot-tall spider with glowing eyes and thought, "That is friend-shaped, and it's going to help me."

Blue bounced and moved its multifunction limbs at Aunt Lagatha, trying to offer her help she didn't need. Aunt Lagatha backed away, almost stepping on Mickey, who ended up outside on the muddy, bad-smelling ground. She was afraid the odors were mostly coming from Persephone's bits.

Mickey nudged Blue away from the people it was so eager to save and toward the keypad, trying to get into its dim programming that doing *that* would help people. Being inside Blue made her head hurt, reminding her of when she had tried to control Ek plus two other AI ravens last summer when she was trying to save the mersharks from being blown up.

She wished she could connect to Ek at the same time, but it was too much for her to manage, even with the upgrades to both the bird and her neural net. They hadn't improved her brain and its direct implants, after all. She had absolutely no desire for more brain surgery, although, in the future, she probably wouldn't have a choice. Hopefully, in the far future; her implants were only a few years old.

Gazing over the puddle of Persephone, Mickey saw Mind Meld Prime, piloted by Geoffrey, idling not far away, guarding Mo, and Ek sat on the lifting arm, partially powered down. Alpha was not in sight;

she hoped Taylor had sent it to rescue Ananda from Yellow at the loading dock.

"Shoo." Aunt Lagatha flapped her hands. "Mickey—"

Mickey turned back. Blue had decided that the keypad would not be helpful and was approaching the people again. If Blue had been an actual spider, she would have threatened it with a rolled-up newspaper. *Bad arachnid.*

She waved at Prime, a kind of "can you help me here?" gesture. Prime rolled forward a few inches toward Mo, who honestly looked terrible, and then rolled back as if to say, *I'm working over here.*

It seemed like hours since Red had killed Doug and injured Pris and the others. And still, no first-response vehicles had arrived. Mo claimed Dr. Lee had blocked calls to 911, but that seemed unreal and honestly too stupid for words.

Mickey leaned inside the corridor and stared at Blue. It occurred to her that Blue probably didn't know Mickey was the human operating it. Why should it? Mickey had never been to Unieda before yesterday and had never operated the spidogs before today. It didn't seem like its grasp of humans as individuals was very good.

"Aunt Lagatha, can you help Mo? It looks like she has a first aid kit. I'll wrangle Blue. Yellow is—" she didn't want to say "gone" because that wasn't correct. "—Not around."

The women switched places, and Mickey approached Blue, who was clicking its mandibles and multifunction appendages at the crowd. It was slightly scary. She wasn't entirely sure that the whole spidog wasn't electrified, especially since it was damaged, but she placed her metal hand on its smooth white back. It didn't respond. Why should it have touch sensors on its back? On the plus side, it didn't immediately electrocute her either.

Mickey shoved at the spidog. "Go that way." Although it was mostly long legs, its body was heavy.

Blue staggered and then righted itself and did a little tap-tappedy dance to turn in place and face Mickey, mandibles and multifunction appendages open.

"I'm not fighting you, you stupid spider. Just go through there and unlock the doors, would you?"

Click-click, went the mandibles.

"Yes, very scary, now go." She pushed with her mind and felt a sharp tug of pain. She had almost reached her limit. It was getting to be time to stick her head in an ice bucket.

She listened to Blue grumbling in its mind about saving the human-blobs as it tiptoed, tap-tap-tap, down the corridor toward the lab.

Trying to keep some part of her engaged with the spidog, she turned to Aunt Lagatha. "Is there some kind of instant ice pack in that first aid kit? I really need something cold for my head."

Another lab worker had also gone outside, and both were fussing over Mo. Mo's beautiful braids were muddy and messed up, and that hurt Mickey to see. Her friend's brown eyes were half open, but Mickey couldn't tell if Mo was seeing her or not. This day had gone so very wrong. She rubbed her forehead with her real fingers, pulling the skin back and forth.

The other lab worker, a man in his midthirties, tossed a plastic packet at Mickey. She caught it effortlessly with her metal hand, read the directions with slit eyes, cracked it open against her metal palm, then lifted it to the back of her skull over the neural net and its burning connections. The temperature of her head seemed to drop ten degrees immediately. Mickey indulged in a full-body shiver of relief.

In the genetics lab, Blue lifted one of its feet and poked at the pad beside the revolving door leading to the corridor to the robotics lab. The flashing red light over the doorway pulsed unrelentingly. That wasn't helping the pain in Mickey's head, nor was the alarm, which had been blaring throughout the campus and probably down the street the entire time.

Blue obviously still didn't comprehend revolving doors. Once again, it started pulling the doors endlessly toward itself, trying to figure out how to get through, although its long, low spider body would not fit the vertical slots.

The rest of the genetics lab staff pushed against the door, heading toward the main building. She sent Blue to unlock the other end of the corridor for them as well; the people Blue was trying to save avoided the spidog, and Mickey felt almost bad for it. She called Blue back as soon as it unlocked that other door.

Once everyone was through, she headed outside to Aunt Lagatha and Mo. She sat on the filthy ground next to her wounded friend. Ek flapped from its perch on Prime to Mickey's shoulder. Mo moved her hand toward Mickey, who took it and laced their fingers together, light brown to medium brown. She had held too many hands attached to broken friends today.

METAL
-36-
Blue

The human-blobs had left Blue alone in the corridor, and the Controller had retreated a bit after sending a vague instruction: *come to me*. What did that mean? If the Controller was in a place, Blue did not know where that place was. Blue really wasn't even sure what the Controller *was*.

However, Blue remembered where Slash had been, with the human-blob back in the canyon. Perhaps Slash needed help to rescue that human still. Outside this corridor, some human-blobs were attending to the ball-blob. But those other human-blobs did not seem to need rescue, remarkably. The ball was no longer leaking, for instance—leaking humans always required help. Another human was in pieces, very leaky indeed, but beyond help. And Squiggle, dear sibling, was also in pieces, leaking quite a bit of odd black fluid.

No one had trained Blue to rescue other spidogs. People were right there, though, and could repair Squiggle when they were done with the ball-human. They could put the black stuff back inside Squiggle where it presumably belonged. Blue assumed some people had repaired Blue after the fight and the fire that had broken its leg, melted its insides and broken its feet, even though Blue had died for a while.

Blue tiptoed back down the corridor through broken glass and made itself into a ball to go back through the strange doors into the building where the long, low container of strange, cold life-forms was. As Blue tip-tapped through that room, it noticed that some of the little life-forms were the same shade of black as the fluid that had leaked from Squiggle, which was odd. Blue made its way down another corridor to the other room now empty of small life-forms, their containers still hanging open after Blue's rescue.

Outside the next doorway was the canyon, and there was Slash and the human-blob—and Arrow Turtle.

The human was down, although it wasn't leaking and had not assumed ball-form. Slash used several feet to hold the human in place and stood backed into the canyon, multifunction appendages raised and clicking, with mandibles also clicking.

Arrow Turtle was a short distance away, sitting there menacingly on its big, round, black rolling feet, its front leg up in the air, ready to crush Slash.

Blue immediately saw the problem. Arrow Turtle could not crush and maim Slash because Slash was standing over the human. By hurting Slash, Arrow Turtle would hurt the human.

If Blue interfered and saved the human, Arrow Turtle would attack Slash and rend Slash to pieces the way the two turtles had torn up Squiggle. If the human escaped under its own power, leaving Blue behind, Blue would also be at risk of Arrow destroying it. Blue was already weak from the fire that the turtle had rained on Blue earlier in the arena, and Blue couldn't run away with any alacrity because of the misfitting replacement leg and feet. Blue couldn't fight Arrow Turtle alone while Slash took the human away, and neither could Slash fight Arrow Turtle alone if Blue took the human away. It was a stalemate.

Arrow Turtle rolled forward and raised its front leg higher.

Blue remembered that it once knew how to fight and searched its programming. The fight sequences were there but grayed out. Blue could only search for life-forms in need of assistance and save them. It could not be a war dog or a guard dog. It could only be a search-and-rescue dog right now.

Blue jumped from the canyon ledge and landed too hard, with all its joints buckling. The human recoiled under Slash. Blue stumbled as the replacement limb gave out beneath it, going down on a couple of its knees. Slash glanced over and then focused back on Arrow Turtle.

Blue tugged on Slash's human-blob, trying to pull it away. The human fought, but that very action caused Slash's feet to slip off and free the human. Blue yanked it, even though clearly that distressed the human. But Blue forced the human to stand up and get behind both spidogs.

Arrow Turtle hesitated, and its arm lowered slightly. It rocked back and forth on its treads. It did not have a face, not the way the siblings did, but to Blue, it seemed as if the Arrow Turtle was focused on Slash, not Blue.

The human wailed loud sounds of distress. Blue shoved backward with one foot, pressing the noisy human against the canyon wall for its own protection. Blue backed up a step, keeping the human on the wall. That left Slash open to attack by Arrow Turtle.

Arrow Turtle rolled forward. Blue could see down its nose, where the fire roiled, ready to be snorted out all over Slash. The world was extremely loud. Inside Blue's head, the Controller was trying to take control again to get Blue to pull the screaming human out of the canyon, away from both Arrow Turtle and Slash. The screaming human was, of course, screaming. Arrow Turtle rumbled. Over everything shrieked the alarm that told the siblings that humans needed help wherever they could be found. Slash, nervous, was tapping all its pointed toes on the concrete ground. Inside the seams of its white carapace gleamed a rainbow of black oil.

Blue's databases were not segregated by war, rescue, or guard functions, so Blue could easily locate information on oil. Oil was flammable and could be used as a weapon.

METAL

Blue could not access protocols on how to use weapons. And this weapon was inside Slash, throughout Slash.

And Blue remembered vividly what it felt like to burn.

Arrow Turtle breathed fire onto Slash, and its heat bathed Blue. Shamefully, Blue tried to back away, stepping on the howling human. Blue did not want to burn again. The human's cries increased a notch. The Controller wrestled Blue for control.

Black oil from inside Slash oozed out of the cracks and crannies in its carapace as Arrow Turtle breathed loud, furious fire, bathing the yellow-and-white spidog from mandibles to toes.

The Controller tugged Blue sideways and forced Blue to drag the human along, keeping its fragile, soft body behind Blue's tough white exoskeleton. Although perhaps the Controller had forgotten, or didn't know, that a turtle had easily penetrated that carapace with fire earlier that day and that Blue was still broken from that attack.

Iridescent oil puddled around Slash's toes.

Blue shoved the human-blob into the far corner of the canyon. It continued to wail and began to beat on Blue's back. Blue lifted the new weird foot and placed it against the human's middle, not very nicely, and pressed firmly. The human stopped hitting Blue.

Arrow Turtle stopped breathing fire. Maybe it needed to cool down or inhale; Blue didn't know. Blue didn't breathe, after all.

The puddle around Slash spread. More oil came from Slash's joints. It did not drip or pour from the joints. It crept, very deliberately, down Slash's legs to join the inky pool.

Arrow Turtle swayed slightly back and forth before Slash, as if waiting to see what the yellow spidog would do.

The Controller tried to get Blue to lead the human away, but the oil's behavior fascinated Blue. It was the wrong temperature, for one thing. It should have been the same temperature as Slash, but it was slightly warmer. Was that from the fire?

Blue lifted one of its multipurpose appendages and inspected the spaces in its own joints. No oil. The human squeaked, and Blue backed into it, making it grunt.

The black puddle coalesced and moved toward Arrow Turtle. Slash seemed unaware of this odd action, but Blue leaned forward to observe. This allowed the human-blob to slip around it and dash away.

Arrow Turtle recoiled from Slash as the human darted by.

The puddle kept creeping toward Arrow Turtle, although the concrete ground sloped in the opposite direction. Blue sent a suggestion to Slash to back up, which the sibling did.

Just before the blackness would have touched Arrow Turtle, the big monster bot threw one last contemptuous gout of fire at Slash, wheeled around and followed the fleeing human.

The puddle drew in on itself and retreated inside Slash. Slash looked at Blue. Blue clacked its mandibles in confusion, having no shoulders to shrug.

Out in the grass, a small life-form hopped. Slash waved its multi-purpose appendages gleefully and sprang into the air. Its white carapace had scorch marks, but its insides seemed undamaged from the fire. Slash landed on the life-form and grabbed it, flinging it high.

Blue was sure that life-form had been inside the building a short time ago. Hadn't Blue just saved it? The Controller was telling Blue to take the small life-form away from Slash, but Slash was having so much fun—oh, there it went, pop. No more life-form. Oops.

Slash bounced away, chasing whatever small life-forms moved in the grass, its carapace scorched black and spattered red. Blue did not want to fight with Slash. Blue was tired.

Metal screeched as Slash threw itself on top of vehicles with glee. More loud sounds joined the cacophony. Blue took a few steps in that direction, but the strange leg gave out, and at the top of the ramp, Blue canted to one side. It pushed itself upright but immediately fell again, and something loose inside fell off.

Blue was gone.

METAL
-37-
Mickey

Ananda, screaming, guarded by Mind Meld Alpha, ran around the corner of the building. Although terrified, she didn't seem injured.

Through a fading Blue, Mickey watched Yellow tear apart a white laboratory rabbit and then run into the parking lot to destroy more cars, setting off a volley of car alarms. A moment later, Blue went dark, and she lost contact.

Yellow rampaged through the lot toward the fence enclosing the Unieda campus. Mickey winced as Yellow trampled over Pris's car, which added its shrieks to the general noise level. Insurance companies in the Northeast were going to be very unhappy after today.

Aunt Lagatha gave Ananda a cursory check, but it was clear she hadn't been badly hurt, although she was holding both arms across her belly. The turrets of both Mind Melds swiveled between the activity beside the broken corridor, where Aunt Lagatha had returned to Mo's side, and watching Yellow, who was almost at the front gate.

Mickey wondered how long their batteries lasted. A Robo Rumble fight was five minutes long. The Mind Melds had been running for what seemed like hours, and their power had to be draining fast. The smaller, lighter spidogs could operate for longer periods of time, no matter what their current function was.

Mickey tried to connect to Blue, but there was nothing. Whatever had happened, Blue was offline.

Ananda looked at Mickey sideways and said rather loudly, "You can stop blaming me for losing the xoggotli now."

Mickey scrunched her face in disbelief and blinked at the non sequitur. Why was she bringing this up now?

On the ground, Mo waved her hand, but Mickey couldn't tell what she was trying to say.

"What?" Mickey said, annoyed, glancing away from Ananda at Yellow. That problem seemed a bit more pressing, as the spidog had reached the fence and seemed to contemplate climbing it.

"I saw it," Ananda declared. She wiped her face with the back of her hand.

"No," Mo groaned.

"Saw what?"

A police SUV pulled up to the guardhouse. Finally. The nasty, mean guard lady actually emerged to lean into the vehicle and talk to the officers.

Yellow crouched in a bush on the other side of the fence.

"The xoggotli, aren't you paying attention?" Ananda cried.

"We all saw it," Mickey replied. "And we lost every piece of it because you let go." She briefly touched her scar where the creature had been inside her.

"I saw it today," Ananda said just as the guard triggered the gate.

"What? Where?" Mickey looked away from the gate.

Mo's hand dropped back onto the damp ground, and Aunt Lagatha bent over her. They said something too low for Mickey to hear.

"Today, aren't you listening to me?"

"Here?" Mickey flashed a glance at the police vehicle as it rolled through the gate.

"In that horrible spider. The xoggotli came out of the spider when it was fighting Alpha and then crawled back in."

"That spider?" Mickey pointed at Yellow.

Yellow jumped onto the police SUV.

"Yes!"

The SUV stopped, and officers got out of both sides.

Mickey ran.

METAL
-38-
Mickey

In hindsight, she probably could have grabbed one of the golf carts, but she didn't know how to operate them, so it wouldn't have saved time. Mickey ran across the damp, squishy lawn, ignoring the walkways, going straight as she could toward the police officers. Ek swooped before her.

Her head was pounding. She had dropped the ice pack. Noise emanated from every corner of the Unieda campus. The police unit's lights were flashing, the red and blue making purple, but thankfully, the siren was off.

The officers, both men, hadn't drawn their weapons. They seemed more curious than frightened by the large white robotic spider on their SUV's roof. The mean guard lady stood in the open gate, her hands over her mouth. Mickey wondered if she even knew what kind of hijinks happened inside the fence or if she was just paid to be obstructive and rude to people trying to get in.

Ek swooped down and tried to knock Yellow off the roof. Yellow swatted at the raven with both of its multipurpose appendages, scoring a lucky hit. Ek tumbled through the air and crashed into the windshield of a nearby car, setting off another alarm.

Stumbling, Mickey tried to connect to Yellow, but of course, Emilio was already in there. Maybe, given time, no headache, and no urgency, she could have ousted the little man and made her way in to control Yellow, but as things stood, there was no way. All she saw was seething blackness.

When she checked the police vehicle again, Yellow had jumped off toward the passenger side, on top of that hapless officer, and was embracing him with its multipurpose appendages. Mickey knew what came next, and she wanted to close her eyes, but she had to keep running. Maybe she could save the other cop. She hoped Mo wasn't watching; her stepdad was a police officer.

"Run!" Mickey shouted, but her breathing was ragged, and the autumn wind blew her words away.

The policeman popped.

The other officer clutched his radio, shouting into his shoulder, running around the front of the SUV, his gun in his other hand.

"Run away!" Mickey gasped.

Something big and hot approached behind Mickey and passed by. Mind Meld Prime. Geoffrey to the rescue.

Mickey stumbled to a stop as Prime, big and menacing, trundled through the lot toward the stopped police car. The surviving police officer had no way of knowing Prime was a good robot, just like he hadn't known that Yellow was bad.

She reached inside herself, dug the tips of her sneakers into the asphalt, and launched herself after Prime. Prime, being wide, had to take an indirect route, but she could run between cars.

Far off, sirens sounded, a lot of them. Dr. Lee was going to be pissed off. Maybe someone in a nearby industrial park had heard all the alarms and called it in despite his precautions.

"Get back in the car!" Mickey yelled at the officer.

Yellow was tearing up the first officer with what could only be described as glee. The second officer aimed his weapon at the spidog. Bullets ricocheted off the curved, reinforced body of the spidog back at the cop. One shot hit him in the leg.

Mickey groaned. More car alarms started as bullets slammed into vehicles. The cop fell to one knee.

Yellow advanced, its filthy carapace only slightly dented, its mandibles clacking, multipurpose appendages raised and ready to grab.

Prime emerged from between two rows of cars and charged at Yellow, who recoiled. So did the officer. The officer shot reflexively at Prime, and again, the bullets failed to penetrate the thick metal armor. Prime tried to nudge the cop aside, but its big metal body had overheated from running for an extended time, and the officer took that as an attack.

Mickey shouted, "The black one is okay! Let it help you!"

The officer leaned away from Prime, his gun still raised. Yellow reached out with its multipurpose appendages to grasp the man. Mickey wanted to cover her eyes, but she kept running, although she knew that she would be too late.

Prime shoved the officer over, not at all gently, and smashed Yellow with its lifting arm. Yellow staggered, curled into a ball, and tried to roll away.

Ek darted down to land on the sprawled officer and raised its wings protectively. Mickey arrived a moment later, grabbed the man by his arm, and yanked at him. Although he was much bigger than Mickey, he slid easily through the gore of his former partner, groaning and swearing at her to let him go.

"Don't be an idiot," Mickey retorted. "I'm saving your stupid life here."

He still fought her.

Yellow tried to roll after them, but Prime smashed its lifting arm into the gore-caked ball of spidog again and again until the tough carapace cracked open, revealing the electronics and hydraulics inside.

And the iridescent black oil.

METAL
-39-
Mickey

Mickey splayed herself horribly on top of the wounded police officer to hold him back from fighting. She stared at the writhing blackness inside Yellow.

And the blackness stared back.

She rolled off the protesting cop and fell to her knees, her metal hand going to the scar on her neck as a sudden searing heat seemed to penetrate it.

The blackness shaped a bubbling bit of itself into an eye and gazed at Mickey. It blinked. She blinked back.

The moment seemed to last forever, but then Prime's arm smashed into Yellow again, destroying its components. Yellow's legs dropped limply. Although Mickey hadn't connected to Yellow, she felt it go out at the very edge of her consciousness.

The oil shifted, not at all dead. It blinked at her again.

No, it was winking.

How had the xoggotli gotten inside Yellow?

Fuck.

-40-
Mo

Thank you for getting us adjoining rooms," Mo said to Pris.

Pris nodded. Doctors had wired her jaw shut, and half her face was bandaged after being rebuilt by the expert plastic surgeons at Yale-New Haven Hospital. She sat propped up in the hospital bed, her head shaved, even skinnier than usual, but Mo couldn't be mad at her for that.

Mo's arm was in a sling post-operation, and her whole middle was tightly wrapped. It hurt to breathe, talk, laugh, move and even eat—maybe she would lose a couple of pounds herself. She had a lot of physical therapy ahead of her; Mickey shared her physical therapist's information with Mo.

Pris used a stylus to write on a tablet suspended on a telescoping arm next to her bed. "No cameras," she wrote, followed by a sad face.

"Not that we could use the footage if we had it. Those spidogs are proprietary."

Pris drew another sad face.

"Hey, at least your fossils are going to be in the Peabody Museum. Dr. Lee is still paying for it, even after everything."

Pris shrugged one shoulder and then drew a sad face with Xs for eyes.

"Yeah, a lot of people died."

They stared at each other. Pris wore no makeup. Her eyelashes were pale, almost nonexistent, her lips a thin white line of pain. Her family was filming a new season of their reality show and had wanted to make Pris's near-death experience a centerpiece, but Pris had never been on the show and still refused.

Pris raised her hand slowly back to the tablet. Her brain had received quite a knocking, but the doctors were sure she would make a full recovery. "Xoggotli?"

Mo bit her lower lip. "Dr. Lee has it—them?—now. That's not good, of course. He's a fellow mad scientist, but I don't trust him." Visions of how the spidogs had acted when animated by the xoggotli would never leave her head. They assumed Red had been infected, too, but somehow Blue had not been.

"Mickey?" Pris wrote.

Mo shrugged. She hadn't been back to Unieda to finish her DNA work since that day. "I don't know. We never found any relatives of hers. She has some has some unusual DNA sequences in common with a couple of the mersharks but she's not a mershark."

"Human, right?" Pris wondered.

"I mean, yeah, she's human, of course."

"Who's human?" Mickey walked into the hospital room, Ek perched on her shoulder.

"You are, Mickey," Mo said.

"Course I am."

Mickey held out her right hand to Pris. She had a brand-new, picture-perfect tattoo of the black axolotl with the bifurcated tail on her forearm as if the creature was sitting there. Pris touched Mickey's fingers with her own and then pointed at the tattoo.

Mickey ran her metal fingers over it. "You wouldn't believe it if I told you."

Mo laughed. "Mickey, we recently saw giant metal spiders kill people. Of course, we will believe you."

"Right," Pris wrote.

"I visited that little axolotl I liked so much before I left Unieda that day," she said to Mo. Mickey turned to Pris. "They have a big tank of them in the genetics lab. The lab workers, specifically Ananda, cut them up while they are alive and torture them."

"That's not quite true—" Mo protested.

"Anyway, I wanted to see it one last time. It crawled out of the tank onto my arm just like this—" she pointed to the tattoo. "And then it, well, it melted into my arm and left this shadow."

"You're right, I don't believe it," Mo said. "But it's a good story to tell about your new tattoo."

Mickey cocked her head, leaning her cheek against Ek, and gazed at her two friends. "Why were you wondering if I was human when I walked in? Back to that stupid DNA test?"

Pris nodded.

"There's something else, though, that we didn't get to tell you yet that Aunt Lagatha and I found in your blood," Mo ventured. She reached out and ran her fingers over Mickey's new tattoo. The black was slightly iridescent and raised. She had never seen tattoo ink like that.

Mickey pulled her arm away.

"You know how there was a xoggotli inside Yellow, and probably inside Red, and they don't know how it got there? Pretty weird, of course."

Pris nodded and then put her hand to her bandaged cheek as if that hurt.

"Well, Aunt Lagatha and I were looking at your blood under a microscope right before everything went to hell that day, and we saw something. She's still trying to figure it out, but I think we know what it is, although we don't know what it means."

Mickey gazed at Mo. Her brown eyes seemed darker than ever before. Ek shifted on her shoulder.

"Mickey, your blood has tiny black globules in it."

Pris sucked in a loud breath. The stylus tap-tap-tapped on the screen scribbling furiously, but Mo didn't look away from Mickey.

"Mickey, the xoggotli is in you."

###

METAL

Equipment Malfunction Kills Three at Local Biotech Firm

Malfunctioning equipment at Unieda Corporation yesterday tragically killed two employees and a first responder and injured a dozen people. The same malfunction prevented employees from notifying emergency services. Help only arrived hours later after neighboring businesses complained to the police about continuous alarms coming from the Unieda campus. Dr. Bao Lee, Chief Medical Officer, alleges industrial espionage by a rival firm. Employees of that rival company were also on the Unieda campus yesterday on what was scheduled to be a collaborative visit ...

The Woman with No Relatives, an Anomalous mtDNA Case Study

By Dr. Lagatha Larsen, Dr. Ananda Patel, Dr. Melissa McLeod, et al.

Abstract: A 28-year-old woman, Jane Doe, exhibits mtDNA that doesn't match any known lineage. Her immediate relatives are unknown as she was abandoned at birth ...

###

About the Author

Gevera Bert Piedmont is a neurodivergent cyborg swamp-witch living on the edge of a frog pond in Connecticut with her spouse, cats, and an impressive collection of rubber lizards. She is the author of *The Maw and Other Time-Traveling Lizard Tales*, the Mickey Crow paranormal series, coauthor of *Airesford* (the other author is an actual zombie), editor of the *Necronomi-RomCom* Cthulhu Mythos duology and Amazon bestselling coeditor of *Horror Over the Handlebars*, an anthology of Connecticut horror. Her next anthology, with coeditor Elizabeth Davis of Dead Fish books, will be *The Atlas of Deep Ones*.

Her novel *Fat Monster* will be published by Nightmare Press in late 2024.

Bert has an MFA in creative writing and belongs to the Horror Writers Association, Connecticut Authors and Publishers Association, and New England Horror Writers. Her (very) small press publishing company is Transformations by Obsidian Butterfly, LLC, and at this time is only publishing anthologies. Connect at Facebook.com/geverabertpiedmont, geverabertpiedmont.com, obsidianbutterfly.com, or her Amazon and Goodreads author pages (check out https://linktr.ee/bybertabird for all author pages and other social media links).

She loves hearing from fans.

Please leave a review on Amazon and/or Goodreads, and follow Bert on both. Authors live on reviews and coffee, and Bert doesn't drink coffee. Thank you!

www.ingramcontent.com/pod-product-compliance
Lightning Source LLC
Chambersburg PA
CBHW050915030726
47503CB00007BB/2299